A HISTORY OF THE FUTURE (2025-2525)

By Gavin Kanowitz

Printed in the United States of America.

Cover Design by Badour Illustration and Design.
Editing by Catherine Jenkins.

Published by
WingSpan Press
Livermore, CA
www.wingspanpress.com

ISBN 1-59594-043-X
EAN 978-1-59594-043-8
First Edition 2006

Library of Congress Control Number: 2006921841

Table of Contents

Chapter 1: The Age of Our Infancy

2025 to 2045: The Great Trade Blocs

This period beginning in 2025, marked the rise and fall of the Great Trade Blocs around the globe. Regional trading alliances developed in the twentieth century, such as the European Union (EU), continued to expand. New blocs, most notably the Asian Economic Union (AEU), were created.

The regrouping of nations, produced new powerbrokers, as access to bloc markets refocused political and economic influence in bloc structures. Initially, the bloc system also served to facilitate the development of the economies of Asia, Africa and Latin America, creating unprecedented prosperity.

However, crime syndicates, including the Florence-based Sons of Medici and the Asian Eastern Triads, ultimately corrupted the bloc framework, employing its trading structure to establish and entrench mafia influence (c. 2030-2060). Numerous financial scandals implicating legitimate public office-holders further undermined the attempt to create more stable free trade.

The three most significant blocs of this era were:

Asian Economic Union (AEU): Founded in 2019, the AEU grew to become the largest trade bloc of the era, comprised of Cambodia, China,[1] India, Indonesia, Japan, Korea,[2] Laos, Malaysia, Nepal, the Pacific Island Nations, Pakistan, the Philippines, Singapore, Sri Lanka, Thailand and Vietnam. By 2040, the AEU had a combined Gross National Product (GNP) of $66trillion (USD), seventy percent derived from manufacturing and production. In 2052, a political disagreement caused a group of nations, led by China, to break away and form the rival Asian People's Forum (APF).

American Federation of Trading Nations (AFTN): The expansion of the North American Free Trade Agreement (NAFTA), ultimately resulted in the creation of the AFTN. The original NAFTA nations—Canada, Mexico and the United States of America (USA)—were joined by the Central American, South American[3] and Caribbean nations in 2012. Australia and New Zealand

---

[1] China annexed the formerly independent nation of Taiwan in 2018.

[2] North Korea and South Korea reunited in 2015.

[3] Both Mercursor, a twentieth-century South American trading alliance dominated by Brazil and Argentina, and non-aligned South American countries, joined the AFTN.

joined the AFTN in 2018, after rejection by the AEU. By 2040, the AFTN reported a combined GNP of $62 trillion (USD), making it the second largest trading bloc on Earth.

European Union (EU): The EU gradually enveloped all European countries by 2020, including Eastern Europe and Scandinavia, in addition to the original Western European nations. A combined GNP of $60 trillion (USD) was reported in 2040, sixty percent derived from trade in information.

Smaller trading blocs included the Russian-dominated New Eastern Bloc (NEB), the West African Union (WAU), the Southern African Economic Communion (SAEC), the East African Forum (EAF) and the Middle Eastern Commerce and Trade Alliance (MECTA).

2025

First manned landing on Mars; Exploration and an overview of colonization

A joint American-European manned mission landed on Mars in 2025. The spacecraft *Enlightenment* and its eight-person crew, led by astronauts Rob Grecio and Anna Tsipsis, spent over two hundred hours exploring the Martian surface. The crew obtained valuable information about the planet's geography and composition, laying the foundation for the later *Ares* Martian exploration programs. Sixteen *Ares* manned flights visited the planet between 2028 and 2044. By the year 2050, Earth computers had generated fully detailed schematics outlining the most minute crevices of such natural features as the Olympus Mons. The Martian moons, Phobos and Deimos, were explored during the 2050s.

The *Ares* missions revealed that the red planet's atmosphere could be easily transformed to create an Earthlike environment and that the planet's surface was rich in iron ore, manganese, magnesium and silver. The first Martian colony was subsequently founded in the Mariner Valley in 2068. Commercial shuttle flights to Mars were initiated in 2071. By 2160, there were twenty-eight colonies on Mars, with a combined population of two hundred and eighty million people. The Martian colonies united in 2186, forming the Martian Federation (MF), whose population grew to five hundred million by 2238. In the early twenty-third century, Martian entrepreneurs and prospectors had profited greatly from the planet's rich mineral fields, increasing the relative economic strength of the MF within the context of the then-existing Human worlds.

Quebec independence

The province of Quebec, won independence from Canada by obtaining seventy-five percent of the 'yes' vote in a province-wide referendum. The sovereign Quebec Republic was established with Quebec City as its capital and Jean Rimbaud was elected as its first president. By virtue of the Blackwill-Redeaux Accord, Montreal was granted the status of an "International City," whose inhabitants were awarded the privilege of holding dual Canadian-Quebecois citizenship.

Black Cloud Syndrome

Population growth and industrialization in the Developing World, caused an increase in global air pollution. By 2025, sulphur dioxide and nitrous oxide levels had reached critical levels in Cairo, Lagos, Manila and Shanghai, a phenomenon leading environmentalists dubbed Black Cloud Syndrome.

2026

Human cloning

The controversy engendered by the cloning of a sheep (Dolly) in 1997, gradually petered out until, in 2026, international bans[4] were lifted with the signing of the Open Genes Agreement. Seizing this newly obtained scientific liberty, Alexi Rokoko, a bioengineer at the University of St. Petersburg, led the first group to clone a fully functional Human being, succeeding in 2032. Rokoko's procedure, Clone Rebirth, overcame duplication resistance caused by genes on the eighth chromosome. Nevertheless, cloned Humans developed poorly until procedures were optimized in the 2060s.

Tamil homeland in Sri Lanka

The Tamils succeeded in winning independence from Sri Lanka. The northern city of Jaffna became the capital of the Tamil Free State, which joined the AEU in 2034.

Hydrogen emerges as "superfuel"

With the gradual decrease in supply of petroleum fuels, other energy alternatives, most notably hydrogen, methane and propane, gained increased usage. By 2026, hydrogen had emerged as a popular and efficient high velocity fuel, creating a class of nouveaux riches known as the Hydrogen Kings.

---

[4] The Global Initiative on Cloning Control, banning Human cloning experiments, was signed and ratified in 2010 by over 150 nation states.

2027

Border clashes in the Baltic; Russian expansion

An economic dispute escalated into full military confrontation between Poland and Lithuania. Polish forces, headed by Zbigniew Hosea, invaded Lithuania and besieged the capital, Vilnius. Russia, fearful of a Polish advance, attacked the Poles, assisted by Latvian and Estonian troops. After six months of bitter fighting, the Poles were driven westward and Vilnius was liberated. Victory increased the reliance of the Baltic states on Russian protection. Russia reannexed Estonia in 2037, Lithuania in 2038 and Latvia in 2041.

Collapse of Persian Gulf regimes

The Ibn Saud dynasty of Saudi Arabia was overthrown by the Secularist Mahan Bloc. Further secular revolts the same year succeeded in removing royal dynasties in Qatar and Kuwait, however, secular revolutions failed in the United Arab Emirates and Bahrain.

2028

Unified Field Theory problem solved

Theoretical physicists Stephane Le Mare and Shlomo Ferstein, published their article "An Epilogue to the Universal Force Linkage Problem," outlining a final resolution to the Unified Field Theory Problem.[5] Le Mare and Ferstein, both members of the prestigious Marseilles Research Foundation, succeeded in linking the strong nuclear force with gravity, to solve the Problem. Their work relied on that of earlier physicists who, between 1990 and 2028, had provided a non-string theory based linkage arrangement for both the electromagnetic force and the weak nuclear force. Completion of the Problem stimulated a more intricate understanding of cosmology and particle physics, presaging the discovery of the querzian particle[6] and greater than light speed travel.

The rise and fall of the Greens in France

France's Green Party leader, Leon Michel, became the first environmentalist elected as a head of state in the western world. A mere sixteen months later, his decision to cut funding to France's fast breeder nuclear reactor program, raised the ire of the barons of French industry, who brought down the Green government and obtained Michel's resignation.

---

[5] Unified field theory postulates that the four forces of nature (the strong nuclear force, the weak nuclear force, the electromagnetic force and gravity) can all be linked together.

[6] See entry for 2070 for a detailed discussion of the discovery of the querzian particle.

First Nations revolt in Quebec Republic
Quebec Republic forces savagely put down Cree revolts, evoking international cries of horror.

The implementation of the Space First Policy
Democratic candidate Philip Newley defeated Republican incumbent Lorraine Bowers, becoming President of the United States. Newley endorsed a more progressive private-sector dominated role for the USA in space exploration. Historians cited Newley's Space First Policy as the initiative which led Humanity to explore and settle deeper regions of the solar system.

War in the Kashmir Republic
The infant Kashmir Republic, having obtained its independence from India in 2022, was attacked by Indian backed Hindu rebel forces agitating for a return to the motherland. When Hindu rebels massacred five thousand Muslim villagers, Pakistan intervened, ending its ten-year period of peace with India.

2029

Birth of Freelands Movement in the USA
The Freelands Movement was founded in Houston, Texas. Freelanders advocated the redistribution of lands in the American interior to the general populace, believing that problems associated with urban poverty could thereby be solved. The Freelands Movement gained strong inner city support and influenced the Democrat Party. Though the proposed initiatives were never implemented, the ensuing dissension in rural areas engendered the Farm Riots of 2033 and provided the foundation for mid-Western alienation from the federal system.[7]

First manned landing on Venus; Colonization of the Morning Star
Astronauts Chi Zihang and Elvis Nakajima, both of the AEU, explored the Venusian surface in protective suits impervious to the acidic atmosphere and high atmospheric pressure. Nevertheless, further Venusian exploration proved to be rigorous, despite the assistance of adaptive technology. The journals of the fifteen *Eros* and *Cupid* missions, from 2033 to 2068, recorded twenty-seven deaths.

The morning star's first colony wasn't established until 2071. Further colonies developed in the 2070s and 2080s, with regular commercial flights

[7] Western alienation continued to grow. See entry 2119 for details of the Second American Civil War.

being introduced in 2096. By 2160, Venus's two hundred and fourteen colonies boasted a combined population of eighty-eight million people.

Initially, Venus's hostile atmosphere restricted settlement to environmentally controlled structures. The advent of atmospheric changing agents in the twenty-second century, such as oxygen-nitrogen generators and pressure droppers, enabled transformation of selected segments of Venus to an Earthlike environment. Eventually, large sections of Venus were adapted, allowing settlement to continue well into the twenty-third century. By 2232, Venusians numbered upward of three hundred million.

2030

Coup d'état in Japan

With military collaboration, the right-wing Bushido Party seized power in Japan. Declared President Ideiko Soto promised clean government, economic rebirth and a more aggressive foreign policy in Southeast Asia. Several members of the Liberal Democrat Party and the New Horizon Party pledged their support to Soto, however, Miro Futuyama, leader of the Social Democrats, demanded Soto's resignation, prompting Soto to place Futuyama under house arrest. The international community condemned the coup d'état, placing a global boycott on the purchase of Japanese goods and products. These sanctions proved unsuccessful and Japan remained an autocracy well into the City State Era following the Third World War.[8]

India's population surpasses China's

Contrary to scientific predictions, world population continued to grow in punctuated spurts. The first Global Census, completed in 2030, revealed the world population had reached 10.4 billion. India's population was recorded at 1.7 billion, replacing China (population 1.65 billion) as the world's most populous country for the first time in recorded history.

2031

Grand European Market opens; Prizes of Slovenia awarded

The Republic of Slovenia completed construction of the Grand European Market outside the capital, Ljubljana, in 2031. At a cost of $50 billion (USD), the Market showcased the latest advancements in science and technology, providing a forum for international high-tech business. To commemorate the inception of the Market, the EU instituted the Prizes of Slovenia, rewarding innovators in the applied sciences. Over the course of the twenty-first and

---

[8] See entry for 2082 for a discussion of the Third World War.

twenty-second centuries, the Prizes of Slovenia gained the prestige accorded Nobel Prizes.

Outbreak of Hashish Wars in the Middle East; MEANA established
Hashish wars between rival smuggling gangs began in Syrian-controlled Beirut in 2031. When two hundred and sixty-four people were killed in one night, the Syrian military authority declared martial law in the city. An emergency meeting of Middle Eastern nations in Istanbul, gave birth to the Middle Eastern Anti-Narcotics Army (MEANA). Twenty-two nations joined MEANA, providing a rare example of regional cooperation.

First Hydrocolony built; Hydrocolonization; Ocean mining
Hydrocolonies were the brainchild of Ramas Amritaj, an Indian engineer who viewed floating settlements as the solution to densely overcrowded living conditions in his native Calcutta. Amritaj's prototypes employed twentieth-century oil rig and deep-sea mining technology, as well as techniques discussed in the novels of Henry Fleshtoldf, a little known twentieth-century science fiction writer.

Mahatma, the first hydrocolony Amritaj designed, was completed in 2031. Its steel girders and gaseous float cushions, provided a home to forty thousand people. *Mahatma*'s success was followed by three similar hydrocolonies: *Vishnu* in Calcutta, and *Gandhi* and *Nehru* outside Mumbai. The latter two hydrocolonies each housed eighty thousand people and included business districts employing the majority of the hydrocolonies' adult inhabitants.

Amritaj's design was adopted in other parts of Asia. Manila, Hong Kong, Shanghai, Djakarta and Tokyo improved on Amritaj's model, in part by anchoring the hydrocolonies to the ocean floor with corrosion resistant super-strength steel. Carrying capacity increased, as did resistance to disturbances like cyclones and typhoons. In 2053, the *Zhing Zemin* colony outside Shanghai housed three hundred thousand people in a self-sustaining environment.

In 2060, Californian architect Rebecca Rubins perfected the Aqua Complex. Using the hydroelectric power of the ocean to generate electricity, this new design exploited magnetic force fields to keep itself afloat. By 2090, twenty-seven Aqua Complexes had been built, while an additional fifteen hydrocolonies adhered to the steel girder structure of the older Amritaj model. A modified Aqua Complex was used for hydrocolonies established in the Mediterranean Sea, North Atlantic Ocean and off the west coast of the Americas in the early twenty-second century. Over thirty-six million people were living in four hundred and fifteen hydrocolonies by 2153.

The location of a population base on the ocean's surface, greatly enhanced the efficiency of deep-sea mining. Coincident with the depletion of land-based mineral resources by the late twenty-first century, iron, zinc, coal, cadmium, chrome, gold, silver and porginine[9] were mined from the floors of the Pacific, Atlantic, Indian and Arctic Oceans. Though these minerals proved difficult and costly to extract, laser digging and ultrasonic mining techniques, developed by the hydrocolonies themselves, greatly improved the viability of these ventures.

By the mid-twenty-second century, hydrocolonies in the Pacific Ocean became the chief centres of iron production and were thus able to maintain a high level of autonomy in the global political framework. Atlantic hydrocolonies off the European and North American coasts, gained similar leverage through the large-scale mining of aluminum and zinc. Ocean mining grew rapidly well into the twenty-third century, by which time it was producing ninety-eight percent of minerals mined on Earth.

Ocean mining and hydrocolonization ultimately formed a crucial foundation for stellar exploration and colonization. Bartholomew Ching, a prominent Chinese geo-historian, later described the development of hydrocolonies as an "unparalleled leap in the Techno-Industrial Revolution of Humankind."

Unfortunately, sea mining also resulted in the alteration and in some cases, the wholesale destruction of certain segments of the Earth's ecosystem. Marine areas once populated by a rich diversity of sea life, suffered a severe decrease in plant and animal populations. The ecological devastation reversed many of the positive gains made during the Clean Seas Programs of the 2010s and 2020s.

2032

Land-speed record shattered

The land-speed record was broken by a Dane, Ole Nielson, in his third run on Utah's Bonneville Salt Plains. Travelling at six times the speed of sound, Nielson smashed the twelve-year-old record held by the Venezuelan daredevil, Santiago Hiero. Nielson used a super-charged hydrogen fuel to propel his vehicle, the same fuel later used by many aerospace vehicles.

Syntho-Blood a practical solution

None Rejecting Synthetic blood became readily available for the first time in 2032. Developed by the Onjami Clinic of Tokyo, Syntho-Blood' was comprised of chemical analogues for erythrocytes, leucocytes and platelet

[9] Porginine, a new super-fuel, was discovered in 2043.

blood cells. The Onjami invention saved countless lives during the Third World War.[10]

Voyager IV loses contact

Voyager IV finally lost contact with Earth in 2032. One of three probes released in the 2020s to explore the edges of the solar system, the probe gathered voluminous information about the planet Pluto, setting the stage for colonization in 2118.[11]

2033

Hydrofood released for popular consumption

The powerful global corporation AquaEat,[12] released its invention, Hydrofood. These water-based food products, were not only rich in free metabolic energy, but were simple to manufacture and store. Hydrofood was credited with nearly significantly reducing hunger levels in Developing Nations. Hydrofood products also played a vital role in space colonization.

Central American Republic formed

A bloc-within-a-bloc, the Central American Republic (CAR) was formed, comprised of Panama, Costa Rica, Guatemala, Honduras, Nicaragua and Belize. El Salvador reluctantly joined seven years later. Although highly critical of this apparent rejection of the AFTN, remaining AFTN members tolerated CAR, as it brought political stability to the Central American region for the first time in decades.

2034

Civil War in China

Triads and Communist militants, attempting to restore Mao Zedong's 'Rule of Law in China', engaged in numerous vicious skirmishes. With over one million dead, the neo-Communist government was unable to stem the violence. Despite their declared mandates, the United Nations and its rival global body, the World Organization of Nations (WON),[13] declined to intervene in China's "internal politics." Ironically, the

[10] See entry for 2082 for a discussion of the Third World War.

[11] Pluto's colonization is described in the entry for 2066.

[12] AquaEat was formed by the merger of two twentieth-century corporations best known for their products Kraft Dinner and Coca-Cola.

[13] WON was formed in 2022, by the breaking away of several European and African nations upset with American domination of the United Nations.

Triads and Communists ultimately collaborated to overthrow the neo-Communists, sharing governance of China until the Third World War.[14]

Odoba gains control of the Central African Federation

Tinus Odoba, a popular religious leader and resistance figure, overthrew the autocratic government of the newly created Central African Federation (CAF).[15] Initially promising to introduce democracy to this large nation, Odoba instead established a new dictatorship, extinguishing the hope that the CAF would bring democracy to sub-Saharan Africa.

Uncontrolled acid fire devastates Los Angeles

An industrial fire ignited by sulphuric acid, destroyed twelve percent of Los Angeles. The frequency of commercial disasters continued to increase, in proportion to escalating global production.[16]

First Manned Landing and Colonization of Mercury

The *Pegasus-12* reached Mercury in 2034. Astronauts Nyrop Carlsson and Lydia Baintree descended to the surface in heat reflecting bubbles. The first space colonies were established on Mercury in 2087. By 2160, the population of the planet's forty-eight colonies was twelve million.

Mercurial colonies were encased in giant reflective bubbles, to protect inhabitants from solar radiation. Mobile colonies capable of sliding around the planet to reside in "cool" areas, were pioneered in 2139.

Formation of the Space Planetary Administration

In 2034, the Dublin Manifesto established the Space Planetary Administration (SPA), and Sven Olafson, a noted astrophysicist, was elected its first president. Headquartered in Melbourne, Australia, the SPA was created by the United Nations, but became an independent organization in 2042. All space exploration, colonization and immigration was regulated by the SPA throughout the twenty-first and twenty-second centuries.

At the zenith of its power, the SPA was divided into five major sectors:

Agricultural Space Academy (ASA)—Headquartered in Cairo, Egypt. The ASA supervised agricultural projects on space colonies and stations,

[14] See entry for 2082 for a discussion of the Third World War.

[15] The CAF was established in 2033 and was comprised of the land areas formerly known as Burundi, Cameroon, Congo-Brazzaville, Central African Republic, Gabon, Rwanda and the Congo.

[16] The industrial degradation of cities, was in part what encouraged Freelanders to demand the redistribution of rural areas. See entry 2029 for details.

ensuring all cosmic settlements became self-sufficient food producers.

International Global Settlement Initiative (Colonial Office) — Headquartered in Rio de Janeiro, Brazil. The SPA's International Global Settlement Initiative was universally referred to as the "Colonial Office." Its administrative body monitored the rights of cosmic settlers in space colonies and stations. The Colonial Office also represented all permanent space colonies and stations in negotiations with their Earth-based controlling powers, the Trade Blocs.

Scientific and Industrialized Space Facility (SISF)—Headquartered in Hamilton, Bermuda. The SISF regulated mineral extraction and scientific space development.

Security Protection Institute (SPI)—Initially headquartered in Helsinki, Finland, the SPI moved to the space colony *Callisto-5* in 2102. The SPI was the first galactic police organization, providing security services to space settlements until the new worlds were sufficiently established to employ their own sheriffs. Penal colonies were established on Mercury in 2094 and on Mars in 2096.

Space Advancement and Education Organization (SAEO)—Headquartered in Louisville, Kentucky. The SAEO provided education and training programs for future colonists, equipping over one billion people with necessary survival and lifestyle skills. With well over a million employees throughout the solar system, the SAEO was the SPA's largest sector.

2035

The Treaty of Friendship; Early product specialization

The NEB, AFTN and EU signed the Treaty of Friendship, ending a bitter twenty-year trade war. The Treaty allocated product specializations to each trade bloc. Trade conflicts were eliminated by diminishing competition, fostering interdependence without sacrificing efficiency. Warren Kirkland, the United Nations Commerce Secretary and the Treaty's mastermind, was, for the first time in history, simultaneously awarded both the Nobel Peace Prize and the Nobel Economic Prize.

Exploration of the Asteroid Belt

For two years beginning in 2035, the *Hercules* missions performed detailed explorations of the Asteroid Belt between Mars and Jupiter, including the large asteroids, Ceres, Juno and Pallas. In 2037, six space navigation stations were established at the edges of the Asteroid Belt to guide travellers.

The Asteroid Belt ultimately proved a rich source of iron and copper. Mining programs on Ceres and Juno initiated in 2078, were jointly managed by British Interspace Mining Corporation and Germany's Dreigan Geocorp.

In 2124, the spaceship *Voyager 3000* collided with a miniature asteroid, killing all crew and passengers. The SPA governing body reacted by implementing the Rearrangement Policy, to clear asteroids from vital space routes.[17]

New world chess champion
Spiro Bubari, the Azerbaijani chess prodigy became the youngest Human World Chess Champion, winning the title at the age of fourteen by defeating Deep Blue VIII. IBM's Deep Blues had not been defeated by a Human player in over thirty years. This event shocked the artificial intelligence community, in particular adherents of the Top-Down school of thought, who had declared victory over the Thinking Chess Computer Problem.[18]

Disintegration of the Canadian Federation
Following the granting of independence to the Canadian province of Quebec in 2025, First Nations won self-government in large parts of the provinces of Saskatchewan, British Columbia and Manitoba in 2035. In 2041, the province of Ontario merged with the state of New York; Nova Scotia, New Brunswick and Prince Edward Island provinces joined the state of Maine. By 2060, the remainder of the Canadian Federation had been absorbed by the United States.

2036

Cure for AIDS discovered
Mikhail Thaslov and Dorothea Woo, biomedical researchers at Johns Hopkins University, announced that they had prevented the replication of HIV using a genetically engineered drug, Soripan. The drug led to the eradication of AIDS in 2042. The cure, however, came too late to save the seven hundred and ninety-one million lives lost from AIDS since the disease was first identified.[19]

Tri-Nation attack on Pakistan
Precipitated by Pakistani support for Afghani resistance movements, Mussaud Khan, the dictatorial leader of Afghanistan, backed by Iranian and Indian troops, attacked Pakistan. Pakistan was defeated in the nine-month conflict,

---

[17] See the entry for 2129.

[18] The Thinking Chess Computer Problem, was the dilemma of whether Humans could build a machine which could not be defeated by its creators.

[19] The AIDS death toll was almost ten times greater than that of the Black Death (a pandemic of bubonic and pneumonic plagues) in fourteenth century Europe.

but only after twenty million people had died when nuclear weapons were used by both factions.

2037

Democracy fails in Malaysia

Right-wing military generals overthrew Malaysia's democratically elected political leadership. A military coup also ended democracy in Indonesia in 2038. These democratic failures were linked to East Asia's growing economic malaise.

The Great Nile Project

Several mini-lakes were created along the Nile River, by employing forced flooding techniques. The lake water irrigated the Sudanese Sahara, greatly improving the region's agricultural capacity. Eventually, the Nile was divided into ten rivers, nine emptying into mini-lakes and the tenth continuing to flow into the Mediterranean Sea.

2038

Terrorists attack AFTN

Liberation America, a terrorist organization opposed to global economic integration, attacked an AFTN meeting, assassinating the leaders of Argentina, Columbia, Ecuador, Paraguay and Venezuela. The unprecedented simultaneous murder of world leaders, drew attention to popular dissatisfaction with the loss of national identities caused by globalization.

Three-year recession begins

The default on large loans to several emerging space corporations, triggered the bankruptcy of the Chase Manhattan Bank. The United States entered a three-year recession that spread to the rest of the AFTN and the AEU.

Tribal Rebellion in Zimbabwe

The Matabele successfully rebelled against Shona domination in Zimbabwe, creating an independent republic. The Matabeleland Republic joined the SAEC in 2040.

2039

Islamic uprising in the Middle East

Syrian-Jordanian Prime Minister Ali Bin Aziz, was assassinated by the Pan-Islamic Fundamentalists in the war-torn Bekaa Valley. The cities of Aleppo, Amman and Damascus were racked by the ensuing violence between Islamic militants and forces loyal to the secular government. Similar unrest occurred in Iraq, Algeria and the Egyptian Republic. By joining forces, the four secular Arab powers ultimately defeated the Fundamentalists, however, Islamic Fundamentals continued to wield power in Yemen and Oman.

Invention of the Psion Ray Probe (PiRP)

A sensitive diagnostic instrument, the Psion Ray Probe (PiRP) employed a high energy Psion particle beam to measure matter densities, identifying the extent of tissue damage, as well as characteristics and possible causation. Eventually, the PiRP allowed doctors to map the spread of pathogens through the body. By the late twenty-first century, the PiRP identified medical practitioners as had the stethoscope in earlier generations.

The first space city

Financed by the AEU and Singapore International,[20] *Confucius I*, the first space city launched into Earth's orbit, functioned primarily as a medical research and residential facility, with a total population of ten thousand. The space city *Solzhenitsyn*, an agricultural commune, was launched by the EU and Russian-dominated New Eastern Bloc (NEB) a year later.

2040

The Robotic Revolution

The years between 2040 to 2095, were associated with the Robotic Revolution. Robots were used extensively in various areas, including medicine, dentistry, mining, clerical processing and machine maintenance. The first robot physicians were introduced in 2040 and by 2063, they had essentially replaced the family doctor. Several robot manufacturers, including AndroProbe, accrued large profits as a result of these projects.

Robots also supported planetary colonization during the twenty-first and twenty-second centuries. Able to function without oxygen, robots built settlements and provided essential services in hostile environments on newly colonized planets.

Dream Phoenix endeavour announced

The Australian government and tycoon Simon Haughton, announced a joint venture to transform the Great Sandy and Gibson deserts into habitable areas. New living space was required to house Australia's large Asian immigrant population. The project was nicknamed "Dream Phoenix," referring to the Aboriginal spiritual belief of "dream time" and the mythical phoenix bird.

[20] Singapore International was an artificial environmental design corporation.

Completed in 2054, Dream Phoenix covered 1.2 million square kilometres. This and similar macro-developments in the Sahara and Gobi deserts, served as prototypes for settlements on newly colonized worlds.

Nuclear meltdown in Indiana

The core of a nuclear reactor near Gary, Indiana, melted down and exploded. Fifty-four nuclear workers and two thousand residents died. For the next twenty-five years, crops would not grow within a one-hundred-kilometre radius. The incident, known as the "Near Apocalypse," shocked America, forcing the Fowler administration to allocate greater funding for research into cold fusion.

2041

Consolidation of art

The Gallery of the Artistic Mind, a multi-million dollar structure, was opened in Rome. Taking over ten years to complete, the Gallery purchased and displayed privately held works of art never before seen by the public. The Gallery was the culmination of a global trend toward the centralization of artistic works for the benefit of a broader audience.

End of monarchy in Britain

With the overwhelming support of the British populace, the Labour government successfully passed a Parliamentary bill, abolishing the monarchy. Only staunch royalists in the Conservative and Liberal-Democrat parties opposed the bill. King William V would forever be known as the last British monarch.

First Moon colony

The first colony on the Moon, *Eden Base*, was completed in 2041. Jointly financed by the AFTN and a group of leading corporations, *Eden Base* was designed to house its population in Earthlike gravitational conditions. It underwent several enlargements from 2041 to 2070, increasing its population capacity by two million. However, during the Third World War, the population was decimated, as various Earth interests attempted to gain control of the Moon, for both its mineral resources and as a strategic military base. *Eden Base* henceforth became known as New Belgium, Humanity's modern battleground.

2042

ANC loses power in South Africa

After ruling South Africa for forty-eight years, the African National Congress (ANC) was defeated in a general election by the United Front (UF), an opposition group representing White, Coloured, Indian and Zulu interests. The UF supported a loose federation of provinces, as well as a denationalization of major industries. These policies hastened the country's breakup in 2050, when the Zulus formed their own state, Kwazulu. White separatist groups later established the Oranjie Vrystaat as their own nation.

2043

Elections in East Africa
Citizens of the Eastern African Forum (EAF),[21] elected Peter Mwetebi's pro-democratic party. Mwetebi brought a new era of Human rights and took a strong stand against corruption in the EAF. The same year, Manis Baroumba of the West African Union (WAU),[22] postponed plans for democratic elections, as member states squabbled over the form of the new political structure.

The Emergence of Regitonics
Parties espousing Regitonic policies, swept municipal elections in France, Italy, Hungary and Poland. Regitonic administrations encouraged government agencies to contract private corporations to deliver social services. Programs as diverse as environmental remediation and drug rehabilitation, were rejuvenated by the prospect of business profitability, stimulating spinoff industries in the process.

Porginine Gamma
Porginine gamma, a new high-velocity fuel, was extracted for the first time from the space between the Earth's mantle and crust. Laser digging, as well as controlled volcanic eruptions and earthquakes, were required. Exxon, British Petroleum, Gazprom and Eurogas established refineries, enabling the use of porginine gamma for space travel. In the 2060s, spacecraft using porginine gamma fuel approached speeds equalling three percent of light.

2044

Operation Biolife
The results of Operation Biolife, the ecological restoration program for the Amazon jungle, was presented by Brazilian Prime Minister Osvaldo da Silva

---

[21] The EAF, established in 2038, included the former nations of Djibouti, Eritrea, Ethiopia, Kenya, Somalia, Tanzania, Tigrea and Uganda.

[22] The WAU, formed in 2030, included the former nations of Benin, Gambia, Ghana, Guinea, Guinea-Buissa, Ivory Coast, Liberia, Nigeria, Senegal, Sierra Leone and Togo.

to the United Nations Committee on the Environment. The report showed remarkable success in curbing ecological damage, by instituting localized sustainable development, coupled with rigorous scientific controls.

American tar sands unlocked

Advanced drilling methods finally unlocked oil hidden in the Tar Sands of the former Canadian province of Alberta.[23] Ironically, despite this success, petroleum was shortly superceded by a new array of porginine fuels. By the 2070s, only sub-optimum vehicles and older machines used oil-based products.

First "landing" on Jupiter

Space Agency of the American Nations (SAAN)[24] veteran Mike Harwell, led the first manned mission, *Armstrong I*, to explore Jupiter. Booster jet packs attached to each crew member's spacesuit, allowing the astronauts to leave the spacecraft and survey Jupiter's gaseous interior. Twenty-one subsequent *Armstrong* missions explored the sixteen Jovian satellites, as well as Jupiter's giant red and black spots.

The first Jovian space colony, *Humania-1*, was established on Ganymede in 2081. *Humania-2* on Europa and *Humania-3* on Callisto, were both founded in 2084. The population of the *Humania* colonies was greatly increased by Earth's resettlement programs in the 2090s. By 2160, there were twenty-three colonies in the Jovian system, with a combined population of one hundred and eighty million people.

Adapting Earth's hydrocolony technology, floater colonies hovering in Jupiter's atmosphere, became viable living environments in the 2120s, each housing one million people. Early warning satellites monitored the planet's lethal storms, allowing floater colonies to escape energy buildups.

2045

The Duprey crisis

French religious leader Cardinal Jacques Duprey, a Catholic moderate, was assassinated in Nantes, the first of fourteen Catholic figures murdered around the world during a seven-year period. The previously unknown New Order of Christ claimed responsibility. An Interpol investigation identified the Archbishop Wotjek Orislaw as its prime suspect. The conservative Archbishop had once claimed that the Church had to be "purged to save itself," however, the evidence was insufficient to proceed with charges against him. Pope John

---

[23] See entry for 2035 detailing the disintegration of the Canadian Federation.

[24] SAAN was the successor to the North American Space Agency (NASA).

Paul IV exploited the suspicions cast upon religious conservatives and seized the opportunity to purge the Vatican of their influence. The assassinations mysteriously ceased in 2052.

Eruption of Mount Fujiyama

The unanticipated eruption of the Japanese volcano Mount Fujiyama, killed one hundred and fifty thousand people. The abysmal failure of hi-tech monitors to predict the eruption, shocked volcanologists worldwide. An earthquake the same year killed thirty thousand people in central Turkey. Pietri Nino, a seismologist at the Earthquake Research Center in Palo Alto, determined that overzealous porginine mining had caused both disasters, by effecting a radical change in continental drift. Nevertheless, business interests successfully resisted calls for regulation of the porginine industry.

Chapter 2: Onward to Space

Various blocs built space stations during the twenty-first and twenty-second centuries. These space stations were classified as follows:

Bio-units: Self-sustaining ecosystems, each housing one hundred thousand people, relieved Earth's population burden in the twenty-first century. Each bio-unit was subdivided into sectors for agricultural production, industrial manufacturing and residential living. Over a thousand bio-units were built during the fifty year period beginning in 2045. Ninety percent of these bio-units were located around Earth, Mars and Venus.

Space forts: The various bloc powers began building space forts throughout the solar system in 2060, beginning with Earth's space perimeter. These space forts housed twenty-thousand troops and were equipped with long-range nuclear missiles and laser batteries. Space forts played a critical role during the Third World War and the conflicts of the twenty-second century.

Sci-units: Space stations specializing in research and development were first built in 2027 and had proliferated by 2070. Scientific researchers from fields as diverse as biochemistry and geophysics worked together, linked to various library and research institutions. Each sci-unit supported three thousand scientists and their families and many operated as mini-universities.

Space stops: Space stops were built throughout the solar system from 2068 onward, to refuel space ships travelling across the solar system. Eventually, space stops also contained docking bays and temporary residential facilities to accommodate long distance space travellers between planets.

Mini-units: Some small space stations were dedicated to specific activities, like communications, weather monitoring or military intelligence. By 2100, crews of twenty to one hundred people were located in mini-units throughout the solar system.

2046

US troops attack South America

American President Bill Shipton, ordered an attack on the Columbian-Venezuelan jungle region in an attempt to extinguish the area's drug trade. Though popular in the USA, this move was harshly criticized by Columbia, Venezuela and other AFTN member countries. While the USA escaped any meaningful sanctions, the effort had no long-term impact on the South American drug trade, which was re-established at manufacturing bases on the new hydrocolonies.

IFEA reports on global economic status

A report by the International Forum for Economic Analysis (IFEA), revealed that China, Korea and Vietnam accounted for thirty-five percent of the world's manufactured goods. African economies showed the highest levels of manufacturing growth at ten percent, double that of most other economic areas. Europe and the USA remained economically wealthy, but were responsible for only eight and seven percent of all manufactured goods respectively, both regions having become largely service-based economies.

2047

Porginine delta causes record rise in energy stocks

Energy stocks on the New York, London, Tokyo, Frankfurt and Seoul exchanges, rose to a new record in anticipation of the introduction of porginine delta, a low-velocity petroleum substitute.

EU and AEU sign Treaty of Friendship

Hostilities between the EU and the AEU ended, with the signing of a Treaty of Friendship in Antwerp. Like the first Treaty of Friendship signed between the NEB, AFTN and EU in 2035, the blocs agreed to selective specialization, whereby each bloc focused on a particular sector of the global economy. Selective specialization encouraged trade and discouraged trade conflict.

2048

Outbreak of Strigmathus disease

Strigmathus, a mysterious disease, killed fifteen miners in a northern Bolivian town. Scientists at the Salk Institute in San Diego, California, identified the cause as an airborne virus. Though the Bolivian government attempted to contain the virus, it spread, killing 2.3 million people in South America and 800,000 people worldwide. Just as suddenly as it had appeared, Strigmathus disappeared.[25]

2049

Gamma Ray Parallelization technology invented

Developed by physicists Barden Maisher and Dorothea Fry of the Free Earth Research Council, Gamma Ray Parallelization (GRP) used parallel gamma rays, synchronized by coordinated matter-antimatter bombardment, to weaken the ionic structure of metals. GRP significantly increased the rate of metal

---

[25] The last known case of Strigmathus was recorded in 2053.

recycling in manufacturing. By 2070, "grazer beams" used GRP to destroy the structural integrity of enemy spacecraft.

UN Secretary-General killed in Punjabi civil war

United Nations Secretary-General and former Punjabi President Mathas Singh, was assassinated by the People's Front of Punjabi (PFP).[26] The PFP began its war to establish a fundamentalist Sikh regime in the Punjab in 2044. Three million lives were lost before the PFP was decisively defeated in 2052.

Introduction of EuroBill 117

EuroBill 117 introduced drastic "competitive wage" cuts, inciting labour strikes, violent demonstrations and mass protests throughout Europe. Supporters of 117, including French Prime Minister Jacques Papierse and his Belgian counterpart, Nikolas Raan, who saw the Bill bringing the EU into competitive alignment with the Asian and African blocs, were forced to resign. German Chancellor Margriethe Riedle and British Prime Minister Peter Tollenby, narrowly defeated no confidence votes in the Bundestag and at Westminster respectively. Strong popular opposition throughout the continent prevented the effective implementation of EuroBill 117.

Manned mission explores Saturn

The solar system's second-largest planet, Saturn, and its moon, Titan, were explored by a joint Russian-Chinese mission under the leadership of Captain Wai Nang aboard the *Gagarin*.[27] As with the previous exploration of Jupiter,[28] booster jets packs attached to each crew member's spacesuit allowed the astronauts to leave the spacecraft to survey Saturn's gaseous makeup. Later *Gagarin* missions surveyed the other Saturnian moons in the 2050s.

In 2102, the first colony in the Saturnian system was opened for Human settlement on Titan. Eventually, Titan's sister moons—Dione, Enceladus, Hyperion, Iapetus, Mimas, Pan, Phoebe and Tethys—were also settled and Jupiter's floater colonies were adopted to hover in Saturn's gaseous exterior. By 2160, there were two hundred and eight million people living in the Saturn system, increasing to five hundred and thirty-seven million people in sixty-five colonies by 2280.

The Saturnian moons, especially Dione, Rhea and Titan, contained vast reserves of porginine fuels. Further porginine deposits, discovered in 2140 within the deeper folds of Saturn, provided even greater reserves.

---

[26] The former Indian state Punjabi, gained its independence as a Sikh homeland in 2038.

[27] The Chinese allowed the ship to be named after the twentieth-century Russian astronaut Yuri Gagarin, in return for Chinese captaincy.

[28] See entry for 2044 for details of exploration of Jupiter.

2050

Hispanic rebellion in the USA

Gangs of youths known as "brigados," ransacked businesses in Los Angeles, Phoenix, San Diego and Dallas. The Riots of Summer in the southwestern USA, later referred to as the Hispanic Rebellion, caused $320 billion in damage and only ended when the National Guard was called to intervene.

Social critics blamed the riots on the poverty and oppression of the Hispanic community which, by 2050, was the largest, but least economically successful, minority group in the USA. The federal government responded by instituting Future 2100, an employment initiative aimed at hiring Hispanic workers in the space industry. This program was credited with turning around Hispanic-American relations.

2051

Merger of transportation giants

The big three automobile companies, General Motors, Ford and DaimlerChrysler, merged to form the Transglobal Automation Corporation (TAC). This largest merger in economic history at that time, was necessitated by increasing competition from South American and Asian automobile producers. Future economic historians identified the TAC merger as a precursor to the rise of Super Corporations.

Human travel surpasses one percent of light speed

The Flyer Series, an advanced aviation program jointly funded by Lockheed and Boeing, was unveiled. *Flyer I* was the first aircraft to fly faster than one percent of light speed. Boeing and Lockheed merged in 2055 to form Airstar International, the world's largest aviation corporation.

Cold fusion achieved

Cold fusion was achieved with the assistance of quark catalysts to facilitate nucleon[29] bonding. Scientists fused two nucleons at room temperature, releasing high levels of energy. Cold fusion techniques supplied energy to Earth's industries, space stations and colonies for much of the late twenty-first and early twenty-second centuries.

2052

The Primax Compactor

The Primax Compactor, an advanced waste disposal unit invented in

---

[29] A nucleon can be either a proton or a neutron.

2052, reduced the volume of inorganic waste by ninety percent by 2061. The Compactor employed magnetic forces to compress matter, creating significantly less voidage[30] than was previously possible. In addition, the Compactor's own compact size allowed it to be used in average households.

Scientific food farms expand
By 2052, scientific food farms produced forty percent of the world's food supply, growing to ninety percent by 2100. Food farms used biotechnology to synthesize food for both Human and animal consumption. As scientific food farms did not require land for food production, eighty percent of the planet's former agricultural lands were made available for Human settlement by 2100.

Manned mission to Uranus
Latin American astronauts in the spaceship *Bolivar-3*, became the first Humans to visit Uranus. Twelve later missions to Uranus, from 2055 to 2075 explored its moons—Oberon, Titania, Umbriel, Ariel, Miranda, and Puck—as well as the lesser satellites.

The first Human colony was built on Oberon in 2109. Due to its violent storms, Uranus itself was not settled, even by hover colonies. The Uranian moons, sites of frequent earthquake activity and few mineral resources, also remained sparsely populated. By 2160, there were 3.5 million people living in settlements and space stations in the Uranus system.

2053

EuroTunnel completed
EuroTunnel, a three thousand kilometre tunnel for vehicular and train travel between the Iberian Peninsula and Scandinavia, was completed, after forty years of construction. Links to cities in Britain, France, Belgium and the Netherlands were added by 2056. The Asia Tunnel joined Japan with Mainland China and Korea in 2058.

First Human landing on Neptune
Poseidon XIV, captained by Tamra Shainer, landed on Neptune. *Poseidons XV* and *XVI* explored Neptune's moon, Triton, in 2056 and 2057. The *Galle* missions, between 2058 and 2062, visited Nereid, Proteus, Larissa, Despoina, Galatea, Thalassa and Naiad, as well as Neptune's rings.

The first colony in the Neptune system was established on Triton in 2111. Hover colonies across Neptune were built by the mid-twenty-second century.

[30] Voidage is the space between solid particles in a system.

By 2160, there were fifteen independent colonies in the Neptune system, with a combined population of one hundred and seventy million people. The Neptune worlds' elaborate network of space stations and communication beacons, as well as its strategic location, enabled the system to become an important hub for interplanetary travel in the twenty-second century.

2054

Pope John Paul IV's Papal Bull

Pope John Paul IV issued a Papal Bull recognizing, for the first time, the rights to abortion and contraception. Church leaders from France, Italy, Spain and Portugal supported the Bull, representing a revival in organized Catholicism in western Europe, which had been seriously weakened by the Duprey crisis of 2045.

However, Eastern European and Filipino Catholics expressed shock and declared an alternative pope, Benedict XVIII, the "True guardian of the Papal Throne." The alternative pope caused the greatest crisis in the Catholic Church since the Great Schism of the Middle Ages.[31]

American Republican Party fragmented

The American political scene was dramatically transformed by the breakup of the Republican Party, into the Nationalists and the Progressive Dynamists. The Nationalists represented patriotic isolationism, deeply influenced by fundamentalist Christian thinking; the Progressive Dynamists remained moderate, favouring Regitonic[32] political and economic policies. Some Democratic supporters were attracted to the Progressive Dynamists, creating a true three party political structure for the first time in American political history.

2055

War in the Middle East

Much to the world's surprise, Israel, Palestine and Syria-Jordan joined forces, against the threatening advances of Islamic regimes in Iraq and Egypt.[33] This new Moderate Front readily defeated Iraq and Egypt at the Battles of Aleppo Heights and St. Catherines, ending overt violence between fundamentalists and liberal democrats in the Middle East for some time.[34]

[31] During the Great Schism, from 1378-1417, the pope resided in the Vatican, while two successive anti-popes ruled from Avignon, France.

[32] See entry for 2043 for a discussion of Regitonics.

[33] An Islamic fundamentalist regime took power in Egypt in 2023.

[34] Secular government returned to Egypt in 2079 and Iraq in 2062.

First multi-digestives for public consumption
Multi-digestive drugs, which redirected nutrient flow to undernourished cells, became publicly available.. The most popular multi-digestive, hydoramine, targeted the absorption of amino acids. Later multi-digestives focussed on lipid and carbohydrate transfer.

2056

ATP production enhanced
Adenosine triphosphate (ATP), an energy rich molecule produced during the body's respiratory cycles, was generated by a non-respiratory electrochemical technique known as triphosphate generation (TPG). Developed by the biochemist Bittesh Mihava, TPG increased the body's energy generation, without additional oxygen consumption. The TPG technique proved essential to the colonization of worlds with limited oxygen supplies.

2057

World's largest democracy becomes benevolent dictatorship
The Indian Path Party (IPP),[35] won an overwhelming majority in the Lok Sabha, campaigning for clean government. The IPP used their majority to grant sweeping powers to the Executive, to address political corruption. The reforms also diminished state power in favour of the Executive. The IPP's popular success in battling corruption, eventually allowed Shami Tendulkar to emerge as a benevolent dictator with little resistance. Tendulkar ruled India for thirty years, creating political and economic stability.

Death penalty abolished in USA
In the case of *Bancroft vs. The State of Texas*, the American Supreme Court prohibited capital punishment, paving the way for the abolishment of the death penalty throughout the USA. Several African and Asian countries followed the American example.[36]

The demise of OPEC
As the price of petroleum rapidly fell after the discovery and refinement of porginine, the economic clout of the Organization of Petroleum Exporting

[35] The IPP was created in 2049, by an amalgamation of the Reconstructed BJP and the dynamic youth wing of the Congress Party.

[36] The death penalty was revived in many countries, including the USA, after the Third World War.

Countries (OPEC) also declined, causing its members to disband. The resulting economic depression in the Middle East lasted well into the 2090s.

2058

Plastodome Crystal completed

The Plastodome Crystal, a complex built entirely from plastic fibre, was completed in Singapore. The brainchild of Manuel Figo, a Portuguese architect, the building was lauded as an engineering feat, as well as a fine example of Plastorealistic art. It suffered little damage in the earthquake of 2065, when the rest of the city was destroyed.

The second Global Census

The second Global Census,[37] which was completed in 2058, reported a world population of 12.4 billion.

Country or Region	Population in Billions	Country or Region	Population in Billions
Asia*	2.4	Europe***	0.6
Africa	2.2	USA	0.5
India	2.1	Russia	0.5
China	1.7	Indonesia	0.4
Latin America**	1.6	Rest of Earth	0.4
GLOBAL POPULATION 12.4 BILLION			

* Asia excludes India, Russia, China and Indonesia, which are noted separately.

** Latin America includes South and Central America.

*** Europe excludes Russia, which is noted separately.

Space junk at critical levels

The UN's Rodriguez Report, authored by respected environmental scientist Camille Rodriguez, proposed plans for the reduction of space junk[38] that had accumulated in Earth's orbit. The Report recommended spaceship hulls be fitted with laser incinerators, to destroy harmful junk in their way. By 2071, a brigade of robotically controlled sweeper planes continuously orbited the Earth, retrieving space junk for recycling.

---

[37] See entry for 2030 for details of first Global Census.

[38] This space junk was comprised primarily of booster rockets, non-functioning satellites and spaceship debris.

Space aviation

Three thousand space flights per year, were leaving or entering Earth's orbit by 2058. This number increased to twenty thousand by 2070.

Gettysburg space city opens

Gettysburg, the first North American space city and the largest at that time, was declared fully functional. Gettysburg housed 100,000 people.

2059

South Africa's last gold mine closed

The last of South Africa's gold mines shut down, as the nation's gold reserves were finally exhausted.

Whale Havens established

The UN's Environmental Earth Foundation (EEF), created ecological havens for whales and other ocean life, providing protection against increasing marine toxicity. Giant filters were used to cleanse several artificial and natural bays.

Moroccan revolution sparks Algerian invasion

The death of King Hassan Ahmed, resulted in a Moroccan revolution. Algeria seized the opportunity to invade Morocco, officially annexing the country in 2060. Algerian President Sayeez Mohammed described the new nation as "the first step toward a Maghreb Republic spanning the Sahara." Troops loyal to the Moroccan royal family, continued to battle the Algerian invaders from bases in Tunisia and Polisaria,[39] with limited American support. However, China provided weapons to Algeria, enabling the Algerians to conquer Tunisia and Polisaria in 2067 and Libya in 2068.

2060

The Sino-Russian War

A border skirmish between Russia[40] and China, over political and economic influence in Mongolia, left five hundred dead. Chinese forces launched a full-scale infantry attack, driving the Russians deep into the Siberian heartland. The Russians then employed tactical nuclear weapons, destroying large segments of the advancing Chinese army; the Chinese responded in kind. The Sino-Russian War continued for three months, ending in a stalemate, however, the first use of nuclear weaponry since World War II, undermined

[39] Polisaria was created in 2032 in the disputed area of Western Sahara.

[40] The Russian economy stabilized in 2010 and its gigantic military was re-established between 2030 and 2060.

decades of international support for global disarmament.

Though the USA officially maintained its neutrality throughout the Sino-Russian War, it was later revealed that American intelligence agencies had encouraged hostilities, by clandestinely providing both combatants with weaponry to prolong the conflict. Ironically, historians have postulated that the outrage engendered by this discovery, created a shared perspective between the Russians and Chinese, which ultimately led to their joining forces in the Third World War.

Scottish independence

Scotland formally gained independence from the United Kingdom.[41] The Scottish Republic continued its economic union with England and Wales, while independently pursuing foreign politics from its seat of government in Edinburgh.

2061

American economy improves

In 2061, the USA experienced an economic boom, equal to that of the mid-twentieth century. In accordance with the first Treaty of Friendship,[42] the Americans excelled in telecommunications and computer services. Global Link, formed by the merger of ATT Electrical, Motorola and Intel in 2057, became the world's largest supplier of electronic information and in turn, one of the most powerful organizations on Earth.

Flyer-2

The Airstar International[43] space plane, *Flyer-2*[44], was successfully test-piloted. Powered by porginine gamma fuel and robot controlled, *Flyer-2* reached a velocity of three per cent of light speed. Tatse-Yakamoto, the giant Japanese airline manufacturer, introduced the *Samurai*, its own high-speed space plane in 2062.

2062

Birth of Populare politics

Populare Philosophy resurrected elements of Marxism-Leninism. Claiming that the failure of Developing World countries arose from the attempted

---

[41] Northern Ireland obtained independence in 2015, reuniting with Ireland in 2023.

[42] The first Treaty of Friendship was signed by the NEB, AFTN and EU in 2035.

[43] Airstar International was a joint EEC-AFTN venture.

[44] Flyer-2, was named after the Wright brothers' plane, Flyer.

imposition of European ideology, Popularists advocated a blending of Marxist-Leninist principles, with local cultural and religious practices.

Populare governments were elected in Bolivia, Peru and Venezuela in 2062 and Columbia in 2064, splitting the continent along ideological lines. In 2065, a war ensued between the Populare Nations (Bolivia, Peru, Venezuela and Columbia) and the Anti-Populare Front, including Brazil, Ecuador, Paraguay and Uruguay. The five-year conflict, left the Populare Nations semi-victorious, but eight and a half million people dead. Populare Philosophy also inspired revolutions in Africa and Asia at this time.

In 2070, the Populare Nations withdrew from the AFTN, to form the Populare Trade Bloc (PTB), seeking trade partnerships with other Populare governments, rather than geographic neighbours.

2063

Porginine discovered in Brazil

Large deposits of porginine discovered in southern Brazil, caused several American corporations to move chemical operations into the region, in turn creating a Brazilian economic boom.

2064

The American Land Reclamation Act

The American Land Reclamation Act became law in the USA. Designed to ease urban tensions, tax incentives promoted the rehabilitation of industrial wastelands into residential areas. Similar legislation was passed in Belgium, France and Germany.

2065

American president assassinated

President Willard Jenkins of the USA, whose Regitonic[45] policies underpinned the Grand American Economic Recovery of the 2060s, was assassinated in Portland, Oregon. The American Tradition, a radical organization opposed to Regitonic philosophy, claimed responsibility.

The Wind Energy Project

An energy production program, the Wind Energy Project was established along the American west coast. The project employed eight hundred thousand wind-driven blades, linked to generator units via a complex power grid. The grid was centrally controlled at a computer terminus in San Jose, California.

---

[45] Refer to the entry for 2043 for a description of Regitonics.

Costing one trillion dollars to build and employing 1.4 million people, the Wind Energy Project supplied the region with eighty percent of its energy needs. Other wind energy projects were undertaken in Angola, Italy and the Philippines during the next decade.

Chile attacks Cape Horn drug traffickers

Drug trafficking, especially in chemically synthesized protomones, reached its peak during the 2060s. In 2065, the Chilean Armed Forces crushed an international drug cartel headquartered on Tierra del Fuego. Despite this rare success, the inability of the world's police forces to control the drug trade, encouraged the legalization of many narcotics during the 2070s.

2066

First manned mission to Pluto

Pluto was visited by Earth's astronauts in the spacecraft *Lowell-1*[46] and Ivan Capurnian was the first Human to set foot on the surface. Pluto's first colony was established in 2118 and by 2160, almost seventy million people were living in fifteen colonies on the solar system's smallest planet. Pluto's moon, Charon, was settled in 2123.

Unrest in West African Union

Tribal conflict in West Africa led to mass violence in Benin, Ghana and Togo. WAU troops quelled the fighting and martial law was imposed as food shortages become widespread.

Super Satellite Program

The Super Satellite Program was established, improving telecommunication links between Moon Bases *Eden* and *Nirvana* and space cities and stations near Earth.

Echoes of Space experiment launched

The Echoes of Space experiment (ESE), a descendent of the twentieth century's Search for Extraterrestrial Intelligence (SETI) program, was launched. Miniature radio telescopes, fitted to high-velocity probes, scanned for radio signals from stars similar to our sun, such as Tau Ceti and Epsilon Eridani, on the hypothesis that those stars would be most likely to contain planetary systems capable of supporting life. Explorers in the twenty-third century validated this hypothesis.

---

[46] Lowell-1 was named after astronomer Percival Lowell, who predicted Pluto's existence.

2067

China tops GNP list

The Chinese GNP surpassed that of the USA for the first time. The top fifteen countries by GNP for 2067, are listed below.

Country	GNP (trillions of $U.S.)	Country	GNP (trillions of $U.S.)
China	28.5	Britain	6.6
USA	28.3	France	6.5
India	11.4	Maghreb Republic	6.1
Japan	10.3	Italy	5.8
Russia	9.4	Korea	5.1
Brazil	9.0	WAU	4.9
Germany	8.7	Australia	4.0
Indonesia	6.9		

Niger Development Project

The Niger Development Project was established, altering the flow of Africa's third-longest river to end an eight-year drought in west Africa. The Project also stopped the spread of the Sahara Desert, transforming parts of it into arable land.

2068

Chemical giants exploit Moon

DuPont and WorldChem, two giant chemical corporations, were granted lunar chemical production rights by the SISF. The corporations jointly established the Lanex Complex on the Moon, to process petroleum, porginine and hyper-strength plastics. The Lanex program encouraged lunar industrialization and settlement for the next twenty years.

2069

Macro-housing in Hong Kong

Eighteen percent of Hong Kong's land mass was cordoned off for the construction of the City of the Celestial Dynasty, a large urban transformation project designed to house nearly two million people comfortably. The City of the Celestial Dynasty increased Hong Kong's population density by three times, without decreasing its standard of living. Financed by wealthy entrepreneurs, this project began a trend in the East towards regulated macro-housing projects.

2070

Querzian particles identified; Ultraphotonic flight possible

Querzian particles were identified in porginine samples by research scientists at the New Hebrides Institute of Physics. By 2092, it was determined that querzian particles, imparted with a critical momentum, created pathways allowing objects following in their wake to accelerate to velocities greater than the speed of light. This discovery ultimately served as the principle for ultraphotonic flight[47] in the mid-twenty-second century.

The initial difficulty was attaining and then maintaining the required momentum for large objects, such as spaceships. Laser bombardment, force-field shearing and extra particle fusion all proved unsuccessful. The Anti-Matter Reflector invented in 2108, allowed a small spaceship to attain critical momentum for the first time.

The reflector bounced energy waves back and forth in an anti-matter bed, creating energy which was imparted to the querzian particles by concentrated wave transfer. At the critical momentum, the querzian particles created a "Relativity shattering pathway,"[48] through which large blocks of regular matter could travel at speeds greater than light. By altering the direction in which the querzian particles were emitted from their source,[49] space flight in any direction of three-dimensional space could be facilitated.

The volume of the querzian particle pathway, depended on a device known as the "Catcher Pole." "Hooking" onto the front of the created pathway, the Catcher Pole manipulated the pathway into a definable size and shape—such as that of a spaceship—whereby all matter and energy contained within the volume could travel faster than light speed.

Speeds equal to one thousand times that of light, would be achieved by the twenty-third century, allowing Humanity to actively explore the stars.

US-China Naval War; The Free Ports Agreement

The Chinese attacked American gunboats in the South China Sea, claiming that the USA was coercing South East Asian nations to boycott Chinese products. The USA denied these charges and backed by the EU nations, defeated the Chinese flotilla off the coast of Malaysia, ending the naval war in two weeks.

[47] Ultraphotonic flight is defined as space flight exceeding the speed of light.

[48] This discovery caused a modification in Einstein's Theory of Relativity, as querzian particles defied categorization as either matter or energy, contrary to Einstein's assumption that all entities consist of one or the other.

[49] Computer-aided plasma magnetic focusing, the process by which querzian particles were redirected, was known colloquially as the "steering wheel."

The USA seized the opportunity to force China to enter The Free Ports Agreement, procuring China's commitment to soften its militant approach in the region, by allowing the USA and EU greater access to South East Asian ports. Chinese powerbrokers, including Nationalist leaders Zing Zeching and Li Wan, vehemently opposed the Agreement until 2074, when Zing seized power. Zing's anti-Western stance increased hostility between the USA and China over the next several years, peaking again when China allied with anti-American Russian forces in the Third World War.[50]

Food wars in India

Food wars tore India's cities apart, claiming over four million lives during an eight-month period of violence. With the support of a large majority of the Hindu populace, the secular government restored order by resorting to the wholesale slaughter of cattle to feed the nation. Hindu traditionalists vented their anger at this sacrilegious outrage, by siding against their secular regime and allying with the Chinese during the Third World War.

2070 and 2072

Belcarz's Child; Annihilation of Neanderthal Man

Two significant breakthroughs in the field of Human anthropology occurred in 2070 and 2072 respectively: the discoveries of Belcarz's Child and the Neanderthal Man Annihilation. In Siberia, Human biologist Jaime Belcarz, discovered the fossil remains of a modern Human child, determined to be approximately 3.4 million years old. This find added 3.3 million years to the existence of modern man, traditionally thought to have occurred only one hundred thousand years ago. In 2084, explorer Pierre Burlliat and anthropologist Yera Yariev, uncovered further Human remains from the same time period as Belcarz's Child. These discoveries caused anthropologists to question our understanding of Human evolution and reassess the steps and timelines involved in the ascent of Humanity.

A less significant, yet important discovery, by biologist Quin Zhen in western China, occurred in 2072. The remains of a Neanderthal man dating back only twenty thousand years, suggested that this species had survived longer than previously hypothesized. The 2079 discovery of the Anatolian Battlefields, rich in stone weapons as well as the fossils of both modern and Neanderthal man, confirmed speculation that a series of battles for control of the Paleolithic plains might have resulted in the annihilation of Neanderthals.

---

[50] See entry for 2082 for a detailed discussion of the Third World War.

2071

Space Shuttle VIII Disaster

Since commercial shuttle flights from Earth to the space stations began in 2045, civilian space travel had grown by one thousand percent by 2070. The industry's unblemished safety record was shattered in 2071, when *Space Shuttle VIII* exploded enroute from Earth to the *Terrania Space Station*, killing two hundred and fifty-nine passengers and crew.

The SPA inquiry into the largest space disaster in history, revealed gross incompetence on the part of the spaceline, Ptolemy Travel Flights. Ptolemy's President, Mervin O'Keach, was sentenced to twenty-five years in prison. Public pressure forced the SPA to impose greater regulatory control over civilian space travel.

2072

Radical judicial reform

Norway abolished imprisonment for all offenses, except murder, and introduced a drug therapy called Psycho-Pharmacological Redirection (PPR). Drugs administered to suppress deviant urges, allowed the criminal's safe return to society. Recidivism was reduced significantly, though some criminals proved entirely immune to PPR. Accordingly, Norway's initial policy was revised, to allow the return of non-responsive criminals to correctional facilities. PPR was soon implemented by many other nations.

2073

Failed coup d'état in Russia; Emergence of the Sporzakov regime

With the world's attention still focused on the USA and China, a coup d'état masterminded by an alliance of Neo-Bolshevik and Populare groups, was quickly crushed by Russia's democratic government. In one week, ten thousand people died in street fighting between government and rebel forces. Russian President Yuri Sporzakov, seized the opportunity to implement martial law, spawning the rebirth of totalitarian autocracy in Russia after eighty years of relatively stable democracy.

Sporzakov administered his country ruthlessly, proceeding to abolish the national parliament and sending secret police to arrest thousands of citizens deemed enemies of the state. Sporzakov began rebuilding the Russian military and increasing Moscow's involvement in the political and economic affairs of the former republics of twentieth-century USSR.

After decades of dismissing Russia as a limited world power, this turn of events caught virtually all political watchers by surprise, creating considerable consternation in the EU bloc and the USA.

2074

The fuel race

Indian-based energy corporation Maraj Chemicals, introduced dodaz, a generic name for a family of porginine-based fuels. Dodaz was used widely for short-distance commercial travel.

Ten years later, the Australian company Bolton Fusion generated another porginine-based fuel, hydrofus, whose later refinements replaced porginine gamma[51] as the principal fuel for interplanetary travel. In 2095, ships powered by hydrofus were able to reach speeds equal to ten percent of light.

Birth of the Biotron

During the twenty-first and twenty-second centuries, the Biotron became the principal unit for mass urban settlement on both Earth and the newly colonized extraterrestrial worlds. Adapting several hydrocolony technologies,[52] the first Biotron was built in Mumbai in 2074. Each Biotron housed thousands of people in a healthy, ecologically adjusted environment, for indefinite time periods.

On Earth, the Alpha Biotron accommodated fifty thousand people, while the larger Beta model housed over three hundred thousand individuals. A typical Alpha model covered a base area of 0.7 square kilometres, extending three hundred storeys up and one hundred storeys underground. Individuals were assigned a cubicle and cubicles were arranged in groups of eight to form an Octraun. Members of an Octraun shared central kitchen, living and washroom facilities. In the developing regions of Earth, and later on new worlds, these living arrangements were relatively luxurious.

An environmental process, dubbed "Octraun node control optimization," linked each Octraun to the Central Computer Terminus, for efficient distribution of heat, air, water and electricity throughout the Biotron.

Every two hundred Octrauns formed a political and administrative unit, known as a Dodectraun. The residents of each Dodectraun elected a governing Council and participated in referenda via an electronic voting system run by the Biotron's Central Computer Terminus.

Externally, the Biotron was linked by monorail and subway to the outside world and eventually, to other Biotrons. Later Biotron models, especially those designed for extraterrestrial worlds, contained offices, industries, food

[51] See the entry for 2043 for the origins of porginine gamma.

[52] See the entry for 2031 for the origins of hydrocolonies.

production centres, retail stores, recreational and greenery sites and other necessities, allowing the unit to maintain a near-complete level of self-sufficiency. In theory, a Biotron resident could live from birth to death in such an environment. By 2100, there were over four thousand Biotrons on Earth; by 2125 there were one hundred thousand.

2075

Peace agreement ends conflict in North Africa

Egypt and Sudan signed the North African Peace Initiative in Khartoum. The treaty ended over twenty years of hostility and also laid the groundwork for more efficient use of shared resources, most notably the Nile River and the mineral wealth of the Nubian Desert.

Chapter 3: Humanity on the Brink

2075-2100: The Buildup, Outbreak and Resolution of the Third World War

Russia resurrects military alliance; Arms race renews

Leaders of eleven[53] of the fifteen ex-Soviet republics met in Minsk. Under the guidance of Russian dictator Yuri Sporzakov, a military alliance was struck and the economic principles of the NEB were reaffirmed. Sporzakov delivered an emotionally charged speech, exhorting the Slavic and Asian peoples to rise again to global power, at the expense of Western nations.

The Slavo-Asian Pact and Sporzakov's rhetoric, produced widespread unease in the West. Anticipating direct military confrontation between the Pact/NEB countries and Western nations, the EU and the USA began a military buildup.

2076

First brain transplant

The first viable brain transplant was performed in 2076, by the Italian neurosurgeon Vincent Feurri. The recipient of the donor brain lived for fourteen hours. Feurri's work relied on flash freezing and selective heating techniques, pioneered by *Eden Base* medical clinics in the 2060s. Neurosurgeons Lo Win and Miero Kamarika continued Feurri's work, rewiring nerves by computer. By the late 2090s, brain transplant recipients commonly lived for ten years or more.

2077

Artificial intelligence popularized

Peocomp,[54] a fifth-generation personal artificial intelligence unit, became a marketing success. Each Peocomp was custom-made to its owner's requirements to provide instruction, organize household affairs or be a companion. Logo Brain, the Texas-based company responsible for developing artificial intelligence technology, was credited with this first use of artificial intelligence for the general public.

---

[53] Latvia, Lithuania, Estonia and Moldavia did not attend.

[54] The name Peocomp was derived from an amalgamation of people and computer.

Moldavia joins Slavo-Asian pact; USA offers support to EU
Russia successfully incorporated Moldavia into the Slavo-Asian Pact in 2077. Fearful of Russia's increasing belligerence, American President Jeffery Smyth, offered the EU the use of two hundred F-46 fighter aircraft and sixty B-88 bombers.

Emergence of the science of brain tectonics
The science of brain tectonics was born at the Piaget Centre for Neurological Study in Toronto, Canada. Brain tectonics studied the brain's action, by directly monitoring the movement of the brain's so-called neuron plates, first discovered in 2063. The investigation of this motion was instrumental in understanding such conditions as epilepsy, mania, pylam[55] and mectian.[56]

2078

Sino-Russia alliance
Russian dictator Yuri Sporzakov met with Chinese premier Zing Zeching in Hong Kong. The two leaders put aside their differences and decided to implement a cooperative economic and military plan. Analysts later argued that Sporzakov and Zeching had decided to divide up their territorial ambitions, so that Russia would be granted free reign in Europe and parts of the Middle East, while China would pursue its imperialistic aims in Asia without hindrance. At the meeting's conclusion, Sporzakov remarked, "There is a need to create a new global power base, independent of the constraints of liberal democracy." Such a power base, Sporzakov claimed, would favour the economic and population settlement demands of the "oppressed" Slavic and Chinese people. For several years, Sporzakov had spoken against what he termed "the economic exploitation of the Slavic people by Western nations."

The EU and USA responded to the Sino-Russian bilateral agreement, by drawing several nations of the Association of South East Asian Nations (ASEAN) Pact, all of whom feared Chinese expansion, into military alliance with the West.

Assessment of global distribution of military power
The Relative Military rankings of the principal international armed forces, as listed in a 2078 edition of *Jane's,* is given below.

---

[55] Plyam is a condition in which overproduction of dopamine causes a painful pressure buildup in the brain. The disease was first identified during the Venusian Space missions. If not treated correctly, Pylam can produce self-destructive psychotic behaviour.
[56] Mectian disease is the rapid onset of brain cell decay, caused by the erosion of neurons as a consequence of techtonic motion.

The unit of measurement is the Military Standard (MS).

1 MS is equivalent to	2 battleships or
	50 tanks or
	1 aircraft carrier or
	15 conventional missiles or
	4 cruiser ships or
	1 killer satellite or
	10 fighter bombers

Country or Alliance	MS Units
Slavo-Asian Alliance	245
USA	237
China	212
EU	195
ASEAN[1]	174
WAU	94
LAAF[2]	95
EAF	62

The development of anti-nuclear missile systems by the major powers between 2020 and 2065, meant conventional wars could be waged without fear of recourse to nuclear weapons.

2079

The gathering storm between the West and Sino-Russia

Through a unanimous vote in Accra, the WAU opted to remain neutral with respect to the continued hostility unfolding between the Sino-Russian camp and the EU-US alliance. Latin American countries split evenly over the decision to choose sides in a conflict that one Brazilian political analyst described as a "Northern Hemisphere Crisis." The Middle Eastern and Maghreb countries also expressed mixed feelings, with Algeria, Iraq and Pakistan siding diplomatically with the Sino-Russians, while Egypt's secular government, Israel and Syria-Jordan backed the EU-US alliance. The EAF opted to remain neutral in any conflict.

Space agency splits: Two new space cities open

A political struggle within the SPA, led to the splitting of the organization and the formation of the rival International Space Agency (ISA), of which the United States and Germany were leading founders.

The same year, two space cities, *Futaria A* and *Mirov*, were established. The former was situated near the asteroid belt, where it functioned as a scientific monitoring base. The latter, an agricultural project belonging to the powerful Russian corporation Vlatchkov Holdings, was located in the vicinity of Venus.

Invention of the Gravo-suit

Denis Champlain, a Quebec engineer, invented the high-tech gravo-suit, that proved vital in the exploration of the outer planets in the 2090s. The suit used micro-stabo generators, implanted in its material fibre, to normalize the gravitational forces exerted upon an individual. The new suits were more comfortable than earlier technologies weighed less and offered better protection against cosmic radiation.

2080

Breakthrough in molecular genetic cleaning

General Electric designed and built the first Deletrious Molecular Remover (DMR). The DMR used controlled X-ray bombardment to clean DNA strands at the nanotech level. DMR was further enhanced in 2090s, by the development of DNA reconfiguration devices, able to remove unwanted atomic interference in individual DNA bases and thereby stabilize the integrity of the molecule against potential decay. Computer enhancement later increased the speed of DNA cleaning *in vivo*, thereby insuring the viable reproduction of DNA in the body. It became commonplace in the early twenty-second century, for people to visit DNA clinics to have their DNA cleaned as a protection against cancer.

War in Europe edges closer

A joint session of the UN and WON was convened in Lima, Peru, after the Russians began massing troops on the Polish and Finnish borders. UN Secretary-General Dominique Lamberaine, invited the Russians to discuss the troop deployment with representatives of the EU. This meeting, held in Geneva, proved fruitless. Russian Foreign Minister Ivan Balchenko, argued that Moscow was supporting the interests of Slavic minorities in both Poland and Finland and would not retreat from its planned action. The world held its breath as the threat of war became more imminent.

Mass space transport

As the dense population of the planet continued to strain Earth's resources and decrease many people's quality of life, cash benefits paid by interplanetary development corporations further enticed would-be new world colonists.

Simultaneously, the Technological Resource Foundation, ASEAN's Engineering Initiative and a consortium of aeronautical companies (Airstar International, Lugvlieg Inc., Tatse-Yakamoto and Airbus), unveiled the *Da Vinci* series of high-capacity spaceships for both commercial and military use. These ships transported large numbers of people (up to eight thousand at a time), at high velocities, to destinations including Mars and Jupiter, furthering the space colonization initiative.

2081

China flexes her muscle

In August, China launched an attack on the independent nation of Nepal. Despite a brave defense by elite Ghurka fighting units, Katmandu fell to Chinese forces two months after the invasion. The UN and WON condemned the Chinese action by placing international trade sanctions on Beijing, however, countries in the Slavo-Asian Pact refused to adhere to these sanctions. In September, Chinese naval destroyers clashed with Japanese battleships off the Korean coast.

The West's guarantees

The EU and US issued the Brussels Promise, guaranteeing the sovereign rights of any country threatened by either Slavo-Asian or Chinese aggression. US president Dianne Bergholm, despite her election less than a year earlier on an anti-war platform, won approval from Congress to introduce compulsory military conscription.

2082

Ukraine joins forces with Russia

Anatol Fuchma, a general in the Ukrainian Armed Forces, took control of the government in Kiev, after staging a successful military coup d'état. Fuchma added his country's name to the Slavo-Asian pact, in spite of Western efforts to keep the Ukraine outside Russia's sphere of influence. He preached Slavic brotherhood and coexistence, similar to Sporzakov's rhetoric.

Soon after Fuchma gained control, construction began on an underground tunnel to enable the shipment of supplies between the Ukraine and Russia.

2082-2086

Outbreak and timeline of the Third World War

August 2082: Russian and Ukrainian aircraft launched a surprise attack on the Hungarian capital, Budapest. A second attack, against Bucharest by

Ukrainian and Belarusian missiles, annihilated much of the Romanian city. The EU and US declared war on the nations of the Slavo-Asian Pact.

September 2082: EU planes strafed Ukrainian troops with volleys of carpet bombs, hampering the Ukrainian advance into the Romanian interior. The same month, Russia occupied Hungary.

October 2082: Slavo-Asian troops defeated EU forces in a series of air battles close to Warsaw.

November 2082: Much of Poland was controlled by Russian and Latvian forces. Finland also fell to Slavo-Asian troops.

February 2083: In a land battle near Prague, the Western powers were decidedly defeated by Slavo-Asian forces. An urgent meeting was called in London, to discuss military strategy to block the Slavo-Asian sweep through Eastern Europe. Prague fell to joint Russian-Ukrainian forces in April.

May 2083: Satellite attacks by American space orbiters on their Russian counterparts, proved successful in delaying the Slavo-Asian military advance. The destruction of their satellites disrupted telecommunications between Russian air and ground units.

September 2083: Laser beams from Mig-58 aircraft assaulted Amsterdam, Berlin and Vienna, killing thousands of civilians. The Western powers responded to these devastating attacks by blasting Russian positions with high-dosage gamma rays. Fighting spread throughout the European continent. Almost fourteen million people died between September 2083 and March 2084, a period known as the "Bloody Months."

December 2083: Vienna, having resisted the besieging Slavo-Asian troops for over seven months, collapsed in the midst of a persistent strategically directed bombing campaign.

January 2084: China successfully invaded and annexed Korea. The ASEAN nations counterattacked the Chinese, with limited effect, as the war extended into their theatre.

April 2084: American and British naval fleets defeated the Russians, in the critical Fury of the Ice Maidens sea battle, fought off the coast of Finland.

August 2084: Chinese and Indian forces clashed along their common border. In a series of search and destroy missions, Chinese paratroopers weakened the manoeuvrability of the Indian armed forces. Civilian deaths in the Asian theatre reached six million.

October 2084: Slavo-Asian troops launched purge campaigns in the occupied cities of Bratislava, Bucharest, Budapest, Gdansk, Prague, Vienna and Warsaw to stamp out resistance movements. This marked the beginning of the war of attrition between EU forces and the Slavo-Asian military machine.

November 2084: Pakistan and Kashmir assisted the Chinese in the Himalayan Campaign, by attacking the Indian army's northwest flank. The mountainous terrain, over which most of this conflict occurred, favoured guerilla warfare.

March 2085: A full-scale pincer attack by Slavo-Asian forces, using troops based at the geographic extremes of conquered Eastern European territory, was defeated by artillery divisions of the German and French forces near the Danube River. In the vicious air-tank battle that followed, the pincer attack failed. Five thousand tanks of the joint Western powers, defeated an equally strong Slavo-Asian force at the Battle of Moravia, a battle in which robotic soldiers were used extensively. The Western powers' victory, marked a turning point in the European theatre, with defeat lowering the fighting resolve of the Slavo-Asian nations.

June 2085: Chinese jet fighters destroyed large segments of Tokyo. Retaliatory attacks by the Japanese produced comparable damage in the Chinese cities of Shanghai, Beijing and Canton.

November 2085: EU and US forces pushed forward in their campaign to drive back the Slavo-Asian armies. Heavy street fighting broke out in Prague, leaving over half-a-million people dead. With the help of the Czech resistance, the Slavo-Asian forces were finally driven from Prague and the city was liberated.

December 2085: Turkish troops, with Western support, invaded Russia from the south, in an attempt to create a second front. Although Iraq assisted the Russians by harassing the Turks, the invasion plan played a crucial role in dividing Slavo-Asian supply lines. The Western-Turkish army emerged victorious over the Russians in fighting at Baku and Yerevan.

February 2086: ASEAN and US forces defeated the Chinese in an important air battle in North Vietnam, however simultaneously, Thai, Burmese and Indian troops were routed by Chinese special forces near Bangkok.

April 2086: Thailand fell under Chinese domination, an event marked by the massacre of over two million civilians by the occupying troops.

May 2086: Yuri Sporzakov ordered the bombings of Boston, New York and Washington, in an attempt to weaken American war support. A leak of the plans to Israeli secret agents, allowed the Americans to anticipate and frustrate much of Sporzakov's intentions, however, both New York City and Washington suffered bomb damage. An attempted Russian landing in Alaska, was blocked by soldiers from the American Ranger Battalion, ending Sporzakov's hope of reconquering the former Russian territory.

August 2086: China and the ASEAN alliance clashed in eastern India, in the largest military battle of Human history. Five million ASEAN and Indian soldiers fought against four million Chinese troops, in what became known as the "Ganges Apocalypse." Three million people died in the nine-week battle, that helped the Chinese gain the upper hand over their ASEAN rivals in the East Asian power struggle.
November 2086: Economic hardship and low public morale resulting from continuous military defeats on both war fronts, helped fuel support for the bloody revolution that overthrew the Sporzakov regime. The new Russian government, together with some member nations of the Slavo-Asian pact, sued for peace, as EU and US soldiers liberated Eastern European territory from Slavo-Asian control.

2087

Signing of the Treaty of Athens

A peace treaty was signed in Athens in January, ending the Third World War in the European theatre. The treaty laid the groundwork for the economic and political restructuring of Europe. Democratic Constitutions were drawn up for the totalitarian regimes of the Slavo-Asian Pact, including Russia, and war crime trials were initiated in Copenhagen. Refugee relocation programs were established to absorb the eighty million Europeans left homeless and stateless by the war. Giant corporations, including Exxon, Nestle and Sinatan (a Munich-based construction company), funded development programs to rebuild Europe's infrastructure, while individual speculators made huge profits during the post-war boom.

Ceasefire in Asian War

In June 2087, a ceasefire was reached in the Asian theatre. Although the Chinese advance had been contained by the ASEAN alliance in India, Zing Zeching's regime proved successful in winning and maintaining control over the territory of the once-sovereign nations of Korea and Thailand. Chinese expansion was restricted, but Zing's new land acquisitions gave him added prestige and moral authority in the eyes of the Chinese populace.

Main consequences of the Third World War

The death of almost three hundred million people in the largest conflict on Earth.

- The end of the Trade Bloc Era and the beginning of a movement toward the City State Era.
- China became the dominant power in the Eastern Hemisphere, although

due to the military-economic challenge offered by India and the prospect of civil war, this domination was not long-lasting. The new territories conquered by China, burdened the country with additional responsibility that proved uncontrollable.

- The United States began a decline that fostered conflict between the federal government and the states.
- The EU dissolved, leaving a Europe comprised of multi-ethnic and multinational cities, stripped of their identities and existing within an undifferentiated continent. Differences between European cities and their North American counterparts became negligible.
- Political and economic power spread to Africa and South America. These continents had avoided the Third World War and prospered afterwards as suppliers to all former war zone regions.
- India split into twelve independent city states, the most powerful of which were Bombay, Calcutta, Madras and New Delhi.

Additional consequences

- The "Annihilation of Budapest" was caused by high levels of chemical contamination, rendering the Hungarian city an uninhabitable biological wasteland.
- Twenty percent of Poland fell under German control.
- Prague became a free city, separate from the old Czech Republic.
- Bulgaria split into three city states.
- Russia declined and dissolved into several city states.
- Turkey occupied over thirty percent of the former Central Asian Republic, principally Uzbekistan and Turkmenistan.

Dawn of a new era in space exploration

An eight-year period known as the "Dark Ages of Space Exploration," ended in 2087. International consortia constructed mining colonies on Mercury to extract chromium, cobalt and vanadium from the vast deposits in the planet's crust.

Solar laboratory built

Planerse Corporation constructed a Solar research laboratory, *The Halo of Aristarchus*, on Mercury. The *Halo* became a leading research facility, providing valuable information on high-temperature planetary colonization, that proved crucial during the Stellar Colonization Era, two centuries later.

2088

Invention of the booster car

The booster car, a dodaz-powered[57] transportation vehicle, capable of carrying one to two hundred people at an altitude of four hundred metres, was patented by Siegfried Hobson. From 2090-2160, this technology forced the redundancy of the road-bound internal combustion automobile, as the principal means of short-distance travel. Roads closed in many cities and the skies around urban centres, soon known as Skyways, were organized to efficiently coordinate the large volume of booster car traffic.

Re-engineering the Martian atmosphere

The SPA shipped large quantities of green leafed plants to Mars from Earth. The plants had been genetically altered to adapt to life in the largely methane environment of the Martian atmosphere. Over a twenty-year period, these plants infused immense volumes of oxygen into the atmosphere. About twenty percent of the Martian atmosphere was ultimately converted to an oxygen-nitrogen mix. The huge cost of separating this working atmospheric volume from the rest of the planet's biosphere, so gains were not lost through natural gaseous encroachment, required technology that only developed in the late twenty-third century. This process, known as Earthification, became standard procedure, giving the atmosphere of other planets an Earthlike character and rendering them habitable.

2089

Ringelbaum inspired to invent force field

A freak meteor shower destroyed part of the spaceship, *Fidelio*. Herman Ringelbaum, a research assistant at MIT, was prompted by the incident to invent the Trapofield, the first workable force field system. The Trapofield was initially used in the mid-2090s for the concentrated exploration of the Oort Cloud Rings. For his work, Ringelbaum was awarded the Prize of Slovenia.

The return of laissez-faire capitalism

With the dawn of the Modern Era of Commercialization, the "buck" ruled again (especially in Africa and South America) and Humanity went wild. The pursuit of money was reminiscent of America's at the turn of the millennium. This period lasted until 2105, when the harsher demands of planetary colonization forced commercialization to become more rational.

---

[57] Dodaz had a unique ability to promote lift, and therefore flight, through the rotary motion of the querzian particles in its fluid, when laser-scanned at a critical angle. The science of querzian particle motion, or querzogenics, showed promise over the next century.

2090

Opening of the Three Religions Tower

The Three Religions Tower, an ornate structure containing a multitude of displays and books on the beliefs and doctrines of Christianity, Islam and Judaism, opened in Jerusalem. The Tower was built with the financial assistance of private donors and eventually grew to contain the largest library of religious texts outside the Vatican. The Three Religions Tower became a leading centre for research and study in Comparative Theology.

Globalization diminished the impact of religious differences on world politics, however, differences in technology and wealth between groups, corporations and cities continued to dictate political direction.

***The Lost Tree of Eden* published**

Michael Verniger won the Pulitzer Prize for his novel *The Lost Tree of Eden*, the story of three explorers searching for the Tree of Knowledge from which Adam and Eve ate. The plot described the explorers' discovery of the tree and their consumption of the fruit, to reverse the consequences of the Fall from Grace. *The Lost Tree of Eden* was unique, in that it was the first novel written in Spacetalk,[58] to win the Pulitzer.

2091

Hase Report released

The Hase Report, authored by economic historian Daniel Hase, was published. The report argued that the Third World War and Russia's economic demise, had been indirectly caused by the gross inequality in wealth between competing regional trade blocs. Hase also argued for the dismantling of the exclusive trade blocs, in favour of a freer policy of global economic cooperation. His report was instrumental in guiding the decisions that led to the breakup of the economic blocs in the early twenty-second century.

Invention of olfactory sensory pads

Mitchell Van Zijk of the New Earth Research Foundation, invented specialized olfactory sensory pads lined with the chemical substance derzium.[59] When inserted, the olfactory pads provided the recipient with an elaborate sensory matrix, allowing the nasal cells to detect previously elusive gases, such as carbon monoxide.

---

[58] Spacetalk was an emerging language spoken mainly by the inhabitants of the floating cities around Earth.

[59] Derzium, a crystalline structure, was indigenous to the diamond deserts of Titan. It also proved useful in radio astronomy.

2092

New Human rights doctrine signed

The Dresden Accord, an updated Human rights manifesto, was signed by all countries of the UN and the WON. The Accord renewed the principles of the Geneva and Helsinki agreements signed in the twentieth century, but placed greater emphasis on the rights of women and children. The Accord was designed to carry more weight than earlier agreements, through the establishment of the International Human Rights Court to monitor infringements by signatory nations. The Accord contained provisions for economic sanctions and possible military action to punish offending nation for gross Human rights violations. Felix Maritino, Secretary-General of WON and the Accord's architect, was awarded the Nobel Peace Prize for his efforts.

The Dresden Accord was adhered to during the City State Era of the early twenty-second century, but with the transition to corporate domination and the true death of nations, the Accord lost its significance, eventually deteriorating into obsolescence by the beginning of the twenty-third century.

2093

Atlantis discovered?

An archaeological dig in Northern Cyprus, uncovered a palace predating all Minoan and Mycenaean ruins in Greece and the surrounding Mediterranean area. The discovery opened an international debate on the origins of Western civilization, with archaeological radicals claiming that the palace was part of a lost city established by colonists from Atlantis.

2094

Elections in Russia bring liberals to power

Democratic elections were held in Russia, with liberal candidate Viktor Taldoz elected president. Taldoz promised and delivered a greater degree of cooperation with the West.

The same year, war villain Yuri Sporzakov was given a life sentence for crimes against the Russian people orchestrated during his dictatorial rule. The sickly Sporzakov died in prison five months after the sentence was passed.

Also in 2094, a pro-democracy party was elected to govern the Ukraine.

Era of speed-thought

Researchers at the Goodview Medical Laboratories, located on the *Roosevelt* space colony near Mars, introduced Human Thought Enhancing Techniques (HTET). Speed-thought processes increased the Human capacity for perception, intuition and the generation of creative ideas. This effect was induced by the stimulation of neurons using micro-electronic devices. The driving force behind HTET development, were corporations that believed new cognitive research would produce more efficient employees.

Neurologists in the 2110s, built on earlier speed-thought innovations, by programming computer-mapping algorithms to electronically break and reconnect neural pathways, as opposed to individual brain cells, further optimizing thought function.

2095

Mass settlement of Yukon and Nunavut

The development of the Yukon and Nunavut territories of North America, allowed for mass immigration to these regions. Left destitute by the Third World War, new immigrants, largely Asian and East European, settled the former tundra regions, where a maritime climate had been environmentally engineered. The settlers contributed to the economic growth of North America, which had been severely compromised by the War. By 2105, twenty percent of the North American population was comprised of post-war immigrants.

2096

Matter accelerated beyond light speed

Matter was accelerated to a speed greater than that of light, using querzian particle technology. The non-matter-energy nature of querzian particles, created the conditions for the Aulbertin Criteria, allowing the violation of Einstein's Special and General Theories of Relativity, without temporal or spatial distortion.

Industry forced underground in Britain

To improve the landscape quality and cope with the problems of decreasing availability of space for industrial zoning, the British parliament passed a bill forcing corporations to site new industrial facilities underground. Despite an initial resistance from business interests, the Bill received support from a public eager for much-needed living space. The US and many European and Asian countries passed similar laws by 2110.

More settlements on Saturn

The SPA unveiled plans for extended settlements on Saturn's moon, Titan. By 2102, the SPA had completed the construction of three independent colonies, each housing one hundred thousand people. The Titan bases were the first of a new generation of space colonies using Biotron[60] design principles, already in extensive use on Earth, in a non-terrestrial environment. In 2110, developers added a Trans-Titan Railway link and a booster car[61] Skyway to accelerate transportation between Biotron units.

2097

Civil war in the Philippines lights up

The Philippine Peoples Brigade (PPB) launched attacks on government installations throughout the country, pushing the southeast Asian nation into crisis. The PPB was essentially a Populare[62] philosophy resistance group, that had been waging war against Domenic Mangadong's Filipino regime since 2079. Although backed by the United States and France, who were hoping to limit Chinese involvement in the region (China actively supported the PPB), Mangadong's government collapsed in 2098 and PPB leader Ernesto Tarsigan seized power as a puppet of China.

2098

Invention of the Microgem

Herschel Leibner, a German inventor, patented the Microgem, a mechanical device allowing the user to store vast amounts of high-density information, by using the spatial angles of molecules that comprised basic nanochips. The Microgem revolutionized the computer data industry, by increasing information storage by a trillion.

2099

Sufi movement on the upswing in the Islamic world

The Sufi movement made tremendous headway, winning popular support in Iran and the Arab world. Guided by the writings of Mohammed Nagabi, the school's spiritual leader and author of *The Chronicles*, the Sufis successfully catalyzed an Islamic renaissance, creating a modernist Islam and shaking off the centuries-old fundamentalist yoke. Nagabi was widely recognized as Islam's finest contemporary scholar, receiving the Nobel Prize for Literature in 2104.

Space colonization: The giant leap

Jan Tamanjiak, President of the Space Academy and supporter of the Burbank Declaration, won the heated debate over its implementation. The Declaration

[60] See entry for 2074 for the development of Biotron units.

[61] See entry for 2088 for details on the development of booster cars.

[62] See entry for 2062 for the philosophy and growth of the Populare movement.

offered space colonists a high level of autonomy and self-government. Some UN member nations criticized the agreement, fearing it would lead to unstable mini-states, jeopardizing the political balance of near-Earth space, however, history has shown that there ensued greater instability on Earth than in the colonies.

2100

Petrus champions world government

Vitulus Petrus, the Harvard-educated geopolitical analyst, in his widely read and acclaimed book, *Toward A Stronger Democracy*, outlined the pragmatic aspects of world government. Petrus' theories, called the "Golden Principles" by his followers, gained substantial mainstream support from 2100 to 2120. Public sentiment shifted from the trade bloc structure, towards singular economic integration. Ironically, the rise of the city state as the primary political unit, led to the obsolescence of Petrussian philosophy after 2125.

Chapter 4: The Age of Breakthrough

2101

Unification of churches

After years of debate, the Neo-Catholic and Anglican Churches united. Church representatives reached the decision at a meeting of church elders in Canterbury and Cardinal Pargonini was elected the first leader of the joint Church. Catholics who opposed the union, broke away to form the Church of the Revelation.

As the Catholic Church had already split in 2054, there were now three branches of Catholicism:

- the Traditionalists, who supported the conservative doctrines of John Paul II
- the mainstream Neo-Catholic-Anglicans under Pargonini
- the Church of the Revelation

The Traditionalists held the Vatican, while the Neo-Catholic-Anglicans were headquartered in Dublin. The Church of the Revelation was controlled from Manila.

2102

Trans-global rail link completed

After a six-year delay occasioned by the Third World War, Inter-Trans finally completed its monorail link, connecting over three hundred of the world's largest cities. The project, which took almost twenty years to complete, criss-crossed five oceans. Porginine-powered vehicles drove the monorails at high velocities, so the journey from London to New York took a mere ten minutes. The building of Inter-Trans, required the cooperation of a multitude of different construction and railway corporations and was Earth's largest engineering project to that date.

2103

Post-war economic boom peaks

European cities damaged in the Third World War were largely rebuilt, according to modern principles. Biotrons[63] and Food Farm units formed the building blocks of their urban environment.

---

[63] See entry for 2074 for details on Biotron origin and construction.

2104

The Blerion reducer

The Kenyatta space city, the first African cosmic colony, was the site of an explosion that initially killed four hundred people. When residents were unable to extinguish the subsequent fire, it destroyed over a third of the colony and forced the evacuation of over ten thousand people.

The disaster encouraged the SPA to demand of operators of any type of space facility, the installation of a highly successful extinguisher known as the Blerion reducer.[64] The Blerion reducer used wavelength detectors to determine the cause and flow pattern of a fire, to eradicate the blaze as efficiently as possible from almost any location on the ship or colony, through the controlled emission of the appropriate extinguishing agent.

Restoration of the monarchy in Romania

A Royalist uprising in New Bucharest succeeded in replacing the democratically elected Romanian government with a monarchy headed by Ion Florenceau, a direct descendant of the twentieth century figure, Prince Michael. This event was not favourably greeted by many continental governments. Florenceau was assassinated during a Romany uprising in 2105 and a nationalist government was restored in Romania. Monarchist regimes, however, took power in the city states of Sofia and Prague in 2106, catalyzing a trend that spread to most of Eastern Europe, the Middle East and North Africa.

Space monopolies disbanded

The Rights Dispute, a famous two-year legal case, was finally decided. In a landmark judgement, The Space Academy voted to reduce the large corporate monopolies that had, until then, almost exclusively controlled space development. This revolutionary decision proved crucial in expanding the scope of space exploration to include new sectors of the general Earth population.

2105

Settlement colonies opened in Antarctica

Two Antarctic cities, named Amundsen and Scott after the region's early twentieth century explorers, opened for population settlement. The inhabitants were drawn from the urban regions of Moscow, Beijing and New York. The cities served as examples of the use of a climate controlled Butatoid[65]

---

[64] The reducer was named after its inventor, Pasqual Blerion.

[65] Named after Brazilian architect Hernando Burtanis.

architecture, entailing the use of large domed structures resting on beds of cylinders, through which the city's heat and air were efficiently supplied, regulated and re-circulated. The viability of such structures encouraged their use in the development of Biotrons on the planetary settlements of Mars and Venus.

Floater worlds established in proximity of Saturn
Construction began on the Rings of Light, a series of five floating cities situated near Saturn. The cities housed over one-and-a-half million people in giant Biotron living units and grew to become the largest permanent space-based structures of the twenty-second century. These cities were constantly modified and upgraded with the latest technologies and remained functional until the middle of the twenty-fifth century. The social structure of space cities in this era was similar to that of state collective farms in twentieth-century Russia, however, in the Rings of Light the "state" was represented by controlling Earth cities or corporations. The cities were built to provide corporations with a working population to exploit the mineral wealth of the Saturnian system.

2106

The end of the Mexican-American War
The two year Mexican-American War, broke out over the collapse of the AFTN. Heavy American bombing of Mexican positions outside the cities of Monterrey and Guadalajara, hastened the collapse of Mexican resistance. The treaty of Tucson reset the boundaries between the United States and Mexico and established a new framework for bilateral coexistence.

2107

End of Islamic rule in Iraq
The Shi'ite Fundamentalist regime that had been in power in Iraq since the 2060s, agreed to hold democratic elections. Sulamein Bajerat, leader of the secular Iraqi Democratic Party (IDP), was elected president. Bajerat ended the eight-year long hostility between Iraq and the Syrian-Iranian alliance.

First theme park in space
Cosmic Shangri-La became the first theme park to operate in near-Earth space. The park offered a number of spectacular attractions, including the Gravo Dip (a hundred-kilometre long roller coaster, powered by a controlled gravitational field), the Simulated Meteor Basher and the Comet Express. The advanced technology and apparent realism of effects used in the creation of the

park, attracted almost thirty million visitors annually. Leisure Entertainment, the company that designed the complex, opened two additional space theme parks in 2112 and 2118.

2108

Launch of Vesalius

Vesalius was a global health development initiative funded by the United Nations and the medical care corporations Dynamic Plus and Lygnex. A total of 1600 medical treatment units opened to the general public in areas of the world traditionally lacking adequate health care. The Life Patch, a primitive immunity technology incorporating many serums into biochemically treated paper, was dispensed at each unit. It provided resistance to two hundred virulent bacterial and protozoan strains.

2109

Disarmament Conference

Representatives of all militarily significant nations attended the International Disarmament Conference in Santiago, Chile to negotiate policies for the reduction of laser and chemical weaponry. They ultimately signed the Olive Agreement, a comprehensive document outlining plans for an era of cooperation between nations. The Agreement provided a specific timetable for the active dismantling of arsenals of mass destruction, which led to a temporary global disarmament between 2110 and 2120. However the rise of city states in the late 2130s, revitalized the arms industry and once again, total disarmament became a distant ideal.

The Martian platinum rush

The Martian platinum rush drew millions of settlers to the Red Planet. Several existing colonies expanded to house the arrivals. Five new colonies sprung up on the Martian landscape by 2120. Most of the platinum was extracted from deposits in surface channels near the equator. Over a hundred times more platinum was extracted from Mars than had been mined from Earth in the twentieth and twenty-first centuries combined.

2110

Turkey defeats Kurdistan and Iraq in ongoing Middle Eastern War

Aided by western capital, Turkey defeated the armies of Iraq and Kurdistan (an independent Kurdish region of eastern Turkey since 2023). The Turkish victory resulted in the breakup of Iraq into the new nations of Meso-Iraq, a Sunni dominated republic, and Shi-Iraq, a Shiite nation state. The same year, Iran suffered an internal crisis sparked by a spiritually motivated Zoroastrian rebellion.

2111

Disintegration of China

United China split into eleven regions following the collapse of the centralized Beijing authority. The breakup was precipitated by the rapid decline of the national government after the death of Zing Zeching in 2104. The Northern region of Manchuria fell under the control of military warlords, while Korea and Thailand regained their independence. A mixture of Confucian democracies and autocratic dictatorships gained power in regions that had once comprised the unified China.

Grid brake system invented

Frederick Drama, a Belgian engineer, invented the grid brake. Drama's brainchild was a grid of interweaving particle jets and reverse momentum fields, capable of decelerating a space vehicle from a velocity equal to five percent of that of light to a stationary position, in one nanosecond or less. The Drama grid brake system served as the primary braking mechanism for high velocity spaceships built between 2114 and 2140. Vijay Drashman's magnetic rotator, an improvement on the Drama model, was used after 2140 to decelerate space ships cruising at near-light velocities.

2112

American anti-tax brigade turns violent

The Wyoming Gun Club, an anti-federalist organization, violently opposed the federal tax hikes detested by Midwestern Americans. The Gun Club, led by ex-Marine Donald Wasseby, attacked and destroyed a US government building in Cheyenne in 2113, killing ten employees. These actions resulted in life sentences for Wasseby and six of his followers, who were seen as martyrs by a growing Midwest anti-federalist movement.

2113

Radical new government in England

Gerald Carberry, leader of England's Anglon Party, founded by highly patriotic renegades from the Conservative and Regitonic parties, took power after winning the general election. Carberry served as English President[66] for

[66] The position of President combined the figurehead status of the defunct monarchy and the old office of Prime Minister. Since the collapse of the monarchy in 2041, the President was the most powerful person in England.

eighteen years. He succeeded in strengthening the English economy, more closely reuniting feuding cities and improving the average living standard.

Drugs in space

Interplanetary Police of the Space Protection Institute (SPI) uncovered an international narcotics ring (specializing in 'Enhanced LSD') on Tolstoy Space Station. Alexander Dimitrov, the ring leader, was arrested and eventually sentenced to ten years in prison.

2114

Anti-federalist forces rise in US elections

Anti-federalist candidates performed strongly in congressional elections in Arkansas, Idaho, Kansas, Nebraska, Oklahoma and Wyoming. Separatist governors were elected in Montana and South Dakota. President Wayne Barkley initiated talks with separatist leaders in Wichita to discuss Midwestern concerns, however, Barkley's refusal to drop tax hikes and his inability to deal effectively with Midwestern grievances caused the talks to fail, as anti-federalist feelings continued to simmer.

Discovery of Ronar Ruins

Explorer Lilian Ronar discovered what became knows as the Ronar Ruins, a rock formation resembling an architectural structure, on the Jovian moon, Ganymede. Ronar claimed the structures were remnants of a settlement from an ancient civilization. The Ronar Ruins remained a mystery until 2145, when the discovery of a second set of related but better preserved structures on the Saturnian moon Rhea, gave credence to Ronar's theory.

2115

Terrorists attack water supply

A radical Islamic organization opposed to any form of cooperation between the nations of Israel and Palestine, destroyed sections of the Middle Eastern water pipeline between the cities of Ashdod and Gaza. The event heightened tension in the region and threatened to reawaken a long-dormant ethnic conflict, however, the apprehension of the responsible parties by the Palestinian Special Forces reduced much of this tension.

2116

The US presidential election

Ashleigh Watson won the US presidential election, aided by low voter turnout in the Midwest. Watson adopted a hard line towards separatist movements in the country, further intensifying the stalemate that already existed between the separatist states and the federal government. In the same election, California and Oregon threw their support behind the separatist movement.

2117

Taxonomic treatment

Immunologist Mitchell Barlow of the Salle Institute for Advanced Research in Disease, successfully and progressively weakened disease-causing viruses, by transferring them between related species. Barlow demonstrated that, in specific instances, by transferring a lethal pathogen from species A into a less harmfully effected but related species B, treating species B and then reintroducing the transformed disease into species A, a dangerous viral infection could be systematically eradicated. Weakening the pathogen by treatment in related species C, D and E following a workup in species B, served as an adjunct to further minimize viral strength before reintroduction into species A.

This procedure proved to be popular with pharmaceutical companies, as its implementation demanded the use of a variety of drugs and was critical in the defeat of many older viral-based illnesses. There was, however, much concern regarding long-term side effects arising from continuous treatment. Between 2140 and 2155, scientists improved Barlow's taxonomic technique, by manipulating the genome of species A to produce a protein, which helped the immune system adjust more readily to the shock of disease reintroduction.

Thailand's conservative government

Thailand's new government began an initiative to clean up the sex industry, which had stigmatized the nation for several centuries. Puritanical laws were instituted to curb the "excesses of the old society." A policy, similar to that of the Chinese cultural revolution of the twentieth century, was introduced to forcefully convert the Thai people as a whole to a new way of life. Ultimately, it failed.

Deep space probe released at ten percent of light speed

The Kepler space probe, travelling at a velocity of just over ten percent of light, departed on a forty-year mission to obtain data about Alpha Centauri, the nearest star to our Sun. A second probe, to Barnard's Star, started its trip in 2119.

2118

Atmospheric floaters

International consortia established floaters in atmospheric habitats around the

Earth. These electronic floaters, which resembled balloons, were designed to filter pollutants from the atmosphere. Five thousand floaters were used in this large scale project, code-named "Nature's Breath." Successive implementation of floater-type projects, from 2118 to 2150, created a temporary improvement in the terrible atmospheric conditions on Earth. They were later used on Mars and the Moon, to pump and recycle oxygen-nitrogen mixtures into their atmospheres.

2119

Life on Saturn

The exploration of Saturn revealed the presence of complex organic molecules, including a self-replicating molecule similar in structure to primitive DNA. In 2123, a research team led by Bacteriologist Bjorn Viren, reported the existence of bacterial organisms living on the planet's gaseous surface.

A species related to blue-green algae was discovered on Neptune in 2127. Eventually, of course, all the solar system's planets were found to contain life, although seventy percent of it was not of the carbon-based form that abounds on Earth.

New World settlement

Space development corporations began to more actively promote New World relocation programs, after large tracts of land were opened for bubble dome living on Venus and the Moon in 2119. The scientific altering of the lunar environment over the previous sixty years, had transformed previously barren areas on the satellite into settlement havens. Demographicists hoped that this new wave of space colonization would eventually ease the problems of overpopulation on Earth. Although corporate-directed programs helped in the settlement of these near-Earth worlds (and eventually Mars, Jupiter, Uranus and Saturn), Government-issued incentive bonds proved more effective in encouraging people to settle the more distant regions of the solar system beyond Neptune.

The Second American Civil War

Fighting broke out in Tulsa, Oklahoma, between federalist and anti-federalist forces, after police killed two tax-withholding separatists in what became known as the Tulsa Slayings. State armies evicted federalist forces from several states west of the Mississippi, forcing a declaration of war by the White House.

The Second American Civil War led to the eventual collapse of the United States as a political entity and the restructuring of power on the North American continent.

The numerical strength of the principal state groupings during this war is as follows.

Allegiance	Number of States	Population
Federalist States	24	290 million
Anti-Federalist States	17	280 million
Neutral States	9	170 million

2120

Battle of the Dakotas

Separatist forces defeated the federalists at the Battle of the Dakotas in April of 2120, however, federal satellites destroyed thousands of separatist aircraft in sky battles over the Ozark Mountains. Several attempts to reach a ceasefire agreement failed and five million people died during the year's fighting.

Funding for the Ronar Ruins

Billionaire Swedish space financier Jonas Sanderson, offered financial support for the investigation of the Ronar Ruins on Ganymede.[67]

The same year, Milan Ivanovic became head of the SPA. Ivanovic backed proposals for a sustainable development policy in space, a policy to limit environmental damage caused by the space boom.

Oort cloud explored

The Halley D'Arrest spacecraft, which left Earth in 2112, reached the Oort cloud and began to broadcast data regarding its makeup. The number of comet bodies contained within the Oort cloud was estimated at two-and-a-half million and the cloud was verified as the birthplace of the solar system's numerous comets. Decades later, stellar missions observed Oort clouds around other stars in the Galaxy and confirmed that these structures were not unique to our solar system.

2121

End of the Second American Civil War

After an eight-month stalemate, the Second American Civil War ended with the signing of the Treaty of Baton Rouge. The Treaty's signatories, each representing one of the original states, agreed to divide the former United States into regional components.

The American Civil War lasted for almost two years and claimed close to seven million lives, with the cities of Dallas, Denver, Houston and New Orleans suffering the heaviest casualties.

[67] See entry for 2114 for details of the discovery.

Asteroid rearrangement

Physicist Philip van Graan, first introduced the scheme to mechanically rearrange the positions of asteroids in the belt between Mars and Jupiter. Van Graan's plan, implemented between 2129 and 2135, aimed to reduce the number of space flight disasters in the "Lanes of Death." Force field lasers, robotically controlled mega-clamps and controlled nuclear strikes were all used to accomplish this Herculean task. Accident rates would drop by a factor of 98% as a result of these innovations.

2122

Aborigine states spring to life

The granting of sovereignty to Australia's Aborigines, led to the creation of localized semi-independent regions in the states of Western Australia and Queensland. An analogous autonomy arrangement was reached in 2124 between the New Zealand government and its Maori majority.

2123

Robot population on the rise

The robotic population of Earth and its space colonies, was estimated at over 250 million. Robots were divided into four categories, according to the nature of their work.

- Heavy-duty robots included all robots involved in difficult, intellectually undemanding, strength-related activities such as machine or building construction, mining and terrain rearrangement, all of which occurred on the macro level.
- Precision-work robots performed detailed micro level assembly work, e.g. electronic apparatus assembly, microsurgery and molecular rearranging.
- Human impersonators carried out much of what was once known as white-collar work. They were modelled as much as possible with the aesthetics and physical features of Humans. Impersonators were used for experimental testing, higher level intellectual work and inter-Human interaction simulation. They were greatly improved in the twenty-third and twenty-fourth centuries during the Age of the Android.
- Thinking machines gained prominence after 2100 and performed insight-related tasks, with the aid of artificial intelligence algorithms. Thinking machines were in many ways similar to Human impersonators, however, highly specialized circuitry allowed them to perform professional services in fields including law, medicine, architecture and engineering.

2124

Death of the USA

As a consequence of the Treaty of Baton Rouge, the former United States of America completed its split into nine independent nations: The Eastern Union, The American Republic, The Free States of Southern America, The Florida Republic, The Midwestern Federation, The Texas Expansion, The California Republic, The Cascade Federation and The Pacific Conglomerate. For details see

Appendix 1: Divisions of the Old United States following the Second Civil War.

The breakup of the United States encouraged the breakup of other nations and heralded the Era of the City State, when the presence of many states of nearly equal military and economic parity, added to the planet's political volatility.

2125

United Arab Armies conquer Syria

The United Arab Armies (UAA) of Nafiz Hassan, completed their conquest of Syria-Jordan in August, 2125. Over the previous five years, Hassan's troops had gained control of the former nation states of Saudi Arabia, The United Arab Emirates, Kuwait, Quatar and the two Iraqi states. Hassan, a Saudi by birth, received popular support from the Arab working class, who sympathized with his intention to resurrect Pan-Arab nationalism. In 2130, the UAA defeated the Iranian Army in the Battle of Tabriz, extending Hassan's power beyond the frontiers of the Arab world.

New colonies on Saturn's moon

The Imperial Japanese Investment House (IJIH) and the African International Bank (AIB), funded two colonies on Saturn's moon, Rhea. Between 2125 and 2140, a further four colonies were constructed on the Saturnian moons Hyperion, Dione, Enceladus and Janus.

2126

The global currency issue

The collapse of the regional trade bloc system at the end of the twenty-first century and the general tendency towards a global economy, encouraged the creation of a universal currency. A meeting of financial leaders in Berne, decided on the adoption of Keynes (named after twentieth-century economist John Maynard Keynes) as the standard global currency. The move towards a single monetary unit alleviated growing exchange rate complexities caused by the emergence of several new nations in North America and China. The use of Keynes lasted for a century, until the International Purchase Power Index (IPPI) completely eliminated currency. The IPPI graded every person according to a financial rating system based on individual wealth; buying power was assigned as points based on a person's IPPI tally.

Cossack rebellion in Russia
Rustin Gamblukov, a former Russian Air Force Pilot, led a Cossack army to carve out a regional mini-state on the Russian steppes, defeating the Russian Militia in a battle close to the Georgian border. Gamblukov's Cossack kingdom lasted only fifteen years, but its breakaway spirit proved contagious. The weak policies of the Muscovite administrators, who had ruled much of Russia since the Third World War, together with a growing rise in ethnic power, greatly bolstered secessionist forces throughout Russia's varied regions. The period from 2126 to 2145, was characterized by much dissension and armed strife across the whole Slavic land mass.

2127

Light speed achieved
Aerospace engineers at a test lab near Mars, accelerated the unmanned spaceship Goddard X-1 to a velocity greater than that of light. The Goddard X-1's outer shell was electro-mechanically altered to protect against the breakdown of the craft's structural integrity. It was powered by a combination of nuclear fusion engines and chemically treated porginine epsilon fuel.

The curse of unemployment
The rapid growth of the robotics industry on Earth, increased unemployment on the mother planet. Cities like Los Angeles, Paris, Shanghai and Tokyo, the four metropolitan areas with the highest robot to human ratios, saw unemployment rates rise to levels as steep as thirty percent. Anti-robot rioting, spearheaded by Neo-Luddite groups, forced the closure of several robot factories in these urban centres. By 2160, global unemployment increased further, reaching fifty percent, as a result of the ongoing robotization of the work sector. Unemployment stress on Earth further accelerated the solar system settlement drive.

2128

Anti-space terrorists hit communication link
Members of the Foundation for a Renewed Earth (FRE), an extremist

group with links to several mainstream anti-space populist organizations, sabotaged part of the global communication linkup connecting Earth with the planetary colonies and space cities. The FRE opposed the high level of capital expenditure in space, claiming that problems on Earth had to be solved before any further capital should be invested in solar system projects. Members of the FRE were guided intellectually by the writings of anti-space philosopher, Virginia Scheeley.

Another milestone in the speed race

James Donnelly, a test pilot for Airstar International, broke the thirty percent of light mark for a Human travelling in space.

2129

Outbreak of the Japanese civil war

After fighting that resulted in almost four million casualties, Najima Okawa, the Grand Taipan of the SONY Corporation, emerged victorious in the armed leadership struggle and ruled Japan for ten years. In 2139, Okawa handed control of the country to separate regional governments representing each of the individual city states.

2130

Human longevity on the rise

The Report on Longevity provided proof that the average lifespan of a person on Earth was ninety-eight years. Lifespan values tended to be higher on Earth than in space, where the average was only eighty-six due to difficulties in adjusting to artificial living conditions. In addition, lifespan values differed by less than ten percent across the broad spectrum of Humanity. People living in Europe, North America, Korea and Japan were at the high end of this scale, with an average lifespan of one hundred and one, compared to ninety-four years for residents of Africa. Improved medical care and better nutrition and living conditions were largely responsible for this dramatic increase in lifespan.

Hippie era on Earth

Noticeable returns to the Hippie subculture occurred in the 2040s and 2090s, but the so-called Fourth Hippie Era on Earth is usually dated from 2130 to 2145. Disillusionment caused by growing levels of unemployment, changing political infrastructures (such as the breakup of the US) and the apparent bleakness of future opportunities for the young, caused many to reject the values of their own period in exchange for the beliefs of the Hippie subculture of the 1960s.

2131

Flooding on the home planet

Large portions of Venice were completely submerged as a result of flash floods caused by icebergs melting within the Arctic Circle. Thousands of people fled to the Southern Alps to escape the waters that flooded the Italian hinterland. Force-field water dykes proved successful in preventing flood damage in Belgium and the Netherlands. The disaster encouraged engineers to begin work on plans to isolate the Mediterranean Sea from the Atlantic Ocean. The project came to be called the Gibraltar Option, named for the force-field barriers installed at the Straits of Gibraltar.

2132

World's largest mural completed

An international team, supervised by esteemed Chilean sculptor Violeta Fortimo, completed the "Faces of Humanity," a sixty kilometre sculpture carved in a stretch of the Andes mountains by a process of laser sculpting. The mural contained over five thousand intricate scenes illustrating the history of Humankind.

The space race continues

Dalton Industries failed in its attempt to corner the Martian iron ore trading market.

Also in 2132, Silvano Salazer broke the space flight speed record for a Human, attaining a velocity equal to forty percent of light. Salazer's daredevil flying skills encouraged younger pilots to push their crafts to their limits, leading to the eventual breaking of the fifty percent speed mark in 2135.

2133

First brush wheel goes into orbit

The brush wheel, a large mechanical apparatus employing trillions of minute hairlike structures to absorb and efficiently store the Sun's energy, was placed in orbit around Earth. Brush wheel structures became a major source of energy storage during the mid-twenty-second century. They proved essential in providing power for most of the more than seven hundred space stations and one hundred space cities that existed in the solar system at the time.

Historic déjà vu in France

Fighting erupted in the cities of Paris, Marseilles and Bordeaux after rioters protested the apparent apathy of the national government in handling the decline of the French economy. Michel Labeau, France's long-standing President, called on the army to crush insurrections led by Neo-Jacobin and Commune Revitalist groups. A year later, following the suppression of this echo of the French Revolution, Labeau introduced a government works program to cope with rapidly increasing unemployment. The program was structured similarly to Franklin Roosevelt's 1930s New Deal.

Curtis Urbain develops the first Gaseous Feeder colony (GFC)
GFCs made use of large gas retraction devices to maintain buoyancy in the gaseous aura of non-solid planets. Urbain's basic GFC model was perfected over the next ten years, producing almost four hundred different versions of the same design. The development of the GFC made it possible to establish large floater colonies on the outer planets of Jupiter, Saturn, Uranus and Neptune, with over a million inhabitants per colony.

2134

The first space corporation wars
In April, a cruiser spaceship registered to Bolzkov Industries, fired on an Almatec Communication's Neptune-Uranus shuttle. Bolzakov claimed that Almatec was using sophisticated espionage hardware hidden on its interplanetary shuttles to interfere with Bolzakov's silicon mining interests on Uranus. Corporate alliances quickly formed and a violent year-long struggle between rival groups ensued. Two hundred thousand people died in the fighting, mainly around the perimeter of Uranus. An eventual truce was reached at a meeting of company officials in Mumbai.

The first space corporate war, although regional in nature, evoked a popular outcry for a decrease in big business involvement in space exploitation. These calls went unheeded, however, as corporate strength gained more momentum towards the latter part of the twenty-second century. Historians attribute the rise of corporate influence in space to the fact that after the collapse of nations, only corporations had the necessary capital to sponsor macro-settlement and colonization in the extended solar system.

Famines ravage sub-Saharan African regions
The famines that killed over four million people between 2134 and 2138, were a direct result of the Central African conflict between the city states of Bangui, Brazzaville and Kinshasa. As a result of famine and war, Africans migrated en masse to the planetary colonies.

2135

Blocking the San Andreas fault

The San Andreas fault was blocked by a large anti-matter energy field to prevent the Pacific and North American Plates from sliding over each other. Anti-matter plugging became the principal means of preventing earthquakes in the twenty-second century. The technique enhanced geological stability in earthquake zones including Armenia, Japan, Old China and Portugal.

2136

United Arab Armies (UAA) attack Turkey

UAA forces launched a two-pronged pincer attack on Turkey. Turkish troops were driven westward by UAA brigades and their Kurdistan allies, while the Turkish capital of Ankara fell to UAA forces in 2137. A joint meeting of independent Middle Eastern nations met in Jerusalem to formulate plans for a local military alliance[68] to put a halt to the expansionist ambitions of Nafiz Hassan. Several European nations offered both military and economic support to this alliance.

2137

Plastomuscle replacement procedure

2137 saw the first use of the Plastomuscle replacement procedure as a treatment for combating muscle wasting from injury and aging. This technique, developed by Linus O'Shea at the Mother Theresa Medical Facility in Calcutta made use of polymer complexes that mimicked the physiological functioning of the proteins actin and myosin in natural muscle tissue. The Plastomuscle procedure represented a significant improvement over earlier attempts at muscle replacement, which concentrated largely on the body's gross muscle structures. In 2138, Plastomuscles were first used in bionic development, particularly for healing individuals who had suffered severe trauma in mining accidents in the Jovian and Saturnian Colonies. Nitroga, a polymer similar to the earlier nylon, predominated in the late twenty-second century as the leading material for artificial muscle contraction and relaxation activities.

UAA expansion continues

The independent nations of Armenia and Azerbaijan, fell to the advancing tide of UAA forces. After four hundred thousand people died in fighting centered around the Caucasian Sea, both countries were annexed by the UAA. Georgia,

---

[68] Known as the Jerusalem Three, the alliance consisted of Israel, Egypt and Palestine.

fearful of the Arab menace, signed military agreements with Romania, Serbia and Bulgaria, establishing the Eastern Pact. In 2138, the Eastern Pact joined forces with the Jerusalem Three to fight the UAA. Pact troops launched a stunning attack against the UAA at the Battle of St. Nicholas' Surprise.

Unidentified Flying Objects (UFOs) sighted in Indian interior

The reported sightings of UFOs in central India were deemed a hoax, until later evidence, released in the mid-twenty-third century, showed that UFOs were actually spaceships belonging to an alien race known as the Pazeq.

2138

First game park on Mars

Private interests opened a large game park on the Central Martian Equatorial Plains, a region that had been ecologically transformed into a savannah habitat resembling eighteenth century sub-Saharan Africa. Animals including cheetahs, okapis and gemsboks were introduced into this artificial world to alleviate population strain caused by the rapid increase in their numbers in the few remaining wildlife preserves on Earth. These animals were almost all extinct by the mid-twenty-first century, until well-intentioned, but badly coordinated, genetic experiments led to a burgeoning of wildlife populations by the early twenty-second century.

UAA advance halted

UAA troops were driven back by a Jerusalem Three counterattack, masterminded by General Yaacov Sharon, a direct descendant of twentieth-century Israeli war hero Ariel Sharon. The counterattack, known also as the Jericho Spearhead, opened the ranks of the UAA's Middle Eastern force, hastening the ultimate defeat of their campaign at the Battle of Amman. The UAA campaign in Eastern Europe and Asia Minor ended in 2139, when Eastern Pact allied forces drove the invaders back, liberating Turkey in the process. A peace treaty ending the war was signed in Sardinia in 2140.

2139

Venusian colony assaulted by acid rain

An unexpected release of highly concentrated sulphuric acid from clouds above the Venusian Colony Cupid 1, resulted in massive damage to the colony. Fifteen hundred people were killed in the sudden acid flood, forcing Human settlement planners to adapt more stringent design constraints regarding the building of newer Eros Alpha and Aphrodite series colonies on Venus.

Chapter 5: A Population Reorganizes

2140-2210: City States Period

The period from 2140 to 2210, was known on Earth as the City States Period. Governmental authority gradually passed from the nation state to the megalopolis. Across the globe, urban metropolises allied with other metropolises, forming strategic and economic fronts, comparable to the city state structure in Ancient Greece. The central authority of the city was considered the third major political and economic development[69] since the end of the twentieth century. Neighboring rural areas would fall under jurisdiction of the city.

The creation of the city state system was a long-term consequence of the resettlement programs initiated after the Third World War. The metropolitan area of each city state had been expanded to provide living space for newly arrived migrants, with cities themselves divided into smaller sub-city units.

The following is a list of ten major cities that played dominant roles in both the political and economic affairs of the city state period: Atlanta, Berlin, Calcutta, Kinshasa, Lima, Los Angeles, Moscow, New York, Tientsin and Tokyo. For details see **Appendix 2: The City States of Earth.**

2140

Earth-Pluto shuttle initiated

The Earth-Pluto shuttle made its inaugural flight in August, 2140. This was the last of a series of interplanetary shuttle programs established to provide regular transportation between Earth and the outer planets.

2141

Sun Probe explores solar core

The Helios Sun Probe, the latest development in high-temperature recording devices, was released into the interior of the Sun. Protected by temperature resistant Eazan Fields, the Helios Sun Probe relayed information about fusion in the solar interior. Analysis of the data revealed that the fusion process was not continuous as hypothesized, but had a discrete nature, with regular patterns of activity punctuated by periods of inactivity. Gersa sub-particles, first discovered in 2067, were theorized to be responsible for this phenomenon.

---

[69] The first development was the Trade Bloc Period from 2000 to 2095, the second was the Transition Phase or Era of Nation Breakup between 2095 and 2140.

2142

UAA leader stands trial

Nafiz Hassan, leader of the UAA, was abducted by a special missions Russian hit squad. In spite of outrage in the Arab world, Hassan was forced to stand trial in Istanbul for war crimes committed against the Armenian, Azerbaijani and Turkish people. After a nine-month trial, Hassan was found guilty as charged and executed by lethal drug injection in 2144.

2143

First use of Tectonic Explosion Dynamics (TED)

Tectonic Explosion Dynamics (TED), a geological technique pioneered in the late twenty-first century, was used to create habitable land in the South Pacific. TED involved the artificial stimulation, by laser or magnetic force induction, of volcanic regions in a tectonic plate for the purpose of generating new islands. Due to the hazards associated with TED, the consortium involved took many precautions, including source-cancellation devices designed to neutralize the buildup of tidal waves. By 2200, an area the size of France had been created using TED techniques. Despite this miraculous land recovery, such efforts had little impact in the war against overpopulation.

Earth's birth rate remained phenomenal, encouraged by emerging corporations who required an increasing consumer market. New technology reduced Human gestation to an average of six months. Fetuses matured entirely in vitro and the onus of child rearing was no longer on parents, but on specialized corporate controlled breeder organizations. Children grew up as parentless units in a giant business market, where their raison d'être was to mature, consume and thereby generate corporate profits.

In spite of the high cost of corporate child rearing, it was considered an investment in Human capital. From the corporation's perspective, the initial capital cost was more than outweighed by consumer purchasing power and loyalty once the child had matured.

Laser beam bisects Martian moon

An accidentally released high-energy beam, bisected the Martian asteroid moon, Deimos. The beam was produced from the prolonged backfiring of a solar brush wheel. Debris from the satellite pelted down on five of Mars' colonies, causing a slight shift in the Martian orbit. However, the use of high strength gersinide walls in the construction of the settlements' framework, protected the Human inhabitants from the rock bombardment.

2144

Dream Phoenix innovations bare fruit

By 2144, ecological development programs stemming from the original Dream Phoenix Project of the twenty-first century, had transformed the desert and semi-desert regions of Mars into grass field habitats.

Founding of Riviera City State

The Riviera City State was opened on the moon. The city was an expensive entertainment playground for the wealthy, recreating in its extravagant self-contained interior much of the glory of its twentieth-century French equivalent.

2145

Advances in manned spacecraft travel

Unmanned flights had been exceeding the speed of light since 2127, however, no Human-piloted craft had achieved this feat. The technology employed in these unmanned flights, could not power manned flights, without the pilot being instantly obliterated. The challenge with high-velocity Human flight was to reduce the external forces accompanying the querzian particle slipstream, as these forces caused organic matter to break down. It was this facet of the design, rather than pure spacecraft velocity, that most challenged scientists researching high-speed Human flight.

The following chronology highlights benchmark breakthroughs in Human-piloted flight from 2135-2145.

2135: A Lockhead 5 spacecraft captained by Ronald Bird, an American test pilot, broke the fifty percent of light speed mark.

2137: The high-speed Henkel 51432 vessel piloted by Juergen Kemps, used a microwave rotary engine to accomplish a speed greater than the fifty-three percent mark.

2141: The Namajika 9000, a ship helmed by Isao Yakomoto, used a combined microwave rotary engine and a querzian slipstream valve, to create booster fields accelerating its pilot to a velocity exceeding the seventy percent mark.

2145: The LD72, a Chinese ship commanded by Li Tong, used an improved version of the querzian propulsion drive to reach speeds greater than the eighty percent mark.

2146

Io rediscovers its volcanic past

Several underground volcanoes erupted on Io, spewing lava across the Jovian moon. Force shields protected the 120,000 colonists resident on the moon's two settlements, however, because of increased volcanic activity, the Io colonies were eventually abandoned in 2148 and its settlers moved to new accommodations on Ganymede and Europa.

Sirius research
A corporate funded space probe departed for the Dog Star, Sirius to obtain more scientific information about the star's system of planets.

2147

The future of weather unveiled
An international scientific and engineering consortium, established several minor weather maintenance programs to provide more rigorous control of Earth's meteorological conditions. Over the next twenty years, mechanical devices were developed to provide a system of checks and balances to counteract potentially harmful hot or cold air fronts. For example, thousands of air reheater and rechurner (ARRs) machines, each using an ultra-violet heat source and turbulent flow inducer, were strategically located in the troposphere. They manipulated air current flow to regulate weather over specific regions.

2148

Mystery labyrinth linked to Ronar Ruins
A unique fifty-kilometre long labyrinth, constructed of a rare quartz crystal, was discovered in a cave system on Pluto. Named the Hades Anomaly, in 2152 the labyrinth proved to be another piece in the Ronar Ruins puzzle. The Hades Anomaly evoked sculptor Georgina Bulkova to describe it as "the most captivating piece of creativity in the solar system."

2149

Formation of Antarctica Confederation
The various city states of Earth's most recently settled continent, united to form the Confederation of the Antarctic. By 2148 there were six major city states on Antarctica and several smaller towns, boasting a total population of eighty million. The removal of over eighty percent of the Antarctic ice shelf to the Martian colonies for water supply purposes during the 2110s and 2120s, freed the Antarctic continent for habitation. The 2149 population values and city state locations for Antarctica, are as follows:

City State	Population	Location
Amundsen	5.5 million	Queen Maud Land
Evans	8.3 million	Wilkes Land
Jawrie	7.5 million	Marie Byrd Land
Oates	7.1 million	Victoria Land
Shackleton	3.2 million	Enderby Land
Scott	8.9 million	American Highland

2150

A philosopher-king in Athens

The Curators of the Ladder of Life, a society dedicated to the philosophical study of Aristotle, took power in the city state of Athens. The Curators had two major political aims: the anointing of a ruler similar to Pericles, the philosopher-king of fifth-century BCE Athens and the establishment of a Pan-Hellenic Empire. The first philosopher king was Dmitras Lokidis, who changed his name to Papademocritus (Father of the Democracy).

Athenian troops launched a series of attacks against the Serbian city state of Belgradus in 2152, in an attempt to win control of the Balkan peninsula. The attacks were beaten back, but the Athenians succeeded in defeating the Albanian city of Tirane and the Macedonian capital of Skopje in 2154. Athenian influence spread to much of Southern Europe, igniting a continent-wide nostalgia for the ancient European classical age.

2151

Introduction of three-tiered urban planning

The three-tiered system, a revolutionary urban planning technique that organized the modern city as a composite of three vertical building levels, was implemented for the first time in the American Midwestern centre of Neo-Metropa. The first level of the three-tiered system was constructed underground and contained the industrial sectors of the new city. The second level was anchored to the surface, stretching over 200 storeys into the air. Office buildings, shopping arenas and marketplaces were located on the second level, alongside residential Biotron structures and other Human habitation facilities. Above the main city, were transportation skyways, shopping and entertainment centres, sports stadiums and Biotron structures populated by higher income individuals. Third level structures were supported by reverse gravitational flux fields, that served as the basis of city construction until the 2260s, when a five-tiered system superseded the three-tiered design.

Approximately three hundred new cities on Earth and throughout the solar system were built between 2150 and 2265 according to the three-tiered approach.

2152

Biotron wars in Calcutta

Armed gangs from different Biotrons in the downtown Calcutta city state, clashed violently over accusations of hijacking of inter-Biotron energy reserves. Approximately 140,000 people died in fighting that spread to a total of twenty Biotrons, turning large parts of Calcutta into areas resembling Second World War Stalingrad. The Calcutta Riots, which were finally put down by the military, encouraged city state officials worldwide to provide funding for specialized law enforcement units.

Known as Urban Dragoons (UDs), this new force was trained specifically to deal with the type of crime and gang warfare most commonplace in the Biotron environment. In spite of increased violence, the positive aspects of the Biotron system still far outweighed the negative.

2153

The March Leap

On the 14th of March 2153, Earth's ultra-sensitive atomic clocks recorded an instantaneous loss of one megasecond. Some scientists blamed the time loss on a readjustment of the space-time continuum around Earth, while others argued that the megasecond loss was caused by a fluctuation in the Earth's magnetic field. In 2198, Luxembourg physicist Johannes Beauchamp, finally settled the forty-five year-old puzzle, by proving that the space-time continuum hypothesis was correct. The March Leap, as it came to be known, provided insight into the mathematical relationship between the four dimensions, paving the way for future time travel.

2154

Discovery of serghese

Serghese, a self-replicating organic molecule, was found in great quantity within the gaseous folds of Neptune. Serghese had the unique ability to selectively retard certain physiological functions and was used by doctors to decrease Human food requirements. The discovery of natural serghese on Neptune encouraged corporate exploitation of this product, leading to the serghese rush of 2154-2166.

2155

Civil war in Baghdad

Fighting erupted between Sunni and Shi'ite Muslims in the city state of Baghdad. The conflict arose indirectly from the power vacuum created in the central Iraqi city, following the UAA's collapse. Turkish paratroopers intervened on behalf of the Sunni, massacring ninety thousand Shi'ites on the third day of fighting. Skirmishes continued for five months before a ceasefire was declared. Cairo city state troops acted as peacekeepers to maintain an uneasy agreement, whereby the 45 million people of Baghdad were divided into separate, independently administered, Shi'ite and Sunni regions.

New breakthroughs in high-velocity travel

Additional techniques developed, beginning in 2155, that contributed to Ultraphotonic flight. These included:

- The Positron-Electron Deorbiting Shunt (PEDS): The use of matter and anti-matter bombardment to produce a pressure drop, translating into the braking force for high-speed vehicles.
- Laser Concentration: Pressure buildup resulted from confining the beams of a xenon-radon laser in a magnetic chamber. The thrust force was then harnessed to accelerate a spacecraft.
- Linear Angular Momentum Flux: A direction-changing effect could be attained by the interaction of an electron stream with high-density pizero particles. The force interaction could then be manipulated to allow for direction changes of the spaceship, as it travelled through three-dimensional curvilinear space.

Chapter 6: Era of Expansion and First Contact

2156-2190: City states merge

The Era of Expansion describes the period in Earth history, when smaller city states merged to form large-scale metropolises. One of the more notable mergers was the unification of Copenhagen, Oslo and Stockholm to form the Scandinavian Peoples' City State with a population of thirty-eight million. Other significant city state mergers took place between Houston and Dallas (Dalhous); London, Birmingham, Liverpool and Manchester (Britania) and Kiev and Odessa (Slavo-Ukrainus).

2157

The light speed barrier falls for manned flight

On May 23rd, Mikhail Sandrovich became the first Human being to travel faster than the speed of light. Sandrovich's craft employed a querzian-positron engine, surpassing light speed within five seconds of stationary takeoff. He and his craft, the Azmatov 5000,[70] were immortalized. Sandrovich showed no ill effects as a result of the flight and his feat was duplicated by Peer Delarouge three months later.

2158

Opening of deep space penal colony

The New Alcatraz Penitentiary, the solar system's largest penal colony, was opened on the dark side of Pluto. The colony was designed to house over one million prisoners, in a series of twelve maximum security Biotron compounds. New Alcatraz was financially supported through a joint funding consortium, established by several city states and space colonies. The Penitentiary remained in existence until the mid-twenty-fifth century, housing some of the most notorious criminals in Human history.

Solar System Census

The Solar System census was completed and published in 2158. An overview of its population figures is given below. The value for each planet system includes the population living on nearby associated cosmic stations.

---

[70] The Azmatov 5000 was named after Petra Azmatov, a leading engineer in the field of flight dynamics.

Planet System	Population (millions)
Mercury	12
Venus	88
Earth	12,675
Mars	280
Jupiter	180
Saturn	200
Uranus	4
Neptune	170
Pluto	70
Kuiper Belt	5
Other space colonies	3

2159

Mysterious capsule discovered

A capsule, the size of a shoebox, was found in the Indonesian jungle region of Iryan Jaya by a holidaying soldier. The capsule contained information regarding an alien race approximately thirty-six light years away, on a planet orbiting the star Arcturus. Skeptics were quick to denounce the find as a hoax, but further investigation proved the capsule's extraterrestrial origin.

2160

Scientists breach Earth's core

A team of geologists reached the centre of the Earth after fifty-five days of laser burrowing. The head of the team, Dr. Bela Saluissan, reported his findings in the scientific journal, *Nature*. These included the discovery of surprisingly large deposits of uranium, porginine and copper in the Earth's core. Mining of the inner mantle began in 2162.

The Alpha Centauri probe calls home

Messages were received on Earth from the Kepler space probe to Alpha Centauri, launched in 2117. The probe gathered vast amounts of information about this closest stellar system to our Sun. Alpha Centauris A and B were found to have eight and three planets respectively, while Proxima Centauri appeared to have no planetary satellites. Three of Alpha Centauri A's planets were similar in size to Earth and a closer investigation of the largest planet revealed the presence of substantial surface water.

2161

Totalitarianism returns to China

A violent *coup d'état* in Tientsin allowed the dictator, Tan Wan, to gain governmental power in China's largest city state. Within a year, Wan's Silver Dragon laser-equipped forces had launched an attack on the rival city state of Shanghai, killing over eight million people in the seven-month long land war that followed. The fighting resulted in the destruction of forty percent of Shanghai and sent millions of city residents fleeing to the countryside. In response to Tientsin's belligerence, the City States of Beijing, Hong Kong and Nanking formed the Confucian Pact in 2162. Despite this opposition, Tientsin successfully occupied Shanghai in 2163, establishing a puppet government in the conquered city state. The same year, Wan declared himself China's true Emperor, recreating Imperial rule in China for the first time since 1911.

Battles in the Melbourne sky

Bandits held the city state of Melbourne hostage by blocking the transportation skyway. After a shoot-out with the city's skyway patrol, two of the eight blockaded zones were liberated. The remaining six zones were freed with satellite firepower that effectively zeroed in and neutralized the bandits' positions, with minimal damage to the skyway's structure.

Discovery of the Kierhaards

Settlers living on floating hydrogen mining colonies in the gaseous milieu of Saturn, were alarmed by a tremor that shook the giant planet. The disturbance was generated by the release of large volumes of highly pressurized gas at an epicentre near the planet's equator. After much speculation, an investigative team led by geologist Sui Tata, was sent into the apparent epicentre to determine the nature of the disruption. After three months of research, the team entered a cavern hollowed into a solid boron structure. Here, in the words of team biologist Justice Kierhaard, they discovered, "the presence of a higher-order life-form that is quite different to any organism on Earth." The string-like species appeared to have an internal chemistry based on the element boron. Further investigation revealed that the species' average lifespan was nineteen Earth years and that it reproduced asexually. The presence of a boron-based self-reproducing DNA-like structure within the beings, provided the crucial evidence that proved them to be living creatures. Psychological and behavioural experts studied the Kierhaards, as they were later named, and learned that the life-form was capable of intelligent communication. Their first appearance on Saturn was dated to eighty-seven million years previously.

The explosion that had rocked the floating Saturn colonies, was caused by the release of a boron-rich vapour by the Kierhaards, in a process repeated every sixty-two Earth years.

2162

Shanghai on the verge of defeat; Global economy in shock
The impending defeat of Shanghai produced mass panic throughout the world economy. Stock markets plummetted in New York, Moscow and Calcutta in the wake of the worst political and human crisis of the twenty-second century. An urgent meeting of city-state leaders was called in Dalhous. The Union of Global Metropolises (UGM) was formed to show international solidarity against Tientsin's aggression. A period of extensive arms development and manufacturing followed the establishment of the UGM, whose mandate was to act as an instrument for collective security, as both the UN and WON had been effectively dysfunctional since the early 2120s.

2163

Light travel leaps forward
Daniel Hastings, the whiz kid of light travel, outlined plans for the development of the famed Starships of Sol (SOSO), a fleet of cosmic ships designed to move over ten thousand people at a time through space at ultraphotonic speeds. Early SOSO models were used for interplanetary travel, but after much success, SOSOs saw service as transportation vehicles for colonists travelling to the Alpha Centauri and Sirius systems.

Crackdown on cosmic fraud
Stephan Ilyunshin and Martin Tassington were arrested in the city state of Naples, charged and later convicted of the illegal sale of large tracts of "Earthified" land to unsuspecting future colonists on Mars. Over eight hundred thousand people lost money in the racket. The result was tighter controls by the SPA on buying and selling property on the new planetary worlds.

2164

Porginine demand causes friction in Asia
The city states of Tokyo and Seoul clashed over porginine mining rights in the Sea of Japan. The conflict led to the estrangement of Tokyo from the UGM and its subsequent alliance with Tientsin to form the Asiatic Peoples' Pact (APP). The APP created a Far East power base, centred on the Tokyo-Tientsin Axis. It expanded in 2165, to include the city states of Bangkok and Saigon,[71] which had

[71] Saigon was formerly known as Ho Chi Minh City, but was renamed in 2034 during the Vietnamese anti-communist Revivalist Period.

both broken away from the UGM after disagreements regarding the over-influence of Singapore and the Java Free State (Djakarta) within the organization.

2165

Barnard's Star probe reports

Earth monitors received the first messages from the probe Gargarin 7, as it circled Barnard's Star, the third closest stellar object to our Sun. Gargarin's reports revealed three planets orbiting Barnard's Star and that the second of these planets appeared to have a biosphere capable of supporting aerobic life. Later investigations, in 2173, revealed that the second planet was indeed populated by several thousand carbon-based species.

Scientists arrested for unethical experiments

Five scientists working on the Bernoulli Research Satellite were arrested for performing unauthorized medical experiments on patients from the Tethys 2 colony in the Saturn system. Albert Steinlitz confessed to undertaking dubious medical experiments, including life and death testing of Humans for unassisted survival capability in methane and sulfur dioxide environments. Other experiments involved the use of deadly heat, administered to subjects in an attempt to replicate the thermal conditions on planets like Mercury. The rogue scientists were eventually convicted and sentenced to terms ranging from twenty-five to fifty years on the New Alcatraz penitentiary.

2166

The Asian War spreads

After obtaining guarantees of neutrality from the Indian city states of Bombay, Calcutta and Madras, Tientsin and Tokyo launched an attack on Hong Kong. The UGM city states, backed by the West, replied to this hostile power grab by declaring war on the APP. However in early fighting, UGM forces were severely beaten by the well-trained Bushido-Samurai regiments of the Tokyo military. In the first three months of the war in China, both the UGM allied cities of Chunking and Canton were destroyed. In fighting on another front, Tokyo launched a successful air strike against the Korean metropolises.

2167

Fall of Beijing

The city state of Beijing surrendered to APP forces in April of 2167. By September, over two-thirds of China was under APP control. In the Korean peninsula, Tokyo's superior air tank divisions, the Honshu Warlords, continued to pound Seoul and its sister cities, Pusan and Pyongyang. The three Korean cities held out for eleven months against Tokyo's overwhelming fire power, before surrendering to the Honshu Warlords.

More APP victories
In November 2167, APP forces, led by the brilliant military strategist Tong Kuo-feng, pushed westwards with the intention of annexing the dissident city states of Sian, Lanchow and Paotou. This was achieved by March 2168. Also in 2167, Tan Wan outlined his manifesto for the re-unification of China under Tientsin's central authority.

2168

Further events of the Asian War
In May 2168, the Human rights organization Global Watch reported that to date, over eighty million people had died in the Asian War.

In June, APP forces successfully attacked the Manchurian cities of Mukden and Harbin. The Mongolian city of Ulan Bator ceased all resistance to the APP in July.

With APP assistance, the city state of Saigon finally defeated the rival Vietnamese city of Hanoi in October. The bloody war lasted for nine months, leaving two million people dead.

A conference called between APP city states and the defeated metropolises in November, outlined plans for the restructuring of Asia. The Korean city states accepted full domination of economic affairs in the Sea of Japan by Tokyo. For assisting Tientsin in the Asian War, Tokyo was further rewarded with political jurisdiction over parts of Manchuria and Mongolia. The Chinese city states were forced to recognize the authoritative control of Wan, who was regarded as the legitimate founder of a new imperialistic dynasty on the Sino-Asiatic mainland. The brief independent city state era in Far East Asian politics had come to an end.

2169-2190

Asian War ends; World economy rebounds
The global economy underwent a post-war boom following the end of the Asian War. Space exploration was an indirect benefactor. Commercial spacecraft commonly reached speeds exceeding the light barrier, while test craft gradually approached speeds two to ten times that of light. There was also a rebirth in interplanetary colonization following the construction of three Biotrons on Jupiter's moon, Ganymede. The Astro 3000 organization, formed as an adjunct to SPA, encouraged financial investment and otherwise promoted interstellar exploration.

2170

Mystery of Jovian moon identified

Jupiter's fast moving moon, J3, was found to possess an inner core that produced large quantities of free-form querzian particles. This source was later tapped to fuel space travel.

Deep space station established

The first outer-solar-system research space station was established, at a distance of one-and-a-quarter light years from the Sun.

2171

The emergence of crustal breathing

Crustal breathing, a heat-releasing geophysical technique using lava to defrost an iced planetary surface, worked successfully in test runs near Pluto's north pole. Application of crustal breathing over the next thirty years, allowed the opening of large sections of Pluto and other icy worlds for Human colonization.

Alpha Centauri system explored

A manned mission explored the Alpha Centauri system, retrieving considerable amounts of the elements rhenium and tantalum to be used as catalysts in porginine-based engines.

2172

Rise of Africa's Princely movement

The Princely movement in African politics began in 2172. By 2200, over eighty-four city states had adopted a Princely form of government. This number had increased to 165 by 2240.

The Princely movement's political philosophy attempted to combine the virtues of scientific progress and technology, with the pre-colonial societal structure of Old Africa. The philosophy borrowed heavily from the ancient Egyptians, Carthaginians and Greeks, as well as the African civilizations of Aksum, Kush and Nubia. Although authoritarian and hierarchical in character, the Princely movement's period of dominance (c. 2195-2290) corresponded with a period of growth and prosperity for the continent. African art, music and sculpture flourished widely in a period that became known as Africa's Golden Age.

2173

The FNES is born

The Foundation for New Explorations in Space (FNES) was established, with its headquarters at Ares colony, Mars. The FNES took over from the SPA the planning, coordination and scheduling of exploration and colonization missions to still undiscovered stellar worlds. The long-term stellar development goals of Astro 3000, the investment consortium, were merged with the FNES in 2175.

Science of invisibility

The ability to create invisible structures became a reality with the development of the Photon Neutralizing Device (PND). PNDs worked by electronically monitoring coloured light waves reflecting off an object and blocking these waves by emitting reverse photons that prevented light reception by the Human retina. Invisibility methods were initially developed to assist the military in covert operations by disguising crucial weapons systems, but were later used in civilian-based industries. Technical training machines used invisibility covering to isolate specific machine parts for study.

2174

Chaos computer system joins interplanetary information network

The Chaos Computer Network System, the end result of a century of research, was finally integrated into the interplanetary information highway. Network users of the Chaos computer accessed the fractal pattern library of the system to obtain information regarding coincidence in fields as diverse as gambling, molecular chemical construction and financial investment.

2175

Nonsense Reasoners challenge conventional thought

Nonsense Reasoning, an intellectual rebellion against the impersonal nature of the space race, gained popularity in most large city states of North American and Europe. Jerdium Suntaxis (aka Harold Tomes), the self-ordained spiritual leader of the alternative movement, combined elements of his own philosophy with nineteenth-century anarchist teachings to create a cult philosophy that gained a strong following among Biotron youth of the 2170s and '80s. Nonsense Reasoners participated in mass protests to demonstrate their grievances against society.

Arms reduction talks fail

Talks designed to limit arms production throughout the solar system, failed after the APP city states (headed by the Tientsin and Tokyo delegations) withdrew from a global conference in Khartoum. Tientsin representative Wangcheng Yui claimed that armament restrictions in the proposed agreement would compromise security within the APP city states. Human rights campaigners argued that such security would not be necessary if city leaders abolished their respective totalitarian police states in favour of democratic government.

2175-2200

Space race heats up

The space race intensified during this era, with over ten thousand spacecraft and probes sent on exploratory missions to over one hundred stars in the Galaxy. The information obtained exponentially enhanced mankind's understanding of the nearby stellar environment. This initial outreach into deep space, the so-called First Phase of Stellar Exploration, was also described as the Period of the Cosmic Probe.

Most probe missions were privately funded by developmental corporations, although city state governments were influential in providing labour (both Human and robotic) for each probe project. Besides exploring new worlds with specialized probes, the mission craft contained robot work teams programmed to build mini-space-docking bays and monitor stations at various radial distances from Earth. These minor star bases contained surplus porginine supplies, used to refuel probes in the vicinity. Space probes were controlled by self-contained mother computers using artificial intelligence to make life-and-death decisions in emergency circumstances. Over five thousand stations and mini-bases were established by these probe exploration missions.

2176

Viral outbreak on Ganymede

A previously unknown viral plague with symptoms similar to the dreaded Ebola disease, killed five hundred people on Tereshkova colony, Ganymede. Medical researchers suggested that the virus had entered the artificial colonial biosphere from a passing comet, which had earlier interfered with the working mechanism of the atmospheric control unit. The hypothesis was proved correct when granules of comet dust tested positive for the virus. The vector transfer of the virus by a comet gave some credence to twentieth-century astrophysicist Fred Hoyle's theory, that a passing comet was responsible for bringing the bubonic plague pathogen to Earth in the middle ages.

2177

First contact: The famed Sirius rendezvous

In this momentous year, the manned spacecraft Livingstone 1 made contact with an extra-terrestrial spaceship close to the star Sirius. Humanity learned with certainty for the first time in its modern history, that Humankind was not the Galaxy's lone intelligence. Information was exchanged between the two parties through the Wittgenstein machine, a logical device that reduced all dialogue to a common mathematical logic. The historic meeting with the extra-terrestrial Tricaver was described years later by historian Marina Ondaatjie as "the awakening of Humanity." As a result of this meeting and others over the following ten years, Humanity was actively drawn into the family of intelligent beings populating the Galaxy, to enter what ultimately became the great game of galactic survival.

2178

Magno-beams first used

Long distance space communication made its first use of Magno-beams. The beams, named after their discoverer, physicist Jakob Magno, employed the symmetrical alignment of dark matter to produce physical conditions facilitating the propagation of waves at speeds exceeding ten thousand times the velocity of light. Magno-beam receptors were installed in all spacecraft and probes built after 2182.

Erma Raing defines Reverse Nationalism

Political Scientist Erma Raing coined the popular phrase Reverse Nationalism, to refer to the decline of the concept of nation and its rebirth under the flag of the corporate political entity.

2179

Political chaos in Britannia

The death of Philip Highberry, Grand Ruler of Britannia, left a power vacuum in the city state that now comprised over twenty percent of the land area of England. Gangs of youths took to the streets to celebrate the death of Britannia's hated leader and created mass anarchy. Violence erupted in the region of Old Leeds when members of Wat Tyler, a Biotron gang with over ten thousand members, attempted a localized takeover. However, the Britannia Air Cadets, a crack regiment of the city state's military corps, put down the rebellion by force.

2180

American States defeat Asian rivals in global conflict

The Alliance of American States, representing the city states of New York, Atlanta, Boston and the Cascadia Union (the amalgamation of Seattle and Vancouver) defeated the city states of Mumbai, New Delhi, Calcutta and Madras in a series of brief mid-Pacific battles. Known later as the Second City State War, the North American city states were successful because of their ability to mobilize powerful corporate funding. Political and economic historians regard the growth of corporate power that followed the end of this bloody conflict as a vital turning point in Humankind's historical development.

Chapter 7: In the Shadow of the Corporations

To read up more on the various Corporations go to **Appendix 3: The Corporations.**

2181

Fallotix addiction a social concern

Mass addiction to the illegal drug Fallotix, a chemical hallucinogen, caused social concern across the solar system. Fallotix effected the Human brain so that the user felt he or she was living in a parallel universe, where all moral judgement of right and wrong was reversed. A crackdown on Fallotix production facilities by interplanetary narcotics police curbed drug production, but the hallucinogen remained a major problem in Human society for the next century, its effect directly correlated with an elevation of serious crime.

2182

The Russian Civil War

Between 2182 and 2184, bitter war raged between the rival cities of Moscow and Kiev. The war had a significant effect on Euro-Asian politics, by encouraging the involvement of such outside powers as Prague (supporting Kiev) and St. Petersburg (backing Moscow). After the bloody battles of Dnieper in June 2183 and Dontesk in 2184, Kiev's forces were finally defeated. The war proved significant in weakening the power of both city states, making them more vulnerable to the influence of the giant corporation, Bolzakov Protech.

2183

Invention of Synthoskin

A viscous chemical compound known as Synthoskin, was developed by scientists Hien Chen and Fielding Bosworth of Venus V Research Labs, to protect Human skin against the harsh atmospheric conditions of planets rich in atmospheric sulphuric acid. Later modifications to Synthoskin allowed for the development of a diffusion mechanism, transforming the skin so it could absorb oxygen in a respiratory manner similar to amphibians. Synthoskin and other artificial respiration aids, allowed Humans to live naturally in the varying atmospheres of newly colonized extra-stellar worlds.

2184

Scientific renaissance in South America

After centuries of technological obscurity, the South America cities of Lima and Santiago emerged as technological powers. Local scientists developed such novel inventions as the Roderigo Communicator, greatly amplifying signals on interstellar communication links, and the Split Finger Shield Blocker, a laser shield that protected planetary worlds from harmful meteorites. The renaissance in Latin American technological innovation was coupled by a significant increase in the standard of living in the region.

2185

GeneralTech takes control of Cleveland and Detroit

Pro-GeneralTech forces, led by one-time computer engineer Tim Guys, overthrew the unpopular governments of the city states of Detroit and Cleveland. This takeover represented the first deviation of a corporate government from the old contract policy to a direct rule approach. Historical revision designed to boost the status of Guys to superHuman proportions, was a consistent characteristic of his regime. He defeated rebel forces in 2187, consolidating his hold on the two cities for the next twenty years.

2186

Russian Civil War ends

The Treaty of the Caucasus was signed between Moscow and Kiev. Dmitri Kozlov, the Muscovite leader, was instrumental in the development of the agreement, which redefined the Moscow-Kiev border, in favour of the Russian city state. Several imaginary lines known as the Volga Frontier, were drawn across this rich heartland to separate the zones of control of other city states including Dontesk, Odessa, Lvov and Volgograd.

Indian city states unite

The India Pact united the city states of Mumbai, Calcutta, Madras and Bangalore, forming the powerful megalopolis of Indo-Dravadi and marking the beginning of the ascension of India to global power. Indo-Dravadi fell under the corporate control of the Sharaputra Group.

2187

Extra Organ Shunting (EOS)

Developed by Lewis Gashow's team at the Pauling Space City Research Facility, EOS was based on the discovery that the addition of a synthetic organ, smaller than the natural organ, but connected to the original, increased life expectancy. EOS shunting reduced the strain the natural organ normally faced through disease, space travel and the aging process. The researchers worked with a group of terminally-ill patients at the colony's hospital and succeeded in prolonging their lives significantly. Although Gashow's research concentrated on the heart, later physicians used his technique on other organs, prompting the growth of a booming mini-organ industry in the twenty-third century.

2188-2194

The Water Wars

In the twenty-second century, there was very little competition in the water market, since start-up free enterprise was dead in most industries and huge corporations controlled every aspect of regular life. With the majority of rivers and lakes polluted or dammed to create Human habitation, access to freshwater became a significant issue. Desalination helped, but many desalination plants, like most other services, fell under the control of a corporation with no qualms about turning off the tap if it suited them. Localized conflicts (water wars) often broke out between city states as the various political powers vied for control of this natural resource.

The Godson Block

Enormous improvements in the breadth of the Human auditory range were made possible by a new technology christened the Godson Block. A micro-scale trapezoidal solid inserted in the inner ear, the Godson Block was constructed of ryzax and its unique shape and material allowed the Block to enhance sound waves so that frequencies normally inaudible to the Human ear could be heard. Ryzax acted as an antenna, emitting high frequency waves to produce a coherent signal that a CPU built into the Block translated into audible information. The Godson Block was invented by Margaret Godson at the Beethoven Institute for Improvement in Hearing on Mars Colony II.

2189

Earth cleanup

The Earth Readjustment Program came into full force as scientists and technicians began the forty-year project of cleaning the Planet's environment to recreate the atmospheric and oceanic conditions of Old Earth. Unfortunately, this project proved too costly and was abandoned ten years later in favour of the more glamorous drives for stellar exploration.

Missions to Alpha Centauri and Sirius Beta increase

Competing corporations increased the number of expeditions to Alpha Centauri and the Sirius Beta systems. These stellar worlds accommodated their first biotron based mining settlers in the years 2223 and 2228 respectively.

2190

Death Retraction

Lionel Bentley introduced and popularized Death Retraction, a medical therapy that successfully cured patients of certain chronic illnesses by pushing the body to the verge of death and then rapidly retrieving it. Bentley argued that certain chemicals produced in the body upon death, were beneficial to health. One such chemical was foximat, a substance that produced resistance to simultaneous neuron collapse; another was rezardure, which prompted a positive mental disposition at the time of near-death. Rezadure was later used to treat patients suffering from neurosis and manic-depression. In Death Retraction, the body was stimulated to overproduce these chemical and a biochemical cascade acted to weaken the effect of the life-threatening illness. However, careful monitoring was necessary to ensure that chemicals such as bortarore, that destroy the internal body mechanism during death, were suppressed.

2191

St. Petersburg expansion

City states had the same ambitions as the older nation states and the year 2191 marked the beginning of the expansion of the St. Petersburg city state westward into Poland and the Baltics. The city of Warsaw was finally absorbed by St. Petersburg in 2215, hence falling under the influence of Bolzakhov Protech.

2192-2252

Noteworthy medical breakthroughs

The treatment of diseases through the application of physics was common during this era. Processes developed included:

- Sub-atomic bombardment: Muon and meson particles (particularly the eta and ki-zoo particles) were used to bombard tumor cells and reduce their cell division capabilities, while simultaneously catalyzing a series of sub-particle reactions to cause cell implosion. This technique was developed by Iri Heraw and Gregor Schmidt at the Centre for Biophysical Research.

- EM Excitation: The stimulation of cells by high frequency electromagnetic waves, produced a biological resonance frequency that was used to revive cells. EM excitation worked by reactivating the ionic charges present in the cell. The technique was developed in 2234 at MIT by a team led by biophysicist George Leonakis. It was widely used for trauma treatment in subsequent wars.
- Quantum Mechanical Effects (QME): This popular treatment was in use from the early twenty-third century onward. Individuals miraculously recovered against overwhelming odds, through the cellular-level manipulation of the probability-uncertainty factor inherent in quantum mechanics. The school of medicine that championed the QME approach was known as the Magicians of Schroëdinger.

2192

Smots Rebellion

Mutant highly aggressive Smots beings, named for geneticist Harold Smots, who designed the original DNA mutations that differentiated these Human mutants, rebelled in New York. Over three thousand people were brutally slain in the four-day period that it took the city's home guard to quell the rebellion.

2193

Hans Thiler's reign over Franco Ini begins

Hans "The Emperor" Thiler, the highly capable Corporate Administrator of Munich-Stuttgart, was appointed Chief Executive Officer of the giant Franco Ini group. The Emperor further enhanced his power in 2195, after his corporation took over the German cities of Dortmund and Bremen, formerly under control of the renegade Kirsch-SAP group. Thiler's reign over the Franco Ini Empire lasted forty-eight years. Historians credited him with building Franco Ini into an extra-global superpower, likening him to a modern-day Bismarck.

2194

The anti-genetic laws

After ascertaining the fallout from the Smots rebellion, several city states implemented anti-genetic laws, designed to limit the amount of fast breeder eugenic trials that had become popular on Earth since the 2180s. Non-viable plant, animal and Human mutants created by this scientific craze, had become increasingly burdensome to Human society.

2195

First mini-black hole sighted

Measurements of electromagnetic radiation in the Galaxy revealed the existence of miniature black holes in space. These cosmic entities, hypothesized by physicists almost a hundred years earlier, were thought to be caused by the phenomenon of sigma particle collapse, a process that resulted from the transformation of various sigma particles into different versions of one another under extremely high temperatures. Miniature black holes were found to have one-thousandth of the density of classical black holes, but their intense gravitational fields had a destructive effect on the hulls of conventional space ships. They were classified systematically according to their size and motion. Although they were initially perceived as the equivalent of natural land mines, by the twenty-fourth century, black holes were used as a reliable source of slingshot propulsion for interstellar travel.

2196-2275

Further corporate advances

Nozeco Transglobal, a large mining consortium, circumvented anti-trust laws to win majority control of mineral recovery and exploration projects in both the Neptunian and Plutonian systems. Nozeco also extended its influence to the more ambitious project of extra-stellar mining, when it unveiled its mineral extraction program for the Alpha Centauri system in 2232.

Other corporations that grew significantly during this period included:

- Peash Inc.: manufacturer of all-purpose ceramo-plastic products
- Biolife Intercosmic: leading space station and colony developer
- Eurb Distilleries: alcohol producers
- Tzof-Witilsk: entertainment magnates

These corporations focused on a single industry and were not generally involved in the contract system. They were consequently nicknamed the Outsiders.

2197

End of dictatorship in Ireland

The O'Driscoll totalitarian regime in Dublin finally collapsed. The 're-democratization' period of the Emerald Isle, under the auspices of the corporations, began.

2198-2250

Art Cosmo Nouveau period

Several artistic styles developed during this highly creative period, including:

- Crystal Mountain sculpturing: Developed by the Titania school and students of the renowned artist Boadicea Ionia, Crystal Mountain sculpturing made use of X-ray and other high frequency EM waves, to engrave patterns into artificially generated crystal monoliths.
- Fractal manipulation: Reverse Entropy Generators, whose motto was "If no solution to a problem can be found then it is necessary to reinvent the problem itself," developed a school of art that made use of chaos system reorganization, to create intricate and aesthetically pleasing patterns from plots of apparent disorder.
- Natural Biomania, aka Life Perversion Art: This art style was developed in the scientific research laboratories of Mars. Natural Biomaniacs used chemical techniques to alter, for the sake of art and art alone, the spatial and structural nature of complex biochemical molecules.
- Sado-confusion: This outlawed and much-scorned art style developed by the dark Jovian-based subcultures, used techniques such as attacking a herd of animals with laser weaponry to produce dynamic confusion patterns. Sado-confusionists, such as Domenic Masterson and Mortimer Parker-Hughes, were independently imprisoned after experimenting with attacks on Humans.

2199

Fire in Mexico City

Over a quarter of Mexico City was destroyed in a toxic chemical fire that forced the evacuation of twenty million people. The devastating effects of the fire hastened inquiries into the hazards of increased city state population densities.

2200

Dongadong steers into Asian power politics

The Asian power elite agreed to relinquish its totalitarian holdings in the cities of Beijing, Tientsin, Shanghai, Nanking and Hong Kong in exchange for a power sharing agreement with the emerging Dongadong Conglomerate. The Treaty of Yin, establishing this joint partnership, was signed the following year. The treaty gave Dongadong and its sister subsidiaries exclusive rights in these metropolises. Later historians regarded Yin as the single most important document in the reformation of the Sino bloc, however, it created bitterness among the Western Chinese, who turned to smaller rival corporations like the Shu and the Tang Yok. The polarization of the old Chinese nation served to further highlight frictions in the Land of the Dragon during the previous century and a half.

2201

Turnover genes

Turnover genes were identified for the first time by Mexican biologists Pete Ramirez and Hettie Leiter. The genes, extracted from the mitochondria of liver cells, had the ability, when properly stimulated, to generate cell reproduction even if disease or trauma had reduced the organ to a few thousand active cells. Organ regeneration by turnover gene therapy became the primary means of organ replacement in the twenty-third century and produced the first major shift away from pure transplant medicine since the advent of extra-organ shunting.[72]

2202

The birth of Particalism

The philosophy of Particalism, developed by pioneer thinkers Reginald Law and Matilda Key, argued that true individual happiness could only be achieved if the soul complement, which existed somewhere in the cosmos, was found and united with the inner being residing within the individual. The search for the soul complement, also known as the celestial find, was defined as a period of blue zoning engulfing the aura of an individual, filling the person with complete contentment. The search for the soul complement by followers of Particalism helped inspire a renewed space race in the mid-twenty-third century.

2203-2220

Breakthroughs in the science of sight

Numerous stimulator devices for the visually impaired were developed during this era, including:

- Window of Sight: This device, used to compensate for total blindness, involved a chemical clock mechanism that caused the periodic release of neurotransmitters to the optic nerve, inducing spontaneous and discrete moments of vision. The Window of Sight machine was the brainchild of Dr. Louis Helms of the Ophthalmological Institute of Mars VII.
- Laser Scanners: This nano-technological laser device, was installed

[72] For details of the extra-organ shunting procedure, see entry for 2187.

behind the eye to collect surrounding information and combine it with light striking the retina. It then transferred an amalgamation of the two sources of sight, creating a viable image that was passed to the brain to produce a picture. Later modifications of laser scanner technology made use of micro-computer processing units installed in the brain to assist image processing. Bionic implants to aid the functioning of the laser were developed between 2230 and 2232.

Other technologies improved the visual acuity of a person with twenty-twenty vision. These included:

- "Onion" Eyes: Improvements to the twenty-twenty eyesight optimum were critical for pilots flying through parts of space laden with asteroid obstacles. The "Onion" Eye was a multi-layered structure overlying the eye, constructed of fine polymers, that through refractive techniques, enhanced the visual ability of the eye by a factor of ten.
- Rod and Cone Perfusion: This procedure improved optical colour and shade definition by substituting treated pre-calibrated fibre optic rods and cones into the retina.

2204

GeneralTech and Franco Ini clash over Martian trading rights

The first of a series of wars between the GeneralTech and Franco Ini corporations erupted over trading rights on mineral-rich Mars. Under the leadership of Hans Thiler's chosen military commander, Steven Raatz, the Franco Ini forces defeated those of GeneralTech in the Battles of Rouge Mons and Pathfinder Landing, forcing the surrender of over half of the Martian assets of GeneralTech to Franco Ini. Wars between these two corporations continued off and on until 2237. GeneralTech was finally driven off Mars in the last of these bloody conflicts, leaving Franco Ini with dominant control over much of the Martian resource wealth. GeneralTech loyalists, fleeing persecution from Franco Ini, eventually settled outside the Earth-based solar system and helped spread Humanity to new planets orbiting other stars. The collapse of GeneralTech's dominance on Mars and the subsequent takeover of its colonies by Franco Ini, was likened by Earth historians to the fall of the Ottoman Empire and the absorption of much of its territory by the British after the First World War.

2205

Reincarnation therapy

Reincarnation therapy, a fashionable form of psychotherapy, attempted to treat mental disorders in patients by probing the unconscious mind to learn about patients' former lives, to explore their effect in the present. Patients were subjected to regression experiments involving hypnosis and brain probing designed to unload the memories of their past lives, usually with positive results. Juan Garze of the Dali-Freud School of Creative Thought and Medicine, was the leading champion of reincarnation therapy. Critics claimed that the success of reincarnation therapy was due mainly to a placebo-like process of subconsciously fooling the brain into thinking it had been cured of a disorder.

2205-2225

Gains in the Java Free State

This period marked the rise of the Java Free State, built around the old Indonesian city of Djakarta, and its development into one of the most important technological development centers in twenty-third century Asia. Unlike many of the city states on Earth the Java Free State would maintain its independence from corporate rule.

2206

Air pollution findings released

Official statistics on atmospheric quality revealed that air pollution values for Earth's city states were eight times the level they had been in the twentieth century. Despite stringent pollution laws introduced during the previous one hundred years, it was determined that the carrying capacity of the Earth was so severely weakened by war and earlier abuse, that the planet could no longer sustain growth. Such findings spurred a further colonization drive away from Earth, toward other solar system planets.

The Grames Planetary Classification

Space geologist Michael Grames's planetary classification method was officially adopted. The description of each planetary type is outlined in **Appendix 4: Grames 2206 Planetary Classification.**

2207

Porax virus outbreak on Callisto colony

The deadly Porax virus killed over seven thousand people on the Callisto colony, Laplace-1. The virus, which escaped through a leaky containment system, was apparently engineered by scientists from the colony's prestigious Jenner Laboratories. The lack of an effective antidote against the pathogen, forced the evacuation of the entire colony, granting Laplace-1 the dubious honour of being the first Human ghost colony in space.[73]

2208

A no-go for world government

An attempt to form a centralized world government to administer Earth and the solar system's Human colonies, failed when several city states, fearful of incurring the wrath of their corporate controllers, chose not to ratify the treaty. World government, even in the form of a limited federation, has yet to be achieved by Humanity, despite the efforts of such believers as the Chosen Unity Proponents (CUP).[74]

2209

Pluto colonies punished

Earth governments enacted sanctions against several member cities of the Alliance of Pluto colonies, after agents discovered that the governors of twelve of the planet's ninety-six settlements were supporting radical anarchistic groups on Earth. Corporate backed invasion squads succeeded in overthrowing the renegade governors in 2213 and replacing them with Earth-friendly counterparts. This series of coup d'états caused such ill feelings on Pluto, that it marked the last time Earth forces covertly became involved in overthrowing a colonial regime.

Fregan Factor research

Nasim Olekby identified the Fregan Factor[75] as the single most important determinant of the rate and extent of aging in Human beings and other higher mammals. Based on his work with rats, Olekby argued that the Fregan Factor could be manipulated to reverse the aging process. By the latter part of the twenty-third century, Fregan Factor investigation became one of the most widely studied areas in biological science. Implications of Fregan Factor research were finally felt during the New Age of Mortality (2380 onwards), when Human longevity increased to an upper limit of two hundred years.

---

[73] An antidote to the Porax virus was developed in 2237.

[74] The CUP was founded in 2202 by Ekiel Brody, who argued that world government was necessary to save Humanity from itself.

[75] The highly organized cellular structure known as the Fregan Factor was first discovered in 2006 by scientists Louise Roe and Yitzhak Bernstein of Intergalactic Space Labs.

2210

Thermohair

Thermohair protection was first used in the Alpha Centauri missions of 2210-2215. It consisted of a low-weight complex composite of plastic-protein (artificial keratin) woven into a meshlike structure. The covering trapped heat to prevent it from escaping the body. Thermohair was temporarily implanted into the Human skin using a series of skin grafts. Later types of Thermohair were installed in the pores to allow normal sweating. A product of Flexicon Corporation, well-designed Thermohair coverings allowed Humans with minimal clothing protection to survive in temperatures of minus fifty Celsius for close to two hundred hours.

2211-2261

The Second Golden Age of Mathematics

During this period, several advances helped elevate the study of numerical logic to a glorious period reminiscent of the Golden Age of the eighteenth century. Most notable among these breakthroughs in Human mathematics and physics were:

- The Approximation Theorem: First developed by the Chang Institute for Numerology and Quantum Mechanics, the approximation theorem, with a proof over 1500 pages in length, was used to bypass the limits of Heisenberg's uncertainty principle and establish a more meaningful theoretical basis for future event prediction.
- Calborm Non-Euclidics: These geometric principles developed by the Laplace Academy on Titan, helped mathematicians understand the synchronized patterns produced by chaos plots.
- Hypermatrices: The brainchild of students working for the Venus-based Turing-Gates Academy of Sciences, hypermatrices were used, in conjunction with infinite recursion principles, to refine solutions for complex economic and social science problems once deemed unsolvable.
- Interstate Mathematics: Used in conjunction with the breakthrough power-variable series developed by Agatha Tonks and her colleagues at the Max Planck Institute-2, interstate mathematics allowed mathematicians to understand the matter-energy conversion principles behind such metaphysical phenomena as ghost-spirit formation and astral travel.
- Multi-dimensional Modelling: Developed By Leornard Laing and Albert Antonelli in the mid-twenty-third century, multi-dimensional modelling

allowed physicists to determine the effects of such phenomena as time-twisting and the three-dimensional warping of particle motion through the space-time continuum.

- Time Mathematics and Futuronics: This branch of mathematics found application in twenty-sixth century time travel. A well-supported discipline, futuronics existed in the forefront of a mathematical revolution that discredited twenty-first and second century mathematics suggesting the impossibility of time travel.

2212

The ugly side of Australian politics

Several months of bloody revolution disturbed the Australian city states of Sydney and Melbourne. The conflicts began when bands of revolutionaries from the secret organization Nouveau Australis, stormed the crumbling Sydney Opera House and kidnapped members of the ruling Startech family. A hostage scenario threatened the stability of the Southern Metropolises as revolutionaries and counter-revolutionaries battled for control of the cities that had been united by the Startechs twenty years earlier.

The military, under the leadership of Christopher Startech, younger brother of kidnapped ruler Fletcher Startech, eventually defeated the revolutionaries at the Battle of St. Ives, but failed to save the hostages. With the help of the elite Aussie 7th Division, Chris Startech eventually declared himself Grand Ruler of Southern Australia, annexing Adelaide in 2214.

Chris Startech's thirty-four year reign was characterized by a growing centralization of power. His government signed a corporate contract with Flexicon TransGlobal to ensure external financial backing for his regime. The restriction of civil rights and freedoms were typical of Startech's autocratic rule. Southern Australia did, however, expand during this period, absorbing Tasmania and several New Zealand and other Pacific city states. These gains increased the size of Southern Australia's population by fifty percent and created a regional imbalance, inevitably leading to localized conflict with several other city states namely Darwin in 2217 and Perth in 2219.

2213-2450

The Great Pioneer Period dawns

During this era, explorers from across the solar system prepared for missions to the multitude of stars near the Sun. This exploration drive met with wide-spread approval and excitement. Religious zealots ventured into space to seek proof of the existence of God, scientists and engineers were lured by the mathematical vastness of the cosmos, while adventurers yearned for thrills beyond new horizons. Low cost querzian particle technology made space travel as practical for crews of five as a thousand. There was much anticipation and revelation, as regular news reached Earth of the latest planetary discoveries and new life forms.

2214-2268

The war against pain

Many scientific procedures to eliminate overamplified pain were successfully developed during this period. These included:

- Nerve stunning (NS): Electronic stunning or deadening of specific nerve pathways responsible for pain sensation, was created through electrochemical impulse generation and directed by electronic mirrors to effect only the targetted nerve cells. Leading proponents of NS included Harthley Bininham and Rhona Gonzalez, both of the Earth-Mars Scientific Cooperation Foundation.
- Pain Returning: This technique transformed the pain sensation into a more pleasurable feeling, more easily tolerated by the body, in a way that would have been eradicated by nerve stunning. This proved a critical point, since the ability to perceive a particular sensation is vital to the well being of the individual.
- Other forms of treatment for pain involved electronic acupuncture, Cerebral Temporary Paralysis (in which the brain was partially paralyzed to disallow pain sensations) and the use of Meilt Creatures, slothlike animals indigenous to Sirius-5/3-1, capable of forming a psychological bond with Humans to remove or reduce internal stresses, including pain.

2215

Turning the clock back in the old USA

Right wing moralists gained strength across the continent by winning control of the governments of the Denver, St. Louis and Virginia Beach city states. In Denver, fundamentalist politicians successfully legislated a series of morality laws based on strict Victorian principles. However, these stringent laws backfired on fundamentalist apologists, indirectly encouraging the mass emigration of people to space colonies and new planets.

2216

The power of the Moisiak Crystal

Wolfgang Smoltz of the Centre for Crystallized Acoustics, demonstrated the importance of complex external longitudinal wave functions in splitting sound waves to create a multitude of harmonics. Smoltz waves, as these energy oscillations became known, were best produced from vibrating Moisiak Crystals.[76] Using electronic sensors, the harmonics generated could be selected or filtered out to provide multi-frequency waves for musical production.

Smoltz's work influenced metallurgical engineering. Using a variation of his method, a family of sound waves with differing periodicity, each matching the frequency of one element of an alloy, could be formed to instantly resonance-crack the compounds. This technique reduced the time for alloy breakdown by a factor of one hundred and created an economic rebirth in the alloy reprocessing industry.

2217

The bridge between nature and nurture

Kelly O'Bannion and Mary Coats, two geneticists at the Mearham Hydrocolony Centre for Genetic Research, discovered an unusual biological compound that forever changed the life sciences. Labelled Coatenian Units, these new compounds were the biochemical bridge linking the genetic and environmental forces that control the body's development and functioning. Biophysicist Mien Kwong further investigated Coatenian compounds and their mechanism of action, detailing their workings in her book, *The Final Link: An Examination of Coatenian Biophysics*.

By the mid-twenty-third century, the study of Coatenian biochemistry became the most discussed scientific issue of its time. Investigation proved Coatenian Units were physically small, fast moving particles, operating on the sub-molecular level. They underwent partial energy conversion and had the ability to record environmental interplay on an individual's body, similar to a computer's memory chip.

Coatenian Units served as the basis for biophysicist Bashir Mehmet's proof of the formerly discredited theory of Lamarkian Evolution. Mehmet showed that the Coatenian Unit could remember the single lifetime environmental adaptations of its organism and, through a process known as Coatenian Molecule Transfer (CMT), pass this knowledge to its offspring's genome.

2218

Sufis expelled

Members of the mystical Sufi sect of Islam were expelled from the Al Mazaar corporation's colonies and city states. A policy of discrimination had been

[76] Moisiak Crystals were first discovered on Jupiter in 2211. They had a unique non-metallic ionic lattice make-up, that could be used for longitudinal sound wave production.

engaged against the Sufis by Al Mazaar's hierarchy for twenty years prior to this expulsion, in an attempt to eradicate the Sufi challenge of Al Mazaar authority. The departure of the intellectual Sufi weakened the corporation politically for the following thirty years, as Sufi refugees carried their knowledge and expertise to competitor conglomerates.

2219

Seventh-generation computers

These machines combined what was at the time high-speed multi-task processing functions (the leading advance of sixth-generation computers) with Humanlike bio-neural capabilities. Brain cells from deceased donors were introduced into Jortran chips, at both molecular and extra-molecular levels, to produce a dynamic composite. For the next two centuries, seventh-generation computers were used in applications as diverse as city control, household management, defence and entertainment. The new generation computers allowed space pilots to control their respective ships more efficiently by enhancing Human-machine communication.

2220-2224

Fuyama Corporation wins Venus

The Balance of Power on Venus shifted in favour of Fuyama Holdings, when the rival Brittanix Corporation was driven off the planet by Fuyama troops. By 2224, the Japanese-dominated corporation controlled sixty percent of Venus's wealth. Despite these critical gains, Fuyama's position remained under threat, especially from Almana and GeneralTech, which remained influential on Venus through the next century.

2221

Brain-think

Mermiran Extra-stellar completed the construction of the central computer known as Brain-think, which controlled all administrative functioning on the Paul Allen Space colony. The citizens of this cosmic structure became the first Human electro-nucleic[77] society. In the twenty-fourth century, the electro-nucleic option was exercised by many colonies, especially those situated in the more remote stellar systems, on the periphery of Human colonization.

---

[77] Electro-nucleic societies were Human colonies controlled entirely by a centralized computer.

2222

Human bioproduction in brief

Human bioproduction, a highly lucrative pharmacological technique employing Human beings as chemical reactors to produce a diverse range of medical drugs, was first tested. The procedure followed these steps:

- Tissue separation: Chemists separated the production-bed tissue from the rest of the organ by creating a barrier, allowing only chemicals necessary for bioproduction to flow into the bed.
- Reaction specific chemical addition: Customized chemicals and non-Human ingredients were added to the production-bed tissue, priming it for drug production.
- Chemical initiation: Starter enzymes ignited drug production reactions. Other enzymes were used as biological catalysts to regulate rates of reaction in the production bed.

The bioproduction process allowed the generation of more Human-friendly drugs. An added advantage was that over one hundred different types of drugs could be simultaneously synthesized in the body of a single individual.

2223-2368

During this period, known as the Era of Human Extra-stellar Colonization (EHEC), over two hundred stellar systems were settled by Human colonists. See **Appendix 5: The Human Colonial Worlds** for details.

Chapter 8: The Pace of our Progress

2224

Laser Centrifugation

Laser Centrifugation (LC), invented by chemist Mashir Ramgeolam of the Mohenjo Daro Colony on Mars, increased the potency of enzymes, hormones and antibodies by spinning them in varying laser centrifuges. Ramgeolam's invention added kinetic energy to the biochemical compound, increasing the probability of molecular collision. In clinical trials, LC-treated enzymes were shown to catalyze reactions a million times faster than non-LC enzymes. The LC procedure gained popularity over the following thirty years, when the medical treatment of deadly diseases of cosmic origin required immediate enzyme/antibody action.

2225

Sub-dividing space

Corporate and independent city state representatives met in Los Angeles through most of 2225 and 2226, to discuss sub-dividing stellar exploration and colonization. The meeting eventually resulted in the signing of the Thousand Frontiers Agreement in 2227, a document whose many ambiguities caused much future conflict throughout the Human worlds.

Discovery of the Czebikian pathway

Scientists discovered the biochemical complex that allowed canines to resist pathogens lethal to Humans. Later dubbed the Czebikian pathway (after its founder trans-species-immunity pioneer Jakob Czebik), the process was successfully duplicated in Human patients through serial drug treatment. It created Human immunity to some diseases normally lethal in Humans, but non-virulent to dogs.

2226

Resurrection of the Olympic Games

The turbulence of the twenty-second century, which ultimately gave birth to the city state system, ended the Olympic games of the twentieth and twenty-fist centuries in 2148. Under the leadership of Chilean entrepreneur Carlos Fernandez, the Olympic Games were revived and expanded to include sports such as Razorball (a sport similar to basketball but played on platforms that extended five storeys high) and Swimchuck (a twenty-third century sport that amalgamated power swimming, wrestling and underwater hockey). The first new games were held in the city state of Kuala Lumpur.

2229

Mercurian poetry and its extraneous influences

Mercurian poetry, which combined multi-sonic synthesis with ancient Incan rhythmic tones, grew in popularity on the Almana corporation's planetary colonies. The giant corporation used the inspirational Mercurian form as a propaganda mechanism, generating a fervour of patriotic loyalty to Almana. Well-respected twenty-third century historian Wayne Troppau, likened Mercurian poetry and its effect on Almana protectionists to the influence of beer hall music on the 1930s German working class. Almana dominated Mecurian politics for another century.

Settlers arrested for alien transportation

Police arrested twelve space travellers in San Francisco for illegally transporting Saturn- based aliens to Earth. Because of their remarkable tolerance to low temperatures, aliens were often used in the cryogenics industry. The smugglers were charged with contravening the Alien Life Protection Act, adopted by several city states to prevent the exploitation of intelligent non-Earth beings by unscrupulous profiteers.

2230

New York police wage war against Bortean clan

New York undercover units defeated gang members of the Bortean clan, which had controlled the city's lower zones. Over 4,000 people were killed in the mammoth clean-up operation, that also saw the death of New York police commissioner Sean Daniels in a retaliatory hovercar bombing.

2231

Armed rebellion on Neptune

The Four Armies Rebellion, orchestrated by troops loyal to the Neptune Floating Colonies, struck against the forces of Hector Hydra. The rebellion marked the first time in the Corporate Era that controlled cities successfully drove out their corporate masters. The Four Armies Rebellion was fought largely with robotic troops. Fighting machines, known as mort animals, were used by both sides in the conflict that caused the loss of over one hundred thousand lives. In a political context, the Four Armies Rebellion provided inspiration for rebels on other Human worlds against the hegemony of corporate entities.

2232

Mass death on Venus IX

Fuyama military strategists committed one of the greatest and most horrendous crimes of the twenty-third century when they secretly altered the oxygen-nitrogen ratio in the atmosphere of the bubble colony Venus IX, killing over twenty percent of the colony's two million inhabitants. Fuyama's involvement in this action remained covert until secret documents, unveiled by private investigators in 2251, brought their crime to light. The corporation's motivation was to suppress dissent on Venus IX, a growing hotbed of opposition to the Fuyama Executive.

2233

Tiger King seizes power in Rangoon

The "Tiger King" Li Win, established his reign in the fast-rising Burmese city state of Rangoon. To counter corporate domination, the Tiger King defeated and annexed the rival city of Mandalay, absorbing it into Rangoon's political structure in 2236. Win further extended his power by signing a favourable alliance treaty with rival city states Bangkok and Hanoi-Saigon. This extension of power allowed him to curb the twin influences of the Indian city states and the Java Free State in South East Asian politics.

2234

Completion of the Gardens of Paradise

The Gardens of Paradise, an elaborate botanical showcase, was completed after eighteen years of design and development. The gardens were built by Martian scientists in a domed setting, to highlight the beauty of Old Earth's nearly forgotten diversity. Over 8.9 million plant species were housed and managed by a crew of eighty thousand biologists and horticulturists.

2235

An overview of Soul Solicitation

Soul Solicitation, a scientific technique for tapping a living organism's energy halo for healing purposes, emerged as a popular method of treatment for psychological disorders. Elaborate processes, based on detailed energy-monitoring techniques incorporating both quantum mechanical principles and photon-harnessing mechanisms, formed the basis for Soul Solicitation.

First devised by biologist Mira Belinsky, Soul Solicitation also exploited the fundamental principles of Kirlian photography, popular in the mid-twentieth century and once dismissed as pseudo-science. In her innovative revival of this discipline, Belinsky showed how different types of energy fields could be mixed to create an optimized field, stimulating the body's natural healing processes.

2235-2285

Musical developments

Throughout this dynamic and turbulent period of Human history, several unique schools of music were popularized. These included:

- Blues Revivalists: Developed in the colonial settlements of Mars, revivalists combined the music of twentieth century blues musicians B.B. King and Bo Diddely, with the local harmonies of Martian soul singing. Blues revivalist music spread throughout the colonial worlds over the next century, reaching its height in popularity around 2245. The leading musicians in this field were Hunter Hawkins, who wrote the popular song "Ares Arrow into my Heart" and Deborah Kling, composer of "Jackson Pollock on a Red Afternoon."
- Classical Wave Motionists: Using computer sonic interplay, this scientifically based style of music pronounced the mathematical edge in great eighteenth and nineteenth century classical pieces. Classical Wave Motion found its greatest popularity among the intelligentsia of the 2270s. Its leading proponents were quantum classicists Jeremiah Burke and Chin Yang, both renowned for their brilliant innovations in the art of pitch-fractioning. using reverse Fourier Analysis.
- Platinum Agers: This school of music, which peaked in popularity in the 2260s, looked to the future as a new Platinum Age of Humanity. Platinum Agers produced joyous, uplifting, fast-paced music, glorifying both space travel and extra-stellar colonization. These compositions employed a vast array of musical instruments. Leading composers of the Golden Agers school included Hata Koronui and Bela Menatak.
- Opera Futura: Opera Futura was popular between 2250 and 2270 and involved performances by skilled singers whose surgically altered voices produced a broader range of pitches. Voice alteration allowed the same singer to perform more than one role in an operatic performance; the tenor and bass parts were often sung by a single individual. Opera Futura productions centred on space themes, with individuals like Korsten Fransch and Fernando Uno emerging as its most celebrated composers.
- Neo-post-romantic: Developing toward the end of the Art Revolution period (2280), this style of music was composed by the first wave of musicians who'd matured in the extra-stellar colonial worlds. Neo-post-romantic music was usually simple, stressing a return to basics and illustrating the

composer's sense of a renewed world. Neo-post-romantics redesigned musical instruments for each song, using materials originating from their home planets, and incorporated into their rhythms beats from the music of the alien Tricaver and Sasong people. Yakori Takamei and Valentina Talimova were the movement's most significant musical figures.

2236

Priska, the new opium

Priska, the opium of the twenty-third century, became the street drug of choice in several Earth city states. This much abused drug synergistically stimulated both the pleasure and nostalgia centres of the brain, inducing a brilliant, but often violent, sense of euphoria.

2237

Advances in botany and plant cell genetics

Jeremy Altexir and Kimbel Varoux of the Watson and Crick Research Foundation, developed and employed a technique of molecular biology to increase DNA variation among the offspring cells of a defined plant lineage. The procedure required use of the micro-manipulation techniques of neutrino bumping (whereby high intensity neutrino beams were used to dislodge base pairs) and cosmic ray focusing, to alter the nature of the nitrogen bases in the DNA molecule, inducing controlled mutations. This procedure assured a higher viability for plant cells in adverse conditions. Cosmic ray focusing, a key to the technique's success, specifically directed ultra-high-frequency EM waves to cause a change in the sub-molecular structure of a compound.[78]

2238

Biological fluid transfusion

Science was particularly concerned with the survival of colonists in worlds with variable atmospheric oxygen content. Alternative body fluid preparation, the development of which was credited to Martian scientist Palirizio Senera at the Vesalius School, required the transfusion of a biological fluid into the body, to alter cell morphology, allowing greater tolerance to reduced oxygen environments. The serum Senera was used extensively by colonists settling the Grus Iota system.

---

[78] The sub-molecular changes induced, included changing cysteine to uracil to thymine, for pyramidine nitrogen DNA bases, or equally reversible guanine to adenine changeovers for purine nitrogen DNA bases.

2239

Experiments in time travel

After thirty years of research, the time travel experiments of Lothair Smallwood and his colleagues at the Hawkings-Weinberg Institute of Cosmological Studies, yielded successful results. Transport beams conveyed matter to a different spatial position in an alternative timeline dimension, creating a crude form of time travel. Because the matter transport machine jumped from one parallel timeline to another, relocating the traveller in alternative timeline dimensions, events altered in the past of one timeline, could not effect the future of the traveller's original timeline. Smallwood's machine, known as the Leapfrogger, won accolades as the era's greatest invention. Its success gave birth to the time travel industry, one of the strongest growth ventures in Human history, when it was opened for exploitation by the public in the late twenty-sixth and seventh centuries.

2240-2280

The Bionic period entered a final phase. The use of machine-like appendages to enhance the life functioning of Humans (bionics) was a key focus over the previous two centuries of Human technology. In 2240, the technology entered its climax: The Great Bionic Period.

The important developmental periods of bionics are as follows:

- Early Bionic Period: Twenty-first century structures relied heavily on metallic super-constructs, prone to breakage and failure.
- Later Bionic Period: Plastics and mesh alloy structures comprised the tension-bearing elements of the bionic system in twenty-second century developments.
- Great Bionic Period: The advanced medical techniques of the twenty-third century, effectively combined polymer strength matrices with living tissue, minimizing rejection and producing a more aesthetically pleasing, physiologically enhanced bionic replacement.

Later work in the field of bionics, under the auspices of Eleanor Smirtzesky of the Aroit Research Facility on Titan, led to the development of fully functioning androids with great tolerance for harsh atmospheres.

2241

Alien abduction

In June, seven cosmic voyagers travelling between the Neptune space cities of Leibnitz and Thoreau, mysteriously disappeared. Although the initial investigation proved fruitless, new evidence surfaced in 2267, proving that the voyagers had been transferred, for experimental purposes, to an alternative phase of existence by an advanced life form.

2242

Ghost particle discoveries

Subatomic ghost particles were discovered by nuclear physicists working at the Martian linear accelerator. These once-illusive particles, whose existence to that point was merely theoretical, can undergo mass alteration through the shedding or uptake of component units, to form conjugates that can interact with other particles. The physicists identified a particular type of ghost particle called the alpha adjunct, which binds itself to the helium nucleus (an alpha particle) and debilitates it so the alpha particle loses its ability for radioactive penetration. Another type of ghost particle, the epsilon D, mimics another electron's size, causing the retardation or cessation of a chemical reaction. This occurs because the reactant ion, unable to violate Paulis's Exclusion Principle,[79] fails to incorporate real electrons into its sub-orbital structure.

2243

Humanosphere

Sociologist James Carmichael, in his famous book *Humanosphere,* coined the term to refer to the sum total of all Human influence and involvement in the Galaxy.

2244

Humanity Unity Agreement signed

Representatives from Earth and all the Human colonies, met on the planet Hercules Xi-3, to sign the Humankind Unity Agreement (HUA). The doctrine born of that meeting, the Hercules Accord, emphasized several important points of agreement:

- Implementation of free and fair trading practices between all Human worlds.
- A commitment to fight piracy, drug trafficking and Human slavery, all of which presented increasing problems in the Humanosphere.
- Block action to foster good relations with the Galaxy's alien nations.
- Limitations on military and industrial spending.
- Joint ventures to undertake new technologies, especially advances in querzian flight.

[79] Paulis's Exclusion Principle is the quantum mechanical law that states that two particles cannot occupy the same space at the same time.

2245

First successful trial of sectional transplanting

Sectional transplanting involved the removal of a sliver of healthy cells from an otherwise cancerous organ, the culturing of these cells in vitro by survival and growth enhancers and the subsequent return of these cells to the organ. Proponents of sectional transplanting argued that the chemicals added to the healthy cells in the growth media in vitro, induced the cells to reproduce at a rate which counteracted or overtook the spreading tumor. Known also as reverse cancer or tumor overgrowth therapy (TOT), the procedure had been developed by Venusian oncologists Toleio Yomura and Franz Rostfeld in the 2230s.

2247

Synthetic DNA

Once reliable techniques for mass production were developed by biochemist Ulf Jorgenstan of the Allied Planets Research Laboratories, production of synthetic DNA bases to resemble the purines and pyrimidines found in normal DNA, became standard procedure. Synthetic DNA bases proved crucial as analogues for the replacement of damaged DNA.

Later discoveries of naturally occurring nitrogen bases on several extra-stellar worlds, eventually swung medical opinion away from the use of synthetic bases toward the use of natural bases for DNA replacement. In the Alpha Aquila worlds for example, DNA containing forty-six types of purines and pyramidines were identified. Further investigation of the many DNA sources across the Galaxy, revealed the presence of a multitude of DNA families that differed from one another according to the type and amount of purine or pyramidine groups found in their genomes. Taxonomists used the variations in purine or pyramidine to construct a rough phylogeny, linking the Galaxy's multitude of organic species.

2248

The fertility drug fentatisis

Fentatisis, a popular drug used to select the number of eggs fertilized at conception, was marketed for the first time. The drug was commonly used when high birth rates were needed to increase populations on new colonies. The use of fentatisis in the colonial period, meant that twins became the most common birth type for women living in the new world.

2249

Photosynthetic restructuring

Photosynthetic restructuring involved calculated biochemical interference in the light and dark photosynthetic cycles, to create different types of carbohydrate monomers. Weynard Wesel of Galactic Alliance Laboratories, produced pentose sugar from a photosynthetic pathway in 2249. Risha Petrokov used a similar technique to synthesize triose the same year. Photosynthetic restructuring allowed the development of new strains of plants, classified according to the type of monomer formed during chemical photosynthesis. The technique also yielded a significant increase in the production of valued carbohydrate monomers, used to form polymers for energy storage. This enhanced the plant's ability to survive in soils of varying chemistry.

2250-2270

More advances in reproductive biology

During this era, biological scientists designed two reproductive methods to decrease gestation time:

- Chemically enhanced embryonic development:

Biological extracts rich in fetal growth hormone and Bersian factors,[80] were added to the embryo in increasing doses over a twelve-week period, to accelerate development.

- Growth structure creation factors:

Specialized nucleic acid-carbohydrate-protein polymer strands, which had been artificially manipulated at the nanotech level, were inserted to direct fetal development.

2251

Space riders

Like nineteenth century cowboys journeying into the openness of the American west, space riders were the adventurers of this era. As the first Humans to explore many of the distant stellar systems, space riders brought with them a sense of daring and courage, best personified in the legendary tales of bravado of Liona Hew (the Vigilante Lady) and Andrew Tentor (the Querzian Fighter)

---

[80] Bersian factors are rich extracts, comprised of over nine hundred compounds, necessary for fetal development. These were meticulously prepared in ratios to increase growth rates.

2252

Human taste sense enhanced

Gustatory modification (GM), a method for greatly amplifying the Human taste range by means of an ionic film placed on the tongue, was invented by Seymour Scheulig of the Neuron Research Division, Katz-Penfield Laboratories on Europa. The ionic film was comprised of a silicon-rich compound called tersium, whose three-dimensional structure allowed the transfer of electrons throughout the film to enhance taste bud stimulation. Gustatory modification proved popular, since it increased Human accessibility to the tastes of foods from colonial worlds, previously indistinguishable to the Human tongue. The four standard taste sensations of sourness, bitterness, saltiness and sweetness, were expanded to over thirty by the GM strip.

2253-2286

Gangster cartels battle in Humanosphere

Two gangster cartels prospered in the Humanosphere during this period. The larger cartel, the Climaro[81] was involved in interstellar drug trafficking, fraud, extortion and the overthrow of local colonial regimes by mercenary soldiers. Its rival cartel, the Hu Wan So, achieved notoriety by smuggling illicit food items, manufacturing weaponry and fabricating precious minerals. Each cartel operated in over eighty percent of the Humanosphere's economies, providing the large black market that existed at the time.

2254

Rigel missions

Trillionaire Jack Frombodi's fleet, the Ships to the Heavens, actively explored the Rigel system. The Rigel system was found to be rich in aluminum and copper wealth and would prove to be a valuable mining site in future Human history.

2255-2280

New drug developments

A number of important drugs were developed during this period, including:

- Mertocinan: This migraine-preventing drug was derived from the Oosokia plant, indigenous to Eridanus Epsilon-413. Mertocinan crystallized or liquefied body salts, depending on blood pressure in the brain, to act as a

[81] This cartel took its name from the twenty-third century Martian Mafia Don Jose de Climaro, who was somewhat of a modern day Pablo Escobar (of the twentieth century Medellin Drug cartel).

prophylactic against migraine onset.

- Bucinol: An acid-based drug synthesized from soil compounds on Cancer Alpha-323, bucinol deprived cancerous cells of oxygen. Used extensively by Humans in the final elimination of cancer in 2275, bucinol was most effective against colon, breast and lung tumors.
- Helepsi: Designed to provide immunity against space influenzas, especially the Anregian and Bootes strains, helepsi was developed from a compound known as Coratch, found on the planet Grus Iota-6/2-3. The drug killed the flu virus by reacting with the amine groups in the pathogen's protein coat, forming an inert shell that rendered the virus harmless. Helepsi therapy was inspired by Alberto Roticello and Harvey Stein of the Harvard Research Council on Space Station 17, who first witnessed the successful effects of the drug on canine and feline viruses in research during the 2250s. By 2262, bacterial breeder colonies were generating large quantities of helepsi. The abundance of the drug over the following one hundred years saved the lives of over 2.5 billion people from space plague.
- Colitnitran: A compound whose origin was the seminal fluid of the yogri animal of Aquila Alpha-7-1/2, colitnitran contained high levels of bromine and iodine. When released into the Human body, these chemicals caused the production of specialized antibodies, required to counteract such tropical diseases as Wershian fever and Goran syndrome, both indigenous to Aquila Alpha-7-1/2.
- Amitran: Belonging to a family of drugs known as genetic defect decelerators, amitran was first produced in 2260 to retard the reproduction of rapidly mutating viruses. The drug was developed from the secretion of the allorella plant of Scorpius Theta-4-4/3 and was hailed as the first real cure for the common cold. Unfortunately, in certain cases, amitran's mutative deceleration action could have detrimental side effects on the body's healthy cells, causing a slowing of cellular response times to changes in the homeostasis.

2256

Germ influx and mutation

Germ outbreaks attributable to extra-stellar pathogens, caused over one hundred million deaths on Earth over the following ten years. Competition with numerous local pathogens forced the extra-terrestrial organisms to diversify, taking on more lethal forms and igniting further mass emigration from Earth.

2257

Janitaus and his Grand Source of Energy

Theoretical thermo-physicist Ira Janitaus predicted the existence of a missing Grand Source of Energy for the universe, claiming this accounted for the difference between numerically calculated energy amounts and actual values for total universal energy. In 2282, physicists at the Adlridge Centre of Mass-Energy Research, developed a series of achy probes[82] to seek Janitaus's theoretical energy source. After twenty years of continuous research, a site thought to contain almost two percent of the universe's energy, was located near a series of giant black holes, almost 1.7 billion light years from Earth.

2258

Prison escape from Quentin Shrubs

A mass prison escape from the penal colony Quentin Shrubs,[83] freed five members of the notorious Rafferty gang. William Poraniuk, the corrupt governor of the Grus Iota-6/3-2 colony Darius-1 granted the Raffertys asylum on this isolated settlement. Poraniuk and the Raffertys combined forces, establishing a crime syndicate called the Circle of Wealth, that grew to rival both the Climaro and Hu Wan So.[84]

2259

Brownian motion computers

Computer engineers Dmitri Ardopdous and Marid Aljahud, both of Marvin Minsky Data Research Laboratories, showed that the Brownian motion of gas molecules in an isolated system could provide an excellent vehicle for the storage and transmission of information.

The principle behind this mechanism, was that as a consequence of the random motion of a gas, an infinite number of permutations, each based on molecular movement in three-dimensional space, could be generated. An individual permutation could be trapped in time and translated to correspond to the equivalent of a single unit of information storage, known as a datum. Infinite permutations equated to infinite data, establishing a high-volume system of memory retention.

---

[82] Achy probes were zero-mass energy-seeking particles, capable of instantly crossing time and space in search of energy sources.

[83] As a result of its web-like architecture, the Quentin Shrubs penal colony, located on the planet Grus
Iota-6/3-2, was also known as the Spindle of Fire.

[84] See entry for 2253 for details of the Climaro and Hu Wan So cartels.

This new method of information storage necessitated a revolution in the communications industry and led to an exponential expansion of database sizes for computer systems in the following century.

2261

Transformation Philosophy

Pasquel Dominguez and Silvana Huber, published a series of articles concerning transformation. A dark philosophy, transformation argued that evil would eventually triumph in the Human soul, as its scope of operation extended beyond the normal defined comprehension only hope for Humanity was to retard this eventual transformation by harnessing metaphysical communications with entities from other dimensions.

Communication with the spirit world became commonplace, thanks to the non-matter energy probes that transgressed existence dimensions. This breakthrough was the first step in the resurrection of metaphysics as a true science.

2262

Madman holds colony hostage

The Human colony of Renfras-2[85] was held hostage by an evil genius known as the Ionizer Madman, who threatened to disrupt the life-supporting atmosphere by introducing harmful ions and free radicals into the settlement's air generating unit. After a ninety-seven day standoff in which several of the Ionizer's demands were met, he was killed by a hit squad. The incident forced the Human worlds to implement tougher technological control laws to prevent sophisticated machinery, such as ionizers from falling into the hands of renegades.

2263

Cell division interference therapy

The first successful trials of cell division interference therapy (CDIT) were carried out. CDIT was based on the principle of stagnis, which involved altering the rate of cell division to offset the action of a potential congenital defect-causing agent on the cells themselves. Leading researchers in this field included Constantine Grabzlski and Viktor Tabchenko.

Grabzlski developed a method of chemically altering the spindle fibres in metaphase I of meiosis, in an attempt to remove imperfect gametes. This enhanced the degree of viable spermatozoa production in males. Tabchenko used an application of quantum physics called electron blasting, to speed cell

---

[85] Situated on Mars, the Renfras-2 colony had a population of 2.8 million people in 2262.

mitosis by a factor of fifty. Jurgen Wigner's invention of the Spongex ball for DNA micro-encapsulation, further advanced CDIT.

2264

Meeting the Zaalilanonex

The Zaalilanonex, a spiritlike people from the galactic centre, made contact with Humanity. Over a thirty-year period, the special relationship between these two species allowed Humanity to gain valuable biological knowledge on issues like life extension and Human anaerobic respiration. Human generations of the twenty-fourth and fifth centuries, used this knowledge to readapt their lifestyles and hardiness to newer types of colonization. Through the Zaalilanonex, Humanity was introduced to many of the galaxy's alien races.

2265-2315

Philosophical developments

During this period, two philosophies grew to prominence:

- Biologics: Based on the belief that the secret to longevity lay in finding the magical difference between life and death, proponents advocated a metaphysical life-death moment trial, followed by an analysis of ways to survive that moment, as a means to enhanced lifespan. Several proponents of biologics actually achieved success this way, increasing their lifespans to over three hundred years.
- Thought-merging: Thought-merging encouraged a generalist as opposed to a specialist lifestyle, as a way of increasing the volume and diversity of thought, in the belief that problems of the individual could best be solved by the randomness of Human thought. Leading advocates included Wolfgang Schmidt, Maria Sanchez-Rodriguez and Axel Pendigrass.

2267

Osteotwisting

Osteotwisting, the science of restructuring bone tissue to achieve various three-dimensional spiral patterns, enhancing bone strength and tension resistance, was developed. Elke Hesgarth of the Bone Muscle Clinic at the Vesalius Institute, emerged as the leading researcher in this field.

Hesgarth developed a product called netarin, made of gellike tubes extracted from peat mosses of a plant from the planet Delphinius Beta-5/2-2. Netarin manipulation transformed a diseased bone internally, while simultaneously maintaining the bone's external structure. The internal spiralling produced by this treatment, permitted greater support for the diseased bone.

2269

Anti-matter targeting as therapy

Anti-matter targeting (AMT), a therapeutic procedure involving focussed anti-matter rays onto a malignant area for tissue destruction, passed clinical trials. AMT was very effective against cancerous cells and cystic growths throughout the body. The technology was developed by eminent biophysicist Simone Chatelier, who also designed the energy trap, a safety guard allowing the capture of harmful gamma rays produced by matter-anti-matter interactions. These captured rays were used in more advanced AMT devices to provide a secondary dosage of heat energy, to annihilate whatever target cells had survived the initial anti-matter onslaught.

2270

Endocrinal synchrony successful

Endocrinal synchrony was a treatment using a series of micro-electric regulating devices placed in each of the target glands, to help synchronize the secretions of the target glands. ES proved to be a powerful therapy for the treatment of hormonal imbalances in the ovaries, testes, thyroid and pineal glands.

2271

The protein enigma unravels

Quintinerary structure proteins, with an additional level of organization to the most complicated Earth proteins, were discovered on several planets in the Bootes system. Classified as super-proteins because of their massive size,[86] these proteins were subsequently engineered to resist PH change, facilitate self-duplication and react to a host of different chemicals at a multitude of sites on the protein body. Later super-proteins were modified to release high combustion energies and used as fuels for short-distance travel. Several protein molecules were also manipulated for structural purposes, forming shear-resistant polymer shields for space ship construction.

---

[86] Quintinerary proteins tend to be 100,000 times heavier than the average Earth protein.

Chapter 9: A Newly-Born People Matures

2273

Human stellar exploration continues

2273 marked the beginning of the next stage of interstellar exploration, in which Human explorers ventured out from the localized Aleph region to explore the surrounding galactic sectors. The following table lists several galactic regions and the years in which they were first explored by Humanity.

Region	First Year Explored	Leader of First Exploration Team
Bet	2279	Dr. Vivian Fan
Chet	2295	Chester Baumgartner
Dalet	2274	Hans Haekel
Fey	2283	Sath Charenoogaroo
Hey	2279	Dennis St. Thomas
Kuph	2282	Ahmed Az Harari
Zayen	2290	Ashley Bandroisan

2274

Anti-Humanism as a philosophy

The growing philosophical movement known as neo-metaphysics, was the genesis of the anti-Humanist rebellion and won accreditation both theoretically and practically in the age of non-intuitive physics. It initiated a hundred-year rebellion, leading to the downfall of Humanism as a central tenant of philosophy. With the diminishment of the role of the individual and the subsequent discovery of metaphysical presences in the Galaxy, the overthrow of Humanism, as evolved by thinkers like Erasmus and Rousseau, was inevitable.

2276

Alien introductions

With the assistance of the Aleph region's Zaalilanonex people, Humans were introduced to six different alien races: the Tebeld, Riota, Fheral, Jyr, Dultas and Kosa.

See Appendix 6: The Intelligent Species of the Known Galaxy for details of these and other alien species.

2277

Vanishing city

The Riotan city of Porak Banatak Goutumo, with a population of 0.8 million, mysteriously disappeared from planet Mafgen-5. The disappearance of Porak remained unsolved for the next 218 years, until Riotan scientist Faq Oumo discovered the high field-density of jazt particles (energy particles that transcend the boundaries of time and space) at the site of the vanished city. Further investigations by Oumo revealed that Porak was built at the locus of collision for jazt particles. Over time, a collision sequence of jazt particles forced the movement of Porak along the time continuum. In 2498, Porak was relocated by Riotan time travellers who had journeyed to the year 4988. The same phenomenon, later called time-space delivery, explained the disappearance of the continent of Lemuria whose remnants were discovered in 2279 in the Pacific Ocean.

2278

Democratic turning point in Kosan history

Democratic elections were held in the Kimpak Alliance of the Kosa Region and ex-general Tarnal Lunt was elected president in a landslide victory, ending two hundred years of rule by the Orak dynasty. Lunt introduced economic and social reforms that eradicated most of the injustices perpetrated by his predecessor, Morkas the Infamous. The Luntian period of democracy molded the Kimpak into the most powerful entity in the Kosan Legion.

New revelation on sunspots

Researchers determined that sunspot cycle patterns are unique to a given star and are caused by the revolution of that stellar body around the galactic center. The type and appearance of sunspots were later shown to correlate with the strength of the gravity field of the nearest mini-black hole.

2279

Alien outreach continues

Human explorers made physical contact with the Izal of the Chet Region, as well as the Shayan of the Zayen Region. As with earlier contacts communication was carried out in binary logic using simple yes or no responses fed off electronic interfaces. Details on the Izal and Shayan are outlined as well in Appendix 6.

2280

Creskew Landing Strip

Hiram Creskew invented Creskew Landing Strips. Force field trapper sheaths, these landing strips could be constructed on almost any type of terrain, providing docking sites for space vehicles.

Humanity meets the last ten of the influential alien species

The Zaalilanonex introduced Humanity to the Fey Region's Gode-Iwi people, the Hey Region's Gald, Lagem and Smertertick nations and the Dalet Region's Bilong, Fogye, Litess, Lol, Noga and Rayoq life forms.

2281-2330

Architectural renaissance

Galdian builders embarked on a number of architecturally innovative projects that eventually earned them the title Master Builders of the Galaxy. These projects included the Celestial Tower, a 315-storey building subdivided into eight subsections, each of which contained a distinct type of Galdian architecture. Two of these were the Meditation Room, a large indoor pleasure palace shaped like a floating hailstone crystal and the Mesomorph, a series of buildings constructed of a flexible polymer allowing them to change shape daily.

2282

Kwan Lee Tan's higa theory

Higa is the intermediate state a substance goes through during transformation from matter to energy or vice versa. By temporarily forcing bodies into a higa state, Kwan extrapolated that material could be propelled at speeds exceeding that of light. Attempts at maintaining the higa state for a prolonged period proved the greatest scientific challenge of the early twenty-fourth century. This feat was eventually accomplished in 2357, with the invention of the cruncher machine. As an alternative to querzian propulsion, higa flight became available at a significantly lower cost for ships traveling at less than ten times the speed of light.

2283-2328

Overview of Rayoqian mercenary kingdoms

Rayoqian mercenary kingdoms, controlled by independent powerbrokers, developed during this period of history in the Dalet region. These kingdoms were autonomous in almost all respects, including intergalactic, foreign and trading policies. The two most significant mercenary stellar kingdoms were

Bosjap and Mikron, named after the stellar systems in which their central authority resided. Between 2289 and 2294, the Rayoqian Central government waged war against the mercenary kingdoms, but was defeated at the battles of the Hax Hafate. In 2294, a loose alliance known as the Independent Rayoqian Planetary Union (IRPU) was formed to act as a security shield for the mercenary kingdoms. The IRPU's existence was short-lived, however, since the Rayoqian Federation's military leader, Basaz Hajn, eventually defeated and reincorporated the breakaway mercenary kingdoms into a reconstructed Rayoqian Collective in 2328, defeating the IRPU at the Battle of Grisqerk.

2284

Mutiny in space

A mutiny occurred on the spaceship Sagrex-5, which was carrying Human colonists destined for the Cancer Alpha system. Although control of the ship was eventually restored to the authorized crew, five thousand lives were lost. The Sagrex incident illustrated the appalling conditions aboard colonial transport ships. After further review, transport ships were forced to comply with a minimum requirement level for their occupants.

2285

War between the Dultas and the Godeiw

An eight-year war erupted between the Dultas and the Godeiw, over settlement rights to the Fey region's Tamarank zone. Known also as the Greater Tamarank Conflict, the war was limited, with both sides reluctant to fully commit themselves to all-out combat for political reasons. Standards of military proficiency were high on both sides, however, with General Waqvas Xe of the Dultas Empire and Godeiwan Commander Logbra Kze Lun earning their places in history on the space battle fields of Tamarank-Alpha and Tamarank-Epsilon. The Dultas eventually emerged victorious, strengthening their resolve to expand into the Fey region and consolidating their military power in the eyes of the rival civilizations in the Bet region. The Treaty of Mout ended the war in 2293, splitting control of the large Tamarank zone seventy: thirty in favour of the Dultas.

2286

Peace between the Bilong and Fogye

For the first time in 171 years, the Bilong and the Fogye discussed peace. The agreement, known as the Peace of Pyer, outlined plans for the Fogye withdrawal from the Denba zone (an area consisting of six stellar bodies whose habitable planets were populated by the Vilma, a sister species of the

Bilong people). The cost of withdrawal was extracted by the Fogye from the Bilong in the form of a fifty percent share of revenue generated by the rich jurian mines of the Denba system.

2287

Lagem poetry

Famous Lagem poet Gatasia, wrote "The Ballad of the Butia," an outstanding piece of verse describing the lifestyle of Lagemian industrial workers. Work contains such lines as 'through the quantum rhapsody does my soul wonder free from the curse of the numbing icons' and 'a cowardly animal crouches below is he I? or are my dreams lost to the Butian underworld?'

2288

Mass exodus from Earth

Social scientist Elaine De May wrote her detailed analysis of reasons for the mass exodus from Earth. De May concluded that six major factors were responsible:

- The lack of personal economic opportunities on Earth, a consequence of the domination of corporate rule.
- The harshness of corporate rule and the collapse of civil liberties.
- Opportunities on the new worlds to develop markets catering to the insatiable demands of the Kosa and the Shayan. (Ironically, many of these initiatives were themselves corporate sponsored.)
- The complexity of life on Earth; the colonies seemed to offer a simpler lifestyle. The new worlds were often promoted as "back to basics" opportunities, offering a meaningful alternative to the technical chaos of Earth. Individual Humans, it was said, could rediscover their Humanity on the colonial worlds.
- The development of religious sects and cults, replacing older more formal religions, which, by the twenty-third century, were in complete decay. At the centre of these new age beliefs, appeared a common philosophy championing the need to separate the cult from the rest of Humanity, by establishing a nirvana in the heavens. The colonies offered these religious groups the chance to pursue this aspiration.
- Earth's overpopulation, war and environmental damage had taken their toll over the previous three centuries. This was further complicated by a baby boom, re-emphasizing Earth's obviously limited capacity.

2289

The peak of the Era of the Cult

The Era of the Cult reached its apex, with almost thirty percent of Humanity claiming membership in one cult or another. Traditional religions were at their lowest level in recorded history, with new age beliefs strongly emerging.

2290

Religious schism in Litessian world

Radical cleric Jod Mankas split from the Church of the Final Finger View, a religious denomination comprising ninety-eight percent of the Litess population, to form the Church of Mankas. Mankas's distaste for the excesses of the Finger View establishment, caused the split. The Litess population polarized into camps either supporting or opposing Mankas. The significance of this event is that it marked the beginning of the era of dual government in Litessian history, with one government for each church, that was to last until 2439.

2291

Further investment projects geared to encouraging Humans to settle the new colonial worlds were established by corporations in 2291 and lasted for forty years. The corporations supported space colonization for two reasons:

- To spread their influence to new worlds and maintain corporate control. It was, however, inevitable by this time that space colonization would occur with or without corporate participation.
- To establish mineral extraction and production facilities on these new worlds that could be sold to the Kosa and Shayan races. This practice, the corporations argued, would insure survival in a galactic order where Humanity was only a minor player.

2292

Time travelers and the Smertertick

Time travellers from the year 4567, visited the three planets in the Smertertick system of Rignus-Kappa (Fey region). The travellers were members of a future people known as the Goish (a life form developed in the fourth millennium from scientific interbreeding programs between the Smertertick and the related Kolivan people). The most startling of these revelations was the problem of the Dread virus, an artificially engineered quark particle system that multiplies at an extremely high rate, breaking down all complex matter in its path. According to the Goish, the Dread virus will destroy over twenty percent of all life in the Galaxy by the fifth millennium. As travellers from the future, the Goish explorers arrived in the twenty-third century to survey the galactic Fey region as a possible temporal settlement frame for forty-sixth century Goish colonists.

2293

Beginning of the end of the corporate era

The Tokkens Corporation, which had been controlled by Ico Jemina for forty years, was thrown into disarray when Jemina's sons rebelled against him. Several city states under Tokkens' control took the opportunity to rebel against their mother corporation. Although unsuccessful, this rebellion laid the foundation for the Liberation Wars of the early twenty-fourth century.

The level of discontent with corporate rule depended on the city state in question. The stifling of individual freedoms did not sit well with many, especially when coupled with mismanagement and the economic hardship of a depression that had begun as early as 2287.

2294

Super-cities

The construction of the twin cities of Rujna and Cgar on the planet Lomly Iota-3 neared completion. These cities were each designed to house over 1300 million Noga, making them the largest urban centres in the Galaxy. Together, the cities covered an area the size of North America. These well-organized Noga metropolises served as the prototypes for a series of super-cities built by the Rayoq, Bilong and Lol in the Dalet region during the twenty-fourth century.

2295

Galactic Peace Program founded

The Galactic Peace Program (GPP), an interspecies organization that had limited success in its advocacy of non-violent dispute resolution in the Galaxy, was formed. The GPP lasted until 2514. During its peak of activity, in the mid twenty-fourth century, the GPP's philosophy was most influenced by Toriv Klenak, a Gandhi-like Rayoqian figure.[87]

2296-2342

Good fortune in New Arabia

The New Arabia colony, also known as Delphinius Beta-5/5, prospered when rich deposits of Shentak dust, a chemical substance used in the production

---

[87] Mahatma Gandhi was a twentieth-century Earth leader who championed the use of passive resistance and non-violent civil disobedience in the move toward Indian independence from Britain.

of high-temperature antioxidants, were found on the planet. This discovery allowed New Arabia to become one of the wealthiest colonies in the Humanosphere.

2297

Alien superpower agreement between the Kosa and Shayan
The Shayan and Kosa, the two powerhouses of Galactic politics, signed a bilateral treaty of friendship that, although initially built on trade, eventually became a military alliance to resist the expansionist aims of the Gald and the Dultas. The alliance lasted through the next century.

2298

Marriage ban
The colony Canis Major Delta-4/4-1 banned marriage, deeming it an outdated institution of no value. Several colonies followed the Delta-4 example, causing a backlash on more traditional Human worlds. Social issues of this nature further divided Humanity, providing a basis for opposing alliances that developed over the next century.

2299

The New Pentathlon
The New Pentathlon was introduced as a sporting event in the Human worlds. The competition consisted of:

- an escape from an underwater facility with computer-designed constraints of a specified difficulty;
- a two kilometre swim against a strong current;
- a dive off a cliff;
- a twenty-kilometre run over a surface sprayed with an artificial adhesive; and a series of jumps over several gorges.

Known also as the Death Run, the New Pentathlon was described by sporting pundits as Endurance for the Crazy.

2300

Further Human colonies
The financial and physical cost of Human colonization diminished each year, as biological and chemical processes became more successful in preparing new worlds for habitation. Entrepreneurs specializing in the transformation and preparation of future colonies prospered, by providing customized living solutions for prospective extrastellar settlement builders.

Artificial gravity machines, which originated in the twenty-second century Solar System Planetary Settlement Era, were now used to simulate Earthlike conditions on the colonies. Most settlements were built as either domed structures or as isolated entities cut off from the rest of the planet by sub-atomic generated force fields.[88] These isolated entities, known as unams, were eventually joined to other unams by linker bridges on the surface of the planet, creating a giant interlinked structure, known as a polyum. Some polyums covered an area as large as Switzerland and housed between five and ten million people. From afar, polyums appeared as giant surface ant colonies. Over time, a single colony might grow to support numerous polyum systems.

Each polyum was designed to be as self-sufficient as possible with respect to its agricultural and industrial needs, taken care of in specialized unam production sectors. It is important to note, especially for those who take comfort from the continuity of history, that the polyum method of colonization evolved directly from earlier biotron systems pioneered over a century earlier.

Smaller groups of unams, or even single unams, were also built on most extrastellar worlds. Often home to single families, individual farmers and traders, these smaller structures, known as monums, were generally inhabited by those living on the fringes of the Human colonial frontier.

2301-2320

Liberation Wars

During this period, the Human worlds were subjected to a series of anti-corporate rebellions that became known as the Liberation Wars. The rebellions were the result of a growing anti-corporate sentiment that had been increasing throughout the Humanosphere for twenty years.

---

[88] Force field colonies were like worlds within worlds. Vast regions of planetary surface were cut off from the rest of the planet and independently modified to take on Human life-supporting characteristics by manipulating such variables as temperature, air content and ecosystem quality. The world within the unam was like its own biosphere. The development of force field technology was accelerated by the dynamic brilliance of the Mersh machine. A mechanized descendant of the twentieth-century cyclotron, the machine worked by accelerating gluons to create a gluon barrier. The gluon barrier was then extended to form the dividing line between a defined volume (the unam in this case) and the rest of the universe. It was possible to escape from the unam by using a stream of anti-gluon particles to create a temporary opening in the gluon barrier. This did not damage the gluon barrier permanently because gluons were constantly generated and recycled by the spinning particles in the Mersh machine.

As vehicles of power in twenty-second and early twenty-third century Human politics, the mega-corporations were responsible for establishing most of the first wave of extrastellar colonies in the Aleph region. These colonies were often well financed, elaborately equipped and designed with the sole intention of spreading the might of the respective controller company beyond the realms of the Earth-based solar system. These plans proved successful in most cases, leading to a burgeoning of power for the corporate elite, especially those of Dongadong and Franco Ini. However, by the mid-twenty-third century, the insistence by corporate executives on the maintenance of a rigid system of centralized control for the colonies weakened popular support for the corporations, with detrimental consequences.

Philosophers including Perkian, Alphonse Leonardo and Rosemary Tanvier emerged as the voices of liberation for the dissatisfied and disenfranchised colonials. In his celebrated work *The New Democracy*, Leonardo urged colonists to rebel and take control of the colonies, while Perkian advocated a return to mid-twentieth century Marxist theory as a way of dispensing with the irrationality of corporate government, a sentiment echoed by Tanvier in her book *The New Cosmic Order*.

Liberation groups, political parties and workers unions adopted the rallying cries of the new philosophers, infusing intellectual theory into an active *realpolitik* initiative. The strength of the liberation movements was further augmented by the growing dissatisfaction of the colonial populace toward the corporations, since the economic depression of the 2290s.

Mass demonstrations directed at corporate officials, erupted on several colonies between 2301 and 2304. Petitions and strikes were called for under the rallying cry of colonial power, while terror groups like the Aquilan Peoples Order (APO) and the Fornaxian Solidarity Front (FSF) lashed out at their respective corporate controllers in a series of bombing and kidnapping sprees in the Andromeda Epsilon, Aquila Alpha, Bootes Xi, Canis Major Delta, Fornax Beta and Lynx Alpha systems.

By 2307, the anti-corporate actions of the rebellious colonies had escalated to a point where eighty percent of extrastellar colonies in the Humanosphere were involved. Rebel groups from twenty-seven colonial systems gathered in a space station in the Canis Major Delta system in 2308, forming an alliance that signified the beginning of the second phase of the anti-corporate rebellion. This new group was known as the Poroit Alliance.

The second phase of the colonial rebellion can best be described as an all-out military conflict. The Poirot Alliance took the initiative in the early phases of the war, striking with lethal accuracy at the disarrayed corporate troops. At the battles of Rigley, Plentithan and Varlkey the corporate forces were systematically defeated by the Alliance's superior fire power. Under the leadership of Catherine Andalgier, a military genius dubbed the post-modern Boadicea, the Poirot Alliance weathered the corporate counterattacks[89] between 2310 and 2312.

Andalgier and her Generals Li Ying, Ambrose Dent and Karl Heinz Leier solidified the Poirot Alliance in 2313, drawing support from anti-colonial groups in the Earth solar system to reshape the military grouping into a guerilla force. For the following three years, this force waged a protracted war of attrition against the corporations. This strategy, adopted in the third phase of the war, proved successful. The corporate alliances surrendered their stranglehold on many of their colonies between 2316 and 2320. New contracts were signed, ensuring full sovereignty for the liberated worlds, in exchange for the granting of favoured (but not exclusive) trading rights by the respective colonies to the former controller company. This system, which survived until the breakdown of the monopolies in the mid-twenty-fifth century, was known as the System of Affordable Coexistence. The Poirot Alliance was eventually transformed into a loose trading confederation of colonies, known as the Human Conformation.

The anti-corporate rebellion marked a major turning point in the history of Humanity. Over two billion people died in the Liberation Wars that, ultimately, engulfed the entire Humanosphere. Historians see this conflict as the end of the era of monopolies and the beginning of a new ideology, placing greater emphasis on individualism and self-determination. While it is true that monopolistic corporate control remained a feature of some thirty percent of colonies in the twenty-sixth century Humanosphere, the rebirth of the nation state in the form of the stand-alone stellar system dominated for some time to come.

2302

Jyr suffer plague scourge

A breakout of a deadly viral plague, Tarbaschian Death, carried by the drami and norkas insect sectors, killed over 3-billion Jyr. A vaccine for the plague was not discovered by Jyrian researchers until 2415. The virus that caused the plague originated in a 4-billion year old isolation organic swamp, located in the Tarbasch Mountains of the newly colonized planet Bruit Phi-4/3 in the Kuph region. As an isolated pathogen, whose genetic material had never before made contact with the Jyr, the virus proved almost invariably fatal to the limited immune system of the unfortunate Jyrians.

---

[89] Fifty percent of the liberated colonies were retaken between 2310 and 2312 by a loose alliance of corporate forces.

2303

Further Human expansion

Mikhael Exdiablo, spiritual leader of the Buhan[90] religious cult, embarked on a pilgrimage with 20,000 followers to the far reaches of the Zayen region. After five years of travel, the Buhans reached the planet Des Kappa-6/3-3. Exdiablo claimed to have seen Des Kappa-6/3-3 in a dream he had in 2286 and had sworn that one day he would lead his followers into this holy land. The Buban settlement was important to Humanity as it created a stepping stone to spreading Human civilization beyond the Aleph region and into the surrounding Galaxy.

2304

Memory breakthrough in Human neuroscience

The development of selective memory transfixion in Humans was announced. Using this process, disturbing subconscious memories were replaced, through neural surgery, with memories of a more pleasant nature. Two procedures were used:

Process A, involved the infusion of foreign memory into the patient's brain, while Process B focused on augmenting existing pleasant memory to replace memory locales vacated by the eradicated unpleasantries.

2305-2325

Alien clothes in vogue

A craze for wearing alien dress swept through Human colonies. Vibrant and influential alienphilic movements emerged, that saw these new cultures as worthy of imitation. During this same period, many Human scholars made educational journeys to alien worlds to study the benefits of newly discovered civilizations and broaden their understanding of the universe and Humanity's place in it.

2306-2435

The Shayan Universe

Between 2306 and 2435, the Shayan transformed into a galactic superpower, whose actions had repercussions in the political atmosphere of the Galaxy. The

[90] The Buhan placed great value in the concepts of isolationism and untarnished growth. Exdiablo lectured his followers on the need for purification and regeneration of the Human soul. He claimed this would best be achieved, if Humanity began anew from a virgin base in an unspoilt region of the Galaxy. What Exdiablo did not realize, was that his leap of faith would encourage others to follow, spurring another mass colonization drive.

rapid development of the Shayan Union sprung from the Philosophers' Rebellion that defined the period of enlightenment in the twenty-fourth century. The introduction of democratic reforms by the Boramp (2306-2329), Fsaek (2329-2362) and Misaf (2362-2388) administrations also helped encourage foreign investment in the Union. Scientists and engineers invented new technologies that ultimately provided the Shayan with a competitive edge. Trader and settlement colonies established beyond the Zayen region, more than tripled the number of interstellar colonies under Shayan control. The immediate growth in Shayan influence was resisted by the Eai and Kefgas nations, but in a series of skirmishes known as the SEK Wars, between 2366 to 2377, the combined forces of these two peoples were crushed. The Shayan Union succeeded in building a military strength to rival its economic power. Shayan generals like Uyers Ram and Shagitoag were immortalized by their victories, as they carried the Shayan form of democracy to the rest of the Galaxy.

2306

Dog racing

Greyhound dog racing was modified so that dogs chased a moving laser beam instead of a mechanical rabbit. By the twenty-fourth century, genetic engineering had transformed the dogs so that they now ran at twice the speed of their twentieth-century ancestors. Often, alien genes were grafted into the dogs' genome to facilitate these desirable changes.

Beyond sport, the medical profession adopted genetic grafting techniques to fight diseases, using alien DNA or protein instead of Human DNA.

2307

A new psychological theory

Argitan Brink developed the Compartmentalized Theory of Psychology (CTP), which argued that relationship problems arise when the compartment (or distinct unit), a person has established with another person, changes. To achieve a higher degree of cooperation with one another, individuals should focus on limiting the extent of these changes. The established psychological hierarchy fought CTP vigorously, denouncing it as running counter to self-expression.

2308-2360

Twenty-fourth century fads

The twenty-fourth century Humanosphere is remembered for its many fads, including:

- Quick Loss Dieting: Weight loss programs using a chemical treatment mechanism to allow obese individuals to shed twenty percent of their body mass in a day.
- Sky Bounce Balls: Charged spherical toys popular with Earth children, Sky Bounce balls could travel the height of the old Empire State Building on a single bounce.
- Spin-Top Houses: Living units, intended for nomadic occupation, Spin-Top Houses could travel at speeds of Mach 5 on a planet's surface. Powered by a spinning action, these houses served as self-contained units and proved popular on many sparsely populated colonial worlds. They were the twenty-fourth century's analogues of the twentieth century's caravans or mobile homes.
- Piping Dens: Modern opium haunts, Piping Dens were popular among the Noteau drug crowd. Noteau addicts were individuals who abused drugs (the most notorious being priska) from new worlds.
- Legalized Sex Farms: Specialized settings for unlimited promiscuous activity, Sex Farms catered to the Roman orgy craze that swept Humanity in the 2350s.
- Simulation Halls: Illusional image rooms, which allowed individuals to replay historical or political events, Simulation Halls were widely used for therapeutic role-play.
- Simulsex: Sex with holographic images was made to feel real using sensory simulation. Simulsex devices were avidly used in the Humanosphere following the 2360 outbreak of a new generation of sexually transmitted diseases that had evolved on the sex farms.
- Space Parachuting: A sport of the rich, Space Parachuting involved an individual being ejected from a space vehicle and landing on a designated spot on an orbited planet. Specialized hover suits and steering gear assisted the jumper's motion, while simultaneously protecting him or her from friction burn caused by atmospheric re-entry.

2309

Bortram on Boutas-6/3

The discovery of a rich deposit of Bortram[91] on the Fogye planet Boutas-6, helped

---

[91] Bortram was an elaborate network of organic minerals, that had been designed by the ancient and now extinct Porew people 40,000 years previously. The Boutas-6/3 deposit was smaller than the Great Salt Lake of Earth, but capable of producing enough organic matter (in the form of proteins, carbohydrates and fats) in one day to feed a population of 200 BLUs (1 billion Life Units) for a year.

refinance many of the near-bankrupt Fogye worlds. The social and political growth of the Fogye was driven by this new-found fortune, which elevated the Fogye as an economic force, not only in the Dalet region, but throughout the Galaxy. Human historians, most notably Lionel Sharpeton, drew parallels between the sudden wealth of the Fogye in the early twenty-fourth century and that of the petroleum-rich Arab nations of twentieth-century Earth.

2310

A vital communications breakthrough

Based on physicist Reichard Wenz's Nobel prize-winning research on R exp N space, engineers developed a communications platform known as dimension beaming. The process worked by sending a signal into parallel space, where its velocity increased exponentially, relative to its universe of origin. The signal was then returned to its originating universe (or dimension), where it had covered a distance of R exp N times the rate it would have covered if it had travelled at its regular velocity in the originating universe.

A distance of four light years could be covered in milliseconds, if the beam was ejected into a significantly faster extra-dimensional Universe (i.e., a universe with a high N number). By selecting higher and higher N numbers, the communications links could be made to travel at faster velocities, so that speeds in excess of one-trillion-trillion times the speed of light were regularly achieved. Although this technique proved to be the major form of communication for the next two hundred years, its application was essentially limited to zero-mass particle travel. The most apparent problem R exp N technology faced during implementation, was signal retrieval from the N dimensional world, a feat that became more difficult as the N number increased. Various sub-atomic relaying functions were implemented to deal with this problem of dimensional loss.

2311

Hypnosleep

Hypnosleep was a drug-induced state designed to decrease the amount of sleep required by an adult Human from eight hours per night to a mere-forty five minutes. Developed by the Sleep Research Foundation on Titan colony, hypnosleep programs became so successful, that their widespread application in mainstream society allowed an increase in the average Human workday from nine to fourteen hours, while simultaneously increasing available leisure time. Drugs used in early hypnosleep programs included Fatizol and Metriban, both of which initially had the side effects of depression and nausea. Alterations in the drugs minimized these negative side effects by allowing rapid eye movement (REM) dream sleep. By the twenty-fourth century, it was common for individuals to spend over twenty-three-and-a-half hours per day fully awake for weeks on end.

2312-2318

Strife in the Rayoq worlds

The Rayoq Federation was weakened by the numerous military and political purges that occurred between 2312 and 2318. Over eighty percent of the Fios party was murdered during this bloody period of Rayoqian history. The purges were ordered by ruling Esbad President Gilkal Shac, in an attempt to consolidate his party's position in the federation. Galactic life activists have estimated that a total of 1.6 BLU[92] of Rayoq, representing 0.4% of the Federation's population, were killed during these purges. A further 750-million Rayoq fled the Federation seeking refuge among the Lol and Noga.

2313

Two planets collide

Shayan astronomers in the Zayen region's stellar system Mos Lambda, observed a unique event: the head-on collision of two of their star's giant outer planets. The planets, Lambda-6/4 and Lambda-6/5, collided after a random gravity swell propelled the latter into the former's orbit.

Planetary collisions are extremely rare. Planets colliding with stars, however, were documented nine thousand times between 2300 and 2500. The most noteworthy of these was the 2486 collision of Gemini Kappa-1/1, a planet three times the size of Jupiter, with its star.

2314

The Riota storage find

Human explorers discovered several storage planets used by the Riota in the Aleph region. The planets were determined to be reserve hubs for food and energy intended for Riotan use in the event of an attack against Humanity. This forced several of the Human worlds, still in the throws of the anti-corporate Liberation Wars, to establish alliances with more powerful alien partners.

2315

Gladiator rebellion

Gladiators from the Ferkan Trang Amphitheatre, the largest entertainment combat region in the Galaxy, rebelled against their Lagem masters. The

[92] Where one Human being is a single life unit, 1 BLU equals 1 Billion Life Units.

gladiators succeeded in overthrowing the Lagem authority on the planet Vorik Pi-7/2 (home of the amphitheatre) and replacing it with a gladiatorial triumvirate led by Giz Wane (a Bilong laser bolt fighter), Borimanus (a Fogyen heat twister) and Celikalph (a Rayoqian chemo-bomber). With the protection of outside parties including the Rayoq and Bilong, both eager to weaken Lagem power, the gladiators survived several counterattacks by the Lagem armed forces. The free planet of Vorik-7/2 became part of the Rayoqian Federation in 2377.

2316

Space-time anomalies

Space-twisting bends of corkscrewlike space-time were first detected by Jonah Moriphagan. These zones proved invaluable to cosmologists, creating linkages between parallel universes.

2317

A new spin on democracy

The colony Fornax Beta-3/3-4 introduced a graduated voting system, whereby votes in an election carried different weights depending on the age, social status and educational level of the individual voter.

2318

A boost for Human science

Renegade Dultas scientist, Numni Notas, introduced Humanity to advanced Dultas technology. It was Nota's generosity that allowed Human scientists to drastically improve their flight technology and resist future Dultas invasions.

2319

An agricultural history of Taurus Epsilon-1/1-3

This was the beginning of the era of crop specialization on the powerful Human colony Taurus Epsilon-1/1-3. Fast-growing ecil and enpa crops became dominant commodities in the economic portfolio of Taurus Epsilon-1/1-3. An allocation system implemented by the ruling Torschow dynasty insured that crop profits were distributed evenly among the colony's nineteen population groupings. The success of the allocation system directly reflected the rapid economic growth of the Taurus Epsilon-1/1-3 economy in the mid-twenty-fourth century, however, by the early twenty-fifth century, the allocation system had suffocated under its bureaucratic weight, finally collapsing around 2420. This collapse devastated Taurus Epsilon-1/1-3. A civil war (2426 - 2438) broke out among the city states of the colony, claiming twelve million lives.

Ecil and enpa did not replace wheat and rice as the two most important crops in the Human agricultural profile. Both crops were exported to the Kosa, who required them for species reproduction. By the late twenty-fourth century, almost eighty percent of the economy of the Human worlds was geared to meeting the needs of such giant powers as the Shayan and Kosa.

2320-2410

Corporations fall; Human colonies mature

A political vacuum was left in the Humanosphere after the era of the anti-corporate rebellions. The centralization of power by a distant elite had failed as the colonies broke free from their corporate masters and, for the first time in their short histories, exercised an unchallenged right to self-determination. Some colonies chose democratic government, others a benevolent dictatorship, while a third group opted for Regitonic systems similar to the types that had existed on Earth in the late twenty-first and early twenty-second centuries.

Historic nostalgia and a recourse to tradition appealled to large sectors of Humanity trying to come to terms with itself in the new milieu of interstellar space, but nostalgia alone was not enough to ensure survival. Humanity was prodded into rebirth, forced to adapt creatively to realities in the Galaxy.

Space historian Etienne Ravoir, called this creative strength Mitama, a term derived from the language of one of the Tebeld people. Colony worlds which quickly learned to understand Mitama reaped its benefits. This was best exemplified by the Alpha Aquila worlds, whose expedited progress and rise to power were a direct consequence of the foresight of its leadership in grasping the central tenants of Mitama.

The advantage of Mitama was felt on both economic and political levels. From the fairly even footing that had existed at the end of the anti-corporate rebellion, the Human worlds were thrust into a flux of differential growth and development; some worlds prospered while others faltered. Humanity was no longer in a league of its own, but in a race with some two thousand extrastellar civilizations scattered across the Galaxy.

Ravoir further distilled this sense by explaining how the era of separate development marked a transition in history, where Humanity changed from a self-focused people content in its own interrelationships, to true souls of the Galaxy, adjusting to the vastness of the cosmos.

It was, however, extrastellar competition that drew to an end the era of separate development less than one hundred years after its birth. Feelings of loneliness and a sense of being overwhelmed by the sheer size of the Galaxy, swept through the Humanosphere. A siege mentality prevailed as Humanity acknowledged its existence in a system in which each individual colony's presence was minuscule relative to the greater whole. Separate development died a natural death, disappearing in the tail winds of the emerging alliance structure, however, the legacy of separate development should in no way be underestimated.

The two thousand Human colonies that emerged from this era, were blessed with a sense of individualism that proved invaluable in the following centuries. The foundations for a strong Humanity were chiselled from this period with the tools of tolerance and cooperation. Humans of different cultural and historical backgrounds, had laboured in tandem to create viable societies, each in their own corner of space.

Altier Bartogas, the noted twenty-eighth century space philosopher, saw the separate development era in Human history as a freak period, inconsistent with the traditional development of most stellar wide civilizations. In other societies, separate development and the decentralization of government occurred much later in their respective histories, after both the alliance and empire eras were completed. For Humanity, the existence of a separate development era at such an early stage of its extrastellar history and the forced acceptance of the Mitama, empowered Humanity with an advantage, greatly decreasing the time for technological catch-up. It was as though, by a strange quirk of fate, Humanity had been given a head start to survive the rigours of its new niche among the Galaxy's advanced civilizations.

2321

Lol holocaust

Worsening internal conflict between different political groups of the Lol, resulted in a nuclear holocaust that left over eight billion dead, eleven percent of the population. The nuclear war was later described by historian Pelal Olal as the "cursed annihilation." The Lol home planet of Borew Theta-4/3 was ravaged by the effects of nuclear radiation, which left the planet desolate. Survivor populations were transferred to the sister planet Borew Theta-4/4 to escape the harmful effects of radioactive fallout. The war weakened the political position of the Lol in the Dalet region.

Chapter 10: Integration and Opposition

2323-2355

Gald time-tracking enterprises

The Gald's Temporal Experimentation business peaked during this period. Specially trained Gald travellers were employed by privately run tracking cartels, to search for solutions to problems by examining real outcomes through the actual playing out of different options in parallel time dimensions. Temporal Experimentation served as a valuable tool in the business, science and engineering worlds, where projects were selected on the comparative outcomes of alternatives.

2324

The Tau Cetus exhibition

Businesses of the Tau Cetus colonies organized an exhibition to make the numerous Galactic peoples aware of the goods and services they had to offer. Such outreach programs were indicative of Tau Cetus's aggressive business policy and allowed the colonies to take an early lead in commercial competition between the newly independent Human worlds.

2325

Monarchy reestablished

Monarchial governments emerged in several newly independent colonies of the Humanosphere, due to a desire for strong local leadership. By 2360, over twenty percent of all colonies acknowledged a monarch as the head of state.

2326

The de-population of Earth

The Earth's population dropped drastically in the twenty-fourth century, reaching a low of 5.6-billion. This trend continued unabated until the mid-twenty-sixth century, when Earth's population stabilized at 3.2-billion.

Ravaged by war and polluted beyond redemption, Earth was deserted by its populace. The shells of cities survived as ghost town hellholes, devoid of hope and home to only the most desperate of Humanity. Rival gangs led by warlords, filled the vacuum once held by corporations and lawlessness prevailed. The planet hung on the brink, heading into the twilight of its turmoil-filled existence.

2329

Dultas and Gald sign the Paisan treaty

At the Jntrnk bridge on the Bet Region planet Degrius Mu-3/3-8, Dultan Foreign Minister Poramitam met with representatives of the Gald, to sign what would become the Paisan treaty. The most important agreement between inter-regional people at the time, the treaty laid the foundation for cooperation between these two peoples and established a loose military alliance known as the Gortran Pact. It was the Paisan treaty, and the threat it posed to the Galactic balance of power, that escalated the movement toward the First Galactic War in 2368.

2330

Earth's political structure

After the anti-corporate rebellions on the stellar colonies, Earth's diminishing role in the Humanosphere became more apparent. Corporations survived on the home planet longer than on the stellar space colonies, but were eventually overthrown by citizens' revolts across Earth and the other solar system colonies beginning in 2330. Subsequently, the corporations were replaced by governors who ruled newly established megastates for the next two centuries. Below is a breakdown of these nine megastates on Earth and, for comparison purposes, their corresponding twentieth-century territories.

Megastate	Equivalent Twentieth-Century Territory
Afrique Grande	Sub-Saharan Africa
Altrasia	China, Southeast Asia, China Sea Hydrocolonies
Atlantuc	Brazil, South-Atlantic Hydrocolonies
Beatranka	Middle East, Eastern Europe, Mediterranean and Arabian Sea Hydrocolonies
Indiras	India, Indonesia, Pakistan, Indian Ocean Hydrocolonies
Lucalius	Eastern United States, Eastern Canada, Western Europe, North Atlantic Hydrocolonies
Oricana	Antarctica, South America (except Brazil), Central America, Western United States and Western Canada

New Pacificurn	Australia, New Zealand, Federation of Pacific Hydrocolonies
Rusograd	Baltic States, Russia, Ukraine, Arctic Circle Hydrocolonies

These territories were united in a loose confederation known as the Earth Peoples' Alliance (EPA).

2331

Galactic Talk Link constructed

Construction began on the Galactic Talk Link, a communications network linking all the Human stellar colonies. The Link used an early type of R exp N information protocol, regulated by a system of forty-five signalling nodes situated at various locations in the Humanosphere.

2332

Tragedy at the Volans Beta-5 colony

Planet Volans Beta-5/4 was swept into a comet storm that destroyed the planet's only Human-inhabited structure. This tragedy encouraged the development of more sophisticated comet and meteor shower detectors and controllers to protect Human colonies from their deleterious effects.

2333

Human-alien interbreeding

Interbreeding between Humans and several other Humanoid peoples of the Aleph Region from 2333 onwards, produced a variety of intelligent hybrids. Careful biological and genetic treatments, usually involving the production of adaptability mutations in the genome of the infants, insured their survival. Although over time these births became more routine, the children were later ostracized by fundamentalists of both communities. The mutants sought refuge in the boundary zones of the Aleph region, eventually forming their own kingdoms and nation states. The table below provides a list of some of these part-Human hybrids, with population figures based on the 2515 census.

Hybrid Species	Base Species	Habitat	Population (2515)
Fizerab	Human/Dorek	Aleph Zone 9-11	35 million
Humanoy	Human/Pilmay	Aleph Zone 67-68	15 million
Quatteran	Human/Quiggis	Aleph Zone 20-23	11 million
Shelikan	Human/Algater	Aleph Zone 9-10	13 million
Valigom	Human/Sasong	Aleph Zone 55	26 million

2334

Revolution in the Godeiw worlds

The Young Godeiw, a militant wing of the Democratic Movement for Godeiw, overthrew the autocratic monarchy of Yamish Ra, establishing a liberal government for the first time in Godeiw history. This new government was overthrown in 2367 by Rais son Fornam, with the assistance of the Dultas. A reborn autocracy known as the Verified Kingship, initially led by Fornam, ruled the Godeiw for the next 112 years.

2335

Resurrection of the House of Gesad

The House of Gesad,[93] oldest order of Transgalactic Psychosaints and astral travellers, wareestablished after 215 years of dormancy. The Gesad was resurrected by stellar psychics living on the Kosa world of Mukan Zeta-3/2, to combat the evil spiritualism of Drendy soothsayers, whose influence over the ruling Dultas class was growing. Members of the House of Gesad were chosen from across the Galaxy by selector monks. In 2365, the two powerful psychic forces clashed for the time in almost half a millennium. Although there was no winner in this battle of spiritual energies, the influence these two houses wielded with the Kosa and Dultas affected interstellar power-politics for the next three hundred years.

[93] Specially selected Humans have been linked with the House of Gesad. Over its 230,000 year history, the order claims to have selected, among others, Confucius, Nostradamus and Siddhartha Gautama (Buddha) as members, endowing each with powers of psychic manipulation.

2336

Izal religious change

The Izalian people were swept up by the Kass religion and its emphasis on monotheism. Although a strong backlash arose from the defenders of the old polytheistic orders, monotheism enveloped the Izalians almost completely by the twenty-fifth century.

2337

Riotan breeder experiments

Breeder experiments by Riotan scientists using rapid twinning techniques, proved successful. Over seven years, the Riota more than quadrupled their population, from 165 to 680 BLU. This accelerated increase in population allowed the Riota to gain political power within the Aleph Region, at the expense of rival peoples including the Tricaver, Sasong and Pilmay. The rapid growth of the Riotan population led to strained relations with Humanity, which in turn developed its own breeding experiments.

2338-2390

Rayoqian exploration initiative

Rayoqian adventurers explored the mystical Spiral Zones of the Galaxy's uncharted Resh region. Coopas Coolt discovered the rotating wormholes of Planth, Legus Xonial and successfully navigated the 450-star Trefdan Bli stellar zone. Tooniaz Poolial, another explorer, spent twenty-eight years studying the quintuple pulsars of Nevinog. Both adventurers emerged with honour from the Rayoqian exploration drive to take their place in twenty-fourth century history. Driven by traders of the mid-twenty-fourth century, the exploration movement allowed the Rayoq to gain an early economic advantage in the newly discovered worlds of the Galaxy's remoter regions. This advantage was short-lived however, soon eclipsed by the growth of the Shayan, Kosa and Godeiw merchant fleets.

2339

Publication of *Boramnk Joos*

Vernax Amgas, renowned Kosa Jurist and psychic philosopher, published the twenty-seven volume *Boramnk Joos*. This mammoth work, which took over sixty years to complete, detailed over ten thousand types of dispute situations and their corresponding paths of resolution. Most noteworthy, are sections dealing with disputes between different types of intelligent life forms in the Galaxy. Kosa diplomats schooled in the philosophy of the *Boramnk* used its wisdom to win critical diplomatic struggles in the Galaxy's political arenas during the twenty-fourth and twenty-fifth centuries. The *Bornnak Joos* was not adopted by Human politicians until after 2450.

2340

Completion of the Tetrabin highway

The Tetrabin highway, a 10,000 light-year long querzian particle blazed route linking the Kuph, Chet and Hey regions, was opened. The highway was jointly administered by six Galactic peoples, the Jyr, Kosa, Gald, Smertertick, Izal and Zweti. A total of 618 space stations were built along the highway to serve interregional travellers.

Spaceships used these highways, rather than travelling along their own paths, for reasons of cost. These blazed querzian highways reduced travel costs by one hundred times, since there was no need to create a new querzian field when a permanent one already existed.

The Tetrabin remained in operation for the next six hundred years and facilitated the dynamic flow of social, cultural and political ideas between peoples of the cross-connected regions. It also served as a model for later space routes such as the Aleph-Bet-Dalets region's Starmak highway, completed in 2432. By the early twenty-sixth century, however, the preponderance of Kosan pirates and Galdian robberships on all highways decreased their usage by neutral travellers.

2341

Formation of the Corporate Unity Front (CUF)

Human corporations which had survived the Liberation Wars, joined forces to create the Corporate Unity Front (CUF), an organization that worked to undermine the newly established governments of the independent colonies, in the hope of reestablishing corporate rule. The CUF's plan was not successful.

2342

The power shift away from Earth

The Aqulia Alpha and Chamaeleon Alpha stellar systems became the first Human worlds to surpass the Earth-based local solar system in overall economic and political influence. Leaders of both systems exercised their power via independently formulated policies that had strong repercussions across the Humanosphere.

In the Bilorm War of 2370, troops from the Aquila Alpha Federation clashed with Earth forces over agricultural rights to the newly discovered planet Tornia Kappa-5/3-2. In 2374, a year-long limited conflict broke out between Earth and

Epsilon Eridanus, over the ill treatment of Earth citizens by Eridanus officials in the Chamaeleon Alpha system.

2343

Jovra win Galdian clan war

Forces loyal to the Jovra Chartel[94] defeated those of the rival Parmoit, ending the sixteen-year civil war that had divided the Gald. A period of regrowth occurred within the Galdian Empire as the new dynasty asserted itself through a series of wars with the Hurgem (War of the Balwart succession) and the Dgloj (Speckled Star Conflict). While reasserting Galdian paramountcy in the Hey region, these conflicts also forced the Smertertick and Lagem to seek alliances with the extraregional forces of the Kosa and Shayan.

2344

The rise of neo-Marxism

Neo-Marxism, also known as Cosmo-Marxism or Fourth Wave Marxism,[95] seized power in the stellar systems Sagittarius Psi and the Bootes Delta, forming the backbone of the Homo Sapian Alliance in the twenty-fifth century.

2345

End of piracy on Drafian Front

Colonies on the Drafian Front were harassed by Human pirates until Chameleon Alpha forces, under the leadership of Stefan Doaks, put an end to the brigados at the Battle of Stellar Ridge in June of the year.

2346-2370

New worlds to colonize

The discovery by Human explorers of a relatively high number of planets

---

[94] The Jovra Chartel was led by the shrewd military tactician Varol Nefrait, who expanded the size of the Galdian Empire to incorporate the stellar clusters of Dnul and Zeberp. This increase in territory to fifty-four stellar systems and their protectorate populations, destabilized the balance of power in the Galaxy as the stellar superpowers, fearful of the Gald success, sought to increase their own domains in the period leading up to the First Galactic War in 2368.

[95] The First Wave refers to the original nineteenth century followers of Marx. The Second Wave was the Marxist Revolution of the twentieth century and the Third Wave was the Populare movement of the twenty-first and twenty-second centuries.

with oxygen-nitrogen atmospheres, expedited a further colonization drive. The reason for the presence of so many planets with an oxygen-nitrogen atmosphere remains a mystery. Some theorists argued that these planets, and Earth itself, may have been remnants of an ancient Human civilization that once colonized the Galaxy. The quest to prove this hypothesis spurred many Human exploration missions.

2347

The Human colonies of the Caelum Gamma-6 system

Mokarno became King of the Caelum Gamma-6 colonies. During his rule, an elite class, the Garytines, was responsible for administering the system's three planets. Favouritism and bribery sparked local rebellions against the Garytine administration, which were brutally quelled. Such actions spread a growing hatred of the King. Mokarno was forced to abdicate in 2385, in favour of his cousin Lembna. The new monarch made it her primary responsibility to restore the credibility of the Caelum royal family.

2348

Further piracy problems

On September 9th, renegade Quiggis pirates attacked the Human colony Saigon-3, located on the planet Eridanus Rho-4/3. A third of the colony's two million inhabitants fled, but the remainder were enslaved and sold on the life form cargo markets of the Aleph region. Attack crafts from several Humanosphere colonies succeeded in liberating the colony, but at a cost of over 20,000 lives. The Saigon-3 massacre represented the first large-scale clash between Humanity and an alien civilization. As a consequence, many of the Humanosphere's colonial worlds became militarized.

2349-2385

Human colonies incur debt

To support technological growth, Human worlds borrowed heavily from the Kosa and Shayan, who took full advantage of this indebtedness in years to come.

2350

Establishment of Sumatra Freedom Colony

Braimang Retch established the Human-controlled merchant world of Sumatra Freedom Colony (SFC) in the Kuph Region. A latter-day Mehmet Ali,[96] Retch

---

[96] Mehmet Ali was a nineteenth century Albanian businessman, who eventually became King of Egypt.

eventually established the SFC as an important base for Human-Kosa trading, with his family ruling the settlement for the next century.

2351

Unveiling of the Death Ray Laser
The Death Ray Laser (DRL), the most powerful weapon in the Human arsenal, was unveiled by scientists at the Samuel Colt Research Centre on Scorpius Theta-4/3-2. The DRL used concentrated laser power to sweep and destroy all matter in an area as large as 100-square kilometres. Similar weapons were developed by the Shayan and Dultas and used in the First Galactic War (2368-2373).

2352

Rebellion fails on Equuleus Alpha
The Tren insurrection failed in its attempt to establish a centralized military dictatorship over the Human-controlled Equuleus Alpha worlds. The rebellion, masterminded by Lucnas Tren, was put down by troops loyal to the ruling Cantashal Alliance.

2353

Massacre on Verkan-2
Godeiw settlers on the planet Verkan-2/2, massacred to extinction the planet's indigenous inhabitants. This grotesque act of genocide was documented by Fogye journalist Armak Ain and published over forty years later in a book entitled *The Forgotten Tragedies*. As a consequence of the book's publication, a series of anti-genocide agreements were signed between the stellar powers of the Fey, Kuph and Zayen regions. The new agreements established the first system of checks and balances to protect the less technically advanced indigenous peoples of these regions. Similar protection agreements were signed in the Aleph Region in the early twenty-fifth century.

2354

Composis philosophy
Proponents of Composis philosophy argued that Humans are composite beings, with a life force controlling each of his or her critical organs: the brain, heart, liver and lungs. Each of these life forces is thought to originate from a different point in the Galaxy, representative of distinct types of spiritual energy. Proponents of Composis achieved remarkable success in the diagnosis and treatment of various neuroses and psychoses, thought to occur when an outside force impinged on the brain's spiritual energy.

2355-2359

Dultas strip mining

The Dultas colonized and mined, to a state of near complete valuable mineral depletion, a total of 583 planets. Their policy of strip mining was implemented by Dultas authorities as a means of providing their empire with the valuable primary resources it drastically lacked. Although the mining proved expensive (costs equalled up to 25% of the Dultas GNP during this period), mineral retrieval allowed the Dultas to stockpile a reserve far exceeding that of other Galactic superpowers. Blue crystal, a source of querzian particles and ambarain a substance more precious than gold, was included in their mineral stockpile.

2356

Sandalius religion on the rise

Missionary crusades dramatically increased the number of adherents to the Sandalius religion. By 2356, over eight percent of Humans were members of the faith. Developed in the twenty-second century, Sandalius encouraged Humans to reject older faiths and follow a new belief aimed at reestablish meaning in a Galaxy where Humanity was no longer the chosen species, but just one intelligent life form among many. Sandalius assumed some aspects of older religions, but was the first theological attempt at addressing Human-extraterrestrial interaction. It was also the first Human-originated religion to allow aliens in its congregation. Detested by religious traditionalists, followers of Sandalius colonized more remote areas of the Humanosphere, seeking refuge from religious persecution.

2357

Humanity's position in the Galaxy

A review by the Institute of Science and Philosophy, revealed that breakthroughs in research and the subsequent advancement of both pure and applied sciences, had helped Humanity narrow the technological gap with rival Galactic powers. A graded listing (from 1 to 10) of the scientific and military levels for several Galactic powers is given below.

Galactic Power	Scientific Rating	Military Rating
Dultas	7.9	8.4
Gald	8.2	7.2
Godeiw	8.2	7.6

Huamnit	6.6	6.3
Izal	8.0	7.4
Kosa	8.5	8.3
Lagem	7.7	8.2
Rayoq	8.1	7.8
Shayan	8.4	8.5

An increase of one point in scientific rating, is equivalent to a ten-fold elevation in effective technological knowledge. A civilization with a military ranking of 8, is ten times stronger than a people with a rating of 7 and 100 times stronger than a population with a rating of 6.

2358

Space station agreement reached

Entrepreneurs from across the Aleph region, reached an agreement to finance a network of independent space stations along the region's periphery. The stations were designed as havens of free speech and free life. Almost seven hundred space stations, each capable of housing half-a-million people, were built from 2358 to 2379.

2359

Shayan invent Light Flash weapon

The Light Flash, a high-intensity spread of electromagnetic energy that could break the force field barrier of an enemy space ship, was invented. The Light Flash was used by the Shayan in the First Galactic War.

Minor players in region unite

Several nations of the Aleph region, the Oljaictriz, the Pilmay, the Quiggis and the Relnaft, met on Triangulum Australae-5/3 to establish a forum for economic cooperation. The organization that developed from this historic meeting was known as the Alliance of Free Planets (AFP). Although the AFP's intentions were initially economic cooperation, over time the mandate expanded to include issues of military significance. The presence of a potentially hostile military force in the Aleph region, was another factor causing the Human worlds to seek allies outside the Aleph region.

2360

Year of revolutions

Within one Earth year, leaders of the Litess, Lol and Noga were overthrown by popular revolt. The new governments in each of these civilizations joined to form the Alliance of Hope (AH). The AH served as a vital foil to limit the expansion of the reactionary Rayoq regime. The appearance of the AH as a beacon of resistance, helped encourage the spread of democracy to the Bilong and Fogye nations.

2361

The rush toward alliance formation

Trade hostilities in the Zayen region came close to setting off a military conflict between the Dultas and Shayan. The Shayan rightly accused the Dultas of interfering with the economics of the Zayen region by flooding the region with precious metals. The crisis, known as the Sha-Dul affair, forced both the Shayan and Dultas to seek allies within the Zayen and Bet regions, bolstering their individual positions. The following table lists various military pacts formed from 2361 to 2366.

Name of Alliance	Alliance Members	Year Established
Argan Pact	Dultas, Eai, Moxon	2361
Horex Grouping	Shayan, Kefgas, Mrptn	2362
Joltam Pact	Shayan, Fheral, Ablatia	2365

The race for military allies characterized future interregional Galactic politics. Much of the fear that gripped the Shayan and Dultas leaderships during this period, was caused by a lack of understanding by each party for the predicament of the other. The rapid formation of military alliances caused panic among other Galactic powers, who then felt compelled to solidify their respective positions through similar alliances. The following table lists alliances formed in the wake of this panic.

Name of Alliance	Alliance Members	Year Established
Forail Constituent	Godeiw, Fooka, Nizem	2363
Group of Four	Rayoq, Bilong, Mizol, Cze	2364
Momant Pact	Izal, Zweti, Boina	2363
Shuklad Entente	Kosa, Litess, Lol, Noga	2367

2362

Kosa mercenaries

The mercenaries of the Kuph region, known also as the Death Head Brigade, had terrorized the outlying Kosa and Jyr colonies for the previous seventy-five years. During this period, the brigades had built an arsenal of wealth and weaponry that allowed them to become a powerful entity in the region. In 2362, the Death Head Brigade was finally defeated and their chief planetary headquarters annihilated by a Kosa strike force. Most of the brigade's leadership was executed, but the terror group's founder and supreme commander, Labnas Bort, escaped to exile in the Aleph region, crash landing unnoticed on the planet Indus Delta-3/2-3. Frozen by his compatriots to avoid detection, Bort awoke almost two hundred years later and repeated his campaign of terror, raiding the colonies of the Indus Delta-3 system.

2363

Peacekeeping for profit

Both the Izal and Godeiw formed Galactic peacekeeping units, which they contracted out to restore calm to zones of conflict. Initially partners, the two groups eventually became competitors in this highly profitable industry.

2364

Non-Earth originating Humans found on newly discovered planet

Explorers found a population of Human beings living on the Dalet Region planet, Rigmora Kappa-5/3-2. The presence of these Humans, who were determined not to have had recent Earth origins and numbered about two thousand, gave support to the Ancient Human Galactic Empire theory.[97]

The Rigmora Kappa-5/3-2 Humans were studied by anthropologists, who identified them as estrus in nature, i.e., their females had a recurrent, restricted period of sexual receptivity marked by an intense sexual urge and only during this period were they fertile. Medical researchers argued that this adaptation allowed these Human females to conserve energy through reduced biological activity, a factor of critical importance on a planet with scarce resources.

2365

Human explorers venture into transitory zones

Human explorers visited the transitory zones, regions of free space on the outer edge of the Aleph region. It was found that the low density of matter in these

[97] For further information detailing the origins of this theory, see entry for 2346.

transitory zones, was caused by the dense flux of anti-gravity waves constantly generated by Galactic movement around the Universe's centre. Of additional interest to scientists, was the increasing growth rate of transitory zones (0.01 light years per year in all directions).

As the zones spread, they generated an anti-gravity field that damaged the structure of the surrounding matter-dense Galaxy, turning affected areas into cosmic Bermuda Triangles.

2366

World markets shudder as prospect of conflict grows

Commodity markets on transregional stock exchanges were shaken by the anticipation of a conflict between the Shayan and Dultas. Wealthy Kosa and Shayan investors moved quickly to invest in such commodities as Blue Crystal,[98] algan wax[99] and suter.[100] The rush to purchase these so-called supercommodities, created further economic panic that spread swiftly throughout the Galaxy, injuring many planetary economies.

2367

Shayan and Dultas head for war

The Shayan broke off all diplomatic ties with the Dultas to protest the latter's growing involvement in Zayen regional politics. Shayan officials placed their forces on full alert, after learning that the Dultas were massing troops and attack-crafts on the Bet-Zayen boundary. For the next year, a state of open hostility existed between the Shayan and Dultas.

---

[98] For details regarding the uses of Blue Crystal, see entry 2355-2359 on Dultas strip mining.

[99] Algan wax was a mineral used for laser shielding.

[100] Suter was a platinum-diamond mineral found exclusively in several stellar systems of the Chet region.

Chapter 11: The Age of Conflict

2368-2373

First Galactic War

Dultas starships launched a surprise attack on Shayan civilian cargo ships close to the boundary of the Bet and Zayen regions. A retaliatory laser attack by Shayan cruiser ships destroyed a Dultas base in the Zayen region killing over 200 MLUs.[101] The rest of the Argan pact backed the Dultas, declaring war on the Shayan and their allies, in both the Horex Grouping and the Joltam Pact.[102] The major events of this six-year war are chronicled below.

November 2368: War began.

January 2369: Dultas forces captured the mineral-rich Vorkan system from the Shayan, giving them a valuable foothold in the Zayen region.

March 2369: Shayan forces were victorious in the battle of Caq, a space-fighter battle fought in the cosmos of the Zayen region's Caq zone.

June 2369: Fall of Yomav, the ancient capital of the Kefgas people, to Dultas forces.

October 2369: Failure of the negotiated ceasefire organized by Izalian diplomat Baltan Aium. Fighting resumed two weeks later.

December 2369: At the Battle of Vlez, the Shayan won an important victory that allowed them to maintain control of the Zayen Region's Algac System.

April 2370: Biological warfare on the planet Min-2 claimed the lives of 40% of the planet's 220-million Shayan inhabitants. Min-2 had served an important role as a throughway for Shayan cargo transportation.

July 2370: Total deaths in the war to this point were estimated at 165 BLUs, with the Dultas coalition appearing to be in control.

November 2370: The Battle Of Tugitac ended in a stalemate, however, the cost to the Dultas military were heavy. The Dultas began revising their strategy from a direct to an indirect approach, the latter involving splitting up the attack forces by creating several diversions.

February 2371: The Flamork offensive, a multifaceted attack by Shayan-Kefgas cosmic fighter units, drove the Dultas from the Vorkan zone of the Zayen region.

June 2371: After a series of Shayan victories in the battles of Kast and Renni, Dultas-Moxon units reversed an apparent military trend by definitively defeating the elite Mertan force of the Shayan.

---

[101] Where one Human being is one unit, a MLU equals 1 million life units.

[102] For listing of Alliance names and members, see entry for 2361.

October 2371: Although this marked the beginning of a second ceasefire, which lasted until Feb 2372, during this five month period, there was also an escalation in the level of espionage between warring factions.

March 2372: Anti-matter camouflaged Shayan spacecraft attacked and destroyed Dultas settlements in the Loshki system, the second largest Dultas inhabited stellar system in the Galaxy. The attack was the largest of its kind in the history of modern warfare. It was also the first attack of the Galactic War in the Bet region. Over 40 BLUs Dultas, both civilian and military, perished in the Loshki massacres. Subsequent to the attack, Dultas morale crumbled as revolutionaries threatened to overthrow the existing leadership. Faced with the prospect of defeat, the Dultas launch a series of all-out counterattacks.

August 2372: Dultas counterattacks failed to break the Shayan defence at the Battles of Lombi and Nadaz. During the same period, the Dultas were completely ejected from the Zayen region. The remainder of the war was fought within the confines of the Bet region.

November 2372: The Shuklad Entente and the Momant Pact declared war on the Dultas and their allies in the Argan Pact. By December, almost all Dultas-held military installations in the Chet and Kuph regions had been evacuated.

January 2373: The Dultas-controlled zones of Celcatel and Riem, fell to the advancing Shayan forces. The Shayan military swept through the Bet region, annihilating most of the Dultas' outer defence. The same month, a coup d'état in Orinas, the Dultas capital, was brutally suppressed by royalist forces.

March 2373: This month marked the beginning of a five-month period of guerilla warfare. Small attack crafts of the Royal Dultas fleet failed to hinder the advance of the giant Shayan military force toward the strategic Dultas-controlled Vesta System.

October 2373: The Vesta Stellar System collapsed and the Argan Pact surrendered.

January 2374: The Treaty of Hjiuty was signed, ending the war.

Under the terms of the treaty, Dultas expansion into areas beyond the Bet region was strictly prohibited. All existing Dultas colonies and settlements in the Zayen region were immediately dismantled.

The defeat of the Argan Pact resulted largely from the Dultas leadership's overestimation of its own strength. The ruling military class was replaced by the less expansionist-minded Cloga Dynasty, ending over 500 years of empire growth. The Shayan emerged from the war as one of the Galaxy's two superpowers, the other being the Kosa. Their trading privileges were extended into the Bet region, formerly the exclusive territory of the Dultas and indigenous Bet region people. The growth of Shayan territory and influence produced a feeling of uneasiness among members of the Forail Constituent and the Group of Four. This feeling manifested in the formation of a series of agreements and alliances designed to limit the power of the Shayan in the Fey and Dalet regions.

During the First Galactic War, 190 BLUs died, including 150 billion Dultas. The war weakened the Dultas Empire for the next century.

The brilliant Shayan Generals Muras Joih and Galbarew Poih, earned a place in the history of space warfare. Muras led the attack on Loshki, while Galbarew was responsible for blocking the all-out Dultas counterattack at the Battle of Nadaz.

The success of espionage tactics during the Second Ceasefire Period, provided the Shayan with the necessary strategic information to counteract and eventually outgun the Dultas.

2374

The Kosan language revolution begins

Language transformation processes were implemented by Kosa authorities to radically alter the nature of the 739 Kosan languages. The campaign was the end result of a forty-year research project, whose principle aim was to simplify the complicated Kosan languages. The re-education of the Kosan populace to use these new language types involved a further century of training.

2375-2397

Tyra raids

The Tyra were another group of Human space buccaneers who terrorized remote space colonies. Well equipped with laser-blocking armor, the Tyra proved difficult opposition, until their final defeat in 2397, by a combined force of Human mercenaries and Kosa troops at the battle of Silver Arch. The vastness of space and the fact that so much of the Galaxy was still uncharted, enabled pirates to avoid detection. As more of the Galaxy was mapped, pirate haunts became harder to conceal and effective counterattacks, such as that of Silver Arch, became more commonplace.

2376

Mammalian metamorphosis becomes reality

Scientific experiments under the guidance of Berla Crombi of the Da Vinci School of Anatomical Research, showed that the activation of key protein and lipid triggers in the body could initiate physical metamorphosis in mammals. Crombi's research, which set the world of biotechnology abuzz, was performed on the Arcturus ground rat. Using a laser beam, Crombi altered the genetic trigger for several of the rat's proteins and then observed the rat's metamorphosis into a new type of rodent.

Another biochemist, Alende Sertanius, expanded the metamorphosis technique to other mammals, so that by 2380, metamorphosis techniques were being used to facilitate animal adaptation to new environmental conditions.

Metamorphosis experiments on Humans were first undertaken in 2391, with the full-scale metamorphosis of an adult male into a Type A Hurora. In 2394, Man Kyi showed that specific additions of ester-based metamorphic drugs, could force the Human body into a cycle of metamorphic changes similar to those of an insect.[103]

2377

The Numeri cults

Flavian Jajipayee published his celebrated book, *Numerocracy*. This book inspired the Humanosphere-centered Numeri cults, whose principal beliefs centered on arithmetic ordering as the prime focus for life's harmony.

2378

Shayan mutiny

A mutiny by troops aboard Shayan battle craft in the Bet region, was suppressed by military police. The mutiny was a reaction against the poor living conditions Shayan troops endured during the Bet region occupation, following the First Galactic War. A decision to advance back pay helped improve troop morale, drastically reducing desertion rates and putting an end to the prospect of future rebellions.

2380

Gwiston forces destroy planet

The planet Entrius in the Leo Minor Beta system, collapsed under the strain of gwiston forces.[104] The planet's 1.9 million Human colonists, were evacuated and temporarily resettled on the planet's moon, Beta-2-A. Ten thousand colonists died in the surprise implosion, generated by a mining expedition's

---

[103] Due to the viviparous nature of Human beings, no egg laying stage was encountered in the Human metamorphic cycle, although a change to an ovoviporous stage, similar to the extinct platypus, was achieved and classified as the Humona D Metamorphic Phase.

[104] Gwiston forces are internal spin forces generated by gwiston particles, that cause the collapse or implosion of a large body, such as a planet.

accidental activation of the gwiston force field. The invention of the gwiston field detector by Shayan scientist Lignas Ro in 2399, helped later miners and geologists avoid accidental activation of a planet's dormant gwiston field.

2381

Fjam rebel against Gald

The Fjam rebellion against Galdian domination brought chaos to the Hey region. The Fjam were an ancient people, whose highly advanced Empire had dominated much of the Hey region from the fifteenth to nineteenth centuries. The Lagem and Smertertick backed the Fjam, partly out of romantic nostalgia for an ancient civilization, but mostly to destabilize the Gald power structure. The rebellion failed after Fjam leader Krkat Kagurtem, was assassinated by agents working for the Sadesk.[105] The Fjam did, however, finally achieve independence peacefully in 2508, during the Age of the Grand Unifier.[106]

2383

Rayoq's new leadership

Sench the Destroyer, a popular and well-loved military and political figure, was elected Supreme leader of the Rayoq. Eager to fill the Galaxy power vacuum left by the defeat of the Dultas in the First Galactic War, Sench embarked on an expansionist policy that enabled the Rayoq to acquire vital stellar territory in the Fey and Bet regions. In his lifetime, the Rayoq increased the size of their stellar holdings by twenty percent. Sench's expansionist philosophy caused great fear for Humanity. In 2385, several Human colonies signed protection agreements with the Kosa and Shayan in the hope of deterring Rayoqian ambitions in the Aleph region.

2384

Earth city state experiments with platonic democracy

A new world platonic society was created in the Earth city state of Phoenix-Tucson. Based on a rotation of the city's ruler each week, giving all worthy individuals an opportunity to govern, the society functioned for three years before succumbing to revolution. Such radical types of government were typical of the decaying Earth, whose remaining population seemed lost, disillusioned and ill-at-ease following the collapse of their corporate entities. Other ruling governments during this period included the nihilistic nation of Toronto and a matriarchal regime in Madrid.

---

[105] The Sadesk was the Galdian military intelligence organization.

[106] See entry 2488.

2385

The Compan make Human contact

The Compan, an alien species from the Zayen Region, made contact with Humanity. Although they were a DNA-based life form, the Compan were unique in that their brains were dispersed through forty different areas of their bodies. This structure allowed the Compan a functional diversity and survival even under harsh or traumatic conditions.

2386

Dultas rulers suppress rebellion

Troops of the Dultas Empire attacked and annihilated rebel forces on the Rim 5 planets. The victory was the first military action taken by the Dultas since their defeat in the First Galactic War. Although they were not expansionist-minded, the empire's ruling Cloga Dynasty did not believe in retreat either. It was generally believed that such inaction had been responsible for weakening such nations as the Fheral in earlier times.

2387

Derivation of the mixing ratio

Linus Roans devised the concept of the mixing ratio to determine the extent of interbreeding between different ethnic groups and its effect on the changing face of Humanity. Using a base value of 0 to represent Humanity in its least polarized phase and 1 to denote its most polarized phase, Roans calculated that as of 2387, the average Human settlement stood at 0.7. The average Human population throughout the settled Galaxy equaled the cosmopolitan nature of late twentieth century New York.

2388

Another rebellion in the Dultas Empire

Cze rebels took advantage of weaknesses in the Dultas Empire to drive the latter from strategic positions in the Bet region's Gorkey Psi stellar system. The Cze rebellion was the first of a series of eight insurrections that toppled Dultas authorities in several Bet region stellar systems between 2388 and 2412. The rebel government on Gorkey Psi joined the Cze-Federation, strengthening the Cze position in the Bet Region.

2389

Android rules London City State

Romnas Regam, a genetically engineered bio-mechanical mutant, seized power in London City State, Earth, after defeating the incumbent authorities (remnants of the Brittanix Corp). Regam's sudden rise to power was opposed by other Earth city states, who feared similar rebellions. Unrest rippled across the planet once again.

2390

War ensues over an Izalian-Zweti love affair

Riots erupted in the Izalian capital of Tlefgan after news broke that Juxes Kooshaign, the Commander-Lan of the Izalian people, was involved in a love affair with Omerak Iln, daughter of head Zweti priest Torak Iln. Although this great love affair was later immortalized in the romantic writings of the Chet region, the Izalian population viewed Kooshaign's actions as a betrayal. Faced with overwhelming condemnation and unwilling to forgo his love for Omerak, Kooshaign resigned his position in 2391.

The events that followed his resignation were critical to Izalian history. Kooshaign's first cousin, Anxes, gained the position of Commander-Lan in 2392. Anxes took the Izal to war [107] with the Zweti, punishing them for their role in disrupting Izalian politics. This ill-timed action weakened the Izal, opening the Chet region to the Shayan and Godeiw.

2391

A regional justice system

The Gald, Smertertick and fifty-six other civilizations in the Hey region signed the Sgtimus Agenda. The Agenda outlined a common judiciary system for citizens of the signatory civilizations. The document represented a major breakthrough in the politics of interspecies cooperation. A similar judiciary system was established for certain civilizations of the Bet region in 2429.

2393-2425

Replay of early twentieth century capitalism

During this period, robber barons profited from the economic laissez faire policies of many Human colonies. Although corruption levels stood high the economy of the Humanosphere worlds boomed.

2394

Advancement protocol established

Many colonies and settlement worlds in the Humanosphere finally agreed upon the advancement protocol, which emphasized the need for treaties of

[107] This conflict was the Izalian-Zwet war of 2393-2400.

friendship and mutual understanding between Humanity and other civilizations in the Galaxy. Bilateral agreements between individual colonies and centralized extraterrestrial authorities, such as the Riota Administration, were encouraged. In 2398, the Canis Major Delta system entered a joint trading agreement with the Izal and similar overtures were made to the Shayan by settlers of the Chameleon Alpha worlds.

Between 2394 and 2420, 118 bilateral agreements were signed between Human worlds and various extraterrestrial civilizations, earning this period of Human history the name of the Humano-Outreach Era. The Humanosphere's advancement protocol proved successful in integrating Humanity into Galactic power politics.

Journey to the center of the Galaxy

Cosmic adventurers Chandra Rama and Violetta Antonelli, embarked on a thirty-year adventure to reach and explore the Galactic centre. Situated almost 30,000 light years from Earth, 25,000 light years from the nearest Human colony and separated from the Aleph region by the Bet and Dalet regions, the task of reaching the Galactic centre had once seemed an insuperable task for Human explorers. Rama and Antonelli succeeded by using a newly developed form of querzian flight known as intergenics.[108] In both the Bet and Dalet Regions, the pair encountered and documented many life forms previously unknown to Humanity. The couple were immortalized in the history of space travel as the Marco Polos of Galactic exploration.

2395

Martian politics at its worst

Political power in the Martian colonies was centralized under the leadership of Trefdan Vaudeville, the wealthy mining magnate who controlled over forty percent of the planet's querzian particle refinement facilities. Life on Mars under Vaudeville and his army of purple shirts improved initially, but the regime abolished the Martian parliament in 2344, thus ending democratic rule on the planet. Vaudeville himself ruled for the next fifty years, establishing a totalitarian regime known as the NeoTrefdats that governed for the next two centuries.

2396-2450

Galdian culture flourishes

Art, music and literary culture flourished on the Galdian Worlds. A new movement

[108] Intergenics occurs when the rare triple-spin of the querzian beta particle is translated into flight energy on the macro level.

known as the Neo-Originists, looked to the classical proto-Galdian civilizations (c.500-1000) for inspiration. Artists like metal sculptor Haberock, Danehlas the playwright of the *Galdian Dust Uncovered* and Livinas who revitalized classical low frequency Medan Music,[109] established their reputations during this cultural revolution. The Galdian Awakening had a widespread impact on the art of the Lagem and Smertertick. Humanity's art was also influenced, as evidenced by the adoption of Galdian canvas techniques into the dominant Taskey School painting style.

2397

Invention of the divisibility probe by Noga scientists

The divisibility probe, a sophisticated instrument measuring only 0.5 micrometres in diameter, became the chief industrial and military tool of espionage during the early twenty-fifth century's Data Acquisition Race. The divisibility probe was named for its ability to self-divide, forming finer and more specific probes to search and process highly detailed structural information for various micro-sections of intricate machinery.

2398

Thieves steal harmful pathogen

Viro-thieves raided the Orgax Microbiological Institute,[110] the largest library and storage facility of deadly viruses and bacteria in the Galaxy. The OMI contained over 100 million different types of viral and bacterial organisms that between them, were lethal to half the Galaxy's population. The thieves made off with over 500 self-contained viral samples that included Heravirus (deadly to Humans), Forlax pathogen (lethal in small dosages to the Izal) and Versap Influenza virus (infectious to the Rayoq). A year after the stunning robbery, the viro-thieves, led by scientific charlatan Olxz Reez, threatened to release the Versap Influenza on the Rayoqian city, Movieteie. Their ploy was unsuccessful and the thieves were captured and executed by Rayoqian special forces.

2399

Tycho Brahe planetary system identified

A Human stellar exploration team led by Rajiv Pataki, discovered a Tycho

---

[109] Medan Music was a musical form developed by a Galdian religious order of the same name in circa 800.

[110] The Orgax Microbiological Institute was founded in 2373 by Rayoq scientists on the planet Dris Beta-3/2.

Brahe-type solar system[111] existing around the Chet region star, Draco Chi. As a result of a phenomenon known as counter gravity release,[112] the local star and ten of the eleven orbiting planets, had been thrust into an elliptical orbit around the system's fifth stationary planet. Existing in the eye of a vortex of forces, this uninhabited planet, Chi-11/5, appeared subtended in a stationery frame of motion in relation to the rest of its stellar system. Over the next century, another three-twenty Tycho Brahe systems were discovered throughout the Galaxy.

2400

The fate of New York City

The Columbus Collective, the student government of New York City, collapsed. The Collective had ruled since gaining power in 2338 after the withdrawal of the corporate entity. The city declined rapidly, falling victim to mass emigration. By 2450, the Big Apple was almost deserted, a harsh consequence of the space colonization drive.

2401

Rayoq-Noga Alliance

In return for a transfer of technology, the Noga allied more closely with the Rayoq, establishing what became known as the Pact of Crinthus.[113]

New trends in Human cities

Human cities in the early to mid-twenty-fifth century tended to be less densely populated than those of the twenty-third and -fourth centuries. A number of architectural styles were revived, including neo-Gothic, futuro-Inca[114] and Ceramic Naturalism.

Nostalgia predominated in the new colonial worlds, with architects and city planners preferring to recreate replicas of Mohenjo-Daro, Ancient Rome, Tikal, Byzantium and Machu Picchu.

---

[111] In the sixteenth century, Danish astronomer Tycho Brahe wrongly theorized that the Earth was part of a system, where all planets revolved around the sun, except the Earth, which was at the system's centre with the Sun revolving around it.

[112] The anti-gravitational property of counter gravity release was first observed in 2314. Even today, little is known about it.

[113] Crinthus is a metal found in the Dalet region's Tersan zone and possessing five times the strength of the strongest Earth steel.

[114] Futuro-Inca style attempted to incorporate fifteenth century Incan design.

2402

Kosa extend local regional influence

A puppet government loyal to the Kosa Regime, vaulted into power in the Mrptn stellar system of Xsaze, establishing Kosa hegemony over 90% of the Kuph region's Mrptn population. The growth of the Kosa power base created fear in other populations in the Kuph region, especially the Bnor, Cze and Jyr, who subsequently formed the Obin Alliance.

2403

Shayan building advance

Shayan builders completed construction of Valanx, the first city built from the mineral Korex, a non-erodible, non-destructible compound found only on the planet Chak Zeta-4/2. The Korex's luminosity gave Valanx a continuous glow, making night and day in the city almost indistinguishable. Valanx city served as the prototype for many Shayan and Fogye cities built during the latter half of the twenty-fifth century.

Overview of Galactic Politics

The Kosa and Shayan were the two most powerful forces in the Galaxy at this time. The Dultas were in decline as they had been since their defeat in the First Galactic War. The Rayoq, Gald and Godeiw, despite being plagued by internal problems, were nibbling at the heels of the Kosa and Shayan. The other Galactic peoples were all fighting for survival and evolving in their own way, with several races forming military and economic alliances with the greater powers mentioned above.

Humanity had shaken off the corporate yoke and was passing through the era of so-called Separate Development, where each new settled colonial world matured into an independent self-sustaining entity. Some of these colonies signed bilateral trading and protection treaties with various alien powers and were prospering from these agreements. However by 2403, except for a few Marxist colonies in the Humanosphere, there was little unity among the different colonial worlds. Galaxy wide, the Human population had grown tremendously during the previous century, driven largely by the need to provide service and production demands of the Shayan and Kosa. The Human population in 2403 was 105.3 billion, excluding cross-species beings and cyborgs who themselves numbered 1.8 billion.

2404

Novel crops

Several new crops were introduced into Human agriculture.

- Butia: A dense, protein-rich crop, butia is similar to soybeans in appearance, but more filling so hunger is satisfied after ingesting only a small amount.
- Dolse: A hardy, fast growing crop, able to grow during any type of season.
- Flort: A sulpher crop that flourished in acid-rich soil. The sub-products of flort were distilled into mechanical fuel.
- Mufinine: A medicinal plant whose bio-products cured forms of the Bootes Simplex disease.

2406

Further technological gains

Double-dealing by such individuals as Vernon Kew and Terry Hartford, allowed the Human worlds to gain control of vital electronic technology from the rival Rayoq.

2407

Kosan leader assassinated

Torang Umain, Galactic Chief of the Kosa, had served as primary administrator for the political and social affairs of his people for seventy years. Because of the fine quality of his leadership, his life had been artificially extended a further twenty-five years. In 2407, however, a power struggle resulted in Umain's assassination. An investigation by the Kosa Security Force's Special Services Division, revealed that undercover Jyr agents were responsible. The Jyr had hoped that the assassination would destabilize the Kosa universe, recently strengthened by the acquisition of Mrptn territory. The Jyr actions hastened the approaching Kosa-Jyr conflict, in which the Jyr were defeated in 2411.

2408

Sex change drug synthesized

The drug Imanin was synthesized by pharmacologists at the Corselius Institute.[115] The chemical's main function was its ability to allow a Human being to undergo a physical sex change by selectively controlling the X and Y

[115] The Corselius Institute was named after Ana Corselius, a leading biochemist of the early twenty-second century.

chromosomes during regular cell mitosis. A complete sexual conversion could be accelerated to occur in one week, with Imanin influencing both the primary and secondary sexual characteristics. Imanin usage was popular during the transgender fad of the 2410s and 2420s, but had subsided by 2430, after the discovery of genetic damage on the autosomes (non-sexual chromosomes) of many of its users.

2409

Drug withdrawal leads to violence on Jyrian worlds
Violent incidents affected the Jyrian worlds after the feel-good drug Zenton was removed from the food supply. The removal was instigated to reduce costs, but as a consequence of the violence, the decision was reversed.

2410 onward

Human Alliance Era (HAE)
The Human Alliance Era marked the next period in the development of Humanity. The era was noted for its breakdown of Separate Development and the grouping of formerly independent colonies into new alliances.

The HAE is also remembered for its qualities of diplomacy, political foresight and wisdom as shown by such individuals as Langley Sound, Fletch Tubervicle and Yves Routaillant, each of whom played a vital role in reshaping Human history.

Seventeen alliances were formed during the HAE. The five most important are detailed below.

Association of Human Colonies and Planets (AHCP): Formed in 2443, the AHCP became the second largest alliance formed during the HAE. Its founder, Langley Sound, developed the liberal constitution upon which the AHCP was based. Colony states in the AHCP tended to be affluent, with a high level of technological sophistication. In time, over 238 planet systems became members.

Homo Sapien Alliance (HSA): The HSA was a Marxist alliance of planetary worlds formed in 2412. Consisting of over 141 planetary systems at its height, the HSA was governed by a legislative assembly representing various communities within the alliance.

Human Federation (HF): As the third largest alliance in the HAE, the industry-driven HF was known for its rigid corporate-orientated structure, modeled on earlier political systems developed during the twenty-second and -third centuries. The HF often earned the ire of other Human alliances by entering into questionable business agreements with alien groups hostile to the rest of Humanity.

Human Peace Initiative (HPI): The HPI was a scientific alliance of eighty planets. Central to medical knowledge in the Humanosphere, the HPI was responsible for many biological breakthroughs during this era. Formed by Fletch Tubervicle, the HPI tended toward neutrality in many of the controversial interalliance issues.
Pax Humana Alliance (PHA): Formed by Yves Routaillant, the PHA linked protective trading and military agreements. With over 350 planetary systems, the PHA formed the most powerful alliance in the Humanosphere.

2411-2454

Shani warriors take power on Godeiw worlds

Led by their matriarch, Nefhizer Nagashez, the Shamis outmaneuvered the Democratic Movement for Godeiw, defeating the latter in the Propaganda wars of 2408-2411. Nagashez's forty-three year rule coincided with a mini-golden age in Godeiw history.

As a military power, the Godeiw rose to rank third in overall Galactic standings during Nagashez's rule.[116] Her support of new innovations allowed the Godeiw to develop an intellectual dynamic to feed its technological growth, bringing prosperity to its people. The period of Shami warrior domination lasted until 2512, when a coup d'état overthrew the Shami Regime, replacing it with a revitalized Democratic Movement.

2412

Dultas loosen grip on protected civilizations

Hoping to stifle a nationalistic fervor among its many population groups, the Dultas decided to grant greater autonomy to fourteen of its nineteen protected civilizations. Despite this apparent relinquishing of power decreed by the Roisan Acts, all foreign or extra-empire relations, including the signing of treaties with external powers, were still overseen by the centralized Dultasian authority.

2413

Ancient civilization of Brabinuly discovered

Ruins from the ancient civilization of Brabinuly were discovered by Kosa archaeologists on planet Decas Psi-2/2 in the Hey region. Further research revealed that the Brabinuly had developed ultraphotonic flight almost forty thousand years previously, allowing them to colonize several planets in the

---

[116] During Nagashez's rule, the Godeiw were still behind the Kosa and Shayan, but ahead of the Rayoq, Gald, Dultas and Lagem.

Hey region. The Brabinuly had made significant progress in the fields of inorganic medicine, metalwork, plastoconstruction and energy field interplay. The Rafghi, outside invaders from an unknown Galactic region, had destroyed the Brabinuly civilization almost ten thousand years previously. Survivors of the Rafghi genocide, only ten percent of the original Brabinuly population, fled to neutral planets throughout the Hey region, mixing with indigenous people to produce among others, the ancestors of the Lagem.

2414

Kefgas settle Earth

Humanoid Kefgas were invited by several city states to settle Earth, which had rapidly depopulated over the previous century. Domed Kefgas settlements were established in the land areas of Argentina, Peru and Chile. The desire by the Kefgas population to settle on Earth was driven by a theology that saw Earth as their religious homeland.

2415

Religious movement spreads through Kosa worlds

The Majana movement, a religion based on zealotry and self-sacrifice, spread through the Kosa worlds. The Majana movement was founded by psychic philosopher Gamriz Nan, whose writings were recorded by his faithful disciples, Oput Van and Wvrek Lim, in the holy book, The Beski.[117] When Nan died in 2304 at the age of 319, his followers, many of whom came from the Kosa military elite,[118] swore to keep Nan's teachings alive by launching an armed crusade across the alliance. By 2415, almost ten percent of the Kosa population had converted to Majana. In the late twenty-fifth century, Majana was adopted by other people in the Kuph region, particularly the Cze and the Jyr.

2416

Lagem scientists complete Giant Candle

Slightly larger than Jupiter, the Giant Candle project consisted of 19,000 linked Queta[119] reactors, generating the energy equivalent of ten suns. This huge network was located in the Tqew zone of the Hey Region. For the next

[117] The name Beski was derived from the Kosa word Besk, meaning to enlighten.

[118] The Fearless Sfibars, the elite fighting class of the Kosa military, were named for their weapon, the Sfibar, an eight-edged sword.

[119] Queta particles are high energy units that continuously absorb energy by selectively annihilating other particles. The particle itself was first identified by Lagem physicist Woohlan Wasin 2389.

century, the Lagem sold their vast energy surplus to any interested buyers, earning revenue to rejuvenate the long depleted Lagem economy. The Giant Candle was copied on a larger scale by both the Shayan and Kosa in the late twenty-fifth century. Queta reactors became the preferred energy source for advanced cosmic powers.

2417-2435

Dultas population increases

For the first time since their defeat in the First Galactic War, the Dultas Empire increased its population. As a result of Latent Stress Population Recovery Inhibition (LSPRI),[120] Dultas population had decreased drastically until 2417.

2418

Rayoq expand into newly discovered Yud Region

A large Rayoq military buildup in the Shaqwaz zone of the newly discovered Yud region took place. The buildup was directed by the Rayoq and their allies in the Group of Four[121] to force the Oita, the dominant life form in the Shaqwaz zone, to agree to relinquish control of the Telnac Extraregional Communication System—the most advanced communication system in the Galaxy—to the Group of Four. Both the Godeiw and the Shayan, who feared the consequences of Rayoqian control over this strategic asset, vehemently condemned the Rayoqian action. The Godeiw kingdom guaranteed sovereignty of the Oita by the Treaty of Buyerflum.

2419

Riotan child leader takes power

The child Omni Rex was elevated to the position of Dektas Dong, universal leader of the Riotan people. Olixan, as he was called, ruled over the Riota for the next fifty-nine years. His period of governorship was distinguished by the growth of the Riotan production base. A lover of architecture, Olixan championed the construction of such structural marvels as the Helvax Ziggarut

---

[120] LSPRI is a physiological reaction, causing a species-wide decrease in fertility. It is triggered by a severe shock to a life form, such as war, plague or famine. If the shock is severe enough, the fertility drop can actually lead to species extinction. Genetic factors determine which organisms undergo LSPRI.A lethal LSPRI response resulted, for example, in the extinction of Dinosaurs at the end of the Cretaceous period on pre-historic Earth.

[121] See entry for 2361.

and the Helical Pyramids of Lorkritan. Communication with other life forms was encouraged by Rex, leading to the establishment of special trans-cultural and trading relationships with the Tebeld and Humanity. Olixan's death in 2478 was followed by a period of internal strife on the Riota planets.

2420

The Godeiw and Rayoq at war

The Godeiw and Rayoq clashed over ascension rights to the Esian[122] leadership. The Godeiw, the local Fey regional power, threw their support behind Joif Jes, champion of the peasant-based Gulmbar Party. The Rayoq backed the more dominant industrially orientated Orsek party, led by Roif Res. In a letter to the Rayoq's chief ambassadorial representative on Esian, the Godeiw warned the Rayoq of the consequences of interfering in the politics of the Fey Region. The Rayoq, however, ignored the warning and after severing diplomatic ties with the Godeiw, continued to support Res and the Orsek party in their struggle for leadership. Events climaxed in the Muhgad hostage incident, in which twelve politicians from the Godeiw ruling executive were kidnapped and assassinated by agents of the Rayoqian Special Force Dinor Rak Division.[123] The assassination prompted an armed response by the Godeiw, beginning the Second Galactic War.

---

[122] The Es are a Fey Region people with strong connections to the Godeiw.

[123] A Rayoqian phrase that translates to "killers of the transgressors."

Chapter 12: Further Conflict

2421-2424

Second Galactic War

The Second Galactic War was fought between 2421 and 2424. The events of this war are chronicled below:

February 2421: The Godeiw launched the first of seven major attacks against Rayoq positions in the Shorktam, Limor and Vekabay zones of the Fey region. Godeiw generals hoped that fatal strikes in these particular zones would force the Rayoq to sue for an early peace. Events proved otherwise.

April 2421: Rayoq Allies in the Group of Four pledged troops to fight against the Godeiw invaders.

May 2421: The Orsek Party, under the leadership of Roif Res, won the Esian leadership struggle. Res offered his unconditional support to the Rayoq.

July 2421: Rayoq defenses held firm against an onslaught of 85,000 Godeiwan spacecraft. The Godeiw were victorious in the battle of Tootan, but were resoundingly defeated by the more technologically advanced Group of Four space battalions at the battles of Reez and Gutnam.

October 2421: The Godeiw withdrew from several bases in the Fey region's Larn and Tablemaz zones in preparation for an assault on the Dalet region's Khoh zone.

January 2422: With assistance from her allies in the Forail Constituent,[124] the Godeiw succeeded in capturing over one third of the star systems in the Dalet Region's Khoh Zone.

March 2422: The Godeiw held onto their new gains in the Khoh zone, despite the severity of a Rayoq counterattack.

June 2422: The Kosa signed a military alliance with the Godeiw. Kosa spacecraft and cosmic battleships attacked Rayoq colonies in the Kuph Region.

August 2422: The Mid-space battle of Termiyud ended in a stalemate between Godeiw and Rayoq forces.

November 2422: The war entered an attrition phase, with both the Godeiw and Rayoq forces launching guerilla-type attacks. The attrition phase lasted for four months.

February 2423: The Human-Dalet region colony Buber-2 was attacked and destroyed by undercover Rayoqian mercenaries posing as Godeiw agents. The attack was intended to draw the Human worlds into the war as Rayoq Allies. Suspicions of duplicity and fear of the consequences of fighting against a

[124] See entry for 2361.

galactic superpower, forced the Humans to adopt a neutral stance for the remainder of the war. This position was heavily criticized by many who felt a response to the death of over 400,000 Humans in the Buber-2 attack was necessary.

May 2423: The Galactic War spread deeper into the Dalet region. The Godeiw increased the ferocity of their attacks against the enemy. Over forty billion Rayoqian civilians were massacred during the first few months of the Godeiw attack on the Dalet Region. Later historians rated the Godeiw attack as was one of the most gruesome events in the history of modern Galactic civilization.

September 2423: Surrender of the Rayoq forces to Godeiw General Tilamp Nag in the Fey Region. Over 188 star systems, comprising ten percent of all Rayoqian worlds, fell into the hands of the Godeiw.

December 2423: Fearful of Godeiw power acquisition in the Dalet region, the Shayan and Izal entered the war allied with the Rayoq.

February 2424: Godeiw forces defeated the Rayoq at the battle of Monx, marking the collapse of all resistance to the Godeiw in three more Dalet region zones.

April 2424: Izal and Shayan troops helped the Rayoq successfully defend the central zones of the Dalet Region. A further seventy billion Rayoqian civilians died in this valiant defence that ended in September.

September 2424: An armistice agreement was reached, ending the Second Galactic War.

November 2424: The Peace of Mrogad was signed. Ninety percent of Rayoq-occupied planets in the Dalet Region remained under Rayoqian control, but the remainder of its Dalet region settlements and all its Fey region worlds were incorporated into the Godeiw framework. Rayoq positions in the Bet region were also relinquished to the Godeiw. The Kosa took all Rayoq-Hey region territories. By the terms of the treaty, over 180 billion Rayoq were forced to live under foreign power.

The magnitude of destruction that resulted from the Second Galactic War was astounding. Both the Godeiw and Rayoq threw all their resources into a war of annihilation. The death toll reflects this strategy. Over 320 billion Rayoq died in the war, mainly as a result of mass extermination programs followed by the Godeiw. The Godeiw themselves lost 90 billion lives. An additional 70 billion people of non-Godeiw or Rayoq affiliation were also killed in the war. The above figures represent a two-fold increase in deaths from the First Galactic War.

The Godeiw were the chief beneficiaries of the war. The performance of their well-trained military machine and field commanders was exemplary. The newly won Rayoqian territory elevated the victorious Godeiw to a position of strength in the Dalet Region. In the short run, the acquisition of planets and population added to the economic base of the Godeiw, strengthening their geo-strategic makeup so it rivaled both the Kosa and Shayan. In the long run, the presence of a hostile Rayoq population under its domination led to insurrection and instability for the Godeiw. Historians referred to the Godeiw territorial acquisitions from the Second Galactic War as the Dalet Region Burden.

Although the problem of Esian leadership succession appeared to spark the Second Galactic War, the direct cause was the expansionist policies of both the Godeiw and Rayoq. As players in the great game of interegional politics, it was only a matter of time before the conflicting aims of these two superpowers clashed.

2426

An approaching threat

The Rafghi, a highly advanced species from the Andromeda Galaxy, undertook the first of several phases in their Galactic colonization program. The growing Rafghi presence eventually threatened the survival of the Galaxy's civilized life forms in centuries to come.

2429

Publication of the *Vortazon*

Kosa scientist Telbibar Torkamagum published the *Vortaxon*, the definitive work on extra-dimensional particle analysis. Torkamagum used the mathematical technique of Merkikan theory to unravel some of the enigmas of extra-dimensional worlds. In doing so, he proved that the known universe was a composite of eleven intertwining dimensions. A brilliant work of science, the *Vortaxon* was to the physics of the day what Newton's *Principia* was to classical mechanics.

2432

Shayan rampage against crime syndicate

The Shayan military launched search and destroy missions to eradicate the Flemak crime syndicate. In a broad sweep through the Shayan controlled Morkab and Balsas stellar zones, the military destroyed the Flemak crime infrastructure. Intelligence gained from the search and destroy missions provided valuable information regarding the existence of a powerful Galactic-wide crime syndicate with origins in the Kosa region.

2433-2436

Final defeat of old Corporations

This was a period of tension between the new Human alliances and several successor organizations to the old corporations. Tensions eventually led to the War of Dominance in which the corporations were again defeated.

2435

Fogye sex industry under fire

Over two thousand Fogye sexual emporiums were closed throughout the Dalet region. Catering to the sexual appetites of over five thousand intelligent species, the Emporiums fell into disfavor after it was learned that half its workers had been drawn into their occupation by a program of abduction and forced slavery. At the height of their popularity, it was estimated that over eight thousand different types of sexual acts had been practiced at the emporiums.

2436-2490

Building mania continues

Investment campaigns helped finance major infrastructure projects in the Humanosphere during this period. The campaigns drew heavily from the wealthy stellar worlds of Alpha Aquila and Taurus Epsilon to establish over three thousand fully serviced space routes and an additional nine hundred interstellar Class I spaceships throughout the Aleph and Bet regions. Entrepreneurs, including Richmond Ying and Paris Nogult, made their fortunes in this forty-year development frenzy that established Humanity as a vital player in the Aleph and surrounding regions. Unemployment in the Humanosphere dropped to a two-hundred-year low of two percent.

2437

Tibetan Buddhism establishes new ground

Tibetan Buddhists identified the next Dalai Lama (Ocean Guru) as the son of a Godeiw peasant. Known as Laga Saan, the new Dalai Lama was the first non-Human candidate ever recognized as the holy reincarnate. Tibetan Buddhism had become one of the fastest growing religions in the Fey Region in the previous fifty years, receiving unusually high support among the Godeiw and Litessian settlers.

2438

An unusual find

Human adventurers James Barkney and Tensley Himes retrieved the riches of Drego from a vault on Drego Pi/2-2, an artificially created spin-off planet in close proximity to the star Libra Alpha. The treasures included the atomic time clock of Gibraz, which according to Riotan legends, had been telling time for the previous three-and-a-half billion years.

2439

The Lagem: Political and economic reorganization

The Lagem worlds were divided into five sectors to increase the potential for each sector to attract new allies, both politically and commercially, in a non-intrusive, non-threatening manner. Over the following century, the competing Lagem segments showed varying technological growth patterns that widely differentiated the economic and social well-being of this once uniform people.

2441

Izalian Voripile religion

This is the year usually given as the birth of the Izalian Voripile religion. Similar to Buddhism in its philosophical underpinnings, Voripile emphasized the importance of a serene and peaceful pathway to true salvation. The religion's influence on the Izalian ruling elite undoubtedly reduced the belligerence of Izalian foreign policy. Historians would compare Voripile to the soothing effects that Buddhism had on the Indian king Asoka, in ancient times on planet Earth.

2442

Shayan policy in the conquered Regional Zones

Shayan developers began re-adapting large sections of the Kalaba, Nurew and Forep zones of the Bet region for colonization by transforming its planets into replicas of their Shayan home worlds. Thousands of planets were redesigned by the Shayan, who saw this as necessary to consolidating their presence in the Bet region. However, Dultas terrorist groups launched attacks on Shayan transformation efforts, delaying completion by five years.

The Shayan initiated similar projects in the Chet and Fey regions. The Shayan advance was beheld with apprehension by the Godeiw, who subsequently made alliances with the Kosa and Es to limit Shayan expansion in the Galaxy.

2444

Lol peasant rebellion

Peasant rebels overthrew the political leadership on several Lolian planets. Dictators schooled in the art of Marxist readjustment philosophy, rose to power in the Lolian worlds,. The most important of these dictators was Pelfark Barx, who ruled the planet Micornia between 2444 and 2456.

2445-2458

The Galdian Crusades

This period was noted for the religious crusades of the Gald. Galdian religious thinkers from the Drambdi and Porschabel stellar systems, financed a series of holy wars against the Dgloj, Hurgem and Smertertick to spread the message of Borkan. Borkan was a religious ideology based on the teachings of twenty-first century Galdian visionary Emlak Shzam, who argued that the Gald could only obtain true peace in their surroundings by merging philosophically with other powers in the Hey region. The Grand Unifier, the most influential figure of the twenty-fifth century, adopted these aspects of Borkan thought into his own theological writings. Success in these wars allowed the Godeiw to capture the Hurgem holy city of Creepius, but heavy losses suffered in battles against the Smertertick, where the Gald were outgunned by the sophisticated Smertertick laser artillery, consigned these campaigns to the trash heap of history. However, the Galdian crusades had the long-term effect of providing a mechanism for the destabilization of the Hey region, making it vulnerable to the advances of the Grand Unifier over half a century later.

2446

Popularization of honeycomb cities

Toward the middle of the twenty-fifth century, metallic super-alloy cities built according to Rayoq and Dultas designs became a noticeable feature of Human urban settlements. Their characteristic honeycomb patterns supported these metallic structures that were often coloured to blend with their environment.

2447

Godeiw bailout of Lolian economy

A huge economic bailout by the Godeiw helped the Lol economy avoid an impending financial disaster bought on by a vast balance-of-payments deficit. This rescue plan by the Godeiw came at a great price to the Lol, since the former succeeded in winning a controlling interest in the Lol economy for the next century. This period became known to the Lol as the Submission.

2448

Change of power for the Dultas

Power struggles within the framework of the ruling Dultas aristocracy polarized the Dultas into two camps: the Regenists, who backed crown prince Hic Loen, and the Transformationists, who supported the young pretender Nilip Vorg. The Regenists succeeded in defeating their opponents in 2448, despite the intervention of the Shayan on behalf of the Transformationists. The Regenists' victory marked a rebirth in the political power of the Dultas.

2449

Civil rights demonstrations in Shayan realm

Civil rights groups marched on several Shayan cities demanding equal rights for the Clega group, the most impoverished population in the Shayan worlds. Equal rights were eventually granted to the Clega in 2456

2450

Rayoq planets split

Weakened by the loss of territory in the Second Galactic War, the Rayoqian-controlled planets split to form the Romnas Conformation and the Bifor Hafate. The former existed as an extension of the old realm, while the latter were transformed into a multi-life form Galactic federation whose population demographics include some of the Noga, Litess and Lol. These territories were re-united in 2491 by the Grand Unifier.

2451

Romnas conformation thwarts coup d'état

In February 2451, a coup d'état almost succeeded in bringing down the newly formed Romnas Conformation. The quick response of loyal Generals Terq and Havihas saved the central government from the insurrection.

2452

Pirate rivalries

Noga pirate king Vlemark Drebz was defeated and driven into exile by rival Galactic marauders from the Poliglak Bandit Brigades. The Poliglaks victory, led by bloodthirsty psychopath Sifoom Frebz It established the basis for a pirate syndicate, whose monopolistic powers spread from the Kuph region to the rest of the Galaxy.

2453

Kosa introduce the Kerax economic standard

Kerax, the precious metal mined at over four million sites in the Kuph region, was introduced by the Kosa onto the open market as a mechanism for standardizing business transactions. Human historians compared the introduction of kerax in the Kuph region to the gold standard of twentieth century Earth. The use of a standardized precious metal for trading purposes also spread to both the Dalet and Hey regions, where the latter used toemp and the former introduced reesam-platinum.

2454

Black hole disaster

A floating black hole in the Dalet region destroyed all four planets in the star system Malemak Kappa. Close to twenty million people from the pre-industrial Relbas civilization on Kappa-3/2 were wiped out in this unforeseen disaster. The black hole, or nemesis star, is now thought to have been the remnant of a localized graviton concentration anomaly that had occurred at the birth of the Milky Way.

2455

Corruption in the Shayan Worlds

Corruption charges brought down one third of the local governments in the Shayan worlds. Cleanup crusades, established in 2449 to deal with growing corruption in the Shayan political structure,[125] were responsible for initiating these charges. An elite class of judiciary officials known as the Rankon Plex, masterminded the purge. The success of the Rankon Plex in controlling intrafederation corruption, allowed the organization to develop an influential role in the Shayan political establishment. Their leader, Amborak Vorm, eventually ascended to power as Shayan President in 2464.

2456

Dultas-Fheral war ends

Peace was finally achieved in the Bet region, ending the ten-year war fought between the Fheral and the Dultas, in the Vouit and Bablican stellar zones. The conflict had ensued over biological production rights to the rich fauna and flora that existed in these zones. A peace congress jointly hosted on the planet Valiraes-Kappa 6/3 by the Shayan and Godeiw split the zones in favor of the Fogye.

---

[125] Corruption had been growing in the Shayan worlds since the First Galactic War.

2457

Rayoq guerillas attack the Godeiw

Rayoqian guerilla groups[126] launched attacks against Godeiw-held Rayoq sites from bases in both the Romnas and Bifor Galactic federations. The attacks occurred unabated for the next sixty years until the temporary liberation of these vast stellar zones from the Godeiw during the Fourth Galactic War. The Rayoqian Ulcer, as the guerilla war was known, retarded expansion of the Godeiw kingdom, especially in the Yud region.

2458

Humans discover the unique Mentan people

Human archaeologists visiting the star system Lignas Ram, announced the discovery of the Mentan, a life form in the Aleph region. The Mentan had adapted to the ingestion of processed food products to such a degree that they were incapable of tolerating natural products. Later studies revealed that the Mentan had been transformed into their curious state by the Buldas people, themselves ancestors of the Tebeld.

2459

Completion of six spinning cities design

Lagem architectural genius Meemota Vlem, released the designs of the six spinning cities of Varna. Still considered one of the wonders of the Galaxy, the cities were built around an artificial gravity center in a sector of cosmic space bordering the Hey region. Several tall, steeple-like biotron spinning cities were built to orbit around the gravity center. Curvilinear highways connected the cities, forming a single unit. The design of the giant space cities has often been described as a perfect example of molecular art, with the whole structure forming an aromatic-ring molecule of benzene.

2460

Noga suppress robot rebellion

The Noga robot rebellion was suppressed by well-trained Jexborath troops. A second rebellion in 2464 overthrew the Noga regime on planet Berkab Delta-3. Led by the giant think-tank computer Pleman Rele III and his network of cyberspace thought-warriors, the robotic armies won control of twenty percent of the Noga worlds from 2464 to 2473, before finally being defeated by the Free Noga Armies in the Carbulassian War.

---

[126] The guerilla groups were mostly comprised of the Rayoq Resistance Movement (RRM) and the Neo-Rayoqian Galactic Warriors (NRGW).

2461

Lagem settlers battle terror gangs

Interspace terror gangs waged war against colonial settlements in the Hey region. In a standoff near the star Valtikibar Psi, troops of the joint Lagem forces succeeded in defeating several terror gangs in a valiant attempt to restore order. Despite the success of the armed mission, terror gangs of roving space marauders played a vital role in destabilizing the colonial worlds of the Lagem for the following thirty years. The terror gangs were led by such infamous personalities as Modar the Slayer and Preskl the Vile. The actions of these individuals and their respective gangs, the Mondal and the Klee, were often compared to the sweeping raids of the Mongols and Huns in early Earth history. Modar the Slayer's conquered territories eventually became the regionally powerful Modarian Collection of Nations (MCN).

2462

Birth of Nasta rings

The Nasta rings, an oscillating force field vortex, sprang into being in the central region of the Galaxy. The product of spin energy from a series of high-velocity particle collisions, the Nasta rings were the first of two hundred rings to form in the Galaxy over the next century. The fusion of these rings may eventually cause the premature cleavage of the Galaxy in three million years.

2463

Litessian scientists cure deadly virus

Litessian scientists on Lexigar Kappa-3/3 announced that they'd found a cure for the deadly Norteek virus. The virus had claimed over eight percent of the Litessian population. The Litess failure to release the cure to the Fogye exacerbated a mounting tension between the two populations.

2464

Kosa engineers invent comet gun

The comet gun, a slingshot weapon that released rotating micro-energetic laser bomb packages, was invented by Kosa scientists. The gun, available in sizes from 0.1 to 300 metres, became one of the most important weapons in arsenals across the Galaxy and was used by both sides in the Third Galactic War.

2465

Association of Human Colonies and Planets (AHCP) splits

Human colonies in the heavily populated star systems of Cepheus Delta, Corvus Beta, Scorpius Theta, Sculptor Gamma and Ursa Minor Epsilon broke away from the AHCP[127] to form the Conformation Front (CF). The breakaway encouraged other Human colonies, including the colonial systems of Chameleon Theta and Draco Sigma, to withdraw from the AHCP. The mass defection from the ranks of the AHCP was prompted by the Association's policy of cooperation with the Riota and Tebeld. The father of the breakaway movement, Thurston French, claimed that the AHCP discriminated economically against Human colonial settlers in favor of maintaining stronger ties with alien peoples.

2465-2490

Further Lagem advancements

The cities of Calixees, Gashan and Taligibor were built during this period of modernization in Lagem history. Settler colonies were also established in both the Pey and Tet regions.

2466-2497

Wars between Human alliances

In 2466, forces of the Pax Humana Alliance (PHA) defeated the Association of Human Colonies and Planets (AHCP), ensuring domination of the Humanosphere by the PHA and its ruling Malvinkian party. Under Tech Helmath, the PHA drove back the Homo Sapien Alliance (HSA) and their Riotan allies to capture control of the Peminak stellar zone in 2468. In 2469, the non-aligned rebel colonies were defeated at the battles of Tema and Veesalk, forcing the surrender of the floating space colonies Scheele and Bessemer to the PHA.

The Malvinik leadership reformed the complex legal system of the PHA, introduced financial controls for their growing economy and established an efficient administrative bureaucracy. Their rule has been described by historians as the Period of Restoration. Helmath's successor, Rino Philpott I, took control of the PHA in 2471. With Philpott at the helm, the Alliance underwent a resurgence in art, music and architectural output.

The Borani Pattern School of metal patch-workers emerged as the most influential art form in the Humanosphere, while the Tevalik form of rhythmic percussion (borrowed from the Tebeld) gained fame in music. Reflecting a

[127] See entry for 2410 for details of the formation of the AHCP.

renewed optimism, architectural styles reverted to those of the twenty-third century stellar exploration race period.

Despite adding a sense of enlightenment and cultural sensitivity to the broader scope of Human culture, Philpott nevertheless proved, like Hemath, to be a warrior at heart. He first conquered the Palivas zones and then the Bolap stellar clouds, establishing a vital Human foothold in the Bet region.

Philpott was succeeded as PHA leader by his daughter, Remali, in 2493. Remali masterminded an expansion drive to establish colonies in the barren Miran, Sentigan and Fleshli zones of the Hey region. Her policy of benevolence and scientific advancement allowed Humanity to take its place as a Second Tier power among the dominant players of the Galaxy.

2467-2470

Workers' rebellion cripples Dultas

The Dultas Empire was burdened by a series of five workers' rebellions during this period. Workers, under the leadership of Kral Braj and Jagadoria, took control of the key Ralfur and Torm zones. Refugees from these rebellions sought asylum in the Shayan-controlled zones of the Zayen Regions. The Dultas refugee crisis remained a critical factor in Galaxy politics. The Kosa accused the Shayan of creating the refugee issue to further weaken the Dultas. These accusations added fuel to the already deteriorating relationship between the Galaxy's two superpowers.

2468

PHA attacks

Armed military units of the Pax Humania Alliance (PHA) launched successful attacks on positions held by part-Human Humanoy rebels in the Aleph region. The Humanoy's military wing, the Righteous League, was violently opposed to the PHA, whom they saw as a front for Human species chauvinism. To stave off what they interpreted as the genocidal plans of the PHA, the Righteous League had first taken up arms against the Alliance in 2461.

2469

The inaugural Galaxy Olympics

The First Galaxy Olympics were held on the Shayan-controlled planet of Derius-5. Over eight hundred competing peoples were invited to take part in these Olympics, which spanned three Earth months. The Shayan leadership used the Olympics as an opportunity to market the strength of their Galactic federation, as well as re-emphasize their domination over both the Bet[128] and Zayen Regions.

Very different peoples of the Galaxy competed against one another by studying their performances against reference points and seeing how each contestant measured against this pre-defined point. Reference points were established through a painstaking assessment of the average physical capacity of the species' general population. The standard deviation issue was taken into account when determining an improvement from a norm, so that species with the most outliers[129] wouldn't dominate the medals. It was further assumed that species who showed the greatest variation deserved to win, since they had a more flexible adaptation profile and were consequently fitter than less variable rival species.

2470

Homo Sapien Alliance (HSA) signs Shayan Treaty

The HSA signed the first of three treaties with the Shayan. The treaty, and its two successors, guaranteed the protection of HAS shipping in the Bet region by the Shayan military. Similarly, Shayan shipping in the Aleph Region obtained a security guarantee from the HSA.

War on drug trafficking proves ineffective

Drug trafficking by merchants throughout the Aleph region reached a peak of activity. The PHA established a special police unit known as the Health Preservers to combat the problem. The Health Preservers launched an all-out war against drugs trafficking in the Humanosphere which lasted until 2487 and resulted in the death of over four million people. At that time, it was commonly noted that drug trafficking had dropped by a factor of only two percent and the Health Preservers unit was disbanded.

2471

Android Worlds: An overview

Android worlds, similar to those that had existed in the Bet, Dalet and Zayen regions since the eighteenth century, developed in the Aleph region. Android leaders, like Olax-5 and Curie-7, liberated their android populations from Human control in a series of conflicts called The First Robo Wars and established android settlements on the Ara Alpha-5, Canis Major Omega-2,

[128] Mass Shayan colonization of the Bet region had been important to Shayan leadership since the end of the First Galactic War.

[129] Outliers are members of a species who deviate from the norm by the greatest amount.

Leo Eta-7 and Lepus Gamma-4 systems. Numbering almost twenty-one billion android inhabitants, the neo-robotic settlements developed into an important part of the Humanosphere. The android settlements remained disunited, with different colonies having varying degrees of contact and cooperation with Humanity.

2472-2505

Kosa prosper from energy windfall

The Kosa Legion prospered thanks to an economic boom in the populous Tralt, Osa and Feewaq zones. The discovery of the energy compound compendium, facilitating the production of cheaper dark matter energy, gave the Kosa an added technical advantage over all Galaxy peoples, including the Shayan, until 2505.

From 2472 to 2505, the Kosa were governed by the League of the Five Metas, a unique meritocracy that allowed the brightest and most competent people from industry, agriculture, military, commerce and service to hold the highest positions in the Legion structure.

2473

Lagem Worlds humbled by computer virus

Formed by the mystic Udess Busd, the Udees Bi cult waged an underground war against supporters of traditional philosophies, arguing that popular Lagem philosophies limited individual thought and blocked expression.

A computer virus created by renegade philosophers of the Udees Bi cult caused chaos among leading Lagem thinkers by interfering with the psychic patterns that make logical communication between individuals possible. Perpetrators of the sabotage were identified using elapsed time probing, a mechanism that uses sub-particle scanning to analyze the matter and energy trails of past events. The Udess Bi continued to wage sabotage into the twenty-sixth century, when they fell under the banner of another powerbroker in the history of the Galaxy, the Grand Unifier.[130]

2474

Free marketers gain control of AHCP politics

The Ornine party won power on many AHCP planets. Instead of offering exclusive trading privileges to the Shayan and Kosa, as had been policy until this time, the free trading Ornine opened their planetary markets to trade with the rest of the Galaxy.

---

[130] See entry 2488 for details regarding the Grand Unifier.

The Godeiw were the first to exploit this new territorial ground, investing heavily in the AHCP economy. By 2490, the Godeiw had acquired the lion's share of the AHCP's commercial infrastructure.

The old Conservative order opposed the AHCP-Godeiw alliance and the Conservatives eventually regained power in 2493. The Conservatives unsuccessfully attempted to roll back Ornine policies and were ousted in 2495 by a neo-Ornine revival, secretly backed by the Godeiw.

2475

Kosa extend influence

Tension Yuus, Minister of Kosan Foreign Affairs, signed a cooperation agreement with the Godeiw, Dultas and Izal. The Shayan responded to this Kosan maneuver by signing a treaty with the Lagem and the Romnas Conformation sector of the Rayoqian legion.

The Kosa instigated this conflict for little reason, other that their leaders' desire to be top dogs. Although they had been sharing this niche with the Shayan for two centuries, the two had been at loggerheads over trade for some time. What began as a trade war, developed into a military debacle.

2476-2482

The Third Galactic War

The Third Galactic War was fought between the Kosa and Shayan for economic, political and technical dominance of the twelve Kuph-Zayen boundary zones. The war spanned six years. The events of the war were as follows:

October 2476: Shayan battleships launched an attack on Kosa floater colonies at the Kuph-Zayen border. A second attack by the Shayan on Kosan shipping, forced a military response by the latter that resulted in the destruction of the Shayan Space City, Polaque-5.

February 2477: The five-month Battle of Belikan. Laser pulse bombs and sub-atomic particle grenades were used for the first time, in a battle that ended in deadlock. Over two percent of the total Shayan Alliance force and one percent of the Kosa Alliance were lost at Belikan.

May 2477: General Torego Sum led Shayan troops to victory over the Kosa's Faptian allies. Three months later, Sum's troops succeeded in routing the Izal at the battle of Terschgian. Sum emerged from the war as one of its greatest military geniuses.

November 2477: PHA troops entered the war allied with the Kosa and scored a critical victory over Rayoq mercenary troops in the Aleph Region. This victory marked the emergence of Human military forces as a credible entity within the Galactic power struggle.

January 2478: PHA troops were sent as part of an expeditionary force to back Kosa alliance units in the far flung Yud region.
April 2478: The Shayan scored a major victory over Kosa Forces in the Dalet region battle of Eva Creg. PHA troops fighting alongside the Kosa were annihilated. The Lol civilization surrendered to the Shayan, ending all Kosa alliance influence in the Dalet region.
June 2478: Confident Shayan forces suffered a major setback in the Bet region when Dultas and Kosa troops ambushed and destroyed the Shayan's 7th division. The Shayan were forced to withdraw from several critical positions in the Bet Region that they had held since the First Galactic War.
December 2478: Hit and run campaigns by the Kosa defeated the more heavily outfitted Shayan space fleet in the Fey region. Kosan General and Commander Al-Insuind, was credited with success for these campaigns.
Mar 2479: Shayan troops launched attacks on Kosa zones along the Kuph-Zayen boundary region. The Cze offered military support to Shayan Alliance troops in the March Attacks, but a combined force of Kosa, PHA and Dultas forces defeated them and succeeded in driving the invaders from the Kuph Region. The Cze involvement in the war ended with their force's surrender to the Kosa Alliance in April.
July 2479: Shayan troops besieged the Kuph region's Sherius zone, as a way of restricting aid to vital Kosa positions in its home region. Sherius was liberated in September, after thirty percent of the Shayan's Kuph Region Expeditionary force was destroyed.
September 2479: Kosa strike forces captured the Albertas stellar zone of the Fey Region. The Shayan and their allies suffered their worst defeat in the war to that point. The Albertas loss lowered Shayan and allied morale for the rest of the war.
January-April 2480: PHA-Android troops distinguished themselves in battle against the robotic regiments of the Riotan armed forces. Four months of fighting resulted in the destruction of the Riota's robo-armies.
February-December 2480: The war entered the Giant Battleship phase, where large interstellar space fleets from both sides fought dogged battles with each other for control of the major routes between cosmic regions. These battles proved costly, but inconclusive. However, a significant amount of knowledge on battleship warfare was gained and used in future wars.
June 2480: Gas attacks by the Rayoq on Izalian positions in the Chet-Dalet region proved highly destructive. The Izalians surrendered control of the frontier region by November.
October 2480: Kosa paratroopers captured key enemy positions in the Tet region, knocking out resistance by the Shayan in this area of the Galaxy. The

paratroop divisions of the Kosa army distinguished themselves in the Tet campaign. They will forever be known as the Kieran or fierce ones.
June 2481: The Shayan reversed their misfortune by unexpectedly defeating the Kosa alliance in the Battle of Totoquatera. Kosa forces were routed by a cosmic pincer movement masterminded by Alleg Dram, greatest of the Shayan's Third Galactic War generals.
September 2481: The Kosa alliance defeated Dram's Shayan forces in a head-to-head battle in the Kaal zone of the Zayen region. The Battle of Kaal proved the largest of the war. The resultant victory by the Kosa Alliance, forced the surrender of the central Shayan leadership and their allies.
February 2482: The last vestiges of resistance to the Kosa alliance were defeated. The Treaty of Allugtar ended he war, which had seen the death of over 150 BLUs.

Although Shayan forces were forced to surrender to the Kosa, the victory of the latter was by no means conclusive. The Shayan lost only eight percent of their territory and remained a Galactic superpower. The Dultas prospered by regaining the lost Shayan territory in the Bet Region and rebuilt their military force.

The Third Galactic War was noted for its transregional scope. Fighting was spread over eight regions, involving fifty billion troops. Hybrand Aines, noted twenty-sixth century Human historian, saw the Third Galactic War as a trial run for more destructive wars that soon followed.[131]

[131] The death of 150 BLUs must be put into perspective. The Third Galactic War was truly Galaxy-wide and the numbers were proportional. One hundred and fifty BLU represented less than ten percent of the combined populations of the Kosa and Shayan. It was also less than the number of people who had died in the Second Galactic War. The war, although enormous by the standards of earlier centuries, was a limited conflict and in hindsight was viewed as a trial run for a future apocalypse.

Chapter 13: The Age of the Unifier

2483

Rayoq World prospers from divohrian find

Divorhian was treated by twenty-sixth and -seventh century Galactic society as a highly precious metal, due to its multiple uses in the space, medical and military industries. Vast divorhian deposits discovered on the Rayoq world Asterius Kappa-3/1 helped contribute to the rebirth of the Rayoq. The absence of divorhian deposits in the Aleph region forced Humanity to import most of its divorhian, placing many of the Human Alliance worlds at the mercy of trade boycotts and embargos.

The Rayoq were a weakened power, having lost the Second Galactic War and one of their larger entities, the Romnas Conformation, losing in the Third Galactic War. But the Rayoq were a tough people and the discovery of their riches of divorhian rekindled their ambitions. With the correct leadership, they could achieve nightmarish power. A new leader was due to arrive.

2484

Catalyst deposits abound in newly explored region

Vast amounts of Lilam catalysts discovered in the newly explored Eiyen region, provided cheap ultraphotonic fuel for the Fogye, Humanity, Litess and Lol, narrowing the technology gap between these secondary civilizations and the primary powers of the Kosa, Shayan, Rayoq, Dultas, Godeiw and Lagem.

2485

Planet Sibora annihilated

Seismic movements annihilated the entire planet Sibora, located in the Dalet region's Rayoq-controlled Deltanius zone. The destruction released a high flux of X-ray energy into the surrounding cosmos. This release, later dubbed the "ground entity," posed a scientific mystery. Metaphysicists claimed that the ground entity was merely a spirit breaking free from its entrapment. Physicists saw the ground entity as the missing energy link that could shed light on the phenomenon of solid body formation in space. Rayoq engineers cleverly harvested almost eight percent of this released energy in giant capacitors, which they used over the following ten years to provide energy to surrounding worlds in the Deltanius region.

By the dawn of the twenty-sixth century, ground entity utilization programs involving the destruction of planets with entrapped X-ray fields were being used in several zones across the Dalet and Fey regions. The hit and miss[132] destruction of planets for such purposes, although highly criticized by Galactic environmentalists, was a boon that could create instant wealth in the affected regions.

2486

Local war

War broke out between the Bnor and Cze for control of the Danofrag zone of the Kuph region. Fighting lasted for five years and led to the eventual defeat of the Bnor Confederation. As allies to the Cze, the Rayoq gained immensely from this war by extending their influence into the heart of the Kosa-dominated Kuph region. The rebirth of Rayoq influence played an important role in restructuring politics in the Galaxy for the next half a century.

2487

Stock prices plunge

Prices on the Galactic Stock Exchange plunged over a two-month period, setting off massive economic panic in the Kuph and Zayen Regions. Investors, eager for security, redistributed their wealth to projects in the Dalet and Bet regions, strengthening the economies in these sectors. The sudden injection of wealth boosted the flagging economies of the Rayoq and Dultas, in turn promoting the rebuilding of their military machines.

2488

The Grand Unifier takes power

The Grand Unifier, a scientifically created chemo-energetic being, was vaulted into the leadership role of the Rayoq's Romnas Conformation following a coup d'état. Genetically engineered by Rayoq scientists during the biologic craze of the mid twenty-fourth century, the 123-year-old Grand Unifier became the most important feature in twenty-sixth century politics. As the developer of the Philosophy of Laon,[133] the Grand Unifier argued that true peace in the Galaxy could only be achieved once all civilizations were united under one being. The Unifier derived much of its philosophy from the rhetoric of numerous Galactic theologies and attained enormous influence

---

[132] Not all planets have hidden X-ray sources and it's impossible to determine whether or not a candidate planet is viable in advance of destruction.

[133] Laon is a native Rayoq language.

throughout the Galaxy as a result of a well-funded, though rigid, policy of active conversion orchestrated by missionary disciples, the Afkroz. Human historians compared the effect of the Grand Unifier on Galactic politics to both the rise of Christianity in the post-Roman Empire era and the growth of communism in nineteenth and twentieth century Earth.

2489

The Grand Unifier's influence spreads in Rayoqian Worlds

The Grand Unifier extended Rayoqian influence over the Dalet Region. In a move of diplomatic genius, the Unifier brought together the Romnas conformation and Bifor Hafate. He also signed the Altefraris Treaty, an important agreement with the Dultas League to restructure trade. The treaty broadened Rayoqian influence into the Bet Region.

2490

Beginning of the economic miracle

Miniature processing and aqueous melding techniques doubled production, reinvigorating the slumping Humanosphere economy. The new economic revolution led to an era of technological advancement that helped Humanity, in particular the PHA and AHCP, reassert their role as the economic powerhouses of the Aleph region. Through poor management and planning, this position had recently been relinquished to the rival Riota. The boom continued into the next century, when greater production levels were required to combat the growing economic and military threat from the Grand Unifier.

2491-2496

Noteworthy oddities

During this era, Human stellar explorers discovered a number of important Galactic anomalies in the virgin Pey region of the Galaxy. These oddities included:

- The neutron star cluster of Tiomades: A system of eight neutron stars, spatially arranged to create a force field equal in strength to that of a black hole.
- The comet-smashing star Aboran: A stellar system that creates five Earth-sized comet nuclei each year, two of which are immediately destroyed by its powerful solar flares.
- The pulsating Javaninex star: A stellar mass that oscillates in volume over a ten year cycle, during which it changes in diameter from 0.5 Sols to 25 Sols.

All these stellar anomalies defied analysis, although plausible hypotheses, ranging from oscillating nuclear fusion functionality to quantum magnetic energy, were put forward as explanations.

2492

Kosan leader assassinated
Terrorists from the Balkitar Guraz militaristic faction assassinated Valimanip Sang, the dominant figure of Kosan politics. Chaos threatened the region over the following three months, until the ascension of the General's Executive under the leadership of Waquis Ralnau. This new era in Kosan history was defined by a renewed militarization, a growing antagonism towards the Rayoq and the philosophy of the Grand Unifier, and a restriction of the democratic rights once vital to the infrastructure of Kosan society. The growing rivalry between Ralnau and the Grand Unifier ultimately led to the Fourth Galactic War.

2493

Signing of the Moranx deal
The Moranx deal was signed, ending all discriminatory tariffs between Human colonies. The deal was seen as advantageous by Human Conformationists, a school of thinkers who wished to see the end of the independent Alliance system and the beginning of a human federation.

2494

AHCP moves closer to the Riota
A series of agreements known as the Parallel Rights Acts drew the AHCP closer to the Riota in terms of sharing political and economic power in the Aleph Region.

Dgloj fall under Unifier control
General Raqent Tobic betrayed his Dglojian people to the Unifier. The Dgloj ceased to be a separate entity and were absorbed into the Unifier Realm. Tobic's name was forever after cursed by Dgloj nationalists.

Lagem split by slavery issue
Abolitionists won elections in the largest of the five Lagem nations despite the efforts of pro-slavery groups. Conflict between the two groups continued to fester when Unifier agents supported the abolitionists.

2495

PHA troops defeat alien invaders
PHA troops led by military figure Sharim el Kimis defeated the alien Bantians in the Plezian wars, liberating over thirty minor colonies from alien domination. The move further strengthened unity forces in the Humanosphere.

Grand Unifier extends local rights
Reform movements sprang up across much of the Unifier Realm, demanding greater rights and funding for local governments. The Grand Unifier, a devout historical scholar who understood the consequences of unrest, eventually complied and granted a limited scope for local governments.

Espionage between Kosa and Unifier
Seventeen Kosan spies were caught and tortured to death by the Unifier-dominated Clivant Secret Police. The event highlighted the extent of the secret espionage war between the Grand Unifier and his Kosan adversaries. Also in 2495, a military alliance was established between the Unifier-controlled Rayoq worlds and the Dultas.

2496

Esian reincarnated warriors battle
Esian scientists brought reincarnated warriors to life in a bid to stem the invasion of the Godeiw. The reincarnates survived for weeks, but were unable to prevent the eventual defeat of the Es.

HSA withdraw democratic reforms
Government instability forced HSA leader Cheng Ding to withdraw some of the democratic reforms made during his predecessor's rule. The move towards a limited autocracy led to a slowdown in HSA political growth in the Humanosphere for the following ten years.

2497

Grand Unifier consolidates power
The Grand Unifier stripped much of the Rayoqian elite of power, even liquidating some of its members. Power was redistributed to a new technocratic class chosen from many of the newer life forms now inhabiting the Unifier's realm.

Further Unifier growth
The Unifier Realm, dominated by the Rayoq and their Dultas allies, expanded into another twenty-three nations to form the Tregum Front. The Front was named after Tregum Yas, mythical leader of the Boiltas people, who'd ruled most of the Galaxy as an earlier Grand Unifier, almost ten thousand years previously.

2498

Kosan expansion
The Kosa expanded their territory in the Kuph region by winning territory from the Boina and Mizol. Kosan power was simultaneously extended into the Bet and Lamed regions. A review by military strategists in 2500 still ranked the Kosa as the most powerful armed entity in the Galaxy, followed closely by the Unifier Realm, the Shayan and Godeiw. Humankind was ranked forty-eighth in a field of over five thousand independent civilizations. Stripped of power, the PHA itself was ranked sixty-third and the AHCP sixty-ninth.

Unifier backs rebellion against Shayan
An Aboriginal land claim deal went sour on Mivhelilab-5/4, resulting in a rebellion by the local Drisian people against Shayan colonists. The planet turned into a theater of isolated conflict when the Unifier offered military support to the Drisian.

The response to the Unifier threat
The Mendos Front, an underground anti-Unifier movement, was established on the Rayoqian planet Hefal Beta-2/2. The Mendos used military sabotage and propaganda to fight the Unifier. Both the Shayan and Kosa supplied limited support for this Front.

2499

Unifier expansion
Forces of the Grand Unifier won major victories over the Iona and Oita in the small Yud region. The military success of the Rayoq created shock waves across the Galaxy.

Shayan-Kosa alliance formed
The Shayan and Kosa put their strategic and political differences behind them to create a military pact to resist further Unifier expansion. In this cold war phase, conflicts between the two groups were limited to specific areas of the Galaxy, a chess game between the great powers, allowing each to assess the other's weaknesses.

2500

The Grand Unifier restructures its realm

The Grand Unifier undertook an ambitious project involving the complete re-organization of economic, political and social realms of all Unifier-dominated worlds into a single system. The new web of organization that replaced earlier structures, focused on the Grand Unifier as the ultimate center of power and took over eight years to establish. Checks and counterchecks were used to subjugate all nodes of power concentration in the web system to the Grand Unifier.

2501

Dultas move into Humanity's principal Region

The encroachment of the Dultas into the Aleph Region caused much concern in the Humanosphere, driving many Human colonies to sign treaties of protection with the Shayan and Kosa. Pro-Human organizations like the Humanitai Society and the Justice Forum for Humania, gained influence in the Humanosphere by profiting from anti-Unifier feelings.

Renegade Dultas ally with Kosa

Derrav Din, leader of the last Dultas holdout planets resisting the Unifier Regime, signed a military-trade agreement with the Kosa. Although Din's influence extended to only one percent of the Dultas powerbase, his defection to the Shayan-Kosa Alliance was taken as a significant moral victory for anti-Unifier alliances.

2502

Rayoq challenge Shayan

Rayoq economic expansion into the Zayen region encountered fierce opposition from the Shayan. Relations between these two great powers continued to worsen, precipitating a break in all diplomatic relations as both parties vied for power.

Schools of Unifierism emerge

Schools of Unifierism emerged in many non-Unifier worlds. Modeled on the structure of twentieth-century American Kremlinologist academies, Unifierists specialized in trying to understand and elucidate the battle plans, strategies and motives of the Grand Unifier.

2503

Unifier revolts spread across Galaxy
In a year of revolts, the Noga, Lagem, Lol and Izalian civilizations were marred by violence, mostly inspired by local pro-Unifier groups.

Publication of the Codex Ron
The Unifier published the Codex Ron, a code of law that eventually applied to all nations in the realm. The Codex Ron placed strong emphasis on the need for a single system of law, taking into account key ingredients of local law among each population under Unifier control.

Human Conformationists make election gains
Human Federation Supporters, a.k.a. Conformationists, won sweeping electoral successes in political campaigns across the Humanosphere. Most notable among these winners were Abraham Abendigo, new President of the HSP, and Amy Yang, who was elected to the same position in the AHCP.

2504

Unifier influence increases
The popularity, strength and mystical sway of the Grand Unifier continued to increase throughout Unifier-dominated worlds. Twelve percent of all Galaxy worlds were now either part of or allied with the Grand Unifier.

Lolian leader flees to Earth
Lolian political leader Wargetz Nemian, was granted refuge on Earth after his home world was overrun by Grand Unifier troops. Sheltered by the protective cloak of Humanity, Nemian continued to lead the Lolian resistance against the Unifier.

2505

Human Alliances closer to unity
Under the guidance of master diplomat General Sharim El-Kim, the PHA, AHCP and HSP alliances were bought together to establish a united front against the Unifier. This pact laid the groundwork for the creation of the Human Conformation.

New weapon in Unifier arsenal
The Unifier developed a legion of psychic warriors to wage war against the spiritual forces of the Shayan and Kosa. Weapons used by the psychic

warriors included the mental manipulation of electrical and magnetic field to create barriers and artificial smokescreens that were designed to hinder the progress of their opponents.

Defense field established
The Rayoq established several force fields around their central planets to protect their core populations against a possible Shayan-Kosa attack.

2506

Unifier and non-Unifier Worlds head for conflict
A joint session of Unifier and non-Unifier World representatives met to lessen tensions in the Galaxy. In November, the Unifier summoned a spirit force to show its mastery over forces of other dimensions. Such spirit-awakening demonstrations occurred regularly until the outbreak of the Fourth Galactic war, when they served as propaganda to demonstrate the futility of opposing the Unifier.

Human Worlds closer to Shayan-Kosa alliance
The Treaty of Veritasy brought most Human worlds into closer military alliance with the Kosa-Shayan Pact.

2507-2509

Events of the Fourth Galactic War
March 2507: Shayan-Kosa forces launched an attack on Rayoq troops in the Beletar sector of the Yud region. The attack was defeated by combined Rayoq-Dultas forces.
June 2507: Invasion of the Aleph Region by the Rayoq. Several zones of the region surrendered to Rayoq aggressions, however, Human Conformation (HC) forces, under the leadership of Barak Kaldaz, defeated the Rayoq in the Capricornus conflicts. The event stalled the Rayoqian advance into the Aleph Region.
July 2507: The Termiak population rebelled in the Shayan-dominated Zayen region, throwing off the latter's yoke in a conflict funded by the Rayoq.
September 2507-March 2508: Period of the mega-battles, most notably the: Andarius conflict, a battle fought for control of the Andarius sector of the Kuph region and won by the Shayan-Kosa alliance; and The Kosa Ralbi, a Bet region conflict in which the Dultas allied with the Rayoq-Fogye to defeat Shayan-Kosa forces.
May 2508: The Dultas achieved a major victory in the Yud Region against the Shayan.

October 2508: The Lagem declared themselves Unifier linked and successfully attacked the Shayan in the Hey region.
November 2508: The HF and several independent Human colonial worlds allied with the Rayoq, plunging the Humanosphere into an internal crisis that saw the Human Conformation at war against Human renegades.
December 2508-April 2509: The mystical sway of the Grand Unifier spread to both Kosa and Shayan worlds. The home fronts of these stellar powers were constantly under internal siege from Unifier-inspired revolt.
May 2509: Human Conformation troops allied with the Shayan launched an attack on Rayoq-controlled colonies and bases in the Zarian Sector of the Dalet Region.
July 2509-August 2509: The Rayoq defeated the Kosa in the Jeman battles. These monstrous conflicts cost over 39 BLU lives and proved critical in turning the war in favor of the Unifier forces.
October 2509: The Shayan-Kosa Alliance was beaten into submission by waves of military attacks spearheaded by the Unifier's Rayoq and Dultas forces. In a desperate attempt to avoid defeat, the Shayan vainly resorted to using biological weapons.
November 2509: This month marked the beginning of the formal surrender of the Shayan-Kosa Alliance. The Fourth Galactic war ended with the Treaty of Volak and the absorption of many Shayan Worlds into the Unifier sphere of influence. The Kosa, however, lost only ten percent of their territory.
December 2509: General Trese, a brilliant military leader and head of the Unifier forces, defeated the HC forces at the Battles of Jauner Phase and Opur. Thirty percent of the Humanosphere was now controlled by the Unifier.

War Summary and Consequences:
The Fourth Galactic War was undoubtedly the most brutal in modern Galactic history. The death total from this war, 1200 BLUs, surpassed the combined totals for the three previous Galactic wars.

Unlike the Third Galactic War, the Fourth produced a clear winner in the Rayoq-Lagem-Dultas Alliance. Historians view the Fourth Galactic War as a war of revenge. Aided by well-equipped and highly advanced Rayoq forces, the Dultas were able to turn the tables on the Shayan, while the Rayoq avenged the damage they had sustained by the Godeiw in the Second Galactic War.

Later historians revealed that the success of the underdog Rayoq-Lagem-Dultas forces over the stronger Shayan-Kosa Alliance was due to secret Rafghi support that the Unifier had obtained from the extra-Galactic Rafghi civilization.

The Grand Unifier reaped the benefits of success in the Fourth Galactic War by greatly expanding its influence from twelve percent of the known Galaxy to thirty-three percent. Unifier-friendly governments were installed in the conquered Shayanian and Kosan worlds and all others defeated by the Rayoq-Lagem-Dultas Alliances. As the most powerful being in the Galaxy, the Grand Unifier dictated political destiny across all controlled sectors. Most of these civilizations welcomed the dominion of the Unifier, seeing the Rayoqian being as a liberator who freed their worlds from the harsh dictatorships of brutal local tyrants.

The following table shows the percentages of population breakdown by political allegiance of all civilizations in the Galaxy after the Fourth Galactic War.

Type of World	Percentage of Galaxy Population	Major parties
Free Worlds (Neutral)	45	Gald, Litess
Anti-Unifier	22	Kosa, Godeiw
Strict Unifier control	13	Shayan
Unifier linked	20	Rayoq, Dultas, Lagem

Please note that the entire Shayan realm was under strict Unifier control. The Shayan were the biggest losers of the Fourth Galactic War.

For Humanity this table breaks down as follows:

Type of World	Percentage of Humanosphere Population	Major parties
Free Worlds (Neutral)	10	HPI
Anti-Unifier	40	HC^3
Strict Unifier control	30	Occupied HC territory
Unifier linked	20	HF and several independent

The Unifier had greater power than any single being had ever attained in ten thousand years of Galactic history. There were those who identified the Unifier as the True Messiah, while others saw him as the devil incarnate. For Humanity, much of the Unifier era was a dark period whose consequences nevertheless affected the course of Human survival.

2510

Captured Shayan and Kosa generals executed

The Unifier tribunals sentenced three Shayan and two Kosa Generals to death for war crimes against the Rayoq and Dultas. Despite threats of renewed fighting by both the Kosa and the Shayan Resistance, these death sentences were carried out.

Drako market established

The Drako Market, a third-party regulated platform, allowed for the exchange of goods between Unifier and Kosa-Alliance worlds. Third parties like the Izal and several Human colonies, benefited financially as middlemen in the Drako system.

2511

Spy networks neutralized

The Grand Unifier cracked down on undercover spy networks in the conquered Shayan Federation. These networks were controlled by Kosan agents, eager to destabilize the Unifier's newly acquired powerbase in the Zayen Region.

2512

Lagem population control program

A program for mass population manipulation and government was developed by Lagem social scientists. Adopted by the Unifier power hierarchy over the following ten years to ensure continued dominion over dissident societies, the program helped control populations that were beginning to reject the central authority of the Unifier's political philosophy. Implementation of the Lagem Control Program, however, increased the bureaucracy on Unifier worlds, a phenomenon that hindered Unifier resistance to the future Rafghi Invasion.

Unifier attempts economic sabotage

Counterfeit currency introduced by suspected Unifier agents caused temporary inflation in the HC.

2513

Post-Fourth Galactic War politics_

Despite losing the Fourth Galactic War, the Kosa Federation rebounded both politically and economically. The Kosa, with the Godeiw, led the resistance to Unifier amalgamation throughout the Galaxy.

Under the leadership of Quat Conkoram, the Kosa Galactic Order was solidified, insuring Kosa domination of the Kuph Region. Armed forces further strengthened the Kosa, bracing its peoples for the possible onset of a Fifth Galactic War that might decide the final fate of the Galaxy. The hostility that existed between the Kosa-Godeiw Alliance and the Unifier worlds created another cold war scenario. The status quo of two superpowers existed in the Galaxy for the first time, ending the diversity that had existed before the Unifier era, when power had been shared among five powers: the Godeiw, Kosa, Lagem, Rayoq and Shayan.

2514

Coup d'état fails to unseat Unifier

A political coup by the fifth column Aoirew Front failed to overthrow the Grand Unifier. Later the same year, the Grand Unifier made a mystical voyage to the extradimensional universe in an attempt to borrow energy from the spiritual worlds. The year-long migration of the Unifier was later described as the Celestial Ouy. Its successful acquisition of energy proved vital in sustaining the Unifier's influence in the Galaxy for years to come.

Unifier attempts to undermine Kosan leadership

Two radical groups, the Kosa Nations Rights Organization and the True Way, united to form the Democratic Alliance, a quasi-political terrorist unit backed by the Unifier, to carry out destabilization missions against the Kosan establishment.

2515

Fighting in Torazeq

Factional fighting split the Fey Region city of Torazeq. While one faction was backed by the Unifier bloc, the other was backed by the Kosa alliance, creating another focus for conflict in the Galaxy's cold war,

2516

Third way alliance formed

Several smaller Galactic powers, the Tebeld, Gald and Littes, formed the Nations Collective, a neutral third way organization of peoples non-aligned with either the Unifier or Shayan-Godeiw Alliance.

2517

Peoples' Declaration issued

The Unifier issued the Peoples' Declaration, a widely distributed code outlining the principles of the Unifier Realm. The Code emphasized the central tenant of Unifier thought, that all beings in the Galaxy are equal and should be treated equally. The Shayan, the conquered HC worlds and other civilizations remained under strict Unifier control. Yet the Unifier loosened its noose on these worlds once its psychic police had curbed resistance to Unifier rule and created "equality." The Peoples' Declaration was more a code for the Unifier worlds of the future, rather than a description of their status at this point.

2518

New domestic policy

The Grand Unifier strove to modernize and improve the standard of living of its subjects. Underdeveloped worlds were targeted for technological infusion. Training schools in the arts and sciences were established across the Unifier sphere and attempts were made to eliminate the problems of disease, famine and poverty. Pro-Unifier Human worlds benefited from these policies, eventually surpassing their non-Unifier counterparts in overall living standards.

Human colonists convicted of alien massacre

Eighty-three Human colonists were convicted of massacring over two thousand indigenous intelligent inhabitants on the newly settled Trauschius Mu-2/2, located on the Aleph-Bet boundary. The massacre broke all HC guidelines, a stringent policy of non-violence toward the intelligent native life forms of settled planets. The indigenous Trauschius were not, however, convinced of the sincerity of the convictions. In 2522, a Trauschius rebellion drove out the only Human colony on Trauschius Mu-2/2 in an attack chronicled in the Colonists Almanac[134] as the Revenge of the Oppressed.

2519

Unifier threats to intra-Human cooperation

The division of Humanity into anti-Unifier and pro-Unifier worlds created great anxiety within the Humanosphere. Clashes between the two parties over issues of colonization and economics, further highlighted these tensions. Although the Grand Unifier chose not to interfere in many of these "local" Aleph Region struggles, its background presence as the powerbroker behind the pro-Unifier worlds was felt throughout the Humanosphere. Rebellions against Unifier domination in conquered Human worlds were dealt with

[134] The Colonist's Almanac is a complete study of the history of Human extra-stellar colonization. First published in 2239, the Almanac has been updated every subsequent year.

harshly through the introduction of slavery, mass sterilization and forced imprisonment. Since these acts were undertaken on behalf of the Unifier by its Human subjects, they engendered feelings of bitter hatred that scarred intra-Human cooperation for centuries to follow.

2520

Deebasch bodyguard at its zenith

The Unifier bodyguard, known as the Deebasch, reached their zenith of power and influence in the day-to-day running of the Realm. Human historians have compared the rise of the Deebasch and their ability to influence the execution of commands in the realm, to the ascension of the Praetorian Guard in Ancient Rome or the Janissaries in the Ottoman Empire.

2521-2524

Developments in the Unifier Realm

During this period, Unifier forces quelled rebellions in the conquered Shayan worlds, democratized local governments and introduced development projects to inject wealth into the lesser-developed worlds of the Realm. The Grand Unifier personally undertook a tour of over two thousand planetary systems in an attempt to stoke the vast personality cult centered around it.

2522

Terror campaigns launched against pro-Unifier groups

The Axmano death squads launched a series of terror campaigns against pro-Unifier advocates in several anti-Unifier Human worlds. The Axmanos were funded by the right-wing Brajania family. Despite their efforts, the Axmanos failed to silence pro-Unifier voices that grew stronger in the following years.

2523

Unifier's settlement equilibrium policy

The Unifier sponsored a policy of intermixing to marginalize the forces of nationalism in Unifier-dominated worlds. Over eight hundred BLU were sent to other planets as a consequence of the Settlement Equilibrium Policy.

2524

Apocalypse "monster" goes berserk

The apocalypse "monster," a dense matter-destroying hadron particle blob, was created by Lagem scientists during a series of experiments carried out on Archaeon Omega-3/1. As a result of a deadly imbalance in the energy fields maintaining its structural integrity, the "monster," originally intended for military warfare, turned on its creators. Fast-matter generators eventually annihilated the "monster," but only after it had destroyed much of Archaeon Omega-3/1, killing ten million Lagem in the process.

2525

Conflict delayed

Tension between Unifier and non-Unifier worlds flared up in a limited conflict in the Anaphroteses zone of the Chet region. This localized conflict, like others occurring simultaneously in the Galaxy, did not develop into anything more catastrophic. The known regions of the Galaxy and Human history were frozen in a state of controlled unease.

Fallout from the Fourth Galactic War still lingered chillingly in the Galaxy's consciousness. Too many lives had been lost and the mood for an all-out war was low in both Unifier and non-Unifier worlds. Political and power struggles in the Galaxy, however, clearly pivoted around the Unifier, the most powerful force in the Milky Way. Historians knew this would change, the question was when.

For the present, there was a stalemate as history rolled toward the future. For Humanity, divided into camps straddling both sides of the Unifier position, there was now a break in the turbulent chronology that over the previous five hundred years had stretched the Human domain to levels never before imagined. Humanity's journey into space included planetary and stellar colonization, contact with the Galaxy's great civilizations, giant steps forward technologically, a vast increase in numbers and a noticeable footprint in the known worlds. Lives had been lost in the Galaxy's Wars, but Humanity was not alone in this. What most counted was that the Human species had taken its place among Galactic peoples. Although still a minor player, Humanity was destined to find a larger role in the Galaxy's history.

Now I, Kanowitz, author of this book, must sit back and collect my thoughts, reflecting on events that have occurred. Some are isolated and independent, but many are linked into a complex web that grows even more intricate with the passage of time and will be chronicled in detail in the next volume of the *History of the Future*.

END OF BOOK 1

Appendix 1: Divisions of the Old United States following the Second Civil War

The Eastern Union (EU): A commercially centered economic union comprised of the former New England States (Connecticut, Maine, Massachusetts, New Hampshire, Vermont) and the regions, states and provinces of New York, New Jersey, Rhode Island, Delaware, Eastern Pennsylvania, Maryland, New Brunswick, Nova Scotia, Prince Edward Island and Newfoundland. Capital city: Washington DC.

The American Republic (AR): This nation's economy depended largely on its industrial production and mining. It was comprised of the former states and provinces of Illinois, Indiana, Iowa, Michigan, Ohio, Kentucky, Ontario, Manitoba, West Virginia and Wisconsin, plus the territory of western Pennsylvania. Capital city: Cincinnati.

The Free States of Southern America (FSSA): A Union incorporating the states of Virginia, Tennessee, the Carolinas, Louisiana, Mississippi, Alabama and Georgia. Capital city: Atlanta.

The Florida Republic (FR): The FR was comprised only of the former state of Florida, whose vast Hispanic population voted overwhelmingly for the right to exist as an independent state. Capital City: Miami.

The Midwestern Federation (MF): Also called the "High-Tech" Federation, the MF inherited the states of Missouri, the Dakotas, Idaho, Kansas, Nebraska, Minnesota, Montana, Wyoming and the former Canadian province of Manitoba. Capital city: Omaha.

The Texas Expansion (TE): This industrial-agricultural nation was made up of the former states of Arizona, Colorado, Texas, Oklahoma, Arkansas, Utah, Nevada and New Mexico. Capital city: Amarillo.

The California Republic (CR): A service and industrial production based economy the CR was comprised only of the former state of California. A new capital was built for the republic at Reagan City Complex, Death Valley.

The Cascade Federation (CF): A resource-based republic formed from the states of Alaska, Arizona, Oregon and Washington as well as the former Canadian provinces of Alberta, British Columbia, Saskatchewan and the Yukon Territory. Capital city: Vancouver.

Pacific Conglomerate (PC): A trading nation made up largely of the state of Hawaii and the islands of Midway and Guam. Capital city: Honolulu.

Appendix 2: The City States of Earth

What follows is a list of ten major city states that played dominant roles in both the political and economic affairs of the city state period. Population numbers are based on 2180 census figures, unless otherwise notes.

Atlanta: As the capital of the influential Free States of Southern America, Atlanta grew to become the largest commercial and information center in the Western Hemisphere. A large population influx from the less viable economic regions of North America increased the population of Atlanta from fewer than 10 million in 2050 to 97 million, recorded almost a century later.

Berlin: Another service orientated city state, Berlin gained prominence for its highly innovative, organized and well-respected aerospace and technological design programs. Population: 86 million.

Calcutta: The Pearl of India was a shining example illustrating the positive transformation of a once poverty stricken urban sprawl into a relatively affluent modern city. Calcutta's city planners revitalized the megalopolis through the wholehearted adaptation of the Biotron system. The city served as a center for micro-electronic production. Population: 157 million.

Kinshasa: The largest city in Africa, Kinshasa's population surpassed that of Cairo in 2105. Kinshasa existed as the center for global textile production during the city state period. Population: 123 million.

Lima: Rapid population growth allowed this former Peruvian capital to become the second largest urban region in South America. Lima was noted for its vast factory resources primarily concerned with heavy industry such as mineral processing and alloy manufacturing. Population: 119 million.

Los Angeles: As the second largest city in North America, Los Angeles surpassed the population of Mexico City in 2075. The city's survival was dependent on its production of luxury items, however, it continued to exist as an entertainment Mecca. Population: 114 million.

Moscow: Although tightly controlled for over forty years by the semi-autocratic Neo-Muscovite Party, Moscow grew in size and importance in the early twenty-second century, when its strategic position between Asia and Europe allowed the city state to assume the role of a Trans-regional Trading Center. Population: 132 million.

New York: The return of a high incidence of crime in this densely populated city state, forced local authorities to adapt draconian strategies. Nevertheless, the city continued to function as a leading commercial and corporate advertising region thanks to its extensive global computer linkup with the outside world. Greater New York in the twenty-second century spread southward to include regions of the Eastern seaboard, like Baltimore, Philadelphia and Washington. Population: 129 million.

Tientsin: Large peasant migrations from the rural areas of China dramatically increased the population of Tientsin. The migrations were inspired by the movement towards scientific urban-based food farms during the late twenty-first century. Tientsin surpassed both Beijing and Shanghai in overall population in 2124 and 2133 respectively, to become the dominant Chinese city state. Tientsin was also noted for its Nutrition Allocation Units (NAUs) that helped coordinate food distribution programs throughout much of the Far East. Population: 169 million.

Tokyo: A city described by Australian-born poet Fergus Hayden as a "Concrete Jungle incubating in a Steel Receptacle," Tokyo served as the leading center of medical research on Earth, but was also admired for its diverse economy. Tokyo had the highest population density of all major city states.
Population: 181 million.

Appendix 3: The Corporations

Almana Enterprise: Argentinean-Brazilian corporation formed in the late twenty-first century by the unification of several South American mining companies. Almana prospered immensely during the twenty-second century, when its mining empire, which was expanded into the African continent, allowed it to gain trade leverage in the interplanetary space colonization initiative of the local solar system. Buyouts of several Colombian and Venezuelan mining conglomerates consolidated Almana's complete control over the economic structure of seventy percent of the South American continent. Like *all* other mega-corporations of this era, Almana began a process of massive diversification in the late twenty-second century to insure its financial survival in the succeeding centuries.
Principal city states under corporate control: Belo Horizonte, Bogota, Buenos Aires, Caracas, Cordoba, Mars XIV (Cite Menem), Mercury III (Bolivar), Montivideo, Recife, Porto Allegro, Rio de Janeiro, Rossario, Sao Paolo, Titan III (El Dorado), Venus IV (Nazca Superias).
Headquarters: Porto Allegro.

Al-Mazaar Resources: A Powerful Middle Eastern entity formed by the amalgamation of several oil and energy corporations in the early twenty-second century. The founders of Al-Mazaar foresaw investment in alternative energy products as the only way of insuring their own economic well being, and therefore invested heavily in the porginine and querzian markets. Financed by European funds acquired through the purchase of companies like Royal Dutch Shell and Agip, Al-Mazaar grew into the largest supplier of fuel in the Human worlds of the twenty-second and -third centuries.
Principal city states under corporate control: Alexandria, Alma Atar, Amman, Ankara, Baghdad, Baku, Beirut, Cairo, Callisto II (Fatima), Damascus, Gaza City, Istanbul, Mars XII (Avicenna), Mars XVI (Islamia), Ramallah, Sarajevo, Tirane, Venus V (Al-Husseini).
Headquarters: Callisto II.

Bolzakov Protech: A corporation whose origins dated to the post-Cold War Re-constructionist period of Russian economic history. Bolzakov Protech was formed by the amalgamation of several military-industrial corporations. The company consolidated its holdings in the Russian nuclear industry of the 2130s, before expanding into such diverse fields as wheat manipulation technology and control systems electronics. Grassroot alliances with the Russian people ensured monopolistic support for Bolzakov Protech in the Corporate Era. For

most of the twenty-second and -third centuries, the company fell under the control of the powerful Mikinsky family, whose forward looking expansionist policies helped spread Bolzakov's influence over several Eastern European cities. In the era of interplanetary exploration, Bolzakov Protech succeeded in establishing and maintaining control of several colonies on the Saturn moons.
Principal city states under corporate control: Gdansk, Kiev, Leningrad, Lvov, Moscow, Odessa, Riga, Rhea I (Onegin), Rhea II (Lermontov), St Petersburg, Talinin, Titan I (Polask), Titan IV (Kievan Rus), Titan V (Yaroslav), Vilnius, Warsaw.
Headquarters: Odessa.

Brittanix Chemo-Fuels: A British company whose origins dated from the fusion of British Petroleum and Imperial Chemicals in 2063. The company expanded rapidly in the twenty-second century, extending its tentacles to control British Aerospace, Glaxo Pharmaceuticals and British Steel. Further expansion into Western Europe allowed Brittanix to win controlling shares in several Belgian, Dutch and Scandinavian cities. The company was one of the forerunners in the interplanetary space race, where it was responsible for developing the Worldwing and Aerojet series of ultraphotonic space planes. Both these spacecraft played extensive roles in numerous space exploration missions that took place in the twenty-third and -fourth centuries. Brittanix gained further notoriety in the twenty-fourth century when it spearhead a vain effort of Reform Policy to return several aspects of government to the people in order to save the corporate system from public ire.
Principal City States under Corporate Control: Amsterdam, Antarctic City IV (Erasmus), Antwerp, Bergen, Britannia, Brussels, Cardiff, Copenhagen, Ganymede I (Anglia), Ganymede II (New London), Glasgow, Liege, Mars VIII (Runic City), Mars IX, (Oranjie), Mars X (Nieu Belgie), Oslo, Rotterdam, Venus VI (Caledonia).
Headquarters: Ganymede II.

Dongadong Trading House: Dongadong was the largest conglomerate to emerge from the Era of Rapid Asian Business Expansion in the twenty-first century. The company originated from the unification of the vast Cheung and Wei trading houses of Shanghai and Beijing. It acquired additional resources by acquiring many smaller trading entities with the assistance of the Tientsin-dominated Chinese government, after the Sino-Civil War of the twenty-second century. Controlled for much of its existence by the Lee family of Tientsin, Dongadong made its greatest advances in the textile and

fabric industries. It made extensive purchases of heavy industrial, plastic and material-preparation factories to expand its production and financial clout. By 2300, it had penetrated almost every facet of Asian influence in the solar system and beyond.
Principal city states under corporate control: Bangkok, Beijing, Callisto III (Nguyenas), Canton, Despina I (Siharnouk), Hanoi, Hong Kong, Macao, Europa I (Zedong), Europa III (Hurachi), Lucknow, Mars VI (Rising Dragon Colony), Mars VII (Lao Tze), Mukeden, Saigon, Shanghai, Tientsin, Tritan II (Khanate), Ulan Bator.
Headquarters: Tientsin.

Flexicon TransGlobal: Flexicon was the first multiregional-multiethnic company to emerge with economic strength from the global corporate race of the twenty-first century. Formed from the foundations of the giant Australian Corporation, Broken Hill Proprietary, Flexicon gained diverse strength in the latter part of the twenty-first century, when it merged with pharmaceutical giant Merck-Frost-Novartis and European automakers Fiat and Volkswagen. Further wealth was generated by the acquisition of African mining houses De Beers and Anglo-American, as well as the French-owned banking establishment Credit Lyonnais. A dynamic organization, Flexicon invested heavily in the space race, where it reaped enormous benefits in the fields of colonial planning and logistical maintenance for both the intra-solar system settlement projects of the twenty-second century and the extra-stellar settlements of the twenty-third century.
Principal city states under corporate control: Adelaide, Astro Belt 1, Astro Belt III, Bonn, Hanover, Bordeaux, Callisto I (New Saxony), Callisto IV (Hegel), Cape Town, Egoli (formerly Johannesburg), Enclidus III (Falling Rock), Europa IV (Thaba Nchu), Europa VI (Bourbon), Europa VIII (Shining Lotus), Guangadong, Jersey City, Kiachow, Leipzig, Lisbon, Marseilles, Melbourne, Novosibirsk, Pluto II (Diaz's World), Pluto V (Nuwe Hoop), Singapore, St Louis, Sydney, Tethys VII (Spielberg Settlement), Titan VIII (Delors Libertie).
Headquarters: Titan VIII (Delors Libertie).

Franco Ini: A powerful banking and commercial corporation formed in 2058, by the merger of Deutsche Bank, Barclays and Banco Roma. The company acquired valuable manufacturing strength in the latter part of the century when it assumed control of Nestle, Olivetti and Saab-Volvo, to grow into one of the most powerful economic players on the central European subcontinent. Further buyouts of Euro Space Agency facilities (in particular Aero-France,

Aerospatiale and Cosmo-Lufthansa) enhanced the presence of Franco Ini in the planetary race. Led by the skillful Hans Thiler in the early twenty-third century, Franco Ini pushed ahead as active promoters of the extra-stellar space race when it spearheaded the drive to explore much of the Orion system.
Principal city states under corporate control: Ariel V (Vivaldi-Luca), Astro Belt V, Ariel VI (Carvaggio), Milan-Florence, Galatea III (Madonna), Galatea IV (Mazzini), Jupiter III-Floating (Pauli), Jupiter IV-Floating, Mars III (St. Bernardo), Mars V (New Bohemia), Mars XVII (Garibaldi), Mars XIX (Goya), Munich-Stuttgart, Rome-Naples, Pluto IV (Medici), Pluto VI (Strauss-Bach), Prague, Turin-Parma, Vienna-Innsbruck, Zurich.
Headquarters: Pluto IV (Medici).

Fuyama Holdings: Fuyama Holdings commanded a presence as the most powerful conglomerate formed in Japan after the merger and acquisition battles of 2140-2160. The company was built around the nucleus of the nine twentieth century Japanese giants: Honda, Hitachi, Matashita, Mitsubishi, NEC, Seiko, Sony, Suzuki and Yamaha. Later takeovers of Dae Woo and Hyundai Chaebols in Korea increased Fuyama's portfolio in Asia, where it represented the principal opposition to the Dongadong Trading House. Guided by the philosophy of the late nineteenth century Meiji Period and inspired by the code of the Samurai, Fuyama's outward looking, aggressive policy often brought the company into open conflict with competitor conglomerates during the extra-stellar space race.
Principal city states under corporate control: Amalthea I, Antarctic City II (Zen), Ganymede III (Tokugawa), Honshu City, Kyote, Osaka, Pusan, Pyongyang, Seoul, Tokyo-Yokohoma, Venus IX (Takamori), Venus X (Hirohito), Venus XI (Il Sung).
Headquarters: Ganymede III (Tokugawa).

GeneralTech: The largest North American enterprise to emerge from the corporate-building era of the twenty-first century. This mega-company was constructed of three sectors that included an automotive division (the old General Motors-Ford amalgamation), an electronics sector (General Electric and Lucent) and an aerospace unit (Airstar, Rockwell, United and Delta). The company expanded into the healthcare and professional services industries in the early twenty-second century, where it profited during the instability of the city state era. As a consequence of the breakdown of federalism during this period, GeneralTech's influence over much of North America remained unchecked. It dominated many facets of life on the continent until its own collapse in the early twenty-fourth century.

Principal city states under corporate control: Cascadia (Seattle-Vancouver), Calgary, Chicago, Detroit, Halifax, Ganymede X (Roosevelt), Inter Saturn-Jupiter (I-II), Luna 1 (Eden), Luna II (Jefferson), Mars II (Diaz), Mars XX (Champlain), Mars (XXII-XXV), Mexico City, Miami, Monterrey, Montreal, New York, Philadelphia, Portland, San Francisco, Soucal (includes Los Angeles, San Diego and Long Beach), Toronto, Umbriel VI (McKinley), Umbriel VIII (Amnesty), Venus I (Clintonos), Venus II (Americanus), Venus III (Goreania), Washington-Baltimore.
Headquarters: Portland.

Hector-Hydra GloboTel (HHGT): Corporation formed in the mid-twenty-second century from the amalgamation of eighteen of the twenty-five leading hydrocolony-based industries on Earth. Hector-Hydra's initial commercial base was the concentrated mining of the great ocean sea beds, where it acquired the nickname of Ocean Overlord. Further experience in non-solid habitation allowed HHGT to lead development of the floating colonies that facilitated Human settlement on the gaseous planets of the outer solar system. Hector-Hydra applied this same expertise in the extra-stellar settlement era of the twenty-third and -fourth centuries, when it became the most influential corporation in the establishment and maintenance of Human colonies on less amicable worlds. Hector-Hydra's control of its city states tended to be more autocratic than other corporations'. Their policies resulted in several anti-corporate insurrections that placed the survival of the corporation in jeopardy. Although HHGT was diverse in structure, a large proportion of its revenues in the twenty-third and -fourth centuries was derived from the processing of cheap porginine fuel analogues, elbitar, javarink and lesamir, all of which were found in the lower atmospheric regions of the giant gaseous planetary worlds.
Principal city states under corporate control: Amazonia, Atlantic Cities I-VII Atlantic X, Atlantic XI, Azovtia (Black Sea), Jupiter Floating Colonies (I,VI,VII,X), Oceania I-VI (Indian Ocean Cities), Neptune Floating Colonies (II,V,VIII,X-XIV), Nile Pharos, Pacific Cities I-XII, Saturn Floating Colonies I-VIII, Yangtze I-III.
Headquarters: Jupiter Floating Colony VI (Aquamesmia).

Mermiran Extra-Stellar: A communications company, Mermiran evolved from the merger of AT&T, Sprint, Microsoft and Mermiran Galacto Communications (formerly known as Verizon) in 2043. Mermiran expanded significantly in the mid-twenty-second century, when it established the first communications network linking the newly founded planetary and space

city colonies with one another in a giant web. The company diversified into energy resources during the same century, when it acquired control of Atlantic Richfield, Pennzoil and Socal. Mermiran continued to prosper well into the twenty-third century, thanks to its engineers' development of faster than light communication mechanisms.
Principal city states under corporate control: Atlanta, Budapest, Callisto X (Hertz), Chorion I (Marconi World), Earth Orbiting Space Cities (II-VI), Uranus-Neptune Cosmic System (a group of nine space cities situated halfway between Unranus and Neptune), Larissa II, Larissa IV (Vendaris City), Mars Orbiting Space Cities (I-VII), Perth, Rejkjavik, Tel Aviv, Venus Orbiting Space Cities (III, IV, VIII,IX), Zagreb.
Headquarters: Larissa IV (Vendaris City[135])

Microgalax: Formed by the amalgamation of Citibank, Bank of America, Century 21 and Rostokov Properties, Microgalax evolved into the largest real estate owner in the Human worlds during the twenty-second and -third centuries. On Earth, Microgalax invested heavily in the land between city states. The company also extended its buyout policy to the rest of the solar system, accumulating vast amounts of land on the southern hemisphere of Mars, on Mercury, on scattered regions of Venus as well as several moons in the Jovian, Saturn and Neptune systems. Microgalax diversified in the early twenty-third century when it acquire control of Allied Steel (formed in 2087 by the merger of US and Bethlehem Steel), Alumico and Polymer Tech.
Principal city states under corporate control: Bangui, Bucharest, Colombo, Dionne (XI-XIV), Harare (Zimbabwe Internationale), Kinshasa, Ganymede (XII-XIX), Las Vegas, Managua, Mars (XXVI-XXIX), New Orleans, Phoenix, Pnohm Penh, Rhea (VI-X), Tegucigalpa, Tethys (V-VI), Venus VII (Hughes Colony), Venus (XII-XV).
Headquarters: Ganymede XIII (Potranum[136])

Sharaputra Developments: As the largest corporation to emerge from India's late twenty-second century economic miracle, Sharaputra grew into a major financial force in the Human worlds. The company acquired much of the Indian subcontinent's infrastructure through a hostile buy-out policy that ended competition from groups in Calcutta and Mumbai. As a conglomerate, Shartaputra used advanced biotechnical production procedures to reduce food

[135] Vendaris City was named after Olivia Vendaris, one of the chief electrical engineers responsible for the design of the querzian particle engine.

[136] Potranum was named after Bela Potranum (2059-2374), Microgalax's trillionaire founder, real estate pioneer and lifelong controller.

shortages that had plagued twentieth and twenty-first century India. It also improved the quality of life for Indians by introducing work programs and Biotron housing to eliminate the region's poverty. Victory in the so-called Food and Poverty Wars, elevated Sharaputra to a godlike status among the masses of Earth's most densely populated region. Sharaputra invested heavily in the United States, where it eventually won control of both the Chevron and Texaco Energy Corporations. By the early twenty-fourth century, severe infighting weakened the structure of Sharaputra and led to its subsequent breakup and eventual decline.
Principal city states under corporate control: Astro Belt Floating Colonies (II, IV), Bengalia, Calcutta, Cawnapore, Dacca, Delhi City, Europa II, Goa, Hydrabad, Kabul, Madras, Mars XI (Ashoka), Mercury II (Akbar), Mercury V (Jahan), Mumbai, Pondicherry, Pluto VII-XI, Venus (XVI-XVIV).
Headquarters: Mumbai.

Tokkens Internationale[137]: As the largest corporation on the African continent for much of the twenty-second, -third and -fourth centuries, Tokkens cultivated successful divisions in agriculture, mineral excavation and space exploration. The company was one of the main drivers of rapid modernization in Africa in the twenty-second century, when it was instrumental, via military intervention, in crushing the twin evils of corruption and poverty.
Principal city states under corporate control: Abiola,[138] Accra, Amarillo Texas, Cabinda City, Callisto (V-IX), Dakar, Freetown, Inter Saturn-Jupiter Space Cities III-VII, Kampala, Lagos, Lome, Luanda, Lusaka, Maputo-Beira, Mars (XXX-XXXV), Nairobi, Porto Nove, Pluto II, Red Sea Floating Colonies (I-III), RwanBurun,[139] Venus VIII, Venus XI, Venus XV (Kaunda).
Headquarters: Venus XV (Kaunda).

Zorgen Investments: Formed by the amalgamation of giant insurance corporations Prudential and Metropolitan in the early twenty-second century. The acquisition of brokerage interests in Lehman Brothers and Morgan Stanley further augmented the corporation's role as the global money-broker in post-nation-state Earth. By the late twenty-third century, the company had expanded by buying out investment houses in Asia, Europe and the planetary space colonies. Unlike most of the other fourteen giant corporations, Zorgen Investments opted out of the city-state-controlling race in favor of a universal

---

[137] Jon Tokkens was the African-American President of the giant energy corporation Exxon, who masterminded the merger in 2099 that created the Tokkens group.
[138] Nigerian city named after late twentieth century political figure Moshood Abiola.
[139] Rwanda-Burundi city state.

financing policy with outreach to all other corporations.
Transformed in 2240 by financial genius Ernesto Zorgen, the company obtained heightened prominence during the extra-stellar era for bankrolling most space exploration missions and colonization programs. Zorgen Investments unique role in the Human worlds allowed it to weather the twenty-fourth century's anti-corporate rebellions to survive until well into the twenty-sixth century.
Headquarters: Mars XV (Milton Friedman Settlement Colony).

Appendix 4: Grames 2206 Planetary Classification

Note that the unit of size, the EV, is equivalent to the volume of the Earth.

Type 1

The smallest type of planet found in the Galaxy. Often covered by ice and frozen methane deposits, Type 1 planets are largely desolate and in most cases uninhabitable. Twenty-second century biological re-adaptation programs helped make some of these worlds more amenable to Human settlement. Pluto is an excellent example of a Type 1 planet.
Size Range: 0.1-0.5EV
Approximate number in the Galaxy: 69,107,240,000

Type 2

Oxygen-nitrogen worlds slightly smaller than Earth, but receptive to Human habitation. Type 2 planets, which are extremely rare, were highly sought after by colonial planners in the twenty-third and -fourth centuries. The race for access to these richly endowed planets often led to conflict between controller corporations. These worlds were the remnant planets of an ancient Human empire that once existed in the Galaxy.
Size Range: 0.5-0.7EV
Approximate number in the Galaxy: 30,000

Type 3

Spanning a greater size range than Type 2, Type 3 planets have a variety of atmospheric compositions. Oxygen-nitrogen, sulphur-methane, carbon dioxide-argon mixtures are examples of some of the gaseous cocktails that defined their make-ups. As a result of their potential for life support, colonization programs also targeted Type 3 worlds. Over forty percent of all planets in the Type 3 range support natural ecologies rich in both flora and fauna species. DNA, complex proteins and carbohydrates were found in the remaining ninety percent of these worlds.
Size Range: 0.7-3.2EV
Approximate number in the Galaxy: 6,800,000

Type 4

Venus-like worlds, with dense atmospheres and characteristically high pressures. Type 4 worlds have often proved hostile to Human settlement,

although the presence of significant mineral resources encouraged temporary Human colonization.
Size Range: 0.8-3.2EV
Approximate number in the Galaxy: 12, 154, 193,400

Type 5

Heat-scorched planets whose surfaces have been baked by the radiation of a central star. Mercury is a fine example of such a planet. As a result of their extreme environmental conditions, only fifteen of these planets were settled by Human colonists by the twenty-fifth century.
Size Range: 0.2-2.5EV
Approximate number in the Galaxy: 49,888,350,000

Type 6

Gaseous planets with solid cores. These large bodies are the most dominant planetary types in the Galaxy. Jupiter, Saturn, Uranus and Neptune are all examples of Type 6 planets. Planets falling under this classification have atmospheric hues that vary from red, to dark-brown to green. A ring system of natural satellites frequently surrounds these planetary bodies. Floater colonies housed Human settlements established on these worlds.
Size Range: 5-10000EV
Approximate number in the Galaxy: 186,212,500,000

Type 7

Volcanic planets with high levels of substrata activity. Type 7 planets often undergo explosion activity that can lead to planetary destruction. The asteroid belt between Mars and Jupiter was formed by the implosion of a Type 7 planet about 600 million years ago. Very difficult to settle, Type 7 planets were colonized only by mining projects that used shock-resistant land-frame structures as the foundation of their colonial settlements.
Size Range: 0.2-20 EV
Approximate number in the Galaxy: 8,345,550,000

Type 8

Asymmetrical planetary worlds with jagged, irregular, but solid form. May or may not have an atmosphere. Several of these worlds were settled by Human terra-forming colonization parties.
Size Range: 0.4-0.9 EV
Approximate number in the Galaxy: 544,400,000

Type 9

Metamorphosing worlds make up the majority of planets found in this grouping. As a result of a semi-solid outer mantle, planets in this category exhibit the phenomenon of flux change that causes crust rearrangement. This produces a varying surface geography that manifests in rapid continental rearrangement,[140] island destruction and re-birth. Due to the shifting crust problem, Human settlement of these worlds was delayed until the late twenty-fifth century, when reliable full continent stabilizing energy fields were developed.
Size Range: 1.5-6EV
Approximate number in the Galaxy: 236,350,000

Type 10

Artificial worlds created from synthesized organic polymers and complex inorganic supermolecules make up the planets in this group. The ancient Bandarian and Calberbesh peoples were responsible for the construction of almost all the Galaxy's Type 10 planets during the zenith of these peoples' respective civilizations over 400 million years ago. Often quite unlike one another in surface texture and atmospheric makeup, some Type 10 planets nevertheless proved to be semi-hospitable to Human colonization.
Size Range: 0.1-0.8EV
Approximate number in the Galaxy: 76,546,000

Type 11

Type 11 worlds include the 11a-Bromine sea planets, the 11b-Mercury worlds and the 11c-liquid Alkali worlds. All planets have one critical factor in common: the presence of a rich liquid resource on the surface of the cosmic body. Although these planets can not readily be settled by Humans because of their toxic liquid foundations, they are often rich in living species that have adapted to life in a liquid environment. Type 11 planets were largely neglected by Human colonial planners although several planets were exploited by hydromechanical mining operations in the twenty-fifth century.
Size Range: 0.02-1.6 EV
Approximate number in the Galaxy: 12,431,220,000

Type 12

Type 12 planets are also known as Fast Spin Geoids. Due to a process known as rapid magnetic interplay, Type 12 planets have an inherently fast revolutionary period around their central star. For example, a Type 12 planet

[140] Continents change shape and global position over a period as short as a thousand years.

of 1EV, situated at a distance of 1 AU[141] from the central star, has a period of revolution equivalent to one Earth week. The overall effect of these rapid revolutions is reflected in the high metabolism of the life species on these worlds, as well as the tendency for some of these organisms to detach their rhythmic biological functions from all seasonal cues. Forced environmental changes bought on by artificial climate control devices were used to make the settled planetary areas more hospitable to Human life.
Size Range: 0.5-3.2EV
Approximate number in the Galaxy: 2,100,000

---

[141] 1 AU = 1 Astronomical Unit, or the distance between the Earth and the Sun, 93 million miles.

Appendix 5: The Human Colonial Worlds

For most of the twenty-third century, these colonies were controlled by their respective establishing corporations. However, by the early twenty-fourth century, successful rebellions broke out against the corporations in what became known as the Liberation Wars. After the wars, the colonies governed themselves during the historical Era of Separate Development.

Corporations originally designed extra-stellar colonies specifically to meet the requirements of their new settings. Modifications of the ambient environment with regard to temperature, pressure and atmospheric gas composition were undertaken gradually, so that each colonized planet was transformed to support its Human population as naturally as possible. The initial self-contained systems existed as temporary features preceding the period of natural acclimatization.

Scientific teams employed by colonization companies thoroughly studied colonial sites chosen for Human settlement. Companies sold colony space to prospective settlers on Earth. Unlike the Interplanetary Colonization era of the twenty-second century, the sale of colonial space in the extra-stellar worlds was not highly regulated. However, groups like the Stellar Habitation Institute (SHI) and the Galactic Peoples Administration Board (GPAB) protected settlers' rights by clamping down on the fraudulent sale of colonial space by stellar junkies and other criminals.

Please note that all population numbers are given in units of <u>millions of people</u> and are based on the 2500 census.

Humanosphere refers to the sum total of all Human worlds and activities.

The number following a star name indicates the number of planets orbiting that star.

All Planets are labeled with the designation (Name)-x/y-z, where x is the number of planets orbiting the star, y is the position of that particular planet relative to the other planet's in its solar system and z is the Type of planet based on the Grames Classification system,[142] e.g. Aquarius Mu-3/1-2, denotes a Type 2 planet that is the nearest of three bodies orbiting the star, Aquarius Mu.

---

[142] For details of planet Types according to the Grames Classification system, see Appendix 4.

Andromeda Epsilon-3

First settled: 2245
Number of Colonized Planets: 3

Epsilon-3/1-2 has mini-plants, known as tacthers, covering twenty percent of the planet's surface. Each tacther is about ten thousand times the size of a streptococci bacteria, but they huddle together in dense colonies that resemble the grasslands of Earth. The planet served as a vital military base for rebel forces during the anti-corporate rebellions of the early twenty-fourth century.

Epsilon-3/2-4 was never permanently colonized. The planet contains a macro-gorge that extends deep into its inner mantle. This macro-gorge, known also as Dawley's Finger, provided geologists with valuable information about the internal structure of solid planets.

Epsilon-3/3-2 is famed for its indigo- and orange-coloured storms that create the unique beauty of this world. Plasma trough beds, the remnants of the planet's recent collision with a high-energy storm field c.100,000 BC, are spread across the planet.

As a stellar system, Andromeda Epsilon proved difficult to explore due to the fields of high energy flares given off by its sun.

Population	**Population Origin**
Epsilon-3/1-2: 318	Epsilon-3/1-2: Australia
Epsilon-3/2-4: 0.001	Epsilon-3/2-4: Multinational
Epsilon-3/3-2: 96	Epsilon-3/3-2: New Zealand, Malaysia

Aquarius Mu-3

First settled: 2245
Number of Colonized Planets: 2

Mu-3/1-2 and Mu-3/2-2 are thought to have evolved from a single mother planet that mysteriously broke apart almost three billion years ago, giving each world the same mineral composition structure. Mica and Pyrite were mined on both planets, as was the electrical superconductor degadan.

Mu-3/1-2 has perfectly sculptured spherical rocks spread across its land surface. It has been hypothesized that these rocks, each the size of a squash court, were used to mark the boundaries of nation states of an ancient civilization that once existed on the planet. The modern Human settlements on Mu-3/1-2 were designed according to strict mathematical optimization patterns, that ironically approximate the design outlay of these ancient spherical rocks.

Mu-3/2-2 contains the famed Valley of Nonexistence, an area about the size of the original United States, in which no life form exists. Although not unusual in itself, the fact that the regions around the Valley of Nonexistence teem with life, runs contrary to logic. All attempts to explore the Valley of Nonexistence have proved inconclusive and it has remained one of the wonders of the Humanosphere.

The Mu settlements differed widely in government, ranging from the hedonist democracies of the planet Mu-3/2-2's western continent to the autocratic penal worlds of the northern continent of Mu-3/1-2.

Population	**Population Origin**
Mu-3/1-2: 265	Mu-3/1-2: Romania
Mu-3/2-2: 374	Mu-3/2-2: Burma, Laos

Aquila Alpha-7

First settled: 2220

Number of Colonized Planets: 7

The Aquila Alpha-7 worlds have become one of the dominant stellar systems of the Human worlds over the course of the twenty-fifth century, surpassing the power of the local Earth-based solar system in 2420.

Aquila-7/1-2 was colonized by both Indian and Japanese settlers. The colony's industrial growth was championed by the powerful Fuyama corporate oligarchy that initially governed the planet as its flagship world in the twenty-third century.

Aquila-7/2-3 and Aquila-7/3-3 have both been settled by East Coast Americans. The former evolved into the trading capital of the Aquila Federation, while the latter served as an industrial base to compete against Aquila-7/1-2.

Aquila-7/4-6 and Aquila-7/5-6 are both giant planets whose moons were settled by mining colonies. Hover settlements populated by Argentine and Chilean originating people are scattered across the surface of the planets' gaseous bodies.

Aquila-7/6-3 is a research planet that has became home to some of the most prestigious Research & Development laboratories in the Human worlds.

The Dirac Quantum Biology Institute and the Rutherford-Cavendish Academy are the most prominent of the over two hundred independent laboratories established on Aquila-7/6-3.

Aquila-7/7-3 has a large population of Korean origin. The central city of Toban served as the capital of the Aquila Federation from 2377 to the present day.

Population	Population Origin
Alpha-7/1-2: 1212	Alpha-7/1-2: India, Japan
Alpha-7/2-3: 1367	Alpha-7/2-3: Eastern US
Alpha-7/3-3: 1318	Alpha-7/3-3: Eastern US
Alpha-7/4-6: 296	Alpha-7/4-6: Chile, Argentina
Alpha-7/5-6: 108	Alpha-7/5-6: Chile, Argentina
Alpha-7/6-3: 541	Alpha-7/6-3: Multinational
Alpha-7/7-3: 223	Alpha-7/7-3: Korea

Bootes Delta-6

First settled: 2219
Number of Colonized Planets: 4

Delta-6/2-4 is known for its high intensity hurricanes and ionic storms. Several cavernous underground settlements were built by Human colonists on this planet in the twenty-fourth century.

Delta-6/3-3 has rich vegetation. Most noteworthy among the planet's plant life is dilphang, a large creeper plant, and poosch trees, an octagon arrangement of eight redwood-like trees around a single base.

Delta-6/5-3 is the population-rich center of the Bootes Delta system. The cities of Euphratia, New Jericho and Damascus Recreate still exist on this planet.

Delta-6/6-2 is an agricultural planet still shared between Humanity and the indigenous leperon primates.

The people of the Bootes Delta star system support a multifaceted economy with strong agricultural, commercial and industrial portfolios.

Population	Population Origin
Delta-6/2-4: 16	Delta-6/2-4: Southern Africa
Delta-6/3-3: 49	Delta-6/3-3: Italy
Delta-6/5-3: 419	Delta-6/5-3: Middle East
Delta-6/6-2: 29	Delta-6/6-2: Spain, Portugal

Caelum Gamma-6

First Settled: 2223
Number of Colonized Planets: 2

Gamma-6/2-3 is the more populous planet. It's geography resembles Carboniferous-era Earth. New Djarkata and Madrid Royale are its two most prominent cities.

Gamma-6/4-2 is an ice-covered world whose climate is similar to that of Earth during the Ice Age. Low temperature crops are grown throughout Gamma-6/4-2. The cities Bering-2 and Spitsbergen-3 have the planet's most significant Human population concentrations.

Population	Population Origin
Gamma-6/2-3: 189	Gamma-6/2-3: Indonesia, Spain
Gamma-6/4-2: 34	Gamma-6/4-2: Russia

Cancer Alpha-3

First Settled: 2230
Number of Colonized Planets: 2

Alpha-3/2-3 is famed for its silver-green oceans and purple vegetation. Its many settlements are built in the classical Greek style of architecture. It serves as the information storage and data allocation capital of the Human worlds.

Alpha-3/3-6 has several floater colony settlements. It is known for its rich sources of methane and hydrogen gases and has several spot-like formations similar to those of Jupiter.

Large cities in the Cancer Alpha-3 system included Bolak-2[143] and Gauss-Folako-1. Both metropolises are located on Alpha-3/2-3.

Population	Population Origin
Alpha-3/2-3: 291	Alpha-3/2-3: East Africa, Greece
Alpha-3/3-6: 156	Alpha-3/3-6: Mauritania, Mali, Senegal

[143] Folako and Bolak were two prominent data statisticians of the twenty-second century. The work of these two individuals laid the foundations of Collection, the data cataloguing science that allowed Humanity to successfully control the logistics of its expansion into the Aleph region.

Canis Major Delta-4

First Settled: 2232
Number of Colonized Planets: 4

Delta-4/1-3 has a moderate climate and is home to the California Recreate system of colonies.

Delta-4/2-3, largest of the four planets, developed into the economic center of this stellar system. It has a rich animal life that includes the urbas, a gold coloured bear-like creature and the svedvibor, a porcupine-type animal with serrated quills.

Delta-4/3-3 is known for its heavy rainfalls and dense tropical jungle vegetation. It has abnormally high oxygen concentrations that often result in destructive fires. Delta-4/3-3 contains the Vestas Paradise series of colonies, including the cities Nirvana-4 and Pax Globulus-3.

Delta-4/4-1, a frozen mineral world, houses numerous Biotron settlements.

Population	Population Origin
Delta-4/1-3: 412	Delta-4/1-3: California, South America
Delta-4/2-3: 223	Delta-4/2-3: Indonesia, Pakistan
Delta-4/3-3: 142	Delta-4/3-3: India
Delta-4/4-1: 9	Delta-4/4-2: NW US, Northern Europe

Capricornus Alpha-4

First Settled: 2236
Number of Colonized Planets: 3

Alpha-4/1-3 is famous for its archaeological treasures. The planet is home to the two-million year-old ruins of Vali, as well as the glass amethyst city of Torkitank.

Alpha-4/2-4 was colonized by religious groups of the Drav I Boorlas Theological Society. Adherents believed in the Five Messiah: Alexander the Great, Cicero, Leonardo da Vinci, Karl Marx and a mystical fifth Messiah who has yet to appear to Humanity.

Alpha-4/4-3's population is centered in the Bismark and Yeltsin settlement colonies. The planet also contains the natural wonder of the Whispering Hills of Futuras.

All the planets in the Capricornus Alpha system are united in a loose federation headquartered on Alpha-4/4-3's largest moon, Andronicus.

Population	Population Origin
Alpha-4/1-3: 180	Alpha-4/1-3: Mexico, Venezuela
Alpha-4/2-4: 91	Alpha-4/2-4: Argentina
Alpha-4/4-3: 43	Alpha-4/4-3: Germany, Poland, Russia

Centaurus Alpha-8

First Settled: 2219
Number of Colonized Planets: 4

Alpha-8/1-3 is a dark, dreary world with an overall mean temperature ten degrees lower than that of Earth.

Alpha-8/3-3 developed over the twenty-fourth and -fifth centuries into one of the most influential planets in the Humanosphere. It contains several major city states of which Virgil, Cicero, Nehru, Nightingale and Confucius are the most important. Alpha-8/3-3 has a diverse Human settlement population ranging from the Eco-Marxists, who settled the continent Engelsia, to the religious Neo-Hussites, who inhabit the island of Rewformo.

Alpha-8/5-2 is an agricultural world. Over three million different crop varieties are grown on this large greenhouse planet, whose pseudo-elliptical orbit allows it to approach the home star in such a way that it receives an optimum influx of radiation for crop production. Scientific farming communities make up most of the population.

Alpha-8/6-3 has become both the economic and political rival to Alpha-8/3-3. The magnificent Cerbian crystal glacier of Angelos-Michalelis is located here, as are the Giant Peaks of Ymir, a group of 2000 mountains each taller than Earth's Mount Everest. Varras,[144] Descartes and Paz are the three most powerful city states.

Population	Population Origin
Alpha-8/1-3: 11	Alpha-8/1-3: Multinational
Alpha-8/3-3: 160	Alpha-8/3-3: Multinational
Alpha-8/5-2: 115	Alpha-8/5-2: Multinational
Alpha-8/6-3: 118	Alpha-8/6-3: South America

[144] The city state of Varras was named after twenty-second century South American political leader Antonio Varras.

Cetus Tau-4

First Settled: 2225
Number of Colonized Planets: 1

Tau-4/2-3 is an Earth-like world known for its deep ravines, gorges, twisting rivers and ox-bow lakes. Early explorers described the planet as the world of many fjords. Tau-4/2-3 emerged as a powerful entity in the Human worlds following the Corporation Liberation Wars of the early twenty-fourth century, however, it was weakened considerably in the mid to late twenty-fifth century by civil war.

Population	Population Origin
Tau-4/2-3: 1241	Tau-4/2-3: Multinational

Chameleon Alpha-16

First Settled: 2227
Number of Colonized Planets: 4

Alpha 16/2-3 has vast deposits of hypermagnetic material located near the planet's poles. The material provides the planet with both a high rotational velocity and an awkward spin pattern. The Alpha 16/2-3 city states have a multifaceted economic portfolio and serve as an important entrepreneurial center.

Alpha-16/5-3 is a strange self-sufficient world, thanks to several thousand nuclear patches scattered across the planet that create natural power generation. The planet is the banking and insurance capital of the Chameleon Alpha system.

Alpha 16/9-2 is rich in borite and flemite deposits, both of which were used extensively in the medical and scientific industries for the development of analytical tools. The planet's jungle-like vegetation contains vast amounts of 'Whirl DNA' plants such as Araskopf, Eotos and Natis.

Alpha 16/12-3 was jointly settled by Human and alien colonists and over time developed into the largest center for multi-species cooperation in the Aleph region. The planet has gas-liquid interface zones as well as many hot springs and geysers.

The Chameleon Alpha planets were united in a federation with the city of Richelieu as its capital. Other prominent cities in the Chameleon Alpha system include Shang, Yuan, New Shanghai and the New Humanity development projects of Alpha-16/12-3.

Population	Population Origin
Alpha-16/2-3: 848	Alpha-16/2-3: France, United States
Alpha-16/5-3: 2326	Alpha-16/5-3: China
Alpha-16/9-2: 315	Alpha-16/9-2: Belarus, Ukraine
Alpha-16/12-3: 4132	Alpha-16/12-3: Multinational

Delphinius Beta-5

First Settled: 2242
Number of Colonized Planets: 4

Beta-5/2-2 is known for its spiral-like plant life and chemical springs. The springs act as a natural tap connecting the planet's surface with its chemical rich sub-crust layer. We now know the springs were built by an ancient civilization that inhabited the planet over a million years ago.

Beta-5/3-3 is a Mars-like world whose surface was manipulated to create Earth-like features. The planet has the largest population of all Delphinius Beta worlds and is noted for its android and robotic research and production facilities. Asimovia and Clarkerius are two of its most important metropolitan centers. Both cities have extensive android populations that originated from research performed in the mid twenty-fourth century.

Beta-5/4-3 is noted for its time research and gravity-manipulating laboratories. The planet reached its economic peak in the twenty-seventh century when breakthroughs in time travel by its scientists made Beta-5/4-3 strategically important.

Beta-5/5-3 has a non-ideal orbit. The planet is heavily populated by religious Muslim settlers and was the site of an important Muslim renaissance in the twenty-fifth century.

Population (Including Androids)	**Population Origin**
Beta-5/2-2: 271	Beta-5/2-2: North Africa
Beta-5/3-3: 1400	Beta-5/3-3: Pakistan, Afghanistan
Beta-5/4-3: 272	Beta-5/4-3: Multinational
Beta-5/5-3: 650	Beta-5/5-4: Iran, Iraq, Syria

Equuleus Alpha-7

First Settled: 2250
Number of Colonized Planets: 3

Alpha-7/2-3 is the second largest planetary body in this system. The planet was heavily colonized in the twenty-third century by Jovian miners. Seen from space, Alpha-7/2-3's high sulphur concentration gives the planet a mustard colour. Specialized sulphur-adapted plant and animal species inhabit the planet. These include the ten-kilometre-long Vermork creeper, as well as the giant sulphur-metabalizing Banpor mole.

Alpha-7/3-3 is populated by both Human and Potitank alien settlements. Unique cooperation projects between the two groups have produced such wonderful structures as the Thrqashian Obelisk as well as the mountain city of Vee.

Alpha-7/5-3 is a planet known for the Medicinal Remarank, a vast natural deposit containing the geologically produced organic compounds blignaw, an anti-carcinogenic drug and dkyrab, an anti-ageing compound. As a result of these deposits, the planet is nicknamed the Fountain of Hypocrites. Alpha-7/5-3's Human population is concentrated in the cities of Wengwei, Rariput and Nandipur.

Population	Population Origin
Alpha-7/2-3: 111	Alpha-7/2-3: Jovian Colonies
Alpha-7/3-3: 221	Alpha-7/3-3: Martian Colonies
Alpha-7/5-3: 115	Alpha-7/5-3: China, India

Eridanus Epsilon-4

First Settled: 2233

Number of Colonized Planets: 4

Epsilon-4/1-3 is a world rich in marine life. It has a wide variety of sea creatures and patterned kelp. The planet hosts over two hundred Human hydrocolonies.

Epsilon-4/2-3 has a yellow day sky that changes colour to orange in the evening.

Epsilon-4/3-4 is known for its rhombus-like shape caused by severe mantle-centered seismic activity. The Headquarters of the Council of Human Architects and Artists is located in the planet's largest city, Turgenev IV.

Epsilon-4/4-2 is an agricultural world noted for its multilevel farming plantations that often reach 200 storeys above ground. The planet had several energy-generating sources located in its mantle, that provided Epsilon-4/4-2 with a moderate climate despite its distance from the central star.

Population	Population Origin
Epsilon-4/1-3: 121	Epsilon-4/1-3: East Africa
Epsilon-4/2-3: 16	Epsilon-4/2-3: South East Asia
Epsilon-4/3-4: 129	Epsilon-4/3-4: Southern China
Epsilon-4/4-2: 96	Epsilon-4/4-2:Saturnian Colonies

Fornax Beta-3

First Settled: 2226

Number of Colonized Planets: 2

Beta 3/1-4 and Beta 3/3-4 were both settled by techno-specialists from the old Earth who helped establish the Regax interstellar channeling system to support Galaxy communications. Fornax Beta-3's pivotal role in manipulating this important invention allowed the system to acquire a disproportionately strong influence in the power politics of the Human worlds.

Population	Population Origin
Beta-3/1-4: 140	Beta-3/1-4: Belgium, Germany
Beta-3/3-4: 156	Beta-3/3-4: Sweden, UK

Grus Iota-6

First Settled: 2241
Number of Colonized Planets: 2, 3 others have smaller settlements

Iota-6/2-3 is the site of the famed Sanger Science Foundation. The planet contains over two thousand island archipelagos with an average of ten thousand islands per chain. Rocky formations form the backbone connecting the islands to one another. Many of these formations were carved as natural suspension bridges by earlier civilizations that once occupied this planet. A partially underwater city known as the Poseidon-Benguela complex, with a population of three million people, was constructed in the twenty-fifth century and linked several islands of the Hornblower Peninsula.

Iota-6/3-2 is a crucial centre of economic growth. Much of the planet's population lives in the city states of Voltaire and Nkrumah. Inhabitants of Iota-6/3-2 have suffered from a variety of natural disasters, of which earthquakes and volcanic eruptions are the most common.

Iota-6/4-1, Iota-6/5-5 and Iota-6/6-5 are each home to small settlement populations.

Population	Population Origin
Iota-6/2-3: 84	Iota-6/2-3: Ireland, Norway
Iota-6/3-2: 646	Iota-6/3-2: West Africa, France

Indus Delta-3

First Settled: 2250
Number of Colonized Planets: 3

Delta-3/1-2 is a rocky planet with little natural water. The planet's hills and valleys make it a perfect location for concealing millions of tonnes of high-tech weaponry.

Delta-3/2-3 is a green photosynthetic world that houses the majority of this stellar system's population. The economy of Delta-3/2-3 is driven by an industrial base supporting its numerous military facilities.

Delta-3/3-3 is an aqueous world whose elevated seismic activity was responsible for generating tidal waves. These waves posed a continuous threat to the planet's hydrocolony settlements. A shunting mechanism was developed in the twenty-fifth century to transport excess water from Delta-3/3-3 to the arid environment of Delta-3/1-2.

Population	Population Origin
Delta -3/1-2: 353	Delta -3/1-2: Mexico
Delta -3/2-3: 186	Delta -3/2-3: France, NE China
Delta -3/3-3: 11	Delta -3/3-3: India (Bengal Region)

Libra-Gamma-3

First Settled: 2238
Number of Colonized Planets: 1

Gamma-3/2-2 is an agriculturally rich world whose soil proved highly receptive to wheat and rye cereal crops from Earth. Wealth generated from the cultivation of these crops allowed farming communities to prosper, earning Gamma-3/2-2 the reputation as the one of the breadbaskets of Humanity. Settlers on Gamma-3/2-2 built large geodesic domes to house their populations. The domes were scattered across the planet's four continents. Gamma-3/2-2 proved of interest to Galactic anthropologists who found fossils in the planet's Terita Quicksand Pits thought to be the earliest examples of mammal-like creatures in the Galaxy. The planet has several major industrial centers, including the cities of Nuovo Kiev, Nebraska II and Vladimir-Dontesk. It also served as the venue for several Galactic Exploration Conferences that took place in the 2270s.

Population	Population Origin
Gamma-3/2-2: 720	Gamma-3/2-2: Ukraine, US Midwest

Octans Beta-4

First Settled: 2242
Number of Colonized Planets: 2

Beta-4/1-3 is an esthetically pleasing planet with beautiful crimson skies and yellow-green alkali rainfalls. The planet became popular as a meditative centre for Galactic transcendentalists.

Beta-4/4-2 is known for its potassium stalactite caves and bromine whirlpools.

The economy of all settlements in the Octans Beta-4 system is driven by the light industrial production of pharmaceutical and artificial intelligence products.

Population	Population Origin
Beta-4/1-3: 32	Beta-4/1-3: Finland, China
Beta-4/4-2: 40	Beta-4/4-2: Thailand

Perseus Kappa-2

First Settled: 2223

Number of Colonized Planets: 2

Kappa-2/1-1 is noted for its thermo-hurricanes. These heat storms cause temperature increases of 40°C to 50°C above the median. Insulated bubble cities protect the population from the harsh temperature swells. Despite its awkward weather patterns, Kappa-2/1-1 was widely settled by Human colonists because of its great mineral wealth. Rich copper, iron and magnesium deposits exist within the planet's molten lava oceans. Most of the planet's mineral resources are controlled by wealthy mining conglomerates.

Kappa-2/2-2 is known for its entertainment and fashion centers. Designer families originating from old Paris and Milan settled the colony in the late twenty-third century, establishing a clothing and fashion industry that became the pride of Humanity. An innovative entertainment industry existed alongside the fashion industry, making Kappa-2/2-2 one of the most dynamic planets in the Humanosphere.

Population	Population Origin
Kappa-2/1-1: 501	Kappa-2/1-1: Southern Africa
Kappa-2/2-2: 81	Kappa-2/2-2: Italy, France

Puppis Rho-4

First Settled: 2237

Number of Colonized Planets: 3

Rho-4/1-2 is a scenic world with large oceans and dense jungles. The planet is home to the Memitax plant, famous for its polychromatic pollen. The Gel Showers of Lumcer are also a noteworthy attraction.

Rho-4/2-3 is a densely populated planet that houses the Kajistan agricultural colonies and the metropolises of Darwinia and Clintorium.[145] It serves a vital role as a pharmaceutical and biotechnological production center.

Rho-4/4-3 is a militaristic world with a vast land defence system used by the Puppis system. It also has a large plastic manipulation industry.

Population	Population Origin
Rho-4/1-2: 33	Rho-4/1-2: Peru, Venezuela
Rho-4/2-3: 218	Rho-4/2-3: Japan, Korea, Vietnam
Rho-4/4-3: 14	Rho-4/4-3: Germany, Ireland

[145] Clintorium was named after twentieth century American president Bill Clinton.

Sagittarius Psi-4

First settled: 2245

Number of Colonized Planets: 3

Psi-4/1-3 was a twenty-fourth century lair for robbers, pirates and other criminals escaping the laws of their respective home planets. Several cities on the planet, Capolania and Riylanus being the two largest, were modeled in the style of eighteenth century European rococo architecture. Known for its exotic cities and free-life philosophy, an active trading market still provides Psi-4/1-3 with most of its wealth.Psi-4/2-2 had many short-lived homosexual and/or bisexual settler colonies. The planet has rich animal and plant life, including the morkas, a dragon-like creature and the vendaveer, a deer-lion-like animal.

Psi-4/4-3 is a world known for its spongy surface. The planet is rich in fungus and moss life forms that give the surface a purple colour that changes to gold as the planet nears its apogee. It is home to a mix of agricultural and industrial Human settlements.

Population	Population Origin
Psi-4/1-3: 34	Psi-4/1-3: Multinational
Psi-4/2-2: 39	Psi-4/2-2: Multinational
Psi-4/4-3: 86	Psi-4/4-3: Italy, Morocco, Tunisia

Scorpius Theta-4

First Settled: 2240

Number of Colonized Planets: 3

Theta-4/1-3 developed into an industrial planet, with over 3000 querzian particle generating reactors.

Theta-4/3-2 is mined by colonists for the minerals Jortak and Fleibo. It has a high earthquake frequency that hindered initial colonization attempts. Super-strength metals form the backbone of all Human construction on this planet.

Theta-4/4-3 is known for its abundant animal life. Animal classes include the vorals, remarkably similar to late Triassic dinosaurs, and the mammalian vrnx creatures.

Population	Population Origin
Theta-4/1-3: 25	Theta-4/1-3: Brazil, Peru
Theta-4/3-2: 12	Theta-4/3-2: Poland, Hungary
Theta -4/4-3: 31	Theta-4/4-3: Canada, Denmark

Taurus Epsilon-1

First Settled: 2221
Number of Colonized Planets: 1

Epsilon-1/1-3 had the largest Human population of any single planet in the Galaxy by the twenty-sixth century. The planet is rich in the heating fuels albatn and jixbi and contains valuable resources of diamonds and other precious stones. Its two largest cities are Amazonia and Indus. The planet has a diversified economy that is one of the strongest in the Human worlds.

Population	Population Origin
Epsilon-1/1-3: 4695	Epsilon-1/1-3: Brazil, India

Appendix 6: The Intelligent Species of the Known Galaxy

This appendix catalogues a selected group of twenty different Alien races who inhabited the portion of the Milky Way Galaxy known to Humanity at the end of the twenty-third century. The names used in this catalogue are those by which each of these species was most commonly known to Earth-dwelling Humanity and are the names used in the body of the text.

These twenty species are spread throughout the eight regions of the Galaxy designated by the Hebrew letters: Aleph, Bet, Chet, Dalet, Fey, Hey, Kuph and Zayen.

Table 1: Important facts and figures about these regions

Region Name	No. of Stars (in billion)	No. of Planets (in billions)	No. of Stellar Zones	Percent of Planets with Life	No. of Intell. Life Species
Aleph	2.2	10.78	56	0.08%	122
Bet	3.6	26.28	37	0.13%	451
Chet	2.1	31.71	81	0.11%	312
Dalet	0.8	1.52	42	0.29%	483
Fey	2.0	15.7	39	0.10%	179
Hey	1.1	7.48	155	0.03%	406
Kuph	4.5	25.65	83	0.14%	981
Uncharted Region 1 (Lamed)	19.3	52.29	76	0.0004%	376
Uncharted Region 2 (Pey)	21.6	6.40	122	0.06%	22
Uncharted Region 3 (Resh)	24.2	10.32	55	0.0005%	9
Uncharted Region 4 (Yud)	15.8	22.50	86	0.01%	556
Zayen	2.5	23.25	95	0.15%	178

Table 2: The principal Alien species originating in each of these regions

Region	Principal Alien People
Aleph	Humanity Riota Tebeld
Bet	Dultas Fheral
Chet	Izal Zweti
Dalet	Bilong Fogye Litess Lol Noga Rayoq
Fey	Godeiw (Gode and the Iwi)
Hey	Gald Lagem Smertertick
Kuph	Jyr Kosa
Zayen	Shayan

Details of the Species

Please note that the biologies of the peoples described are organically based unless otherwise specified. 1 BLU = 1 Billion Life Units. A Life Unit is a Humanocentric definition equal to a single Human Being. **All population values are for the year 2400.**
The histories of each species summarized are of events prior to the twenty-third century only.

The civilizations examined in this Appendix generally have multi-faceted economies consisting of a broad scope of agricultural, industrial and commercial endeavors, however, to illustrate the key differences between Galactic peoples, only those economic areas that the civilization is noted for excelling in have been elaborated on.

Military Ranking is based on a scale from 1-10.

Aleph Region

Riota

Population: 165 BLU

Galactic Habitat: The Riota occupied ninety-two different stellar systems by the twenty-third century, all of which were located in the Aleph Region. The four main Riota stars are Aquarius Alpha, Ara Zeta, Canis Minor Alpha and Camelopardalis Beta. These stars alone provide the living environment for thirty percent of the Riotan population. The Riota thrive in tropical worlds, rich in both fauna and flora.

Physical Features: A full-grown Riotan adult stands approximately 2.5 metres tall and weighs around 350 kilograms. Despite this size, Riotans are capable of extreme feats of agility, stealth and flexibility. Riotan adults have a mottled pink and brown skin with thick hair surrounding the pink regions. They resemble two-legged horses in form. The Riotan birth process involves a regulated system of advanced twinning that results in the formation of two beings differing only in left-right symmetry locations of all vital organs. Riotans possess razor-sharp hand-like appendages that they use for hand-to-hand conflict.

Military Ranking: 6.4

Primary Points of Interest: The Riotans achieved considerable success in the Galaxy as trainers in technology and the sciences. It was Riotan scientists, ironically, who spread space flight technology to the Tebeld, later one of their biggest competitors in the Aleph Region.

The Riota had success in the fields of diplomacy and political negotiation. Riota political schools, or Aeras Academies, were often called upon to solve interstellar crises.

An advanced industrial people, the Riota specialized in the production of a multitude of products. Among these was regam, the boron-based alloy whose widespread use in the twenty-second and -third centuries echoed that of plastic on twentieth-century Earth.

Riotan cities were built using a honeycomb structure, but tended to be sparsely populated.

History: The Riotans learned the secret of interstellar travel in the eighteenth century, when they were forced to defend their home worlds against the ravages of the Dultas' invasion of 1795. Through hit-and-run techniques known as Rys Raids, the Dultas were driven from the Aleph sector by the Riota, who established an hegemony over the vacated region. Their monopolistic power lasted for four hundred years, until the ascension of that other Aleph Region player, the Tebeld.

The Peliforam Institution, an oligarchic grouping, governed the Riotan worlds after the eighteenth century. Their rule over the Riotan Federation can be subdivided into three phases, each dominated by a specific dynasty. The Ralivat ruled from the eighteenth to the nineteenth century; the Kameek from the twentieth to the twenty-first century; and the Sheregain from the twenty-second century onwards.

Riotan political leaders included such notables as Shelamp Sagn, the First Perliforum Institution leader and Belbitam, a diplomatic genius who established several of the leading Aeras Academies.

Tebeld

Population: 237 BLU

Galactic Habitat: The Tebeld is the group name for over 300 related species that developed independently in 9000 stellar systems spanning the Aleph region. Tebeld groups had long lived on planetary systems with extensive wooded or marshy environments to provide plentiful water and organic material. The Tebeld originated from an advanced race who originated near the Galactic center and settled the Aleph and Bet regions of the Galaxy over two million years ago. War, famine and disease caused great anarchy among the original settler Tebelds, leading to losses of knowledge and civilization and the consequent regression of many of these isolated cultures to a bronze-age level of technology. This knowledge was, however, reacquired through interaction with the Riota.

Physical Features: The largest population Tebeld, the T-alphas, are hairy, have two heads (a major cephelus for cognitive thinking and a minor cephelus controlling basic motor functions) and are 1.5 metres tall on average. T-alphas are capable of spontaneous, but reversible, metamorphosis to a slime-like form that conserves energy allowing adaptation to temporary changes in the environment. Mood changes can also induce the spontaneous metamorphosis sequence. The nature of the metamorphosis continues to perplex scientists. Gestation involves a surrogate mother who helps nurture the developing zygote during the early stages of pregnancy. Death in T-alpha organisms is induced by the liberation of large doses of toxins accumulated in the brain throughout the individual's lifetime. The average lifespan of a Tebeld is nineteen Earth years.

Military Ranking: 5.7

Primary Points of Interest: Over 200 types of government exist within the Tebeld universe, of which the Dom Process, a legacy from the original Tebeld populations, is the most popular.

The Dom Major, a being specially trained from birth to use spiritual and intellectual powers to govern, is worshipped as a god by the people and capable of communicating with alternative energy and conscious levels through the medium of the Tej. Acting as an absolute monarch, the Dom Major's insights into the non-material world give the individual a mandate of unquestionable control.

Festivals and feeding rites are often enacted to pay homage to the Dom Major. A gathering of leading community figures, known as the Thir, moderate communication between the populace and the Dom Major.

- Historically, the Tebeld were renowned for their hunting abilities, often using their advanced hunting skills as mercenaries to even the most technically advanced civilizations of the Galaxy. Four types of hunters existed in Tebeldian society: Scoragis: Phase I hunters. Attacked and killed serpents, insect-like creatures and giant worms.
- Braz: Phase II hunters. Attacked herbivores and swimming carnivores such as the Barcha.[146]
- Lokoi: Phase III hunters. Specialized in hunting medium-sized land-living and flying carnivores that include the Xey.[147]
- Mopaq: The most highly skilled Phase III hunters. The Mopaq specialized in hunting Giant Strang[148] and Impu.[149]

Tebeldian hunters moved up this graduated hunting hierarchy according to a strictly determined measure of individual prowess in hunting ability.

History: Tebeldian populations on their respective planets showed a common pattern of development that repeated itself cyclically. A period of great famine, lasting for fifty years, was followed by a five-year war between the planet's Dom Majors. An era of dictatorship of the Supreme Dom (lasting seventy-five years) succeeded the war era, and was itself followed by a period of technical progress that completed the cycle. A cycle lasted one hundred and fifty years before repeating. Contact with advanced civilizations from other worlds disrupted the cycle after the twenty-third century, creating uncertainty and instability in the political, economic and social structure of the Tebeld worlds.

---

[146] An invisible fish whose meat was rich in life-sustaining nutrients.

[147] A Pterodactyl-like bird capable of eating a Human.

[148] A dragon-like creature that could eat as many as eight Humans in one meal.

149 A highly mobile creature, the fast reproducing and developing Impu existed on all Tebeldian worlds and was introduced to its current habitat, like most other beings, by the ancient ancestors of the Tebeld.

Bet Region
Dultas

Population: 1976 BLU

Galactic Habitat: The Dultas inhabit all zones of the Bet region. Dultas population colonies are also located in the Fey, Yud and Zayen regions. The center of the Dultas Empire is on Dultanas Lambda-5 in the Bet region's Vorkel zone.

Physical Features: The Dultas are divided into eight different sub-species, each identifiable by a unique eye colour, ranging from silver to maroon. Dultas beings have an average height of 2.5 metres and the equivalent strength of five Humans. Adult Dultas males have two horns protruding from the back of the head. The incisors are rotating teeth whose churning and cutting motion aid in the food ingestion process of the Dultas. Hydrochloric acid-producing salivary glands further assist digestion. The reproductive process of the Dultas includes the transfer of the infant to the wombs of five host mothers before final birthing. This process, still observable, was adopted over time by the Dultas as a way of reducing congenital birth defects.

Military Ranking: 8.5

Primary Points of Interest: Centrally controlled by the High Emperor and the Exclusivity Council, the 195 different Dultas nations were each distinguished by language and cultural differences.

The High Emperor oversaw the Exclusivity Council, which in turn administered the day-to-day running of the Empire. Each of the fifty-nine positions in the Exclusivity Council represented a particular sector of the Dultasian political infrastructure (Agriculture, Defence, Finance, etc.). Lower councils, known as Timinos Forums, acted as regional agents of governments for each of the Dultasian worlds. The head of an individual Timinos Forum, known as the Timinant, was directly responsible to a selected member of the Exclusivity Council.

The Dultas were feared throughout the Galaxy for their destructive military imperialism. Dultasian society had been structured as a military state, bearing remarkable resemblance to nineteenth century Prussia or ancient Sparta. Lead figures in the Timinos Forums and Exclusivity Council traditionally rose through the ranks of the military.

The Dultas military was divided into several sectors, including the:

- Corsgluf: Hit-and-run flying soldiers who attacked using fully armoured micropods.
- Molbitus: Fighting troopers who manned the 100,000-strong fleet of

battle cruisers.

- Neigian: Foot soldiers with bionic implants to optimize their fighting ability, they were armed with blast guns and protected by light metal-textile suits.
- Vaiy: Pilots in the Dultas airforce who flew a selection of over two hundred types of ultraphotonic fighter planes.
- Uribi: Computer-controlled henchman who acted as suicide soldiers in the first wave of Dultasian armed attacks.

History: Rigelam Piot founded the Dultas Empire in the eighth century BC using the ancient military schools of Foigal as his base of strength. In the War of the Nobles, Piot's forces ousted rival challengers and won control of the ancient court of Dultana. He ruled the Dultas Empire for the next five centuries before the Flambian Order of Warriors sacked the capital city of Nilaep, situated on the giant continent Velipar.

The first Flambian overlord of the Dultas Empire was the brutal tyrant, Keeshap. During Keeshap's one-hundred-year rule over the Dultana, he succeeded in uniting the rebellious western continent tribes of Bazil and Cley into the Dultas Empire. Keeshap II and his successor, Keeshap III, continued the warlike policies of the original Keeshap, defeating the rival Flambian Order. During the latter part of Keeshapian rule, the Dultas developed ultraphotonic flight and by the first Century BC were exploring the local Vorkel zone.

Keeshapian rule over the Dultas Empire terminated with the death of Emperor Gaoishap VI in 87 AD. The Coohia Dynasty, a noble house from the Leepar continent of the home planet, succeeded the Keeshapians. The Coohia were known for their autocratic rule and intolerance towards conflicting thought. Their age of rule was characterized by destructive terror campaigns and is considered by historians to be a dark era in Dultasian history.

The Coohia were overthrown in 523 AD by a series of citizen rebellions that erupted on several planets in the Vorkel zone. A civil administration ruled for the next two centuries, during which time the Empire spread to the Bet region's Campasgnion and Oolas sectors. In this same era, Dultasian science, art and architecture flourished and the empire reached its first Golden Age.

Internal strife and corruption ended the civil administration and it was replaced by an aristocratic dictatorship known as the Eelas. The Eelas ruled the Dultas Empire for 1087 years (715-1802), an era characterized by a renewal of military orthodoxy. The Dultas succeeded in winning control of the Bet region's Pilkam, Nightgew and Davildav zones after successfully defeating their arch-rivals, the Fheral and Moxon, in a series of military conflicts over more than five hundred years.

The Eelas Dictatorship was finally overthrown by a series of leadership assassinations masterminded by a rebel group known as the Commanders of Vaiy. After the 1802 murder of Demaish, the last Eelas leader, the Commanders of Vaiy succeeded in quelling all opposition to the imperial structure by establishing a rule of law that continued to the twenty-third century. The military resurrected the ancient positions of the Exclusivity Council and High Emperor, expanded the Empire to control a significant portion of the Bet region and initiated a policy of exploration and colonization, further increasing Dultas influence outside the Bet region. The military also reunited Dultas colonies that had drifted apart during the Eelas dictatorship.

Fheral

Population: 231 BLU

Galactic Habitat: Like the Dultas, the Fheral occupy over ten thousand colonies in the Bet and other regions of the Galaxy. The principal Fheral worlds are Raminotas Kappa, Begia Felugia Delta, Ciprank Phi and Veritook Eta.

Physical Features: The Fheral are powered by external battery-like organs known as Teega, attached to the back of the individual. The Fheral resemble hunchbacked chimpanzees in form. They stand about one metre tall, have dense hair and an ovoviporous type of gestation that parallels that of Earth's extinct platypus. An oxygen/nitrogen atmosphere, rich in fluorine compounds, is the optimum respiratory environment for the Fheral.

The Fheral have a unique aging process that appears to be the reverse of most other organisms in the Galaxy; they start life in the elderly form and regress physically (not mentally) to their infant form. This process is known as clemequ.

Military Ranking: 6.8

Primary Points of Interest: Fheralian societies are governed by a liberal democratic system. Elected councils known as Oorangia, govern individual Fheral colonies. The Galaxy's Fheral colonies are split into six federations, of which the Fheralian Peoples Alliance, the Union of the Fifth Front and the Noz Respwk Legion are the most powerful.

The Fheral have a diverse economy that has made great strides in agriculture,[150] chemistry[151] and mechanics.[152] It is, however, in the field of

[150] Fheral agricultural advances include the improvement of high-energy simplex fruit production methods.

[151] This species developed the wheelix energy-storing molecule that can trap and selectively release large quantities of energy for biological function.

[152] The Fheral invented the cycloptic jaw device used for efficient excavating in deep mining.

zoology that the Fheral have earned a Galaxy-wide reputation. The Fheral single-handedly bred almost ten percent of all animals in the known Galaxy, many of which created enormous economic wealth for the Fheral. Approximately forty percent of all Fherialian worlds exist for the sole purpose of animal breeding. The zoological gardens at Timurasz Gamma and Valishu Iota are brilliant testaments to the zoological endeavours of the Fheral.

Some notable species bred by the Fheral in captivity included:

- Onii: a fierce feline with a strong resemblance to both the Earth cheetah and antelope.
- Baoem: an organism that resembles the Earth jellyfish, but is five times larger in size.
- Northe: a metallic, green-hued organism that can secrete over fifteen thousand different dyes.

History: The Fheral were formerly the chief rivals to the Dultas in the Bet Region. Their elevated status in Bet Region Galacto-politics was reached after a series of eight civil wars between the independent Federations, ending with the signing of the Peace of Lopax in 2142.

Legendary Fheralian leader Harmen Sham, gained notoriety in the mid-twenty-second century for his military exploits against both the Dultas and Roulas, another Bet region people, who were eventually conquered by the Dultas in 2278. Harmem Sham was also the founder of the Fheralian Peoples' Alliance.

Ventran Shang, another notable Fheralian leader, pioneered the development of radiation weaponry that prevented the complete takeover of the Bet Region by the Dultas in 2215. Shang was also a leading figure in the Fheralian zoological movement.

Dilbartan Sham, a twenty-third century descendant of Harmem Sham, pioneered methods of intricate planetary transformation to facilitate Fheralian zoological goals. A dynamic political leader, Dilbartan Sham is often spoken of as the Mother of the Modern Fheralian Political State.

Chet Region

The Izal

Population: 287 BLU

Galactic Habitat: Izalian settlements are found throughout the Chet region. Colonies have also been established since the twenty-first century in the Dalet and Fey regions.

Physical Features: Izalians have a furry body covering, three pairs of eyes[153] and scales on their chests. The species has a strong digestive system, capable of breaking down compounds as diverse as polymers and metals. Izalian hardiness allows them to tolerate high levels of methane and other toxins that would be lethal to Humans.

Izalian females are fertile only five days during each Earth year.

Izalians and Humans share a genetic link to a common ancestor from the Plampar Alpha-3 system of the Chet region's Zornan zone. The average lifespan of an Izalian is 102 years.

Military Ranking: 7.4

Primary Points of Interest: The Izalian Legion is a decentralized alliance of Izalian planets and colonies. Izalian populations living on a planet are subdivided into units called Shua, each containing ten thousand individuals. The Shua is headed by an individual called the Shuatang, who reports directly to the Oma (Planetary Administration Council). The level of democracy within a Shua is strong, although, in Izalian society, there is more emphasis on the well-being of the community than the individual.

There have been several attempts to further centralize the Izalian Legion, but the success of such policies has been minimal. Ironically, the independence of the respective planetary Oma councils has contributed to the gradual decline of the Izalian Legion by allowing for the formation of conflicting alliances by respective Oma groups with external partners. These alliances are often at war with one another.

Izalian society has advanced as the result of a policy of Active Scavenging. Izalian raider parties act as technical parasites, reaping knowledge from other civilizations by both espionage and covert thuggery. Temporary alliances of convenience have often been established with other civilizations during the course of Izalian history as an efficient means of acquiring knowledge. The philosophy of building on the original knowledge of others is known as the continuum principle. Espionage procedures developed by the Izal have been highly effective in achieving their aims. The Pizaria, another Chet region people, were one of the most adversely affected victims of Izalian espionage schemes.

The Izalians are a highly adaptable people who have thrived on their aptitude for reforming new technologies to meet their own needs. This characteristic has allowed them to achieve prominence in such diverse industries as metal smelting, waste material recycling and energy resource management.

As a military force, the Izalian Legion is known for its advanced Galactic

[153] The third pair of eyes is thought to have evolved directly from the Pineal gland.

Power Station Fleet, a sophisticated robotic army, as well as a fearsome array of atmospheric suction bombing and hover vehicle attack crafts.

History: According to legend, an ancient Humanoid race, the Jucto, left the planet Plampar Alpha-3/2 on a long voyage to discover the mythical Jesmiang diamonds and escape the ravages of overpopulation afflicting their home planet. Those groups left behind by the so-called Jesmiang Quest developed into the Portifan,[154] while the travelers themselves evolved into the Izalians. Over a three-thousand-year period of waning technically, the Izal suffered a severe loss of scientific knowledge, most importantly in the field of space flight.

Near the beginning of the modern era, the Izalian civilization was resurrected by a low-grade form of ultraphotonic flight capability. Over the next millennium, several thousand Izalian colonies were established within a 100 light-year radius of the originating planet, Plampar Alpha-3/2, creating what eventually became a loose federation of Izalian settlement worlds.

The Izalian League was formed in 294 AD as a military alliance resistant to expansionist efforts of the other Chet region species. Six wars have been fought between the Izalians and the rival Portifan nation. These conflicts have weakened both the Izal and Portifan.

Izalian civilizations have also been afflicted with epidemic plagues that have killed significant segments of Izalian populations across the Chet region.

Zweti

Population: 125 BLU

Galactic Habitat: The Zweti occupy planets in seventy percent of the Chet region. Colonies also exist in the Bet and Dalet regions. The average Zweti-occupied planet is about the same size as Mars, but has vast areas of rich temperate grassland. Specialized organic compounds are used to transform the atmosphere of a newly colonized planet to meet the breathing requirements of the Zweti.

Physical Features: The Zweti have a natural evolutionary history similar to that of Earth spiders. Zweti adults have several types of body coverings, ranging from thick bristles to hair to fur. Short bursts of energy generated by the planctias gland in the abdomen provide fuel for body metabolism. The Zweti reproduce viviporously at birthing locations spread throughout their cities, with an average of four Zweti young emerging per egg hatching.

Military Ranking: 5.7

Primary Points of Interest: The Zweti were the founders of the Library of

[154] The Portifan are a sister species to both the Izal and Humanity.

Absolute Truth (LAT). Located on the Zweti controlled planets of Kalburgan Kappa-7/3, Dilovak Alpha-3/2 and Minorik Beta-4/1, the LAT contains all free knowledge available to civilization. Human scholars have likened the LAT to a modern-day Library of Alexandria. The Colonial Network of the Zweti world planets is sophisticated and decentralized. Each occupied planet in the Zweti network exists independently in a political and social context, but is tightly bonded by economic dependency.

The dominant Zweti religion is Torky, which places heavy emphasis on building construction, growth and development. Therefore, Zweti worlds have large areas resembling well planned concrete jungles. Inter-sheets connect Zweti cities to one another. An average Zweti planet contains one hundred uniformly sized city states, each of which has a population of around two million.

History: Zweti history traditionally focused on defense of the LAT. The scholarly Cults of the Diflgew and Primok, Chief Guardians of the LAT, have led six campaigns over the last four hundred years to defend the library against barbarian invaders from other systems.

An adventurous people, the Zweti have been cosmically active since the fifteenth century. The expansion of the Zweti realm since the twenty-second century has come at the expense of weaker Chet powers, specifically the Llu and the Blogar.

Dalet Region

Bilong

Population: 356 BLU

Galactic Habitat: The Majority of the Bilong inhabit worlds in the Borteriak and Shilmey zones of the Dalet Region. Bilong worlds tend to be tropical with predominantly cloud and fog coverings. This type of climate has acted as a shield, blocking external monitoring of the Bilong by other species, adding to the mystique surrounding Bilong civilization. Terqop Mu-3, Sliva Psi-1 and Negrex Tau-4 are the three most important Bilong inhabited stellar systems.

Physical Features: The Bilong are amphibious. No fossil record substantiating their evolutionary history has ever been discovered. Death occurs through spontaneous combustion occurring when an individual reaches the age of 101.53 Earth years. Bilongs resemble the Earth octopus in form, except they have nine tentacles that allow them to hover gently above the ground surface when away from the comfort of their swamp-like home environment. They achieve hover flight through air turbulence generated by symbiotic organisms living in their tentacles. Spugas structures (ram-like horns) protrude from Bilongs' forehead and extend over one metre (half the length of the individual). These structures are used for personal defense by both genders.

Military Ranking: 5.9

Primary Points of Interest: The Bilong are a spiritual people whose lives are governed by a Buddhist type of philosophy known as the Sanity of the Soul. Industrially, the Bilong have proved to be great innovators in the design, construction and modification of spaceships and Bilong engineers were frequently contracted throughout the Galaxy.

Types of ships pioneered by the Bilong over the last four hundred years include:

- The Ritarius: A cosmic vessel that adjusts shape continuously in response to its surrounding environment.
- Robotic Warships: Designed in cooperation with the Noga, these highly mobile ships were of great value in later Galactic wars.
- Bistablockers: As mass transportation vessels, these jumbos were capable of transporting over 0.5 MLU people.

Another important Bilong industry is the development of aeltinium smelters that manufacture life-support for artificial geoid moons. Political power in Bilong society is controlled by the Newo class, selected for their high level of understanding of the Sanity philosophy.

History: The Bilong developed as a powerful force in the Dalet region after their defeat of the Rayoq in the Deniashas Wars of the eighteenth century. The experiences of this war helped stimulate industrial production that laid the foundation for the spaceship design programs that grew to maturity in the twentieth century. In the twenty-first century, spaceship production fell under the control of the Pasgatio class, who used their influence to accumulate more wealth. The collapse of the Pasgatio class in the political uprisings of 2119, led to a more equal distribution of economic influence and a return to the Sanity of the Soul philosophy as directed by the Mewo class.

Fogye

Population: 377 BLU

Galactic Habitat: Urikeeps Alpha-12, Dalnam Gamma-5 and Role Theta-9 are the three most significant Fogye inhabited stellar systems. The Fogye prefer worlds with a mean temperature of -50^{0}C year round.

Physical Features: Fogye adults have cone-shaped heads, tapered toward the top. The species is small; an average adult is only 1.3 metres tall. The

Fogye have seven genders, of which four are infertile. The act of conception involves the synchronization of all three fertile genders. Recent attempts to turn one of the infertile genders into a breeding group in hopes of increasing the declining Fogye population, has achieved some success.

A Fogye being has a pair of eight-lobed ears, four noses (each situated on a single quadrant of the face) and a toothless mouth. Digestion is aided by sulphuric acid produced by the anti-freezing system of the Fogye. The Fogye have an extremely low nutrient requirement, due to the efficiency of their bodies in preventing energy loss. They change hair colour to match their particular environment and in response to heat, metamorphose for protection into structures known as pseudophages.

Military Ranking: 7.1

Primary Points of Interest: The Fogye are renowned for their artistic genius. Several great schools of art acclaimed throughout the Galaxy began in the Fogye sphere, including:

- The Sea Bottom Carvers: An artistic sect that creates complex patterns and designs on the floors of the Molant[155] Seas.
- Space Illusion: This discipline entails the creation of giant holographic images in space, stretching hundreds or thousands of kilometres. An ancient art form, Space Illusion was used as a protective mechanism to ward off enemy vessels from attacking Fogye worlds.
- Psychotechs: This branch of art involves the mind manipulation of structures and sculptures.
- Combatronics: These art pieces are generated by chaotically combining realist works of early Fogye masters.

Industrially, the Fogye are famed for manufacturing cold-produced products, most notably pharmaceuticals, surgical tools, life-support systems and hypothermophilic plants.

The four infertile genders perform all industrial, administrative and artistic functions in Fogyean society. The three fertile genders exist only to breed.

History: By the twenty-third century, there remained a total of 456 nations in the Fogye Collective. These nations existed as independent political and economical entities.

The Fogye transformed from an industrialized people to an art-centred collection of nations in the nineteenth century. This period coincided with the growth of liberalism in Fogyean society and the collapse of the old order. The movement away from full industrialization cost the Fogye dearly

[155] A chemical found on several of Fogye worlds allows liquid water to exist until it drops to a temperature of -100° C.

in the Dalet region's power struggles, where they lost over three-quarters of their territory to the Rayoq, Litess and Bilong. As members of the Alliance of Free Nations, the Fogye have survived from the twentieth century onward by seeking protection from the Galaxy's great powers in exchange for artistic merchandise. This policy is known as the Patron system.

Litess

Population: 552 BLU

Galactic Habitat: Most Litess populations are found in the Talagoriak and Rofoes sectors of the Dalet region, where they occupy 317 planets. Each planet is divided into domains that fall under the strict control of a territorial tribe. There is no central unity among Litessian groups in the Dalet Region and political power is divided among tribes and clans.

Physical Features:_The Litess have greyish faces with luminescent eyes. Two auxilliary limbs protruding from the thorax add support to the primary limbs which extend from the abdomen. Acetone and fumaric acid, in combination with propane gas, are necessary for Litess respiration. Litessians are characterized by their pronounced feet.

Military Ranking: 6.1

Primary Points of Interest: The Litess are a devoutly spiritual people who follow the Final Finger View of the universe. This philosophy places great faith in the coming of a messianic figure who will resurrect and enrich the Galaxy. Fanatical cults dedicated to the Finger View, have complicated the political landscape of the Litessian sphere of influence.

The Litessian economy is strongly geared toward manufacturing. Gas transportation, liquid purification and tool and dye construction works are the mainstays of almost all Litessian societies. The industrial refining of such heavy metals as thorium, uranium, cobalt and lig[156] has added much wealth to the Litessian worlds. However, manufacturing has also contributed to the pollution of such planets as Illam and Rinovar, which after two hundred years of dense population support, became uninhabitable in the twenty-third century.

As a result of their negligent industrial practices, the Litess have earned their reputation as Polluters of the Galaxy. The search for new pollution-free worlds on which to establish production facilities has been a major factor in driving the Litessian colonization initiative in the Dalet Region.

---

[156] Lig is a metal found exclusively in the Dalet region and used extensively as a chemical catalyst due to its high surface area to volume ratio.

History: Litessian history is one of brutality and violence. In the seventeenth century, the Litessian mother planet, Richglaw, was the site of a bloody civil war that resulted in the death of forty percent of the planet's population. The civil war was followed by an era of space exploration in the eighteenth century, which in turn was eclipsed by the Stellar Gang War Period of the nineteenth and twentieth centuries. The Order of Tribal Domains established on newly colonized planets in the twenty-first century used the Land Principle formula to divide territory according to tribal preferences. Unfortunately, the poor method used to carry out land division created bitterness that came to a head in the Hilliside Warrior Struggle on Jewlitar Rin in 2141. Because of such infighting, the Litess became susceptible to attack from other species, including the Rayoq invasion in 2189 and the struggle against the Noga in 2247.

The Lol Confederation

Population: 471 BLU

Galactic Habitat: The Auius and Shifan zones of the Dalet region had the greatest concentration of Lolians in the twenty-third century.

Physical Features: The Lol are giant insectoid beings that 2.6 metres tall and resemble Earth cockroaches. A thick armour-plated fibre, perforated with tiny respiratory pores, covers their skin, while an acid-based blood circulates inhaled gases to their various body tissues.

Razor-sharp secondary hands are used to cut apart food for ingestion, while a corrosive alkaline saliva assists in initial digestion. Lol physiology allows their organs to be removed from their bodies for an indefinite period without significant effect.

The average Lol lifespan is forty-seven years and each adult produces some fifteen offspring during its lifetime, of which only a third survive to maturity.

Military Ranking: 6.6

Primary Points of Interest: The Lol are known in the Dalet region as the Copy Cat People, a name they have earned for their policy of mimicking the political systems of civilizations deemed most effective at any given time. Such a process of government selection has caused the Lol to oscillate between autocratic and democratic institutions. Over the last five thousand years, the Lol have had eight hundred different types of government.

The Lol not only mimic the governments of other civilizations, but often resort to copying other civilizations' cultural heritage. Almost every advanced civilization that has come into contact with the Lol has been mimicked in accordance with the Copy Cat Principle. These include Earth's age of the

Moghul Maharajas, Victorian Era, Second World War and early space-race periods.

The science of mimicry is such an integral part of Lolian society that they have gone to great extremes to rearrange their cities, cultural establishments, way of life and even appearance to accurately mimic target civilizations. A Copy Cat Simulation could last up to fifty years and was controlled by the Loc Designer, who used drugs and other hallucinogenic agents to alter the population's mindset so they could tolerate and participate fully in the simulation.

The Lol are also specialists in the industrial process of miniaturization. This technology has valuable application in the fields of matter-decay preservation, gross material compacting and synthetic gravity induction. Techniques such as photon injection and neutrino blasting can reduce an object the size of a car to that of a matchbox by altering the subatomic distribution of spuon particles within the matter's quark matrix. Miniaturization accounts for over forty percent of the Lol GNP. Other fields of interest in the Lolian economic portfolio include: Rapid-Gel manufacturing, building construction and cosmetics.

In the twenty-third century, the Lol worked on the reverse of miniaturization, the science of mass maximization. Through the manipulation of the sub-particle structure of material items, the Lol succeeded in increasing object volume by a factor of ten. This allowed for the development of more practical easy-to-use items with no additional material costs.

Lol military strength lay in the effective use of mechanical cutting machines, killer X-ray devices and tactical nuclear warhead batteries. The armed services of the Lol Confederation was mainly a defensive force, however, espionage programs allowed the Lol to acquire valuable technology from competing space civilizations.

History: Initially a farming civilization specializing in rearing the goat-like bliba and the bovine pust, the Lol were driven to industrialization following the Faseh civil war of 1487. The Lol space colonization drive began in 1523 with the settlement of the Velpan Delta system by Lol colonists from the planet Ainite Omicron-3. The Copy Cat Principle was adopted in 1899 to limit the growth of centralized power in the Lol sphere of influence and introduce fresh ideas into the political, economic and social fabric of Lolian society.

The Lol learned the technology of miniaturization from the now extinct Urelib civilization in the seventeenth century. The knowledge they gained from this apprenticeship allowed the Lol to achieve a much coveted position in the Galaxy's economic politics. The Lol were involved in several military and economic alliances in the Dalet region, but their lack of mastery over more sophisticated dark matter space flight limited their colonization drive to this region.

Noga

Population: 43 BLU

Galactic Habitat: Noga Populations were distributed over fourteen planets and 754 space colonies in the Dalet Region during the twenty-third century. Their planets tend to have dry climates with sparse vegetation and little animal life.

Physical Features: Nogas are generally over 2.5 metres tall. They possess a hard exoskeleton with high electrical conductivity that allows them to carry a potential of 400 volts. The DNA-RNA complex of the Noga includes a unique type of genetic material held together by a complex amino acid[157] known as savans. Removal of a mere one percent of the savan from a Noga will result in instant death, however, the stabilizing effects of the savan molecule allow Noga DNA to reach lengths three to four times that of mammalian DNA.

Nogas are capable of changing parts of their bodies from a liquid to a solid and vice-versa. Blood pressure can be made to vary by a factor of 1000 times to assist this physical transformation.

Military Ranking: 5.1

Primary Points of Interest: The Noga have a reputation as the finest robot manufacturers in the Galaxy. Several types of robots are produced by the Noga for Galaxy-wide distribution, including:

- Industrians: Used for large-scale production of heavy equipment.
- Armifors: Military robots used widely in the Third and Fourth Galactic Wars of the twenty-fifth and -sixth centuries.
- Androbods: Skillfully designed by Noga engineers to resemble other life forms, Androbods are expensive.

Besides robot manufacturing, the Noga are heavily involved in the production of both metal colouration devices, enabling the change of hue of a metal internally to avoid the need for expensive painting, and mass molecular synthesizers.

The Noga worshipped a being called Hinas, who according to legend, unified the Noga people almost ten thousand years ago.

The Noga military force was renowned for its fully robotic Shagai attack fleet.

History: The Nogan home planets of Anefrian and Linx were controlled by Magno Gangs until a revolution in the fourteenth century. The Chimbo

---

[157] By 2300, 190 types of amino acids had been identified by Human scientists, nine times the amino acid population that existed on Earth.

Technicians, who established scientific government, also introduced robot manufacturing to Nogan society.

The Chimbo were opposed by the Chaos Warlords, who attempted unsuccessfully to overthrow the former in the nineteenth century. Nuclear war between these two groups resulted in the death of ninety percent of the Noga population in 1953. Order was restored in the modern Noga state at the beginning of the twenty-first century.

Spurred by such inventions as the robot manufacturing Philib machine and other micro devices that increased production, the Noga redefined themselves as a competent industrial force in the Dalet region, where they wielded influence through the Joint League of Industrial Nations (JLIN).

Rayoq

Population: 1414 BLU

Galactic Habitat: The Rayoq are the superpower of Dalet region politics. A widespread civilization, Rayoq colonies can be found in all regions of the Galaxy. However the highest Rayoq population densities are in the Shex, Forea, Gultinar and Civer zones of the Dalet region. Rayoqian cities have the distinct feature of being built to rotate mechanically around a central core, insuring optimum sunlight intake for the domed city structures. The cities themselves rest on electrically charged plates.

Physical Features: Rayoqian adults resemble giant Earth snails in shape and form, except they can move incredibly quickly as a result of the rigorous muscle action of their pseudopod organ. A hard outer covering protects the Rayoq from dangerous levels of radiation, often a feature of their habitat worlds. The Rayoq can tolerate the respiration of all known atmospheric gases, making them one of the most versatile life forms in the Galaxy. Rayoqs are also capable of emitting pulsar rays in self-defense. The biggest weakness of Rayoq physiology is their lack of well-developed three-dimensional vision. Their sight must be augmented by sophisticated optical equipment.

Military Ranking: 8.1

Primary Points of Interest: Rayoqian society has been molded on the dual concepts of exploration and development. Rayoq explorers were the first species to visit worlds outside their home region. The Rayoq were also innovators in the exploration of neutron stars and the colonization of high-pressure worlds.[158] The Rayoqian exploration drive was motivated by their religious philosophy of the Seed of Deliverance, which argues that the survival of the Rayoq as a people was

[158] Some high-pressure worlds have atmospheric pressures exceeding one thousand times that of Earth.

best ensured by maintaining habitats in a diversity of locations throughout the Galaxy. Consequently, Rayoquian science has produced tremendous advances, especially in fields relating to the preservation of life under adverse conditions. Mechanisms invented for this purpose include:

- The Carbo Gauge for measuring and generating basic organic compounds.
- The Bizmum Reader, used by the Rayoq in the exploration drive of the twenty-second and -third centuries to locate lethal poisons and toxic chemicals.

History: The Rayoqian worlds were joined in a strong federation that has existed since the eleventh century. The federation's history can be divided into four periods.

- The Pure Rayoq Era (eleventh to fifteenth centuries): During this period, the Old Federation was divided into five sub-federations, constantly at war with one another. Rayoq, the largest sub-federation, was the eventual winner in this power struggle.
- The Plintan Period (sixteenth to nineteenth centuries): This was the first era of exploration. During this period, the strong leadership of both Plintas III and Plintas IV insured Rayoq domination of the Dalet region.
- Elbiratus Period (twentieth to twenty-first centuries): Elibatius II and his successors quelled rebellions by aristocratic groups who intended to destroy the Old Federatioh's infrastructure. Along with Plintas III and Plintas IV, Elbiratus II is considered one of the greatest Rayoq leaders.
- Quasi-Liberal Period (twenty-second to-third centuries): During this period, Rayoqian politics was dominated by three parties, the Fios (Conservatives), the Esbads (Radicals) and the Omor (Moderates).

Fey Region

Godeiw

Population: 979 BLU

Galactic Habitat: The Godeiw is the name given to the nation formed by the unification of the Gode and Iwi peoples. The Tervas zone of the Fey region was the exclusive home of the Gode until their mass expansion in the sixteenth century. By the twenty-first century, Gode colonies had spread to all eighteen zones of the Fey Region and two zones in each of the Hey and Dalet regions.

The Iwi are almost totally contained within the confines of the Fey

Region. The most important Godeiw planets are Lopvares, the administrative capital of the Godeiw kingdom and Jesparez, the kingdom's most populous world. The Godeiw kingdom is the most powerful entity in the Fey Region, containing fourteen hundred populated worlds.

Physical Features: The Gode body resembles the Human skeleton in shape and structure. Such an appearance has earned the Gode the nickname among Humans as the Walking Dead. They possess the innate ability to spend long periods in hibernation. Gode beings end their lives when their offsprings sacrifice them.

The Iwi are a cannibalistic people who resemble walking cacti in shape and form. They have a specialized hepatic system centered around a vacuum pumping liver and a brain that continuously rotates around the central nerve stem.

Military Ranking: 8.8

Primary Points of Interest: Gode planets tend to have a jungle-like vegetation, which the Gode maintain with their skills in the root restructuring of tree networks, rapid forest growth and bio-adaptation. Known for their beauty and mystical qualities, Gode worlds are the envy of most civilizations in the Galaxy. Despite this love affair with the biological, the Gode have restructured their society along commercial lines. Insurance dealing, Galactic investment and commodity trading form the cornerstones of Gode economy.

The Iwi live in more Spartan conditions. Unlike the elaborate stone-glass-vegetation architecture of Gode cities, the Iwi prefer clay buildings as the sub-structures of their metropolises. They also tend to inhabit more desolate planets with arid or semi-arid environments. The Iwi are specialists in mechanization and favour heavy industrial production as opposed to the light manufacturing preferred by the Gode.

The Gode-Iwi Alliance, which became the Godeiw kingdom in the twenty-second century, is not an alliance of equality. As power brokers in the pact, the Gode tend to dominate the more passive Iwi. This relationship is most evident in the economics of the Godeiw kingdom, where real power is centered on the financial conglomerations principally controlled by the Gode.

The Godeiw King, ruling from the capital planet of Lopvares, is the principal authority, although planetary governors, or Clinasts, have considerable power in the territorial regions they controlled.

History: The Gode developed as power players in the Fey Region during the sixteenth century. From this period until the beginning of the nineteenth century, the Gode were involved in a series of military campaigns that expanded their Empire at the expense of the rival Filbar, Deliv and Ranosian peoples of the region. Under the Palthoras monarchial dynasty, which existed from the nineteenth to twentieth century, the Gode enjoyed a golden age that ended with the corrupt rule of the Lorez dynasty.

Gode strength was reasserted by Albatang the Great, who reclaimed much of the territory lost by the Lorez and built the foundation for a second Godeian expansion in the Fey region. The descendants of Albitang eventually masterminded the alliance that led to the foundation of the Godeiw Kingdom in the late twenty-second century and also to the acquisition of the large industrial base that has helped diversify the economy and made the Godeiw one of the great Galactic powers.

Since the mid-twenty-third century, the authority of the Godeiw kingdom has been supported by the Shami Warrior military class, who have been challenged by two groups: The Iwian Peoples Alliance, a militant organization that sought to free the Iwi from the domination of the Gode; and The Democratic Movement for Godeiw, a powerful group that operated covertly and publicly to force the downfall of the Godeiwan monarchy and hasten its replacement by a Democratic Government.

Hey Region

Gald

Population: 128 BLU

Galactic Habitat: The Gald inhabited fifty planets in the Flarmey and Penscki zones of the Hey region. Gald planets tend to be small (about the size of Pluto), mountainous in nature and contain large cavernous systems that provide the backbone for the dwelling units of the Galdian inhabitants. Located below this cavernous system is the Albick zone of the sub-crust that serves as the industrial base of production.

Physical Features: The Gald brain is divided into three hemispheres, a feature that allows them to be very adept at the skills of verbal comprehension and word fluency. Physiologically, the Gald alternate from one generation to the next. One generation takes on the lanky form, while the next generation boasts stout stumpy features. Variation in height can be as much as one hundred percent from 1.5 to 3 metres tall. The Gald have a tube-like body frame that moves forward by means of a vertical peristaltic thrust. Gald skin is protected by barbs that function as an internal parasite-cleansing mechanism and secrete acid for self-defense. Metal products are used in the digestive process to assist in the breakdown of complex proteins and carbohydrates found in the Galdian diet. Communication between individuals occurs through a mathematically coded language.

Military Ranking: 6.8

Primary Points of Interest: The Gald developed a solid reputation as the Galaxy's leading trackers and transporters of goods. Long-range shipping sustains almost forty percent of the Galdian economy. Over three hundred shipping and tracking consortiums were operated by the Gald by the end of the twenty-third century, accounting for a fifth of all Galactic shipping revenue.

The mass organization needed to mastermind such work, provided the impetus for the modernization of Galdian society and also contributed to a culture of crime that permeates almost all avenues of their socio-economic framework.

Galdian politics has traditionally been controlled by representatives of the trading hierarchies who meet regularly in the Planius Reas, the Gald Parliament. Control of planets in the Gald sphere is divided among the shipping cartels. The cartels exercise their authority through the militant Fectro Forces.

On the technological side, the Gald invented such devices as the quantum tracking probe[159] and the fast-flow transportation device that uses baro waves[160] to transport materials to destinations across the Galaxy. Supporting these processes is a mechanized system known as the baro wave generator, with strategically placed nodes at many Galactic locations.

History: The ascension of the Fectro Forces and their cooperation with the tracking companies, has been in place since the early twentieth century. In the twenty-second century, the Gald sphere of influence was rocked by a series of unsuccessful revolutions led by the Marchi-Tuoro, a libertarian organization influenced by the ancient Galdian thinker Elp Marchi, whose philosophy had a strong similarity to that of the ancient Chinese thinker Lao Tze. As a military industrial power, the Gald rank behind the Lagem and Dgloj in the Hey region.

Lagem

Population: 2135 BLU

Galactic Habitat: In the twenty-third century, the Lagem were the most populous species in the Galaxy. Although there was a significant Lagem presence in the major regions, the species' highest settlement concentration was in the Draval, Kista and Markemas Zones of the Hey region.

Physical Features: The Lagem are a combination inorganic-organic life

[159] The quantum tracking probe can precisely locate the position of any transported article in the Galaxy within a few seconds.

[160] Baro waves are an energy form transcending space and time.

form spawned from the robotic colony of an earlier experimental people established on Elibartius-5 of the Dravel zone. Resembling early prototypes of twenty-first century Humanoid robots, but with small tails, spinning eyes and U-shaped heads, the Lagem are capable of detaching their body parts then reconstituting themselves in a new form to suite any task. The Lagem are not only efficient reproducers, but also have a mechanism that optimizes their nutrient intake-to-waste ratio.

Military Ranking: 8.2

Primary Points of Interest: The Lagem economic focus is on banking and investment. Their control over much of the Hey Region has historically been negotiated through their administration of a vast financial network known as the Creesh.

Lagem society respects equality, with no class divisions, mirroring in many ways the ideal Marxist society envisioned in nineteenth century Earth. Profits from the Creesh system are evenly distributed among inhabitants of the Federation of Lagem Worlds according to the philosophy of Galack or Benevolent Materialism.

The Lagem began to diversify their economy in the nineteenth century by venturing into such varied pursuits as inter-species sex, gladiator fighting and macro-roulette, which together account for ten percent of the Lagem GNP.

Most Lagem worship the spirit of the scientist Clmn, who according to legend, engineered the original robots of the Elibartius-5 colony.

History: The Lagem have possessed the knowledge of interstellar flight since the late seventeenth century. Originally a military people, the Lagem waged a successful war on the rival Alac people for control of the Hey region in the nineteenth century. With a strong bias toward big government, the Lagem managed to avoid the nationalistic and tribal wars that plagued several other experimental species. Rivalry with the Kosa and Shayan led to limited conflicts in the twenty-first and -second centuries, that further increased tensions in the Hey region. Fearing an unlimited war with the Shayan, in the twenty-third century the Lagem followed a policy of neutrality that eventually crumbled.

Lagem domestic politics focuses on several issues, most important of which is the reform of the Creesh system and the creation of work-promoting programs, such as rotating all jobs in the workforce every two years.

Smertertick

Population: 202 BLU

Galactic Habitat: Smertertick settlements are found in the Ligreted and

Filopanian zones of the Hey region. Forty percent of the Smertertick population live in the Ligreted Ci Gamma-3 stellar system, the ancestral home of the Smerterticks.

Physical Features: Globular in form with an obvious protrusion at one end for a cerebral body, the Smertertick have a complex structure. They walk on a series of forty feet. Reproduction takes place by means of budding, similar to the asexual reproduction of Earth bacteria. The Smertertick were in fact a bacterial form that grew in size over time (from one micron to one metre) in response to climatic changes. The species has an elastic skin and secretes a sticky polymer for personal protection. Smerterticks are known to live as long as 315 Earth years.

Military Ranking: 4.3

Primary Points of Interest: The Smerterticks are a non-violent people and their economic livelihood centers on the production of glass materials for industry and construction. Four types of glass structures have been pioneered by the Smertertick.

- Alical: A super-strength glass used to distribute the load in construction. Alical glass is capable of supporting vast stone weights.
- Biobase: A biologically friendly glass that if ingested, acts to protect parts of the bodies of some species from acidic corrosion.
- Laserglo: A glass structure containing five liquids encased in a mesh network. Produced by the bombardment of salaphoid glass[161] by laser action, Laserglo is widely used in several fields of aesthetic design where it is appreciated for both its unique structure and brilliant form.
- Reproglass: This cheap glass is widely used by the Smertertick. It is named for its capacity for self-reproduction under proper environmental conditions.

The Smertertick live in glass cities. They have a small, but efficient, armed forces whose strength is based on a series of minor space stations that can metamorphosize into battleships. The colonies and settlements of the Smerterick worlds are closely united under a meritocracy government centered on Ligreted Ci Gamma-3.

History: A series of dictatorship dynasties ruled the Smerterick population from the eighteenth to the twenty-first century. During the rebellion of the glass makers in 2088, the last of the dictatorship dynasties was overthrown and replaced by the leadership of Reparius Shi. It was Shi who introduced

[161] Salaphoid glass is a natural product of ligreted Ci Gamma-3.

the meritocracy government and established the basis for a competitive Smertertick economy that brought the civilization into the twenty-second century as a significant player in the Hey region. Since the twenty-third century, two forces of note have been active politically in the Smertertick worlds: the Isolationists, who want to divorce the civilization from all politics in the Galaxy; and the Fundamentalists of Bos, who seek to move the Smertertick toward the worship of the ancient glass scorpion deity, Bos Perfalgius.

Kuph Region

Jyr

Population: 184 BLU

Galactic Habitat: Jyr settlements are still wholly located within the Kuph Region. Mioq Beta-7 and Cilidon Omega-4 remain the two most populous Jyrian stellar systems.
There are a total of 432 planets in the Jyr sphere of influence, each governed independently.

Physical Features: The Jyr have pinkish-orange skin covering their reptilian-like body. Their spinal bone protrudes from their back in a parabolic arch and helps support the body in conditions of extreme gravitational pressure. The average Jyr is a metre tall. The Jyr have a complicated organ system that appears to operate interchangeably, so that if necessary, the heart can work as a kidney and vice versa. Such an advanced internal mechanism has insured great longevity for the Jyr. Reproduction among the Jyr is a very complicated procedure and requires the assistance of the related Kloq and Bratx peoples during both conception and gestation.

Military Ranking: 5.4

Primary Points of Interest: The Jyr live in giant terrainean structures that resemble Earth's anthills.

Jyrian life centers on the religions of Meras and Sorium, both of which believe in the continuous exorcising of demons from the host body to insure the individual's survival. Meras and Sorium are believed to be two supernatural beings who continuously fight for control of the Jyrian soul. Soul cleansing ceremonies are used to resolve this conflict within the individual and prevent the rebellion of the conscious, a state of mind in which one being is particularly dominant over the other, a situation that if not checked, can lead to death.

An industrial people, the Jyr excel in such diverse operations as halogen mining (particularly chlorines and iodines), agrarian tool manufacturing and exotic dye production.[162]

History: The Jyr were once a highly advanced civilization whose society fell into disarray in the eighteenth century after the Halkonian dynasty seized power. The rise of the Meras and Sorium religion in the nineteenth century created a situation that ultimately led to a rebellion against the Halkonians and the subsequent breakdown of the centralized Jyrian power base. These events caused the creation of the independent planetary system that existed in the twenty-third century.

Kosa

Population: 1615 BLU

Galactic Habitat: The Kosa are the most powerful civilization in the Galaxy from an economic, military and political standpoint. Over 50,000 planetary systems in all regions of the Galaxy are controlled by the Kosa Legions. The majority of the Kosa population resides in the Chemhuk, Eagatuz and Hilapeer zones of the Kuph region.

Kosa planets tend to be about twice the size of Earth, having a two-to-one land to sea ratio and a temperate climate.

Physical Features: The Kosa are a Humanoid people who originated from the ancient Aelitius civilization. The average Kosa adult reaches a height of 1.8 metres and has an extremely muscular framework. All births by Kosa females occur in the breach position. Head-first births result in infant death, as the trunk of the newborn infant has to adapt to the environment before its head and sensory organs can begin functioning. Three to four infants are born at once, but females are physiologically limited to two pregnancies in their lifetimes. The Kosa have a much lower body temperature than Humans and possess only four digits per limb. They have little hair and a rough outer skin with strong resistance to extreme temperature fluctuations.

Military Ranking: 9.2

Primary Points of Interest: The Kosan economy, like that of the Galaxy's other great powers, is highly robust. Areas of specialty exist in the electronic and material fields. A strong financial sector further boosts the Kosan economy. Their chief mined products include iron, vanadium and berischium.[163]

The Kosa have developed a reputation in the Galaxy for their ability

[162] In particular the production of Brizundoa, a base pigment in dyes used throughout the Galaxy.

[163] Berischium is a mineral element resembling wood, but is at least a thousand times stronger than the most compressed Earth hardwood.

to trade and sell information. Galaxy-wide information exchange bureaus operating through networked systems allow the Kosa to create a trading forum for the distribution and relocation of goods. The same information forum is used by the Kosa to extract valuable data for strengthening their position in the Galaxy. Kosan society is heavily influenced by regional corporations who play a vital role in assuring the stability of the Alliances.

The Kosan planets are divided into fifteen alliances of which the KPL, the KSG and Kimpak are the most powerful. Although these alliances have frequently been at war with one another, during times of peace they unite under the banner of the Kosa Legion. The movement for Kosan democracy has been very successful in ensuring a broad liberal consensus favouring the freedom of thought, word and action in the Legion's worlds.

History: Kosan populations started to expand throughout the Kuph region in the seventh century AD. Initially united under the Plaze (c.900-c.1100) and Vekota dynasties (c.1100-c.1300), the Kosa split into three alliances in the early fourteenth century. These were the Allied Front, Bolqw Group and the Yomes Structure. The alliances battled one another for domination of the Kosan sphere of influence throughout the fourteenth to sixteenth centuries before the arrival of Alnauj Refz of the Yomes Structure, who succeeded in uniting all Kosan populations across the Kuph region under his domination.

The Era of the Yomes Structure brought much wealth to the Kosan sphere until the fall of Refz's dynasty to Kosan barbarian forces in the eighteenth century. The development of the information age in the nineteenth and twentieth centuries was paralleled by the division of the Yomes Structure and its evolution into the fifteen alliances.

Initially established as a series of economic groups, the Alliances grew into military pacts during the twenty-first and -second centuries. Quick to adapt to changing political and economic conditions, the Kosa proved highly adept at promoting and selling their culture to the rest of the Galaxy.

Zayen Region

Shayan Union

Population: 1389 BLU

Galactic Habitat: The Shayan are an advanced silicon-based life form who inhabit all the Zayen region. There are an estimated 70,000 planets under Shayan control. The Shayan prefer planets slightly smaller than Earth, with a rich gaseous-silicate atmosphere and silicon-based flora and fauna. Kwareltius Gamma-5 and Michona Psi-7 are the most populous of all Shayan planets.

Physical Features: Standing 3.1 metres tall with an average weight of 105 kilograms, the Shayan are a lanky people with acute senses and strong extra-sensory perception. The Shayan nervous system is about ten times as sensitive to stimuli as the Human nervous system. All Shayan are part of a single gender that reproduces asexually. The Shayan have small wings attached to their backs that allow them to glide like birds through the air at low levels. They are a carnivorous people with scissors-like probosci they use to feed on other silicon-based life forms.

Military Ranking: 9.2

Primary Points of Interest: The Shayan have a rich economy, surpassed in the Galaxy only by the Kosa. The Hilec class are the chief industrialists in this economy, while the Tengar function as its main traders. The Strangt are active in all facets of industrial production, most notably holography, memory chip manufacturing and planet transformation.

Despite being silicon-based, the Shayan farm both carbon and silicon animals and have the largest agricultural economy in the Galaxy.

The gingan, a cow-like animal that produces the rich carbohydrate seeri, the fulab, an antelope creature known for its high levels of adrenalin, and the rugaj, a non-chlorophyll based plant-animal that produces oils used in industry, are three of the most lucrative creatures farmed by the Shayan.

The Shayan government is run as a strict federation headquartered on the star base Elvaran Kappa-5/3. The President, an executive of nineteen leaders, governs the federation, while the 150,000 member representative council communicates across the Zayen region to debate federal decisions. Additional levels of government are responsible for administering local affairs.

The Shayan military force is known for its highly mobile space fleet, battleship flotilla and cosmic mine-laying and mine-detection capabilities. Shayan settlements established on the colonized planets form a grid that when viewed from space, look like a giant spreadsheet.

History: The Shayan Union grew to prosperity in the eighteenth century after defeating the rival Kefgas and Billokam in the early wars of the Zayen region. Under the dominion of Lowab Shelefaanon, the Shayan Union spread throughout the Zayen region absorbing several hundred smaller nations into their ever growing sphere of influence. The Shayan growth period continued throughout the nineteenth, twentieth and twenty-first centuries, despite popular rebellions by independent settler colonies and local autocrats against the increasing role of technology in Shayan society.

Since the mid-twenty-second century, Polibae Shelefaanon, a descendant of Lowab, has worked to integrate non-Shayans living on the periphery of the Union into the broader spectrum of Shayan society. This policy of integration has had mixed results, with some groups responding favourably, while others object to the strong role of the central government in setting economic policy.

Appendix 7: Life form types that exist in the known Milky Way Galaxy

Alumitoids: Aluminum-based organisms that are rigid in shape and have robotic features. Alumitoid bodies also have a high cellular magnesium and copper content. They are found mainly in the Dalet Region.

Casgains: Slime-like organisms composed of high fat and cholesterol superstructures, they originated in the Forbasch and Plamtoes zones of the Galaxy's Hey region.

Diamanoids: A very dense carbon-based crystalline life form. Most diamanoids can metamorphose into graphite if necessary.

Fiticites: These iridium-based life forms often have pointed or jagged shapes.

Glymoids: These creatures have a crystalline structure that can take on a tetrahedral or icosahedrons form.

Hosgramins: Hydrogen-helium organisms, their sub-atomic interactions lead to alpha decay that provides energy for their metabolism.

Javolites: Sulfur-based organisms that use iodine and astatine to form cellular networks.

Mesomorphoids: These "super elastic organisms" are composed chiefly of bringbew, an inorganic, stretchable compound.

Nugoids: Organisms composed of a radioactive matrix, Nugoids are rich in elements from the lanthanide and actinide series of the periodic table.

Oragamin: Life forms based on a germanium version of DNA known as oragat. Oragamins are found largely in the Crstam zone of the Kuph region.

Organoid: A group of organic-based life forms, including Humanoids. Organoids are found throughout the Galaxy.

Percotoids: Living entities containing the rare compound percitonic acid. Percotonic acid acts as an agent for metabolism, forming molecular complexes that react selectively with various biochemicals to sustain life.

Pyres: Fire-like organisms that continuously ignite an external chemical source, usually on the skin, to yield energy. Pyres are often surrounded by an oscillating flame that resembles an energy halo.

Rigmoid: These organisms have an intricate three dimensional structure and a complex indefinable shape. The chemical rigmoinix, present in large amounts in the Zayen Region, acts as the linking agent holding their body structure together.

Rltoes: These organisms have a high degree of life specialization in both the structure and functioning of individual body parts. This feature is maintained through the manipulation of gyman particles.
Safamin: Specialized life forms that use the noble gases (neon, argon and radon) for biochemical functioning.
Trygoes: Silicon-cellulose organisms that use plasto-electric charges for mobility. They reproduce through a complicated diffusion-regulated technique of ion exchange.
Urltoids: Giant organisms (often thirty metres in height) composed of ultra-light trachyan fibres (silver oxides with garmium molecules). Most urltoids live in suspension approximately fifty metres above their specific planetary surfaces.
Zytins: Energy-matter life forms, Zytins can convert from one an energy to a matter life form and back again depending on their environmental constraints.

Printed in the United States
48720LVS00002B/97-162